Scots Honor

A Sam McKay Novel

K.M. Hardy

Copyright © 2020 K.M. Hardy

All rights reserved. No part of this book may be reproduced or transmitted in any form or by any means, electronic or mechanical, including photocopying, recording or by any information storage and retrieval system without permission in writing from the publisher.

Picaty Press —Tooele, Utah
ISBN: 978-0-578-75666-0
Library of Congress Control Number: pending
Title: Scots Honor: A Sam McKay Novel
Author: K.M. Hardy
Digital distribution | 2020
Paperback | 2020

This is a work of fiction. The characters, names, incidents, places, and dialogue are products of the author's imagination, and are not to be construed as real.

Dedication

To my husband: who never doubted I could do this.
To my kids: I hope you'll follow any dream you have.
To my Gran: you kept me writing.
To my Editor Margie: thank you for all of your help and support
during this process.
And, because she'll kill me if I don't say it, I love you mama!

Chapter One

"EVERYONE SHUT UP AND GET DOWN! DOWN ON THE GROUND NOW!"

It was Tuesday, March 12th, 2018, and the entire building of En Passant Bank was filled with the sounds of screaming. No one could have suspected when they woke up and headed to the bank in the heart of Cleveland, Ohio, that they would be caught in the most terrifying moment of their lives. But once the ball got rolling, there was no stopping the chaos that had erupted. Tellers crouched down as they were pulled from behind the counter; civilians huddled together; two children cried in fear as they clung tightly to their mother.

"Where is he?!" the head of the crew shouted to his men.

"I found him, he's over here!"

Looking to his left towards the bank manager's office, the head walked over and yanked him and the customer he was with out of the room.

"Alright," he chuckled, "now we're in business."

~~~

Thirty minutes later, on the roof of the building across the street, SWAT Sniper Jones sat and watched through the tiny window at the top of the bank's doors the horrific scene unfolding: twenty hostages and six men dressed in black business suits and ski masks armed with automatic rifles.

"They've got all of the hostages sitting on the floor, but one of them is sitting in a chair away from the others, sir," the sniper radioed in. "It seems like the leader is interested in him. Three of the others are surrounding the other civilians, one lookout in front and another in the back."

"Can you describe who's in the chair, Jones?"
~~~

"I can do better than that, sir, and just tell you who it is: Brian Cairne."

~~~

"Jones, say again?" Chief Humbar started to sweat.

"The hostage that is in the chair is Brian Cairne, sir. I'm positive."

"Shit!" the Chief exclaimed at the news. Turning to his Lieutenant, he barked. "Get Sam over here, now!"

"He's already here, sir!"

The stocky man turned to see his friend and trusted colleague, Sampson Angus McKay, running over, his Kevlar vest in hand. Towering at almost six and a half feet tall, the black-haired man had to stay crouched to avoid getting his head blown off. It almost made him an easy target. But no matter how many times the Chief saw him do it, it still boggled his mind that a giant Scotsman wanted to be a cop.

Sam crouched next to the Chief and looked over the hood of the car. "Wha' we got, then?"

"Six of them, armed with automatics, twenty hostages, one of which is Brian Cairne. They've singled him out."

"Who?"

"Brian Cairne, the steel millionaire."

"Ach, I'll take yer word for it." Sam quickly slipped the vest over his suit. "Has anyone made contact yet?"

"No, we waited for you."

"Alrigh', well, le's ge' started."

The two men looked over their shoulder at the giant black van behind them, watching as Sam's trusted team set to work connecting their surveillance equipment. Not a minute later, they signaled for Sam and the Chief to join them.

"It's ringing!"

Sam quickly grabbed the phone with a quiet "Thanks" and took a deep breath as he listened to the line. After two rings, it was answered.

"Who the hell am I talking to?" a deep voice spoke.

Calmly, Sam answered. "Hallo, my name is Sam McKay."

"What the—you're not American?"

"No, I'm afraid not."
~~~

"Well, what the hell kind of accent is that?"

"I's Scottish. Are ye the man in charge?"

"Scottish, interesting. Well, caballero, yes, I'm the man in charge."

"Alright. Do ye have a name I can call ye?"

"You can call me Gerry," the voice growled.

"Very good, Gerry. Looks like ye've go' a verra interestin' situation goin' on, made a lo' of cops around here a wee bit nervous."

"Yeah, and I'm about to make their day a lot more interesting if my demands aren't met."

"Alrigh', tell me yer demands and I'll see wha' I can do."

"We'll get to that. First, let me give you the full scenario: I've got twenty people here, some of them are women and children. And I will not hesitate to shoot any one of them if you screw with me. Is that clear?"

"Aye, tha's very clear. I donnea want to screw ye, Gerry, I want t'help ye."

"Good, then get me a bus out front in ten minutes and tell these cops to stand down."

"I promise ye I will look into the bus, but I cannea tell anyone t' stand down," Sam answered calmly.

"Do I need to shoot someone already, Sam?"

"Gerry, please listen to me. There are a lo' of frightened people in there, and the cops need to be nearby in case any of them needs help when this is all over. Alright?"

No matter the hundreds of times he'd been in a hostage exchange before, the silence on the end of the line as he waited for a response always made a bead of sweat appear on Sam's head. Just as he began to wonder if he had been hung up on, Gerry responded.

"Alright, fine. But the cops have to stay where they are."

"Aye, ye got it."

"I want that bus out here in ten minutes."

"I will get ye a bus as fast as possible, bu' I need something from you too. Ye said ye've go' some women and children in there. Why donnea ye let them go?"

"No no, bus first and then we'll see about hostages. You call me back in two minutes, caballero."

Before Sam could reply, the call ended. Putting the phone in his pocket, he turned to the Chief. "He wants a bus here in ten minutes."

"We can get one en route from the station but it'll take at least twenty."

"He won't settle for twenty, we're gonna have to do bettar." Sam turned back to his team of three: Derrick Rivera on the phone systems, Simon Abler on the computer, and Julie Russell looking at the blueprints of the building. "You guys go' anythin'?"

"Amazing," Julie muttered as she looked over every page of the prints, "this bank should be completely impervious; there's no way to breech it other than the front door. The two back fire escape doors would set off alarms, and there's no way to bypass them unless you're at the main computer in the manager's office."

"All of their security cameras and systems are intact," Simon added, pushing his glasses up on his face. "Nothing was tampered with. It looks like a good old' fashioned bank robbery, not too sophisticated."

"But they singled out Brian Cairne?" asked Rivera. "You saying it was just a coincidence that he was at the bank today?"

"I don't know, it's your job to figure that out." Simon sighed. "I'm just the computer guy."

"Alrigh', enough." Sam interrupted them. "Here's wha' we know so far: the suspect is callin' himself Gerry, and he's go' a Latino accent. A' the moment, Gerry's calm, which tells me this isnea his first time robbin' a bank. Julie, go coordinate with SWAT on a way to ge' into the buildin'. Simon, see if ye can ge' the security camera feed up. Rivera, find a quicker route for the bus."

"Oh, great," Chief Humbar said.

Sam turned to where he was looking to see a middle-aged man in a three-piece suit walking through the lines of policemen towards them with a couple of security guards just one step behind him.

"Who the hell is tha'?" Sam asked.

Humbar was stunned. "You're kidding, right? That's Jackson Green: Cairne's son-in-law, CEO of En Passant International Bank, Ohio's Congressman, and golden boy planning on making a run for President. Honestly, McKay, don't you ever watch the news?"

"I'd rather be out on my boat. Ge' rid of him, will ye?"

Chief Humbar nodded and quickly walked over to the approaching politician.

Brian glanced around the room nervously. *Of course, the one day I give my security man the day off is the day I'm being held up in a bank,* he thought. Looking over to the hostages cowering in fear, he felt more afraid for the mother and her two small children who made him think of his own family. The older girl had to be seven, like his youngest grandson, AJ, and the boy couldn't be any older than three. As their mother clutched them tightly, barely holding herself together, Brian's heart ached to see them so petrified. Calmly, he raised his hand.

"What the hell do you want, gringo?!" One of the robbers barked, pointing his gun at him.

"Just to help make the situation a little more bearable for the children," Brian answered him calmly. "I noticed in the manager's office there is a bowl with some candy. Would it be alright if I got a piece for the kids?"

The robber stared at him blankly before answering, "Are you kidding me?"

Brian shook his head. "No, sir. They're scared, and a crying child would make everybody feel more uneasy. Some candy might help them stay calm."

Another tense moment of silence followed before the robber turned to the others and began to speak in a rapid-fire manner, though Brian couldn't understand a word of the language. Finally, the robber walked into the office and retrieved the mentioned bowl. Shoving it into Brian's hands, he motioned towards the kids. "Do it, but be quick and don't be an idiot. Got it?"

"Yes, sir," Brian nodded and gently stood up, walked towards the children, and squatted in front of them. "Hey, guys. It's gonna' be okay, don't worry. Here, would you like a caramel?"

The children hesitated before their mother whispered, "It's alright, you can take one."

Gingerly, the kids reached out and took some candy, unwrapped them, and quickly placed them in their mouths. Brian smiled and set the bowl down in front of them.

"I've always thought that candy makes everything better. Why don't you guys hang on to that?"

"Thank you," the little boy squeaked.

"Alright, that's enough! Back to your seat!" the robber barked.

Brian stood up and slowly returned to his designated spot. Looking back towards the mother, he nodded after she mouthed a "thank you." Now that he'd had a chance to help, the tension in the air eased some but only a little. Looking out the small window next to the large doors, he prayed that this nightmare would be over soon.

~~~

Sam called the bank again. It was answered after two rings.

"Hallo, Gerry?"

"My bus on its way, Sam?"

"The closest one is twenty minutes away, but I'm tryin' to ge' it re-routed so it'll be here sooner."

"That's not what we agreed on, caballero. I let you keep the cops and you promised me a bus."

"And the bus is comin', i's just gonna' take a little—"

"Meanwhile you've got all these poor, scared people sitting here with a crazy guy holding a gun pointed directly at them. Should I start with the kids?"

Sam heard the sounds of screaming in the background and felt his blood start to boil. Taking a deep breath, he answered, "Gerry, I donnea control the traffic. I promised ye a bus, and a bus is comin'. There is no need to hurt anyone."

"Chicos, agarren a la niña!"

"NO!" a woman sobbed, "No, please don't! Please!"

"MOMMY!" a little girl screamed.

"Gerry, listen to me!" Sam barked a little louder than he would have liked. Quickly, he composed himself before continuing, "Gerry, righ' now nobody has been hurt. But if somebody *does* get hurt then tha' lands completely on you. Ye start killin' people and I cannea stop these cops from bargin' in there and shootin' ye right where ye stand."

Gerry remained silent, so Sam pressed further.

"Now I promised ye the bus, and i's coming as fast as possible. Donnea hurt anyone, and ye'll be able to leave here alive. Ye go' that?"

More silence followed and Sam held his breath. When he heard the same woman crying, "Oh God, thank you! It's okay,
~~~

sweetheart!" he sighed in relief.

"Alright, Sam, you just bought yourself fifteen minutes." Gerry hung up.

"Rivera, where's my bus?!" Sam barked.

"It's coming, stuck on 71," Rivera answered.

"What are you people doing out here?!"

Sam turned to see the man in the suit standing at the door of his van and yelling at all of them with Chief Humbar directly behind him.

"Shouldn't you be 'breaching the building' or something?! Why are you just sitting here and giving this terrorist what he wants?!"

"Congressman, I'm going to have to ask you to leave the scene and let us handle this," the Chief said coolly.

"Forget it, Humbar! My father-in-law's in there! I'm not leaving until he's safe!"

Sam piped in, "Congressman Green, righ' now there are six men, fully armed and ready to shoot, with twenty hostages. Their leader has already threatened to kill a child, and I guarantee that if we donnea handle this delicately, he will do tha' and much worse."

Sam stared the man down before adding, "This is a very high-risk situation. There is nothin' tha' ye can do here. For yer own safety, please go back to yer home or at least stay out of the way."

Green glared before straitening his jacket. "Alright, fine. Just get my father-in-law out safely or I will ruin you, do you understand?"

"Sam, I got them!" Simon exclaimed.

Sam waved the Congressman off without a backward glance and turned his attention back to Simon.

"I was able to hack into the security camera systems, now we can keep an eye on everything."

The two men watched the pixilated images closely, looking for signs of weakness or openings. Sam paid close attention to the older gentleman in a chair that was being closely guarded by one of the robbers and interrogated by another.

"Tha's gotta' be Gerry," Sam pointed to the imposing figure in front of Mr. Cairne.

"What do you think he's saying to him?"

"I donnea know, but it looks like shit might hit the fan soon. We've go' to get these men to let their guard down a little."

"Hey Humbar," Rivera chimed in, "you've got eyes up on the

building, why not have your snipers take them out?"

"The windows are too small for Jones to have a good clear shot; he'd only get one of them at best. The last thing we should do is antagonize this guy."

"Aye," Sam nodded. "Bu' all the same, ge' yer guys ready to breach. And ge' a few more snipers up there with yer man jus' in case we can take them out when the bus comes."

"You got it." Chief Humber turned and walked towards the waiting policemen.

~~~

"Boss, we're almost ready!"

Brian nearly choked as the man calling himself Gerry grabbed him by the collar and yanked him out of his seat.

"Everyone, *atención*!" Gerry shouted, immediately commanding the hostages' attention, "You will follow my associates to the back of the bank and do as you're told. If any of you feels like being a hero, raise your hand, and we'll shoot you now."

The crowd responded with whimpers.

"Very good. Everybody up!"

The hostages did as they were told and followed the three men in charge of guarding them whilst Brian was met with the barrel of a gun to his face.

"Now you and me, Mr. Cairne, are going to take a little walk…"

~~~

"Boss, something is going on in there," Jones' voice called from the radio.

Chief Humbar raised it to his mouth, "What is it, Jones?"

"It looks like they're moving the hostages to the back of the bank. They've moved everyone out of my sight, I can't see anything."

"It's going out of range of the cameras, I can't tell what's going on either," Simon added.

Chief Humbar looked to Sam (who was already re-dialing the banks phone number). "What do you think? Breach now?"

"No, too risky, we cannea see wha' he's doin' with the hostages." Sam raised the phone to his ear. "Le' me see if I can ge' him to give some up, first."

Suddenly the air shook with the ear-splitting sound of an explosion. Everyone within fifty feet of the bank dropped to the ground as dust and debris flew every which way. Not a moment later, Chief Humbar jumped to his feet and yelled, "Breach, now! Go, go, go!"

Dozens of SWAT members entered, their guns up and at the ready. Sam looked out the back of the van and watched the scene unfold. Out of the corner of his eye, he saw Julie run back to the van.

"What happened?" She demanded. "We had just barely found a way to come in around the back!"

"They had moved the hostages and two seconds later came the explosion. That is the extent of our collective knowledge," Simon answered her.

Julie rolled her eyes and stood next to Sam, who was staring at the entrance to the bank with a hardened expression. The same familiar defeated feeling rose up in him, as would usually happen any time he had failed to end a hostage situation before it got violent. Although he could only count on his hand how many times that had happened in his career, it didn't stop the sinking emotions he felt. Time seemed to stand still as he watched the paramedics rush inside, already knowing there would be significant collateral damage.

"Sam?" his radio buzzed.

He lifted it to his lips. "Aye."

"It looks like we got played; they never had any intention of using the bus."

Without a word, Sam marched forward, taking in the scale of the destruction as he walked. While most of the hostages were unharmed other than a bump on the head, including the two children, there were a few that required immediate medical attention.

"Sam!" Chief Humbar called, "Over here."

Sam walked over to where the Chief was kneeling over the body of an older gentleman with a bullet wound in his forehead. "Tha' Brian Cairne?"

"Yeah, the bastard shot him at point blank range after locking the others inside the vault. While everyone else rushed towards the explosion, they escaped through the bathroom windows."

"So, they're already gone?"

"I'm having my guys pull ATM cameras in the area, see if we can find out where they went."

"How soon will ye be able t' tell wha' they took?"

"Sam, it's a mess in here. It's going to be a while before we know anything." Chief Humbar rose to his feet and clapped Sam on his shoulder. "Look, you did your part. Get out of here, we'll take care of the rest."

Sam stared at the executed body for a moment longer before turning and abruptly walking back to his team. All three of them stared as he came closer until finally, he said, "Brian Cairne's dead, Gerry pu' a bullet in his brain."

"Dammit," Rivera said softly.

"There wasn't anything you could have done, boss," Simon added.

"Yeah," said Julie, "guys like that can't be reasoned with."

Sam didn't respond. He began to remove his vest when he heard his name being shouted through the crowd and coming closer.

"Sam! Sam!"

"Oh, for God's sake," Julie moaned. Turning towards the source of the voice, she barked, "Can't you take a hint, Terry?!"

The short, boyishly handsome man known as Cole Terry grinned at her. "A journalist never rests, Miss Russell."

"Ye're no' a journalist, ye niaff, ye're a bloody blogger. Go find yer lead somewhere else, Terry," Sam growled. "I've go' nothin' for ye."

"Would you describe the situation as unique, Sam?"

"Hey, Jackass, he said no comment!" Rivera barked.

"I didn't hear him say that," Terry continued, "was there anything about the perps that struck you as odd? Any ideas on what they were looking for? What can you tell me about the hostages? Was there anyone of significance among the hostages?"

"Christ, Terry, I ough' to have ye charged with harassment! Ge' the hell ou' of here!"

Suddenly two officers who knew Sam appeared and began to escort the annoying reporter away from the van. The team of four began to pack up their gear. Sam had barely put his vest away when the sounds of struggle coming from behind him caught his attention.

"Now' wha?" He wondered aloud and turned to see Jackson Green pushing every cop that stood in his path out of the way, until he was face to face with Sam, fuming.

"Where's my father-in-law?!" Green demanded.

Sam took a deep breath. "Congressman, I'm verra sorry, but Mr. Cairne didnea make it."

He watched Jackson take a step back and cover his mouth, "Oh my God …"

Sam stood there, unsure of what to do. Finally, Julie took over.

"Congressman, this is a lot to take in. Why don't you sit down?"

"No!" Green shouted and turned his attention back to Sam. "You did this! You said that you would stop this before it escalated! What am I going to tell my wife?!"

"Tell her tha' we did everything we could," Sam answered calmly.

"No, no you didn't. And I'm going to make sure you don't get the opportunity to screw anything up again!"

"Okay, Green, that's enough," Rivera walked forward. Taking the man firmly by the sleeve, he tried to lead him away from the group when the Congressman's security force stepped in and pushed him off.

"You're finished, McKay, do you hear me?! Finished!"

Sam blocked out the sound of the politician's threats as he finished packing his gear. Finally, the threats ceased as Green was led away from the scene.

"Unbelievable," Julie muttered. "Seriously, nobody gets just how hard our job is."

"I know," Simon added, "you'd think they'd understand we're facing crazy people all the time, and we don't control the outcome of anything."

Sam said nothing. He watched Rivera walk back and climb into the driver's side of the van, then out of the corner of his eye, he saw Chief Humbar approach.

"Green give you an earful?" he asked.

Sam nodded. "Wouldnea be the first time."

"Yeah, well, I heard him from clear over there threatening to completely ruin you. I wouldn't be too sure he won't follow through on that."

"Ach, ye know how it is with these rich types," Sam shrugged. "Always promisin' they'll ruin others when they're in the heat of the moment. It'll be fine."

"All the same, you better stay clear for a few days until he cools off." Chief Humbar stuck his hand out to Sam's and shook it. "Thanks for your help."

"Aye, I'll send ye the bill."

The two men said their goodbyes before Sam jumped into the passenger side of the van. Rivera drove off towards their headquarters, located in Beachwood. It was a modest office; a suite that was a part of a strip of stores. Occasionally some passerby would walk in, mistaking it for a printing store, but one of the little team would simply guide them out of the door and back on their way before returning to their desks.

All four of them had worked for different agencies at one point before their operation was set up. Simon Abler, a young and lanky African-American with thick rimmed glasses, had been a White-Collar Crime computer specialist for the Federal Bureau of Investigation. Recruited at the age of 20 after he had been caught hacking into a pharmaceutical company—he was attempting to expose the animal tests they had been conducting—when he was caught at a protest. Julie Russel was a tall, fiery redhead with creamy pale skin and green eyes. Once a member of SWAT, she was well on her way to becoming the youngest lead entry officer on record in Ohio at age 26. Then one day she had been near fatally shot in the back, right next to her spinal cord. Left paralyzed for almost a year, she had attended physical therapy faithfully until she finally learned to walk again. The incident had unfortunately destroyed her career physically, and she was forced to retire to a desk job until Sam discovered her, and she became the team's strategic specialist. And though their shorter, sculpted Latino-American partner, Derrick Rivera, stayed with the operation most of the time, he was technically a liaison for the FBI when he wasn't on a surveillance assignment. His main responsibility was to oversee their private operation and coordinate with law enforcement officials within a 100-mile radius. Despite his hot-headed nature, he was more of a big brother to Julie and Simon and very quickly considered a part of the team. The three of them butted heads regularly when they worked together, but when they met each other for a drink there was always laughter. There was perhaps no closer group of people.

Sam handpicked every one of them when he set up their modest operation. With a decorated career with SWAT as a part-time hostage negotiator, his sudden career move to open a private agency two years before had left the people around him scratching their heads. Long ago, in what seemed like another life to him, he was a detective in Helensburgh, Scotland, in a little village called Rosneath. Upon meeting Meredith Staton, a dark haired and curvy American who had come to Scotland for a summer break trip with her friends, he moved to America to marry her and (largely due to a glowing review from his old partner in Rosneath) became an Internal Affairs Detective. While most IA Detectives would leave behind a terrible taste in any law enforcement official's mouth, Sampson Angus McKay had the strange distinction of being an IA Detective who did not. His towering height intimidated most everyone that met him, but his deep-set, gentle brown eyes helped to soothe his gruff exterior. At forty-three years of age, he had a worn face and a bulky but toned body. Most women (and sometimes men) that he met on the job thought him handsome. In every investigation he ever conducted, was thorough, fair, and level-headed. Though there would always be some cop who felt they had been jaded after an investigation ended, the majority of the policemen and women Sam came into contact with appreciated his respectful manner and accepted the outcomes. Three years later, he decided to accept an opening in SWAT and quickly rose in the ranks. To anyone who did not know him personally, he appeared calm and reserved. But to his team, he was a grumpy enigma. All four of them: a family.

"'You got mail!'" Simon smirked, setting a small stack of envelopes in front of Rivera.

"Why is it I'm the only one on this team that handles the paperwork?" he grunted.

"Because if we screw it up then the team gets disbanded," Julie smirked. "As the FBI guy, you get the honor of making sure that doesn't happen."

"You know you could always help," Rivera glanced back at Simon.

"Oh no, I'm not good with paper. Paper cuts," he lifted his hands and smiled. "I'd bleed out everywhere and die, then you guys couldn't hack into programs or make online pizza orders."

"You're right, it'd be *impossible* to replace you," Rivera rolled his eyes.

Sam was at his desk in the back, hiding behind a few police reports. Though he would never let his team see it, he was smirking at their banter as he skimmed over details of various robberies, looking for similar MOs, in case they had seen the crew at En Passant before. He didn't have very long to look when he noticed Rivera in his peripheral vision.

"Somethin' to sign?" he asked, not bothering to look up.

"No … I'm sorry, Sam. I didn't mean to see this. It was just in the rest of the mail."

Furrowing his eyebrows, Sam looked at Rivera and accepted the opened envelope. While Rivera retreated to his desk, Sam unfolded the contents. In large bold letters at the top, he read: **DIVORCE AGREEMENT**, already filled out, courtesy of Meredith. Upon seeing that she fully intended to have sole custody of their twelve-year-old son, Oliver, Sam slammed his fist on his desk.

The rest of the team jumped at his sudden outburst. Concerned, but knowing full well not to approach him in a time of anger, they watched him grab his jacket and car keys before storming out the door.

"Derrick, what the hell was that?" Julie asked.

Rivera sighed. "Meredith served him papers."

Simon looked over. "What about Oliver?"

"She's pursuing sole custody."

Julie shook her head disdainfully. "That bitch."

Chapter Two

One year later

"Ladies and gentlemen, we are now making our descent into Glasgow International Airport."

Sam opened his eyes, exhaustion from the lack of comfort in the tight coach seat on the redeye evident. *One o' the joys of bein' as tall as a damn tree*, he thought. He opened his last bag of airline cookies as the pilot continued over the intercom:

"The time is 7:39 a.m., and if you thought to pack a coat, you'll definitely want to put it on before you walk outside, as it is a windy 5.5 degrees Celsius, that's 42 degrees Fahrenheit for our American friends traveling with us. There's a slight drizzle of rain. On behalf of the crew and myself, we'd like to thank you for flying with us today, and we hope you enjoy your time here in Scotland."

The moment the captain turned off the seatbelt sign, everyone on board stood up except for Sam. Sitting in a seat at the very back of the plane, he waited for everyone else to leave before gathering his carryon and making his way towards the terminal. After getting through customs, he had retrieved his suitcases and was headed towards the nearest bus stop when he heard a familiar voice.

"Sam! Oi! Over 'ere!"

He turned to see the origin of the voice and smiled. "Thomas McFarland, wha' the hell are ye doin' here?"

"Hannah called me," the bristly blonde man smiled in return. Though Thomas wasn't quite as tall as Sam, he was considered a giant among men, and not even Sam would want to catch himself in a fight with him.

"Of course, she did. I tol' her I'd take a bus and no' to trouble herself."

"Ach, well, tha's yer baby sister for ye," Thomas clapped him on the back. "She wanted to come and ge' ye herself bu' couldnea find a substitute. And it's been slow down a' the docks lately, so i' wasnea much trouble."

"Ye drove over an hour to come and ge' me, man."

"Well, when you put it to me tha' way, I'll be expecting a pint a' Jackie's la'er."

Sam chuckled. "Aye, alrigh'. How is the ol' bassard?"

"Still as mean an' ugly as ever, but he finally did somethin' smart and hired a pretty new lassy. Pub fills up mos' every night now, thanks t'her."

"Dancin' girl? Never though' he'd do tha'."

"Ach, no. Waitress; pretty t' look a' and pretty t' talk to. Many a' man have been tryin' to ge' a kiss since he hired her, but not o' one's ha' any luck."

Sam loaded his bags into the back of Thomas' old, rusty Hillman Imp. "I cannea believe ye still have this piece of shite."

"Oi, haud yer wheesht when ye talk to Hillary. She's a classic."

"This thing'll never ge' us back to Rosneath," Sam sighed. "Maybe I shoulda' taken a bus."

"Sam, shu-up and ge' in the car."

Before long, they were driving next to the River Clyde and headed for home: the village Rosneath in Helensburgh.

"Back to this girl," Thomas began again. "She's American."

"American? In Rosneath?"

"Aye, anno ye have a weakness fer them American lassies." Thomas waggled his eyebrows at him. Sam rolled his eyes and Thomas continued. "She keeps to herself, mostly. Never see her except for when she's workin' at the pub or in the market."

"She go' a name?"

"Aye, Liz. I heard it once when Jackie was callin' for her. So have ye go' a place to stay?" Thomas asked. "I may no' have much room in me wee flat, but ye're welcome to the sofa."

"No thanks, pal, I'll be stayin' at the cottage. Hannah said she's go' it fixed up fer me."

"Too right."

"Listen, Hannah said she kept me bike. Think we can stop by on the way?"

"Ach, i's at me flat, Hannah dropped 'er off fer ye las' week."

"Thanks. Ye still shaggin' Helen?"

Thomas beamed. "Aye."

Sam chuckled. "Ye ever gonna' make an honest woman of her?"

"The day that bassard Barney makes me a captain, an' if she'll ever say yes, aye!"

A moment of silence passed between the two men until Thomas cleared his throat. "So … how's Oliver takin' it?"

Sam turned away and looked out the window, his preference not to discuss the matter very clear.

Thomas nodded. "Aye, ye got it."

"Does the radio still a' least work?"

Thomas smirked and turned it on to his favorite local station. Sam hated the ridiculous modern pop music the man liked. In fact, he was convinced Thomas liked it just because it annoyed him. But he simply turned his head and looked out at the lush green mountains. The remainder of the drive, Thomas talked about everything that had changed and everyone who had died in the village the past twelve years since Sam had gone. Sam listened though his mind was pre-occupied with everything that had happened in the past one: Meredith had gotten what she wanted in the divorce, including sole custody. If that wasn't enough, Jackson Green had made good on his threat and had Sam's Hostage Negotiation team completely disbanded.

Rivera had gone back to surveillance full-time and had pulled some strings for Simon to get rehired at the FBI, though it was in the IT department, much to the young man's annoyance. Julie was able to secure a position as a strategy asset for SWAT. Though she enjoyed it, the downside was she was still not allowed to do much field work, if any. Sam was completely discredited, stripped of all of his achievements. There wasn't an agency around that would touch him, let alone give him a job. Even his friend Humbar wasn't permitted to hire him, though the stocky man fought hard until there was nothing left he could say. In effort to be closer to his son during the horrible divorce, Sam had tried for jobs other than law enforcement; he was good with his hands, there were options. He had even sought jobs outside of Ohio. But due to the economic state (at least that's what everyone told him), he could never get past the first interview. After six months without work, and with the divorce being finalized, his green card no longer held any weight, and he was 'politely' asked to leave America and return to Scotland. Now he was back in his home country. And despite the terrible circumstances that forced him back, he had to admit that he missed it.

After they had stopped by Thomas' flat near the docks to pick up Sam's bike, they made their way out of the heart of the village and further into the hills on The Clachan road. Sam stared at the richly colored trees and inhaled the crisp, woody scent; memories of being a child and climbing those trees flooded back to him. They pulled into the drive of an old white house with bright blue trim that had paint peeling everywhere, and Sam couldn't help but smile, *It's just as I remember.* Despite having not set foot in it for so long, he never had the heart to remove the key from his key ring. He half expected his father to have changed the locks at least once before he died four years prior, but was pleasantly surprised to learn that his key worked as it always had. Walking in to a hallway, he looked to his right at the sitting room: faded ivory walls with wooden beams lining the ceilings, a floral sofa, wooden tables, and a fireplace. Further down the hallway was the kitchen and a door that lead outside. Just before that, there was a set of stairs that led to the three bedrooms up top.

"Alrigh' there, big man?" Thomas called.

"Aye," Sam answered before walking back to the car.

"Come now, admit it t' me, ye missed us."

A swarm of tiny bugs resembling the mosquitoes Sam had gotten very familiar with in America flew around his face and he swatted them. "Aye, bu' I dinnea miss these little bastards! Damn midges are terrible!"

Thomas gave a hearty laugh as he reached his hand out to shake Sam's. "See ye a' the pub later?"

"Not tonight, pal. I jus' go' back, and I need some sleep in a good bed."

Thomas let out a booming laugh. "Aye, ya do look like a dug lickin' pish off a nettle."

"Shu-up," Sam rolled his eyes and laughed in reply.

"Tomorrow then?"

"Aye."

Just before Thomas drove off, he rolled down the window and called, "It's good to have ya back, big man. Spendin' so long with them Americans, ye go' a shite accent now."

Sam couldn't help but roll his eyes before he waved him off. Walking back inside of the house, the first thing he did was walk back into the kitchen to see what food he might need. Hannah had thought ahead to buy him some bread, cookies, milk, and even tea, but not much else. Setting the kettle over the fire, he took his suitcases up the stairs and into the first bedroom on the left. It was once his father's bedroom, and it was the biggest of the three, though it didn't look it with the large bed consuming most of the space. The only other furniture was a chest of drawers against the wall with a window, a flimsy portable closet next to it, and a little side table. He had barely gotten one suitcase unpacked when he heard the kettle screaming and quickly went to attend his tea before coming back to unpack the other suitcase.

After storing his suitcases in one of the other bedrooms, Sam discovered that it had finally stopped raining. Deciding there would be nothing else to do the entire day, Sam rode his bike back into the village and towards the market.

While most single men would have settled for the bare basics, one thing Sam could pride himself on was what a great cook he was. Though Meredith did alright during their marriage, she was prone to burning things now and then, so a few nights a week he would cook instead. Not that he ever told her he didn't like her cooking, as she was sensitive about that fault. Now, as he placed the many items he had selected in front of the clerk, he almost wished he'd taken the opportunity to insult her that way but quickly snuffed the feeling out. *It wouldnea have helped anythin'.*

"Ach! Tha' cannea be Sampson!"

Sam looked over to see a portly man with painfully thin white hair and a bristly mustache slowly walk towards him and couldn't help but smile. "Hallo Mr. Stewart."

"Ye donnea work for me anymore, son. Ye can call me Andrew now." The man smiled and offered his hand.

Sam shook it gladly and remembered a time when his father and Andrew Stewart owned the only grocery store in Rosneath; when he was a young lad finishing school, he spent his afternoons stocking the store and making deliveries for some of the locals. He remembered the man before him appearing bigger. When he was sixteen, Sam cleared Mr. Stewart by a few inches, and now he stood nearly a whole head taller than him.

"Ach, no, ye'll always be Mr. Stewart to me, sir."

Mr. Stewart laughed. "How long has it been, laddy? Eleven, twelve years?"

"Aye," Sam nodded. "Been a while."

"Wha' on earth ye doin' back here? Last I'd heard, ye and yer brother were happily livin' in America. Heard ye'd even settled down with tha' American woman tha' came here."

Sam nodded. "Well, I havenea seen Josh for a long time, now. And this last year my marriage ended in divorce."

Mr. Stewart tapped his fingers together nervously. "Oh, I'm sorry lad. I dinnea know."

The bell hanging next to the door rang as another person walked in, and Sam was grateful for the awkward moment being dissolved. He followed Mr. Stewart's gaze as he addressed the new patron.

"Afternoon, lassy." The older man smiled.

"Hello, Mr. Stewart," she smiled.

"I have a package for ye tha' came this mornin'. Give me just a wee moment, i's in the back."

"Thank you," she nodded and her eyes briefly met Sam's before she pushed a few loose strands of hair over her ear. She turned her back to him to look at the display of fresh berries.

She was of medium height with dark hair twisted into a braid falling down her back. And despite the many layers she was wearing to fend off Scotland's cold climate, Sam could tell there was a womanly figure underneath her clothing. He watched her for a moment before the clerk's voice brought him back to the present. "16 pounds, please."

Sam paid for his groceries and loaded them into a paper bag before walking out the door and back to his bike. Groceries stowed in the front basket, he began his ride home, doing his best to avoid any larger than normal holes in the road. Once or twice, he pulled to the side to let a car pass, as the roads in Rosneath were not very wide. He couldn't help but chuckle as he thought of the many times he had complained about the drivers in Cleveland who were going way too fast and would speed past him on the highways. Only now did he appreciate the irony, as he was slightly annoyed by the tiny roads and the drivers who were slow in Rosneath. It had just started to drizzle again by the time he got to the cottage, so he rushed inside before the paper bag could fall apart.

Though it was barely mid-afternoon, Sam was already ready to go to sleep. Unpacking everything that he bought, he settled on a can of lentil and vegetable soup and some bread with marmalade for an early dinner before he retreated upstairs and collapsed on top of the covers.

~~~

The next day, Sam had already started a daily routine for himself: he woke up early, went for a light run before returning to do at least 50 situps, showered, and fixed himself a full Scottish breakfast consisting of eggs, beans, mushrooms, tomatoes, toast, and black coffee. As he polished off the last few bites, he circled another ad in the classified sections of Rosneath's paper. Though he technically did not have to worry about paying for the house as it was left to him, Josh, and Hannah, there was only so much money he had available, and most of it was spent flying back to Scotland. Not to mention, he knew he would go absolutely crazy without a job to keep him stable. After learning there wasn't an opening for a constable at his old police station, his options were down to: a gardener for the MacKenzie's, a mechanic at Virgil's, or working with Thomas down at the docks. After he washed his dishes and left them on the drying rack, Sam grabbed his coat, hopped on his bike, and road into town.

The gardener position had already been filled by the time he got within range to call the MacKenzie's; the docks advertisement turned out to be old news that for some reason had not been removed from the paper; and as Sam pulled into the yard at Virgil's garage, he watched the man he assumed was the manager shake another man in a suit's hand, and he was less than hopeful.

Once the man in the suit had left, the manager called to Sam. "Ye here about the job openin'?"

"Aye. Am I too late?"

"No' at all. Can ye replace a fuel line?"

"Aye," Sam nodded and parked his bike. Following the man into the garage, he saw a tiny, red four-door car up on the lift.

"Go on, then," The man nodded to the car.

Sam didn't waste a moment; removing his jacket and rolling up his sleeves, he took a quick look under the carriage and looked for the offending line. When he found it, he ran his fingers across the rubber to check for damages. Unable to find any, he furrowed his eyebrows.
~~~

"Hey, man," he called. "Is the fuel line blocked or somethin'?"

"No, why?"

"Well, if I dinnea know bettar, I'd say i's brand new."

Sam looked over to the smiling man who immediately chuckled. "Well done, laddy. Can ye start tomorrow?"

Sam laughed. "Aye."

"Wha's yer name, big man?"

"Sam."

"I'm Virgil; good to meet ya, man. Come talk in me office."

"Hey, wha' was really wrong with the car?"

"Needed a new tire," Virgil laughed before he walked away.

Within minutes, Sam had all of the paperwork filled out and a jumpsuit that barely fit his tall frame. Virgil told him he could only afford to have him three days a week in the afternoons, plus Saturdays, but Sam was happy for the chance to do something and didn't mind not being full-time. Stopping only at the post office to mail a letter to his son, he took the long road through town and spent his time re-familiarizing himself with Rosneath's streets and people. By mid-day he began to feel hungry and stopped in front of his favorite, Chippy's, for some fried fish. By mid-afternoon, it had started to rain, and he headed back to the cottage. Along the way, he noticed a tan colored car pulled off to the side of the road failing to start. He intended to stop and help, but as he was just behind the car, the engine turned over, and the car was moving again. He barely caught a glimpse through the rear window, but he could tell that the driver was definitely female. Before long, she was far enough away that he didn't have to worry about her stalling again, so he continued home.

The white car in the driveway caught his attention. He didn't have to wait too long to wonder who it belonged to as his sister came bounding out of the house and ran into his arms.

"God, I cannea believe ye're actually here!" Hannah exclaimed joyfully.

"Came all this way jus' to see if I was lyin', did ya?" he teased.

"Shu-up and hug me," she laughed. "I'm so sorry I wasnea able to pick ye up meself."

"Ach, is alright." Sam smiled and hugged her tightly. "How are ye, lass?"

"Hungry," she pulled back. "an' I saw that ye've already been shoppin'."

"Aye, you stayin' for dinna'?"

"I already peeled the potatoes."

Sam chuckled at his baby sister's antics. She was still the same bright and bubbly person she'd always been, and he was grateful that nothing had changed her in his time away. She had just turned twelve when he'd moved to America, and though they had kept in touch through letters and later email, sending each other photos all the time, seeing her in person made him happier than he'd been in over a year. She spoke about her work as a teacher in Stirling High School and how her students gave her a better appreciation for their father, her mother, and all of the trouble they'd put the two of them through. Sam heartily laughed and agreed. Curious as to how his former step-mother was, Hannah assured him that Paige was happy in Edinburough and sends her regards to Sam. When Hannah asked him about Meredith and Oliver, Sam gave her the basics but immediately turned the conversation elsewhere. They spoke of their other brother Josh briefly, mostly agreeing how neither of them had heard from him in years.

"You donnea think he's ..." Hannah stopped herself.

"Dead?" Sam filled in for her. "Ach, no, dinnea worry abou' that. I checked for his name in the system regularly to make sure he wasn't. The last I'd seen, he'd been found guilty of possession, and he's serving five years in an American prison."

Hannah looked down at her plate of food sadly. "Well, at least we know where he is."

Sam nodded and took a drink of his wine. "Ye gotta' stop worryin' abou' him so much, Hannah. Josh made his choices."

"He's still our brother, Sam."

"Aye, tha' he is, and I'll be the first one to help him when he's ready to change. But until then, he's go' consequences to deal with. Now, change of subject, don't think I didnea notice tha' wee ring on yer finger there."

At the mention of her engagement, Hannah beamed and brought her hand forth to show Sam.

"It happened last week, I dinnea wanna' tell ye over email since ye were comin' home anyway."

Sam held her finger closer to his eyes, feigning close examination. "Boy's a tight Scotsman isn't ... ahh, there's the diamond."

"Shu-up," Hannah pulled her hand back and pushed him. "I think i's beautiful."

He laughed and nudged her. "I was startin' to wonder if Zander would ever make ye an honest woman. I'm happy for ye."

"Thanks, me too. His mum wants a big white weddin' at the family home in Edinburgh."

Sam took another sip of wine. "And ye don't?"

"Ach, no. Too many people, half of which I donnea even know, and the whole thing jus' becomes a big show fer everyone else." Hannah sighed. "Ye've done the white weddin'; give me one reason why I should do it."

"Lo's of free stuff."

She laughed before grabbing Sam's wrist to glance at his watch.

"Ach, I gotta' be headin' back. Gotta' give the kids a test in the mornin'."

"Can I have a ride to Jackie's?"

"Aye, come on."

The rain was pouring as they carefully drove into town. Hannah pulled in front of the old pub and she hugged Sam tightly. "I'm so glad ye're back."

"Aye, me too," he smiled and gave her a squeeze. "Be careful, now. And congratulations to ye and Zander."

"Thanks. Say hi t' Thomas fer me?"

"Aye, I will," he nodded before running up to the door. He stayed behind to watch his sister drive off only for a moment before walking inside of the old building. It had been twenty years, and Jackie's hadn't changed at all: the barstools still had ripped leather and padding spilling out the sides; the juke box was still in the far corner; the air still smelled of cigarettes and ale. In fact, the only difference was the wood tables and benches had more condensation stains all over them than he remembered. Sam wasn't the least bit surprised.

"Sam! Over here, big man!"

Sam looked down the bar and saw Thomas waving to him before everyone else in the bar turned to see him. Suddenly his name was being shouted, and dozens of people were walking over for a handshake. "I's good to see ye!" "When did ye get back?" "How was America?" were the most frequently asked questions he had to answer before he could finally sit in the stool next to Thomas.

"Sampson McKay, as I live and breathe."

Sam looked over the bar to the short, bald headed man that was Jackie. The grumpy man looked him over once before grunting, "Twenty years and ye're still an overgrown bampot."

Sam nodded. "Aye, and ye're still ugly."

Jackie scowled in response before placing his hands on the bar. "Wha'll ye have?"

"Ale."

Jackie opened a bottle of Guiness and retrieved a glass. Setting them down in front of Sam, he turned and walked away to his other customers. Thomas couldn't help but chuckle.

"I donnea think he's forgiven ye for tramplin' his bloody flowers yet."

"And why should he? It was only twenty-five years ago." Sam muttered as he carefully poured his ale.

Thomas chuckled before nudging Sams shoulder. "Oi! Tha's the girl!"

"Wha' girl?"

"The American I tol' ye abou', tha's her!"

Sam turned to where Thomas was looking and recognized the woman instantly. Medium height and slender, her dark brown hair still twisted in a braid that fell down her back, wearing a white high-neck sweater and tight jeans, but it was the same woman from the grocer the day before, and there was no mistaking it.

"Tha's Liz," Thomas whispered giddily.

Sam nodded his appreciation before turning back to his drink. "Shoulda' gotten us a table."

"They were all full when I go' here," said Thomas. "Now ye can see why."

"Ye better no' bring Helen here with ya, if ye're gonna' keep lookin' a' the lassy like tha'."

Thomas laughed before turning back to his own drink.

A few minutes later, the pub erupted with loud shouts and crude remarks. Curious, Sam looked over to the door.

"Oh, bollocks," Thomas muttered.

A rough group of five big men came walking through the door and stopped in front of a fully packed table. Within seconds, everyone who had been sitting there vacated it, and the group slid in.

Sam furrowed his eyebrows, "Is that …"

"Aye, Ben Abernathy and his group of miscreant numpties."

Sam scoffed. "No' much has changed, then?"

"Only one thing," Thomas nodded towards the door again.

Sam looked to see a willowy blonde woman wearing a tight green dress walk in and immediately sit in Ben's lap. "Is tha' … Victoria McDuff?"

"I's Victoria Abernathy, now."

Sam turned back to Thomas with his mouth dropped open. "She actually married that arsehole?"

"Aye," he nodded. "Ten year ago."

"Well … her taste is shite, bu' she looks great."

Thomas chuckled. "Well, I can tell ye she donnea look like tha' on the every day. I think she heard *you* were back."

Sam had barely taken another sip of his ale when Ben and his men started getting louder than usual. He looked over to see the fat one he recognized as Wyatt Clowney with his hand on the American waitress' wrist. She was pulling away from him without much success. Sam looked around for Jackie and cursed the man's no-care attitude, as he was nowhere to be found. Without wasting another moment, he left his seat and walked over to the table.

Wyatt leered at her. "Come on, luv, jus' one?"

"Let go of me, now!"

Wyatt laughed before feeling a large hand land on his shoulder that squeezed him until he yelped in pain and released the waitress' wrist. He turned and bellowed, "Who the hell do ye—" before stopping himself and staring wide-eyed at the man standing over him.

Sam glared Wyatt down before turning his attention back to the woman. "Lass, le's have a round of scotch for these good men on me, an' they won't bother ye anymore."

Liz rubbed her wrist and nodded before quickly running back to the bar.

"Sampson McKay."

Sam turned his attention to the groups leader and nodded. "Ben."

"Son offa bitch! Ye look like hell, big man!"

Sam looked over at Liam McClennon, a pencil thin man with flaming red hair that he kept tied in a disheveled pony tail. "And ye still look like a squirrel's nest."

Liam's booming laughter only added to the tension in the air; the remaining patrons had grown silent and were watching the scene at the end of the pub, wondering what would happen next.

"Sam, I hope ye havnea forgotten the Lawder twins?" Ben pointed to the remaining two men sitting next to Wyatt.

Sam nodded to the dark, grisly men, "Aaron, John."

They nodded in return.

"And of course, you cannea have forgotten this beauty here," Ben nodded to the woman still sitting in his lap.

Victoria looked Sam over and purred a low, "Hallo, Sam."

"Hallo, Vicky," he replied to her. When Liz appeared with her tray, he gently took it from her, "Thank ye."

Liz walked back to the bar without a word, and Sam gave every man and woman at the table their drink.

"Why dinnea ye pull up a chair, Sam? Entertain us with yer adventures in America," Ben said before taking a sip of his free scotch.

Sam looked squarely at Ben before answering him. "Perhaps another time, lads."

Thomas, who hadn't moved an inch from his spot at the bar since Sam walked over to that table, stared at the scenario. Finally, when Ben chuckled and the other men picked up their drinks, Sam walked back to the bar. Thomas took a long sip from his own ale, relieved that the situation was finally diffused.

Sam set the tray back on the bar in front of Liz. "Ye alright, there?"

"Yeah, thanks," she nodded, picking up the tray and wiping it down.

Reaching for his wallet, Sam retrieved a fifty-pound note and set it in front of her. "Keep the change."

Grabbing the money a little too quickly, Liz placed it in her pocket and kept her eyes on the large man as he walked back to his seat.

Chapter Three

Nearly three weeks had passed since Sam settled in; he spent most of his time fixing up the cottage if he wasn't working at the garage. Every Thursday he rode into town to pick up his pay from Virgil, stop at the market for groceries for the week, as well as any supplies he needed for the renovations. Most evenings were spent at Jackie's with Thomas, but occasionally he would stay in for the night and read a book instead. Though he sent a letter to Oliver every Tuesday without fail, Sam had yet to receive a reply from his son. Still, he kept sending letters and assuring him that he loved him. Things were peaceful, and he couldn't find it in him to complain too much.

On a particularly cold Saturday, Sam was at the garage finishing an oil change. He slammed the hood of the car he'd been down and handed the keys to the woman in the lobby. "Alrigh', lassy, ye're clear. Tha'll be 40 pounds."

The woman handed him cash, smiled, and left with a polite, "Thank ye."

Sam was concentrating on updating the books when the door opened again, and the smell of tropical perfume wafted to him. He raised his eyes to see a familiar blonde woman in tight leggings and a form fitting dress top. "Hallo, Vicky."

"Hi, Sam." She smiled and walked over and took a seat in the chair across the desk from him.

"Wha' can I do for ye?"

"There's a ligh' in me Jetta been flashin' for a few days now."

"Well, les' have a look."

He followed her to a new, foreign silver car. Victoria climbed in and turned the key before moving out of the way for him to see the light.

"Ach, yer tire pressure's a little low, s'all it is."

"Oh, good, I was worried it was somethin' serious."

"Pull up to the pump, I'll have ye outta' here in no time."

She did as instructed, and Sam set to work checking each tire and filling them as they needed.

"This job seems a little below yer skill set, if I've heard righ'," Victoria said.

"And wha' have ye heard?"

"Tha' Sampson McKay was a big shot in America, had yer own office and everythin'."

He scoffed, "Ach, whoever tol' ye tha' was way off. I was a cop: hostage negotiations."

"Still, muss'a been much more excitin' than pumpin' air in tires." She winked at him.

"Work is work," he grunted, "cannea be too picky. And wha' about you, Victoria Abernathy?"

His obvious dig at her status didn't phase her. "Aye, I go' married."

Sam screwed the last cap in place before standing over her. "There, ye're all set. Five pounds."

Victoria retrieved the money from her handbag and flashed him a coy smile as she handed it to him. "Thanks, Ben's shite with cars."

"I remember," he nodded and walked back to the office. He could feel Victoria's eyes on him, but he wouldn't turn around. Rummaging through the file cabinet, he heard her come in through the door and glanced over his shoulder.

Sitting down in the chair across the desk again, she continued, "So how are ye gettin' on?"

"I'm alright."

"You stayin' at yer ol' place?"

"Aye."

"I've seen ye at the hardware store sometimes."

"Have ye, now?"

"Aye, Ben has me there pickin' up shipments all the time."

"Wha' for?"

"He runs his own business, buildin' houses."

Sam finally found the correct paper he was looking for and returned to the desk; not looking up, he answered, "Good fer him."

"Wyatt, Liam, John, and Aaron work for him, too."

"Do they?"

"Aye. Ben does alright; loves workin' with his hands."

"I be' he does."

"Well, I guess ye'd remember wha' all he can do with his hands, wouldnea you?"

Sam grunted a reply.

Victoria leaned forward on the desk. "Are ye ever gonna' look at me, Sam?"

Sighing, he set his pen down and his eyes found hers. "Wha' do ye want from me, Vicky?"

"At the moment, a conversation."

"We're havin' one."

"Then how abou' a drink?"

Sam returned to his work. "I dinnea think Ben would like tha'. And ye're a married woman now."

"Aye, bu' I'm no one's property. And I'd like to have a drink with an old friend. Ye're off in ten, le's go to Jackie's."

Sam finished writing on the paper and filed it away, "Another time, maybe."

Sam left the office and walked towards the old boat in the far stall. Though he heard Victoria huff from her hurt pride, he refused to look at her as she walked to her car and sped away.

~~~

It had been an uncharacteristically warm day, and there wasn't a cloud in the sky, giving Sam the perfect opportunity to renovate the outside of the cottage. The sun was starting to set as he finished hammering down the last new shingle on the roof, when Thomas pulled up.

"Need a hand there, big man?"

"Sure, jus' take me ladder to the back, will ye?"

Thomas chuckled. "I've come to take ye to Barney's. He's barbequin' tonigh'."

"No' tonight, pal. I've gotta' clean up a bit."

"Ach, just jump under the water a minute and get yerself dressed. We're all goin' to the pub after to watch the big footie match, ye cannea miss tha'!"

Sam smiled at the offer; watching a football match between Scotland and England was tempting.

"Ach, alrigh'. Give me ten minutes."

Thomas helped him put all of his tools away and stayed in the
~~~

sitting room while Sam showered and dressed before they headed to Barney's house. Just about everyone he would usually see at Jackie's was there, along with most of the men Thomas worked with at the docks. He and Barney exchanged a little banter throughout the evening, but Sam mostly kept to himself and enjoyed the food until it was time to head to the pub.

Already packed full with everyone itching to see the game, the crowd gathered around the back corner of the bar and stared at the small television hanging near the ceiling. Quickly, Sam and Thomas slid into a table where they could still hear the announcer and see a little of the game.

"What can I get you guys?"

Sam looked over to see the American woman with her hair in a braid. "I'll have a beer."

"Same," Thomas nodded and shouted at the TV. "ACH! Come on!"

Liz chuckled and set to work bringing the two men their drinks before returning to cleaning the glasses.

The football match hadn't been on longer than ten minutes, but Jackie's was already overflowing with heated testosterone.

"Ach! Murphy wouldnea know how to score if a woman came righ' up and spread her legs for 'im!"

"Awa'n bile yer heed, ye great bampot! He's still better than tha' dobber McCaffey!"

"Yer off yer heid!"

Someone swung the first punch, and Sam couldn't help but laugh at the ruckus people were making. Not in the mood to be involved in the fist fight, he sat back and watched. Even Thomas began to join in and called to him. "Oi! Ye gonna' help here?!"

"Ye can handle yer own!"

"You nancy!"

Sam laughed even louder and raised his beer to Thomas as he knocked out his first man.

With the sound of a loud clanging, everyone stopped the fighting and looked to the bar where Jackie was waving his faded but still shiny brass bell back and forth and yelling above the crowd, "Alrigh'! Tha's enough! There'll be none of that in my pub tonigh'! Behave yourselves, the lot of ya!"

Immediately the crowd settled down and turned back to the match.

Thomas broke away from the rest and joined Sam at the table again, his nose trickling a little blood from a good punch someone had managed to give him in the chaos.

"Ye got a little love bite, there," Sam pointed to the dripping appendage.

"Bugger off."

Only one more punch was thrown during the first half of the game, but the man responsible was immediately escorted out. Sam and Thomas were on their second beer by the time the crowd had started to get really antsy: England had made three goals, and Scotland had a pitiful single goal.

The noise started to get to Sam, and he stood up from the table.

"Oi, where ye off to?"

"Gettin' some air."

"Ach, ye've spent way too much time in America," Thomas chuckled and took another sip of his beer.

"Shu-up," Sam rolled his eyes and walked outside.

It was a peaceful night; other than the sounds of shouting coming from the pub, he couldn't hear anything other than the sloshing water from Gare Loch. Staring at the water made him think of the many times he'd taken Oliver out for a spin on his old boat. The first time the boy tried to steer the outboard motor was something to laugh at, but Sam never let his son see him chuckle. Thinking of Oliver made Sam grow melancholy; despite his angry feelings towards Meredith, he secretly hoped that they might be able to work through their problems. If not for their sake, then perhaps for Oliver's. Sam quickly buried his sad feelings and went back to staring at the water. The loch would be a little too cold for his liking to go sailing at the moment, but when it would warm up further into summer, it would be a different story.

His serenity was interrupted when the door to Jackie's opened and more shouting rang through the air. He turned to see the American waitress stumble out and run around the bar. When he heard the sound of her vomiting, he grew concerned and decided to find her when he saw Liam McClennon walk outside of the bar as well.

"Sam," Liam looked surprised. "Wha' ye doin' out here? Shouldnea ye be watchin' the match with the others?"

Sam narrowed his eyes at the disheveled red-head. "I could ask ye the same thing."

"Ach, I jus' came out for a cigarette."

"Everyone smokes in Jackie's, pal." Sam growled, "He's go' ashtrays all over the bloody bar."

Liam sputtered for a moment, "I … was hot. Now ye gonna' let me smoke in peace or no'?"

Sam brushed past him and went to the back of the pub where he saw the waitress holding her braid back. She was coughing and sputtering. He quickly knelt beside her and gently took her hair in his hands, causing her to jump in surprise.

"Is alrigh', is alrigh'," he soothed.

"Who are you?! What're you doin …" she slurred her words before turning to throw up again.

Sam grasped her arm and held her steady until she finished. "Okay, ye're alrigh'."

"Ugh … I feel dizz…" her eyes began to roll to the back of her head.

"Hey now, donnea pass ou' on me now. Jackie's no' gonna' like his only waitress drinkin' on the job."

"No … no drink …"

Realization hit Sam, and he cursed under his breath. He picked her up and carried her back into the bar to find Jackie standing near the door.

"What the hell's go' into her?" Jackie asked as loud as he could, the crowd's yelling still drowning out his voice.

"Does she have a drink back there?"

"Ach, no. She never drinks on the job, jus' water."

"Shit," Sam whispered to himself. "Do ye know where she lives?"

"I think I got her address in me files somewhere back at the house."

"Ach, is there somewhere in th' back she can rest?"

"No."

Sam rolled his eyes. "Forget it. Oi, Thomas!"

Thomas peered out from the table and quickly ran over to Sam, his eyes wide at the peculiar situation. "Ye need a priest?"

"Verra funny. Get yer car, I'm takin' her back to my place."

"Whas' the matter with her?" Jackie asked again.

"For a pub keeper ye're really daft, Jackie." Sam growled at him. "She's been roofied. Quit bein' such a tight Scotsman and hire a damn bouncer, so this shit doesnea happen again."

For once, Jackie didn't argue with Sam. Satisfied that he had made his point, Sam carried the only waitress out the door.

Thomas quickly pulled the car around and tried to help Sam carefully climb into the passenger seat, the unconscious woman still in his arms. "Shouldnea we take her to the hospital? Ya said she's been drugged."

"She's tossed most of it behind the pub; she'll sleep off the rest and be fine."

"Ya havenea even finished unpackin' the house, big man. Where she gonna' stay?"

"She can have my bed, and I'll take the couch." Sam adjusted, attempting to make the precarious position he was in less uncomfortable. "Hurry up, will ye? She's heavier than she looks."

Thomas slammed the door shut and jumped in the driver's seat. Once they had pulled up to Sam's cottage, he opened the door for Sam while he carried Liz up the stairs and into his bedroom.

Sam tucked Liz in and checked her pulse. Satisfied that it was strong and she was sleeping peacefully, he checked that the window was locked and shut the door behind him. Thomas followed him back down the stairs.

"Ye sure about this, big man?"

"Aye, I know a date rape drug when I see it. She'll be fine."

"Who the hell would do tha'?"

"Twenty quid says Liam McClennon."

Thomas stopped short; his eyes widened. "I dinnea even see him at the pub tonight."

"Me neither, but he came walkin' out after she did. And he was flustered when he saw me."

"Ye really think tha' means he drugged her?"

"With Liam's history with women, yes."

"Tha' bassard," Thomas rolled his eyes. "Ye gonna' tell a constable?"

"I cannea prove it. But the next time I see him, I'll make sure he knows not to try that shite again." Sam walked Thomas to the door. "Thanks, pal."

"Aye, g'night."

Sam shut the door behind him; after retrieving a thick blanket from the linen closet, he got a fire going in the fireplace and picked up his copy of *The Old Man and the Sea*. Once during the evening, he walked up the stairs to check on his guest and make sure she was still breathing before returning to his reading. When his eyelids started to grow heavy, he set the book back down on the table, turned out the light, and fell asleep to the sounds of the crackling fire in front of him.

~~~

The following morning, Liz woke up with a headache. Opening her eyes slowly, she looked around her and started to panic from the realization that she was not in her flat. Tearing the covers from her body, she felt a small sense of relief to see that she was still wearing the same clothes from the night before, and nothing had been removed. Taking a deep breath, she looked around and assessed her surroundings.

The room was small and quaint. A dresser sat to her right underneath a small window, and to the left of it, up against the corner of the room, was a rollaway closet of sorts. Upon seeing the button-up shirts and shoes underneath them, not to mention the faint smell of oil and sweat stemming from the bed sheets, she knew instantly that she was in a man's bedroom. She looked to her left and saw the small side table with a glass of water and a bottle of aspirin on top of a note that said: *"Don't be afraid, I'm downstairs whenever you're awake."* She released the breath she'd been holding, feeling a tiny bit more comfortable at the situation she found herself in. Whoever it was that had taken her to his house, she had the feeling he wouldn't harm her. Dry swallowing two aspirin before chasing them with a little water, Liz slipped on her shoes and meekly opened the door to the hallway.

There were three other doors, one of which was open to reveal the bathroom. Steam was still wafting out of it and Liz guessed that her host had already showered, as she couldn't hear the sound of running water. Peaking inside, she sighed in relief to see it was in fact empty. She heard the sound of a pan clanging on the floor followed by a soft, "dammit," and she jumped in surprise. Leaning over the balcony, the sound of something frying and the smell of coffee reached her nostrils. Her stomach grumbled in hunger. When she heard a man's voice humming, a shiver flew up her spine. Knowing it was time to see who her rescuer, or captor, was, she slowly
~~~

descended the staircase.

Turning on the last step, she saw a very tall man working over a stove with a tea towel swung over his shoulder. More smells of bacon, toast, and eggs reached her, and she licked her lips. She suddenly found herself walking to the kitchen without realizing it, until she was in the doorway.

Sam reached for his coffee when he saw someone out of the corner of his eye. He turned to see his guest up and out of bed, looking all around her before looking directly at him. He couldn't help but chuckle inwardly when he saw her visibly relax upon seeing him.

"Mornin'," he nodded to her. "How's the head?"

She nodded in return. "Fine, thanks."

"Do ye want some coffee?"

"Yes, please."

Retrieving a mug from the cupboard, he poured her some and gestured to the kitchen table. "There's cream and sugar over there."

Liz tentatively took her coffee from him with a very quiet "thank you" and went to sit down while the man continued to cook.

"Did ye see the aspirin I left for ye?"

"Yes, thank you for that." The headache hadn't totally gone away yet, and she rubbed her temples.

Sam watched her carefully as she nursed her coffee. When the toaster popped, he left the items on the stove alone to fetch it. Not moments later, he had fixed a plate with eggs, bacon, potatoes, and toast together and placed it in front of her, along with some silverware. Sliding the butter and a jar of marmalade next to her, he turned back to the stove to fix his own plate.

"Tuck in, a full stomach will help ye feel better."

Despite her headache and slight nausea, the plate of delicious food in front of her made Liz's mouth water. Picking up a piece of toast, she smeared a little butter on it and took a small bite. When her stomach didn't retaliate, she picked up her fork and took a bite of the potatoes. She peered up through her lashes when her host joined her at the table and began smearing butter and marmalade on his own toast.

Sam could feel her eyes on him and cleared his throat. "I'm Sam."

"Yeah, you're the guy that helped me with those jerks at the bar. I guess this is the second time you've saved me, now."

He smirked, and Liz smiled. Taking a few more bites of food, she swallowed the uncomfortable lump in her throat. "Um … I wasn't … I didn't have a drink at the bar … did I?"

Sam set his fork down and swallowed the bacon he'd been chewing on before facing her. "No. Some arsehole slipped a drug in yer water."

She nodded. "I thought it tasted a little funny. When I started feeling dizzy, that's when I ran outside to try and … well, get it out."

"Smart girl. Unfortunately, ye dinnea get it all, though."

"Did you … hold my hair?"

"Aye."

Liz looked down, and her cheeks turned bright red in embarrassment.

"Dinnea worry, I've seen much worse."

"I'm so sorry."

"Ach, is alright. Ye needed help; nothin' to be ashamed of."

Liz smiled shyly.

Sam took another sip of his coffee. "So how are ye enjoying yer first time bein' a bartender?"

She looked up. "How do you know this is my first time?"

"Because a seasoned one would know to keep her drink under the bar where no one could reach it at all times." He smiled at her.

"You're a bartender?"

"No, I was a cop. I know a thing or two."

Her eyes widened. "Oh …"

"Jus' be more careful from now on." Sam took a hearty bite of potatoes.

She nodded and returned to her own breakfast. Spearing a bit of egg, she said quietly, "I'm Liz, by the way."

"Nice to meet ye, Liz."

"You too, Sam."

Sam had finished his breakfast quickly, but Liz could barely eat half of it before insisting she was full. Taking her plate and cleaning everything up, they walked to the door together, and Liz looked down at her feet nervously.

"Um … my car's still at Jackie's, I think."

"Aye, my friend helped me bring ye here. Well, I have to go into town anyway. Would it be alrigh' if I walk with ye?"

Liz gave him a small smile and nodded. "That'll be fine."

"Good. I's a cold mornin', do ye need a coat?"

"If it's not too much trouble."

Sam made quick work of retrieving his thick, woolly coat and a smaller one that belonged to Hannah from the front closet. "Tha's me sister's, bu' she won't mind ye borrowin' it."

"Thank you, this is nice."

Sam locked the door behind him, and the two of them walked down the road together. They hadn't gotten very far when a car horn honked behind them. Sam groaned and rolled his eyes to see Thomas pull up to them in his rusty Hillman Imp.

"Oi! Ye two need a lift?"

Sam walked over and placed his hand on the hood before turning back to Liz. "Liz, this is Thomas. He's the one tha' helped me with ye last night."

"Oh, um … hi," she waved nervously.

"Dinnea worry, lassy," Thomas smiled at her. "I look mean but underneath all this gruff, I'm nothin' more than a kitten."

When Liz laughed at Thomas waggling his eyebrows at her, the tension in the air was dissolved, and Sam turned back to her. "Jackie's is a wee bit of a walk from here, a ride would get ye there faster."

She smiled and nodded, "… Okay."

Sam opened the door for her, and she climbed in the front passenger's seat. "See ya later, pal."

"Aye," Thomas nodded.

Liz looked to Sam. "Thank you again, Sam."

"Ye're welcome." Patting the roof, he watched the car take off down the road, and he turned back around to retrieve his bike.

With no work shift that day, Sam rode to the hardware store and began wandering the aisles for interior paint and brushes. Staring at the swatches, he decided on a light sky-blue color for the sitting room. *Hannah always loved this color,* he thought to himself as he grabbed a large can of it. Also grabbing a tin of dark wood stain and some rags to apply it with, he had just finished checking out and was loading his bags into the basket on the back of his bike when he heard loud, boisterous laughing coming from across the road.

He looked up to see none other than Liam McClennon and Wyatt Clowney sitting at a table in front of Chippy's store. Wyatt was gorging himself on three baskets of fried fish and chips, and Liam was sipping a beer while he munched on his own basket of food. Upon seeing the ratty redhead again, Sam abandoned his bike and marched over.

"So, we'd just finished, and then she says 'wha' the hell kinda shag was tha'?'" Liam boomed.

"What di' ye tell her?"

"Only that …" Liam stopped himself when he saw Sam marching over to him. "Sam! How are ya, big ma—"

Sam punched Liam squarely in the face before he could finish his sentence, knocking him out of his chair and on to the ground. He glared at Wyatt, who didn't move other than to raise his hands in a quick defeat, before turning around and returning to his bike.

Liam pushed himself off the ground and reached for his nose as he felt something wet trickling out of it. Barely touching it, he winced in pain. "Oi! Ye broke my nose, you bassard!"

Sam didn't look back. He simply hopped on his bike and began peddling home.

Chapter Four

Liz was at the grocer's, but her mind was on the incident at the bar a week before. Ever since that night, she had followed Sam's advice and kept her refreshments hidden where no one could touch them. There hadn't been a problem since. That didn't stop her from looking at everyone she served with suspicious eyes, however. Every man who talked to her at work made their attraction to her more than obvious by asking for her number, or a date; more than once she was even asked for a kiss. The only time they hadn't asked was when their wives or girlfriends were with them, though the women noticed any time their men looked at Liz as more than a waitress. Their jealousy obvious, they would quite literally smack any ideas out of their heads. She still didn't know who it was that tried to drug her, and while she wondered, she knew there was nothing she could do about the situation, so what was the point?

As she walked, she thought how the only men who hadn't tried to proposition her were Thomas and Sam. Though she hadn't really spoken with either of them since the morning after that horrid night, other than when they came to Jackie's, they were the only people she felt comfortable with since she'd moved to Rosneath. She wondered if she could even consider them her friends.

Her thoughts were interrupted when Mr. Stewart walked over with a letter in his hand.

"Good mornin', lassy," he smiled at her cordially. "This came for ye yesterday."

"Thank you, Mr. Stewart," she smiled in return before taking the letter from him.

"Ye're a long way from home, aren't ye dear?"

"What makes you say that?"

"Ach, is none of my business. I jus' notice how every week ye send a letter to Pittsburgh, and there's always a letter comin' to ye from Pittsburgh. Seems to me, ye ought to be in Pittsburgh."

Liz quickly stuffed the letter in her pocket. "Thanks for getting this to me, Mr. Stewart."

"Of course," he smiled and walked away.

Liz turned the corner and pulled the letter out again. Though she knew she should wait until she got back to her flat, the temptation to just open it and read it then and there was overwhelming. She was about to cave when another customer turned onto the same aisle as her. Stuffing it back in her pocket, she resolved not to look at it again until she was safely inside of her home.

~~~

With Thomas's permission, Sam had borrowed his car in order to haul some of the bigger supplies he needed from the hardware store back to the cottage; a few wooden beams to fix the back porch, exterior paint, as well as soil and some flowers in their pots in an attempt to revive the garden in the front. He was just finishing tying the beams down to the roof of the rusty thing when he noticed a shadow coming from behind him out of the corner of his eye. He didn't bother looking over his shoulder.

"Tha' wasnea a very polite thing to do, ye know." Ben Abernathy walked around to the other side of the car and looked at Sam directly. "Punchin' me best mate, like that."

Sam didn't even acknowledge Ben's presence as he loaded the remaining supplies into the car.

"Ye've only been back wha', two months now? And already yer stirrin' up trouble. Wha' are people gonna' think, Sam?"

"Does it look like I'm concerned abou' wha' people think?"

"No, I suppose not. But then again, I shoulda' known bettar'. Ye've never cared wha' people though' about you."

"Too right." Sam slammed the door and walked around to the driver's side. "Now excuse me, I've go' a house to fix up."

Ben blocked his way. "Let me level with ye, McKay. I'm no' all that concerned about ye knockin' Liam to the ground. We both know he's done more than enough in his life to deserve it. Bu' wha' I am concerned about is you and Vicky."

Sam didn't flinch. "There is no 'me and Vicky,' Ben."

"Too right, there's not. And there better no' be. No' unless you really want tha' rematch."

Sam scoffed. "I's you who wants a rematch, Ben. I won tha' fight
~~~

fair and square, and ye know it. As far as yer current reason to hate me goes, if this is about her comin' to the garage, all I did was fix her tire. I fix cars, pal. We're gonna' run in to each other from time to time."

Stepping up and getting directly in Sam's face, Ben growled, "Jus' leave her alone. Yer time with her is done; she's mine now."

Sam squared his shoulders and glared him down. "Ben, relax. I donnea want her anymore than ye want me to have her."

The two men refused to move their stances until the sound of a car horn broke the tenseness. They both looked to see a constable stopped in front of them. "Oi! Are we havin' trouble, lads?"

"Not at all, constable. I was just leavin'." Ben gave Sam one final look before he turned and walked away. Satisfied that there wasn't a situation to address, the constable left as well.

Rolling his eyes, Sam got into the car and drove off. He made quick work of unloading his supplies, covering the wood with a tarp, and fastening his bike to the back of the car before driving back into town towards the garage for his afternoon shift. He had barely walked into the garage when Virgil came out of the office.

"Oh, good, ye're here, laddy. Jus' go' a call about a dead battery out near the Burn by Back Road in Clynder, lassy needs a jump."

"Aye, I got it," Sam nodded. Making quick work of getting into his too small jumpsuit, he grabbed the keys to the only truck Virgil had and headed out of Rosneath and onto B833.

What would take him about a thirty-minute bike ride only took him ten minutes driving to get to Clynder. Turning on Back Road, he followed pavement until it broke off into a little dirt path that followed the Clynder Burn stream for a couple of miles. The path and stream were surrounded by trees, barely giving the truck enough room to maneuver. Sam drove along slowly before he finally saw a familiar tan car sitting in the middle of the road. Parking the truck and reaching for the jumper cables, he smiled to himself to see Liz get out of the driver's side door.

Seeing Sam's face made Liz laugh incredulously. Pushing her loose hair over her ear, she mumbled, "Unbelievable."

"Is savin' ye considered a full-time job?"

"Ha-ha. I've been having trouble with this thing ever since I bought it, I guess it just decided to die today."

"Aye, les' have a look."

Liz popped the hood and watched Sam spend a few minutes beneath it.

"Yer battery's no' the problem. Serpentine belt's shot to hell."

"Okay, I have no idea what that means, so I'll take your word for it."

He chuckled. "It means I cannea fix it here. But I can fix it back at the garage. I'll have to tow ye."

The sky rumbled with thunder, and the two of them looked up to see a sky pregnant with heavy clouds.

"We bes' hurry."

Sam deposited the cables back inside the truck and retrieved some straps and a chain. In no time at all, he had the back of the car hooked up to the front of the truck.

"Alright, just keep the car in neutral and keep the steering wheel straight. Once we're outta' here, I can really tow ye back to the garage."

"Got it," she nodded. Following his instructions, Liz placed the car in neutral gear and in minutes they were off of the dirt path and back onto pavement. A few minutes later, Sam had the truck flipped around and her car tied tightly to the back of it, bumper to bumper. The ride back to the garage was pleasant enough, and before long, she was sitting in the office at Virgil's while her car was being pushed into an open stall. A few moments later, the owner Virgil walked over to her.

"Afraid we dinnea have a belt right now, but I can have one here tomorrow mornin'."

"Okay, that'll be fine."

"If ye need to get anythin' outta' yer car ye can go on, now."

"Thank you," she nodded and walked inside of the garage.

Sam was still poking and prodding everything under the hood when she opened the passenger door. When she pulled out an easel and a canvas as well as a pack, he ventured a guess. "Ye paint?"

Liz smiled. "A bit."

"Wha' do ye paint?"

"Landscapes and objects mostly, but sometimes I'll do portraits."

He nodded in approval. The thunder cracked loudly, and they both looked outside to see large raindrops start pouring down.

"Oh, great," Liz sighed in frustration before turning back to Sam. "Listen, I can't walk home with these or they'll get ruined. Is there somewhere around here I could just leave them until tomorrow? Like a locker or something? It's just I don't want to leave them in my car where somebody might get to them, you know?"

"Aye, I get it, but I dinnea think tha'll fit in any of our lockers."

She looked back outside. "Okay … how long do you think this storm will last?"

Sam walked over and took a quick glance at the sky. "This one'll be a while. Probably go on through the night."

Sighing, Liz opened the door to load her things back.

Shaking his head, Sam called to Virgil. "Oi! Can I borrow the truck tonight, pal?"

"Aye, too wet to walk!"

"Thanks!" Sam turned back to Liz. "I'm done in a couple hours, do ye wanna' ride?"

"Oh, no. I don't want to impose."

"Ye'll catch yer death in this storm. Then I won't get paid when I fix tha' belt tomorrow."

His teasing caused her to laugh before she looked at her feet. "Um … are you sure?"

"Well, if ye wanna' walk in buckets of water, I won't stop you."

"Alright, alright," Liz rolled her eyes. "Yes, I would like a ride please."

"Brilliant. Go wait for me in the office, will ye? I've go' an engine to fix."

He walked past her to an old boat sitting in another stall, and Liz made herself comfortable on the only cushioned chair available. With nothing else to do, she plugged in her headphones and listened to some music to pass the time. Thomas had come sometime during the day and picked up his car; Virgil left two hours before it was time to close; and only one other customer showed up needing to top off their fluids. It was still pouring rain by the time Sam was finished and was locking everything up. When he walked into the office, Liz had fallen asleep in the chair, and he gently laid his hand on her shoulder.

"Hey, time to go."

Liz rubbed her eyes and yawned. "Sorry."

"Ach, yer fine."

Once he had finished locking up the office door, the two of them ran to the truck through the rain; Liz secured her things in the backseat, and Sam loaded his bike into the truck bed before they were ready.

"Where do ye live?"

"I'm renting a house out by Camsail Bay."

"Tha's just past the road to my place." He engaged the windshield wipers at full speed as they drove.

Sam slowly made his way out of town; a few members of the village ran across the road now and then. The rain came down so heavily it was difficult to see. Finally, he got out of the heart of Rosneath just as another loud crack of thunder sounded over them.

"Good heavens …" Liz whispered in awe. "Do you think it might be a hurricane?"

"Ach, no, dinnea worry."

The sky burst bright with another flash of lightening followed by a loud crash of thunder. Liz had to cover her ears from the noise. "I think I'll worry a little bit."

The road forked, and Liz pointed to the left. The storm didn't let up as they followed the road, and Sam could barely see out of the windshield by the time they pulled in front of a small wooden cottage. Liz covered her painting with her coat while Sam brought in her other items and the easel. Once they were safe inside, she quickly removed the soaked cloth and sighed in relief.

"Good, it didn't get too wet."

Peering over her, Sam couldn't help but admire her work: It was a perfect depiction of the stream she was stuck at earlier in the day only in much brighter colors. Though he didn't know much about art, he had seen enough from the hundreds of times Meredith had dragged him to art galleries to know it reminded him of a Van Gogh painting; the colors were splattered heavily on the canvas. Taking a moment to look around him, he noticed a few other paintings in the same style. There was one of a shepherd leading hundreds of sheep in the hills, another depicting a ship at a dock, there was even one of a little store in town that he recognized.

"Did ye do all of these?" he asked, more than impressed.

She blushed and nodded.

"Ye're very good."

"Thanks."

Another loud crack of thunder sounded, and the lights went out.

Liz reached into the drawer of the table in the hallway and pulled out a flashlight just as Sam looked out the door to see the roads beginning to collect water, but not quite enough to completely flood them.

"I best be goin'," he said.

"You're kidding, right? It's cats and dogs out there. You should at least wait until it lets up a little bit."

He looked back at her, questioning her offer.

"It's no problem. I'll make you a cup of tea to say thanks," Liz smiled at him, though he could barely make it out with the flashlight pointing directly at him. "Listen, I need to go upstairs and change out of these soaking clothes. Can you get a fire going?"

"Aye, I can do tha'." Sam turned to his left and walked into the small sitting room where the fireplace was. Stripping out of his wet coat, in no time at all, he had a fire crackling away, and he stayed close to warm himself. With the light bouncing around the walls, he was able to truly look at his surroundings.

While the outside of the house was older, he could tell that the inside had been updated in the recent years. The carpet still smelled new, and the walls appeared to be a light grey, at least it looked light grey in the dim light, with white moldings. There was a bright red couch facing the fireplace with a small glass table in front and a desk against the wall to his right. On the other wall was a fog stained glass window where he could barely make out the outline of the truck with a tiny bookshelf underneath it. A little too modern for his taste, but it was a comfortable room.

Sam heard Liz bound back down the stairs and looked up; she had changed into a sweatshirt that was far too big for her, and she wore some tight leggings underneath, her hair still wet but pulled into a ponytail. She turned the corner and walked towards the kitchen, and he followed. It was much smaller than his with barely enough room for a two-person table against the wall. A small refrigerator sat next to the sink and pantry while on the other side was a two-burner gas stove. As Liz lit a match to get the flame going, he poked around the cupboards for some tea and cups.

"You don't have to do that; I can take care of it."

"I donnea mind." He opened one cupboard and found very little inside of it: Liz had a package of shortbread cookies, a lot of canned soups, and a little tin of black tea. He pulled down the tea and searched for the pot and mugs again, but Liz found them first and set them on a wooden tray. He then turned to the fridge to see a small carton of milk, a few eggs in a basket, and a loaf of bread. *She dinnea eat much*, he thought to himself. He reached for the milk and looked at Liz skeptically who ignored his prying looks as she poured the boiling water into the pot. Tea ready, he picked up the tray and carried it to the sitting room, and Liz grabbed the cookies before following him.

"Thank you, again, for bringing me out here," Liz said. She took a cookie from the bag before handing it to Sam.

"Is' no' a problem," he nodded, eating a whole cookie in one bite.

"So," Liz cleared her throat and sat back on the couch. "I've only seen you around for a couple of months, but I'm getting the impression from everyone that you used to live here?"

"Aye," Sam replied, his mouth full.

Liz smirked and gave him the chance to swallow before she continued. "Well, since we're just trying to kill time, let's talk about that."

He chuckled. "No' much to tell."

"Were you born here?"

"Aye."

"When did you leave?"

"Abou' twelve years ago."

"Was it a girl?"

Sam looked at her directly. "Aye. Now les' talk about you. Where ye from?"

She shifted uncomfortably. "The U.S."

"Where?"

"Recently, New York."

"How long ye been livin' in Scotland?"

"Eight months."

"And what do ye think?"

"It's very … wet."

The two of them chuckled and returned to their tea.

Though it was difficult to see in the dim lighting, an object behind Liz caught Sam's eye: a flowerpot with finger paint all over it. He guessed that wasn't her artwork as it didn't look the same, it was much more childlike. Inside of it was a strawberry plant that had a few young berries growing, nowhere near ripe enough yet. But what was really curious to him was the name painted in bright white letters on it.

Nodding his head to it, he asked. "Ronald?"

Liz looked over her shoulder to see what he was talking about and froze. Quietly, she set her tea down, walked to the plant, and turned it away from him.

Confused, but understanding that the subject was not open for discussion, Sam took another sip of his tea. The lightening flashed, and the thunder clapped again over them. The rain continued to crash down over the house with no sign of slowing down.

"I think you were right, and this storm isn't going to stop tonight," Liz commented.

"Aye," Sam set his tea down. "Guess I bettar be goin' then."

"Is it really a good idea to drive in something as bad as this?"

"Ach, I'll be fine."

At that moment they heard a crash outside. Liz ran to the door and opened it to see that a large tree branch had snapped off and fallen in front of the road. Sam stood behind her and let out a frustrated sigh. He was ready to go out and move it when he heard Liz clear her throat.

"I have some extra blankets upstairs, if you want to give me a minute."

He furrowed his eyebrows and looked at her. *Is she lettin' me spend the night?*

She seemed to sense his question because she turned to face him. "A huge tree branch just broke off; it could have hit you, if you'd been out there."

"Ye hardly know me."

"Yeah, but … look, do you want me to make you a bed or not?"

Taking one more look at the damage outside, Sam decided he wasn't in the mood to risk catching his own death and nodded. Liz locked the door, and the two of them returned to finish their tea. While he took the tray back to the kitchen, she took the strawberry plant upstairs to her bedroom and pulled out two blankets and a pillow from her closet before going back down again. In no time at all, she had made him a bed and found him washing her cups in the sink.

"I can do that."

"I's alrigh'."

She smirked, already able to tell that, as they got to know each other, there would be many moments they would be stubborn with each other. She grabbed a tea towel and started drying. With everything finished, they walked back to the sitting room, and Liz cleared her throat. "Well, I'm gonna' go to bed. Do you need anything else?"

"I'm alrigh', thanks," he waved her off. "Goodnight, Liz."

"Goodnight, Sam."

Sam watched her walk up the stairs and allowed his gaze to linger over the only parts of her body that weren't hidden by the sweatshirt. Once she was out of sight, he walked into the living room towards the tiny bookcase that sat under the window. There wasn't a very large selection there to choose from. Most of it appeared to be modern works of fiction he'd never heard of before and a few that he had. *Wouldnea have pegged her for a Harry Potter woman,* he smirked to himself. Deciding to give a small blue book a chance, he settled into the couch and listened to the rain while he read.

Upstairs, Liz lay awake in bed. Even though she felt like she could trust Sam, that didn't stop her from locking her door before undressing. Now that she was alone, she pulled out the letter she'd placed in her nightstand. The envelope had a few water stains on it from the rain soaking her pants, but the letter inside was only wrinkled from being stuffed in her pocket. Using her flashlight, she smiled and felt tears of joy brim in her eyes from seeing the familiar crude pencil writing that said, *"Dear Mommy."*

~~~

The sun shone through the stained-glass window directly onto Sam's eyes, and he cringed. Grunting, he sat up and rubbed his face when he heard the sounds of someone talking coming from outside.

"Come on, you stupid ..." Liz's voice trailed off.

Curious, he slipped on his shoes and opened the front door to see her trying to move the large branch which completely dwarfed her. Amusement at the sight pulled the corners of his mouth up into a smile. Putting on his coat, he walked out to her.

Liz neither saw nor heard Sam as she tried to pull the branch again. Heaving with all of her might, she pulled and pulled until the smaller branch she'd been holding on to slipped out of her hands and whipped away from her. The momentum whipped it back and caught
~~~

her in the leg.

"Ouch! Dammit!" she hissed and rubbed the now tender spot.

Sam's laughter came from behind, and she turned around.

"Hey, I'd like to see you try and move this thing."

"Ach, no problem." Sam bent down and heaved, lifting the branch up only a few inches but just enough to let him move it a few feet before he had to set it down again. With another deep breath, he repeated the action until he had successfully cleared the pathway for the truck.

"Show off," Liz mumbled. "Do you want some coffee?"

"I need some breakfast," Sam replied as he felt his stomach rumble.

"I've got a couple eggs and some bread, but not much else."

"Yeah, I need more than wha' ye've got in tha' kitchen." Sam walked towards the truck but turned back to Liz. "Come on, ye cannea live offa' canned soup three meals a day."

Laughing, she followed. "When you cook like me, yes you can."

"Better artist than a cook, eh?"

"That's right."

Sam laughed and drove them to a small café in town near the garage. While he ordered a full Scottish plate and coffee, Liz ordered a smaller bacon and egg-stuffed roll and coffee.

"So...did you sleep well?" Liz asked.

"Aye. Comfy couch, ye have there."

Liz smiled and nodded. "Good."

"Listen, I was gonna' take ye to the garage after this and get tha' belt replaced. Shouldnea take me more than a half hour."

"Okay, thank you. That'll be great."

"Ye workin' at Jackie's tonight?"

"No, I'm actually driving to Glasgow tonight."

"Wha' for?"

"I've got a plane to catch."

Sam furrowed his eyebrows in curiosity. "Where ye goin'?"

Liz smiled but didn't answer.

He chuckled. "Alright, ye dinnea have to tell me. Are ye comin' back?"

"Yeah, in a couple of weeks."

Sam grew really curious about her agenda but kept his questions to himself. The waitress returned, carrying their plates, and the smell of bacon and sausage hit his nostrils. Greedily, he dug into his breakfast.

"What's your last name?" Liz asked him, genuinely curious.

"McKay. Yours?"

"Jordan."

Sam looked up. "Liz Jordan? It suits ye."

"Thanks, Sam McKay," she blushed and took a bite of her roll.

Chapter Five

Within a week of Liz's hiatus, the crowd at Jackie's quickly thinned. Sam found it much easier to get a booth at the pub, and he couldn't help but laugh inwardly at the melancholy air surrounding Thomas and his fellow bar mates every evening. More than once he would hear somebody murmur: "The lassy was the only good thing abou' this place." Jackie would hear it too and smack whoever said the comment upside their head and follow with, "My ale was enough for ye before she came along; is' enough now."

"Come on now Jackie, why'd ye le' her go?"

"Awa'n bile yer heid, ya doaty nance's! She'll be back in a wee while!"

Listening to the frequent banter between Jackie and his customers never grew old for Sam. But every mention of Liz made him all the more curious about her. Despite his curious nature, he was never one to pry into other people's business. But the way she hid herself wherever personal information was concerned intrigued him. He couldn't help the feeling prickling the back of his neck the more he thought about it. After two weeks of Liz being gone, one morning he couldn't stand the curiosity any longer.

"I'll be back, pal," he said to Thomas as he got up from the table.

"Aye, dinnea be too long or I'll finish breakfast without ye!" Thomas laughed and downed his ale.

Sam walked outside, retrieved the phone he rarely touched from his pocket, and looked up a number he hadn't called in months.

~~~

Derrick Rivera was sleeping soundly when the shrill, obnoxious ringtone of his phone started to sound. He jolted up and began reaching for his pants when he answered it groggily. "Rivera."

"Did I wake ye?"
~~~

His eyes opened wide at the familiar voice. "Sam? Jesus, do you know what time it is?"

"Wha' happened to the whole 'early to bed, early to rise' bullshit ye believe, Rivera? Gotten lazy since I been gone?"

Rivera glanced over his shoulder at the woman sleeping next to him and smirked. "Not exactly. What's up?"

"I need a favor."

"Okay, sure."

"Can ye run a background check on someone for me?"

Derrick furrowed his eyebrows. "Yeah, sure. Give me a second to find a pen … Okay, what's the name?"

"Liz Jordan."

"Liz … Jordan … Is Liz short for something?"

"I dinnea know, try Elizabeth, Eliza, whatever else ye can think of."

"Okay. Any special reason I'm doing this?"

"Aye, I'm curious."

"And we all know how you don't like being curious," Rivera chuckled. "Alright, I'll see what I can find out and send it to you."

"Ye still go' my email?"

"Do they even have computers in that little village of yours?"

"Watch yer mouth, Rivera."

"Ha. Okay, I'll get this to you as fast as I can … It's good to hear from you, Sam."

There was a pause over the phone before he heard Sam clear his throat. "Aye."

The call ended, and Rivera set the phone back down on the nightstand. He smiled when he felt an arm slide over his torso.

"Mmmm …too early …" Julie whined. "Come back to bed."

Rivera rolled over and pulled her flush to him. Caressing her face with the back of his fingers, he smiled when she flinched at the loving gesture.

"Stop it, you're tickling my nose." She swatted at him.

"You're cute when your nose wrinkles like that."

She opened her eyes and looked at him incredulously. "Really?"

He chuckled and leaned down to kiss her.

When he pulled away, she yawned. "Who was on the phone?"

"It was Sam."

She shot her eyes wide open and looked at Rivera in a panic

before he laughed. "Relax, Jules. We don't work for him anymore; it's not like he can say anything about it."

She relaxed a little. "Yeah …I guess that's true. … How did he sound?"

"Fine, I guess?"

"What did he want?"

"He wants me to run a background check on somebody."

"Who?"

"Her name's Liz Jordan."

"Oh, good grief," she moaned and rolled over. "That's just sad."

Confused, Rivera snuggled up behind her. "What's sad?"

"He's having you do background checks on the women he meets now? That's terrible!"

"Oh, come on," he laughed and leaned down to kiss her shoulder. "He didn't tell me why he wants it, he just said he's curious. Besides, you know Sam, he doesn't do anything like this without feeling like there a reason to."

"Yeah …I guess you're right. What time is it?"

"Almost 5:30."

Groaning, she pulled back the covers and sat up to stretch. "Guess I might as well get up."

"Right, you've got that big seminar at the university today."

"Yeah, woo hoo!" She rolled her eyes.

Just before she stood up, Rivera ran his fingers over the bullet wound next to the base of her spine.

Julie quickly got out of bed and away from him at the gesture. "You know I don't like it when you do that."

Taking a deep breath, he let the subject go. He heard her turn the knobs to the shower and called, "Can I join you?"

"Sorry, stud, no time for round two."

"What if I promise to behave?"

"You never behave. Why don't you go make coffee?"

Rolling his eyes, Rivera reached for his boxers and slipped them on before walking to the kitchen.

~~~
~~~

"How's it goin', laddy?" Virgil called to Sam, who was bent over the engine of the old boat.

"Jus' … about … done." Sam wiped the oil from his hands and turned to start the engine, which quickly roared to life.

"Ha! I gotta' admit, I'm a wee bit more than impressed! The ol' girl's been sittin' here fer five years, hadnea been able to get her goin' in all that time."

"Well, she's goin' now," Sam smiled. Shutting the engine off, he jumped out of the boat and walked over to Virgil to give him the key.

"Well, ya obviously know your way around boats?"

"Aye, a bit. You gonna' see if she's seaworthy?"

"Ach, I wish I could. I'm too old to be doin' tha'."

"What'd'ya have her for, if ye dinnea want to use her?"

Virgil laughed, "A hobby. Always tol' the Mrs. I wanted a boat to go fishin'. She said if I could find one that wouldnea rob us of house and home I could get one. So, when a bloke was sellin' this ol' girl for 500 quid, I jumped at the chance. Little did I know, she needed to be completely rebuilt."

Sam laughed as well and walked over to the sink to wash his hands; they had finished their work quickly, and Virgil decided to close early for the day to get the boat home, allowing Sam an early afternoon off. He decided being on the water wasn't a bad idea. After a quick trip to the grocer's, he headed home and decided he would use his following day off to have a little fun instead of remodeling the house.

The next morning, he woke bright and early and packed sandwiches, beer, and cookies before he got on his bike and headed to the docks. It was a beautiful, sunny day, and it appeared everyone had the same idea as there were plenty of people out on sailboats enjoying the weather. Fortunately, when he talked to the manager at the rental station, there was one sailboat hybrid with a cabin left, and Sam had no problem paying the full day fee to use it. In no time at all, he had gotten far down the loch where it wasn't so crowded before he brought it closer to the shore, slowed the boat down, turned off the engine, and made ready to hoist the sail. He had just finished unraveling it when someone in a little cove on shore caught his eye and he smiled.

Liz was focused on a canvas that showed bright blue waves crashing on the mud and pebbled shore when she heard a boat drawing nearer. Looking up from her work, she laughed to see Sam getting closer. "Hey, sailor!"

"Hallo!" He called to her and carefully brought the boat in to a sandy bar. "Ye paintin' waves or boats today?"

"Waves," she turned the painting to show him. "But it's not done yet, won't be done for a while. Nice boat, is it yours?"

"Ach, no, jus' borrowed it. Perfect day to go sailin'."

"I bet it is."

"How was yer trip?"

She gave a beaming smile at the question. "It was great."

"Jackie's hasnea been the same withou' ye. Most of his customers were threatening to never come back if ye weren't there."

Liz scoffed and rolled her eyes.

The gentle waves began pulling the boat away from the shore and Sam thought fast. "Ye ever been?"

"What? Sailling? Oh no, I've never even been on a boat before."

He smiled. "Do ye wanna'?"

"Oh, um …" she looked back and forth between him and her painting.

"Do ye gotta' be at Jackie's later?"

"No, I don't go back until tomorrow."

"Ach, come on then. I've go' sandwiches and beer."

Liz looked at her painting once more before smiling. Making up her mind, she nodded. "… Alright, just give me a second to get this stuff in my car."

"Hurry up, or I might drift off without ye!"

Liz carefully placed the wet painting on the front seat where the sun could shine on it before stuffing her easel, pack, and wet brushes into the back. Doors locked, she ran back out to the boat where Sam was standing at the front with his hand outstretched. She had barely placed her tiny hand in his large one, and he lifted her up in one pull. She yelped in surprise.

"Come on, girl," he chuckled. "The tide's turnin' me sideways and we'll get beached if we dinnea move!"

Liz started to feel a little uncertain until Sam took the wheel and placed the boat in reverse. Slowly, they drifted away from the shore until they were far enough out of the little cove for him to turn around. Once they were out and away from the shore, she watched him set to work connecting the fabric of the sails to different lines.

"What should I do?" she asked, looking around, uncertain what help she could give if any.

"Keep yer hand on the wheel, make sure we donnea crash into the shore, and le' me know if anyone gets too close to us."

Liz nodded and gripped the wheel tightly. Sam looked back at her and couldn't help but feel amused at her nervous demeanor. As soon as every sail was hooked up, he began to pull the lines to raise them.

The wind caught the mainsail, and the boat lurched beneath them. Sam was prepared for it, but Liz yelped again in surprise. He chuckled and walked back to her.

"Relax, lass. Yer startin' to make *me* nervous."

"Yeah, yeah. You want to take over?"

"Ach, yer fine."

She was shaking as she held onto the steering wheel. "Wha—what do I-- what do I do?"

"Well, if I were ye, I would turn the boat soon so we donnea crash into the point up there."

Liz opened her eyes in a panic when she saw the stretch of land he was pointing to in the distance closing fast. She began to turn the steering wheel as quickly as she could until he came up behind her and placed his hands over hers.

"Slow down," Sam laughed. "Water isnea like the road, Liz. I's always movin'. Ye won't turn immediately, but ye cannea keep turnin' the wheel or we'll capsize. Give it a moment, keep yer movements slow and smooth, get a feel fer the water."

She breathed a sigh of relief when the boat began to turn away from the point and out deeper into the loch.

"Okay … Okay … slow and smooth …" she gulped. "I haven't felt like this since I first learned how to drive a car."

Sam kept his hands over hers and helped her steer until they were far away from the shore and further out in the water. When she finally started to relax, he stepped back and let her handle the boat solo. "Jus' watch the boom."

"The what?!"

"Tha' thing," he pointed to the long, bottom part of the sail that swung next to them as the wind shifted. Sam couldn't help but laugh at the way she ducked beneath it.

Though it took time, Liz began to enjoy the exhilarating feeling that came from sailing. The wind whipped through her hair and billowed the sails, giving them what she thought was really good speed. Just as she became comfortable with everything, Sam walked onto the deck again and began pulling another line.

"Hold on!" He told her as he hoisted the jib.

The second sail made the boat go even faster, crashing through the waves and whitecaps. Even though Liz wasn't expecting it, she was much more comfortable with the sudden change and laughed as she felt the water splash up the side of the boat. She watched Sam as he sat down on the deck and get comfortable while she steered. Occasionally he would look back to give her a thumbs up or ask if she was alright. She would smile and nod, and he would go back to relaxing while she steered. The air was still cold despite the warm sunlight, and it was freezing on the water, but she hardly noticed with the way her adrenaline was surging.

When they started to get out into more open water, Sam stood and began to lower the sails back down.

"Wow!" Liz exclaimed joyfully. "That was incredible!"

He laughed. "Aye. We've gone far enough, les' take a break and eat."

Sails lowered the sails. Surrounded by water with no chance of crashing into anything, he led Liz down into the cabin. It was tight inside with cabinets and a table and bench combo built into the wall on the right, a short set of stairs that led to a tiny closet-sized bed near the front, and a second steering wheel and radio to the left. Sam had to stay hunched over in the small room, his tall frame making it impossible to move about too much. Liz couldn't help but smirk at the sight of the large man in such a tight space. She made herself comfortable in the booth while he opened up the brown paper bag he'd brought and laid out three ham and cheese sandwiches, a couple of beers, and a bag of chocolate and vanilla swirl cookies. He handed her a sandwich and a beer.

"Three sandwiches?" She asked.

"Aye, I get hungry." Sam ate nearly a third of the sandwich in one bite, and Liz smirked again before taking a dainty bite.

Through a lot of laughter and talk, they ate and drank until all of the food was gone (at least all of Sam's was) before going up top to sail some more. Once he had the mainsail and jib raised again, he took over the steering wheel, and they cruised all along the loch for hours, getting further and further away from Rosneath. They spotted some seals and their pups along the way, so Sam dropped the sails so Liz could watch them until the animals decided to go fishing and dove into the water and out of sight. The sun started to get lower by the time he'd realized how far away they had gotten from Rosneath, so Sam dropped the sails and turned on the engine, and they started heading back. By then, Liz really began to feel chilled and folded her arms across her chest tightly, grateful she had decided to bring a sweater with her despite the sun. Sam wore jeans and a t-shirt, and she envied how comfortable he looked.

He turned to look back at her and chuckled. "Ye gettin' cold?"

"Little bit," she nodded.

"So, I suppose you dinnea wanna have a swim, then?"

Liz's eyes nearly popped out of her head, and Sam had to stop himself from laughing at her.

"There's no way this water is warm enough to swim in!"

"Ach, course it is!" he waved her off.

"It's been raining or snowing almost every day for months! We've only had like, what, maybe three warm days in all that time? It can't possibly be less than freezing!"

"Exactly, sun's had enough time to melt the ice."

Liz's jaw dropped. "You're insane!"

"I'm Scottish," he waggled his eyebrows at her. "We wild swim regularly, tha's why we're so tough."

"Yeah? Well, I'm American; we don't do that. And obviously, we're wimps."

Sam laughed. "Ach, fine. Forgo' to bring me swimmin' trunks anyway."

Liz laughed and poked him in the ribs.

"Hey!" He grabbed her wrist and pulled her closer. "Jus' for tha', *you* can steer us back."

"I don't even know where we are!"

"Ach, come here." He placed her hands on the steering wheel. "Who knows when I'll ge' to do this again, so we bettar enjoy it now."

With how close he stood behind her, Liz could smell hints of oil and gas that obviously came from working in a garage. But underneath all of that, he smelled like leather and sweat. It was so uniquely him, and she found herself leaning in closer. She told herself it was because of how cold she felt and the warmth of his body that made her snuggle closer to him as they puttered home, but the way her heart quickened from feeling his hands over hers insisted differently. She rolled her neck and shoulders. Somehow her head ended up laying against his chest, and she froze. But she couldn't find it in herself to pull away.

Sam didn't mind how close she was; he had only intended to help her steer and keep her a little bit warmer than she was during the ride, but in the moment of her laying her head against his chest and placing her body flush to his, he found he was enjoying the feeling and didn't question it. Taking a deep breath, he thought he could smell pears and a little hint of vanilla, soft and sweet just like her. He suddenly felt heady from the closeness and swallowed hard. He could tell she was nervous by how tense she felt. *Don't do anything foolish,* he chided himself.

The sun was just starting to set by the time Liz spotted her car and pointed. "There."

"Aye," Sam nodded. He put his hand on the throttle and slowed the boat down as they entered the cove. Once they were close enough, he turned off the engine and let the boat coast into the sand bar until they were brought to a sudden stop.

Quietly, they walked to the front of the boat and Sam took Liz's hands and lifted her down and onto the wet ground beneath them.

"It was a nice day," Sam spoke first.

"Yeah, it really was," she smiled at him and quickly looked down.

He noticed the tinge of pink in her cheeks but decided not to mention it as he cleared his throat. "I best be gettin' the boat back to the docks, else they might think I stole it."

She laughed. "Okay. Thank you, Sam. I had a lot of fun."

"Aye, me too. G'night, Liz."

"Goodnight," she nodded and quickly ran out of the muddy ground and to her car.

Sam watched her drive away before he put the boat in reverse and began puttering further north towards the docks. By the time he had pulled the boat into the marina, it was completely dark. He was the last customer to return the keys, and the manager charged him an extra hundred pounds sterling for keeping it an hour longer than agreed. *It was worth it,* he smiled to himself as he rode his bike home. Feeling cold by the time he walked in the door, the first thing he did was get a fire going in the fireplace before putting the kettle on and sitting down to read another chapter of *The Old Man and the Sea*. Try as he might to concentrate on his book, the scent of pears and vanilla was still fresh on his mind.

Chapter Six

More than a week later, Thomas was helping Sam unload various pipes and plumbing equipment from his car and into the cottage.

"Christ, man, why the hell do ye need all this?"

"Because my house's plumbing is old as shite," Sam answered and picked up a particularly heavy box. "And if I dinnea replace it soon it'll come through me ceilin'. Is' times like this I miss bein' in America."

"How's that?"

"Excellent plumbing."

"Well, they'd need it, wouldn't they? There's always a stick up their arse over somethin'."

Sam chuckled. "Help me ge' this upstairs."

"Aye. So, are you and Liz shaggin' now?"

Sam scoffed. "No."

"Ah, so ye dinnea fancy her then?"

"I'm gettin' old, bu' I'm not dead, Thomas." Sam rolled his eyes. "Of course, I fancy her."

"So wha's the problem? I though' ye like them American girls."

"She's no' interested," he answered as they set the box down in the bathroom.

"Ha!" Thomas' voice boomed in laughter. "Yer aff yer heid. The lassy's been livin' in this town for nearly a year, and yer the only man she's actually looked at like she wants to shag. Ya may no' be dead, but yer a blind numpty."

Ignoring him, Sam walked back down the stairs and towards the car to unload more, but Thomas followed him and kept talking.

"I'm jus' sayin', she's pretty, she's single, and she obviously fancies ye. Ye should a' least try."

"No point in tryin, pal."

"Ach, wha' is it ye used t' always say? 'No matter how hard i' gets, ye have to try?' Sounds like ye need a taste of yer own medicine, man."

"No' this time," Sam answered gruffly.

Thomas quit laughing. "Listen, pal, if this is abou' Meredith—"

"Is' not."

"Then is it abou' Oliver?"

Stopping in front of more tools, Sam sighed. "He hasnea written me back. I've even tried to send him a few emails bu' …He blames me for the divorce."

"Ye think tha' if you go after Liz, Oliver will hate you more?"

"Aye, I know he will."

"Then tell him the truth about his mum."

"And risk him losin' the relationship he has with his mother?" Sam shook his head. "No, I cannea do tha'."

Thomas rolled his eyes. "Damn yer pride, man. Ye cannea spend the rest of yer life bein' a martyr, no' even for the boy. And he's no' talkin' to ye anyway. So, stop bein' such a Jessie and take the bloody woman to dinna'. Hell, bring her as a date to the Spirits Festival on Saturday!"

Sam picked up the last of the supplies and marched past Thomas and into the house.

Thomas sighed. "Okay, fine. Come on, le' me buy ye a pint."

"No thanks. I've go' a bathroom sink to fix. Enjoy." Sam didn't bother looking over his shoulder as he heard the sound of Thomas' car pull away from the cottage and head down the road. Instead, he picked up his wrench and hammer and began working on the rusted water pipes. Try as he might to focus on the task he'd set for himself of removing and replacing the bathroom sink that day, his thoughts kept turning to his teenage son. It had been nine months since Oliver had even spoken to him, despite Sam living back in Scotland for only three. Though part of him wanted to tell Oliver the whole truth about Meredith's extramarital activities leading to their separation, the knowledge of how much the boy loved his mother stopped him from doing that. *I wanted t' fix things …I wish I could at least tell him tha'* …But per Meredith's usual fashion, she didn't give Sam the chance to cool off from everything that happened and made the final decision for the both of them.

Between his anger at Meredith and how absurdly long it was taking to get every pipe loose, Sam impatiently began to hammer away at the pipes when his hand slipped, and he brought the hammer down on his thumb.

"Ach! Shit!" he hissed to himself.

At that moment, the doorbell rang. Still grumbling over his sore thumb, Sam yanked the door open ready to yell at whoever was on the other side but quickly stopped himself.

Liz stood on the porch holding a paper bag that was beginning to stain with oil; she was a little startled at Sam's angry demeanor but quickly recovered and smiled. "Hi."

"Hi," he said, surprised to see her. Curious, he nodded towards the sack. "Wha's tha'?"

"Your order."

"My order?" Sam furrowed his eyebrows.

"The food you sent Thomas in to town to get. He told me to tell you that Helen called him about an emergency, that's why he couldn't bring it back."

Sam eyed her curiously. "…So, he called ye, then?"

"No, actually I was leaving the store when he stopped me. He asked if I remembered where you live and if it wouldn't be too much trouble for me to bring this to you. You're on my way home, so … here."

She handed him the oil-soaked sack and turned to leave. "Enjoy."

Sam laughed and shook his head. "Liz, I dinnea order anythin'."

It was her turn to furrow her eyebrows. "But Thomas—"

"Is a nosy bampot. Dinnea ye notice tha' there's more than enough for two in here?"

"Well, I know how hungry you get, so I didn't think anything of it." Liz smirked.

"Too right, I probably could eat all tha'. Bu' seein' as how yer here, care to join me for a free lunch?"

"Sure," she giggled.

Sam moved to the side and ushered her to the kitchen in the back. "Alrigh', les' see here …fish and chips."

"Thomas is quite the romantic, isn't he?"

He laughed. "Ye wanna beer?"

"Yes, please."

Retrieving two beers from the refrigerator, Sam opened them both and handed her one before clinking his with her.

After taking a big drink, Liz reached for a fry. "So, what are you working on now?"

"Upstairs bathroom."

"Something broken?"

"No, jus' old and out of date."

"Sounds fun …"

They ate in silence and the air became thick with awkwardness. Sam cleared his throat. "…Ye goin' to the Spirits Festival on Saturday?"

"If by 'going' you mean working, yeah," Liz chuckled. "Jackie's going to have a booth set up there where I'll be helping him tend bar for the whole thing."

"Ach, of course. He's still tryin' to make his own whiskey, eh?"

"I guess so. He's hoping it'll get more attention when people come to his booth. You going to come?"

"…Aye, I might." He smiled at her.

A light tinge of pink spread across Liz's cheeks; pushing some loose strands of hair behind her ear, she looked away from him. "…This is very weird, isn't it?"

Sam smirked. "Aye, a bit, but no sense in wasting a free Chippy's. I guess is' hard to hold a conversation with someone you dinnea know much abou'."

"Especially when you're not on a boat where you can just tease each other about the weather."

Chuckling through a large bite of fish, he nodded. "Aye. Alrigh', I'll start. So, I've tol' ye I was a cop."

"Yeah."

"Well, I was actually a hostage negotiator in America."

Liz perked up and her eyes widened. "You lived in America?"

"Aye, for twelve years."

"…So, was the girl you left this town for American?"

"Aye, she was my wife."

"Was?"

"We divorced last year."

"Oh, I'm sorry." Liz shifted anxiously and swallowed the rest of her fish. "Did you have any kids?"

"Aye, a son. His name's Oliver."

She smiled. "That's not a name you hear very often."

"T'was my wife's choosin'; she loves art much like ye. Her favorite book is *Oliver Twist*."

"Charles Dickens, a woman of taste."

Tired of talking about Meredith, Sam cleared his throat and changed the subject. "Alrigh', now is' yer turn. Tell me about yerself, Liz Jordan."

The way her hands retreated to her lap made it easy for him to assume she was uncomfortable, but he kept his eyes trained on her.

"Not a lot to tell, really."

"Ye ever been married?"

"Yeah, I was married for a while but …not anymore."

He eyed her curiously. "…Wha' happened?"

Liz wrung her hands and fingers. "…He died."

Sam watched her carefully, trying to read her body language. Though his curiosity was begging him to probe further, he held his tongue and changed the subject. "So why move to Scotland? We donnea exactly have sunny beaches, ye know."

He noticed how her shoulders relaxed at his new question. "I've always wanted to see Scotland; it's pretty here."

"There's much prettier places in the world to be, not to mention more with the times."

"Maybe I wanted to slow down a little bit."

"Oh, in tha' case ye definitely came to the right town."

Liz laughed and ate another fry. "I like it here. The people are nice, and nobody's trying to find out anybody's business."

Her curious comment made him feel a bit guilty, remembering how he'd asked Rivera to look into her for him, and he thought about calling him to tell him never mind. Before he could think more on it, Liz stood up.

"Well, thanks for letting me share lunch with you, but I'd better get going. I've got some groceries in the car I've got to get home."

"Aye, of course." He walked her to the door. "So, see ye in a few days at the festival?"

"I'll be there," she smiled and walked away.

He waved to her as she drove off when he felt the phone in his pocket buzz. Looking at the screen, he smirked when he saw a message from Thomas that read: *Good fish?* He texted back: *You're a meddling nance.*

~~~

Saturday morning had Rivera walking into his apartment after a
~~~

long, tedious week of finishing an observation assignment and filling out paperwork. After finally having a stroke of luck with the suspect he'd been watching for nearly three months, he was able to give the lead over to the FBI's investigators and move on to a different surveillance assignment. That was after all of the documentation was finished first of course, which was his least favorite part of the job. His phone buzzed in his pocket, and he pulled it out to see an email notification from Simon. As much as the young man annoyed him with his sarcastic wit, he couldn't lie to himself and say that he wasn't happy to see him when he gave him Sam's request. Thinking about the conversation made him chuckle.

"Ooh, I love it when the boss wants me to spy on people!" Simon had clapped his hands together like a child and pushed his glasses up his nose. Turning to his computer, Rivera watched him pull up a few various programs he couldn't even begin to understand. "I'm *so* tired of telling people to try rebooting everything, so this'll be *much* more fun! What's the name?"

"Liz Jordan."

"And she's in his town … what's-it-called."

"Rosneath, yeah. But he didn't give me anymore—"

"That's more than enough for me!" Simon clacked away at the computer giddily. "As soon as I find out something, I'll let you know!"

"Okay." Rivera walked away, careful to hide his smile from the young man. *God I've missed him.*

Opening the email now, he snorted upon reading Simon's message:

Took a little digging, but I've got your Liz Jordan! Turns out she's actually Liz Harper, and she's on the run :O scandalous! Tell Sam I'm sending him hugs! S. Awesome Abler

Attached was a file containing everything Simon was able to gather on this woman. After forwarding the email to Sam, Rivera strode into the kitchen where he knew a beer would be waiting in the fridge. But when he opened it and saw the little brown paper lunch bag he'd made for Julie before he'd left still sitting there, he sighed in frustration. Ignoring it, he grabbed the beer and slammed the refrigerator shut.

~~~
~~~

The sun shone brightly in the afternoon on Saturday. The town was alive and quite literally buzzing at the Spirits festival. Highland Gathering Park was lined with canopies and tables as people from all around Helensburgh brought their own distilled whiskeys and bourbons for everyone to sample and hopefully buy, though a few people took the opportunity to bring homemade baked goods to sell instead.

Sam walked through the savory smells and bustling activity, politely turning down everyone who offered him a sample of their homemade alcohol and stuck to his cup of ale. Thomas, on the other hand, was more than happy to sample everything that was handed to him without any thought of buying a bottle. After an hour of taking a few dozen tiny shots, he was already a little tipsy. After taking a shot from Jackie's booth (with Sam and Liz stealing a glance and a smile at one another), Sam led him to the section where the baked goods were and sat him down at a fold-out table just as the sun was beginning to set.

"Easy, pal."

"Ach, I'm fine …I need a bloody pie!" Thomas pointed to the booth behind them. "Pigeon!"

"They only have pork or chicken over there, Thomas."

"Sounds perfect! Ge' me a bloody pork pie!"

Chuckling, Sam walked over to the booth that was being manned by a young redheaded girl who reminded him of Julie. "Ye go' any pork pie?"

"Aye." The young lady pulled out a knife to cut a slice from the large pie sitting on display. "How much?"

Glancing over his shoulder at his drunk friend, Sam turned back and said, "He's gonna' want more than a slice."

Setting down the knife, the young lady picked up a smaller pie that was enough to feed a family of four. "Will this do?"

"Aye, perfect."

"Twenty quid."

Sam reached for his wallet, but a familiar hand flashed out in front of him holding money. Looking to his side, he saw Victoria standing there with a smile on her face as she paid the girl. "Le' me."

The young lady, obviously not caring about the tension that flowed back and forth between the two of them, took the money without question and said cheerfully, "Have a lovely evenin'!"

"Thanks," Sam nodded to the both of them and took the pie back to Thomas.

"Ach! How'd ye know I wanted pie?" Thomas slurred his words together.

"Lucky guess, pal," Sam smirked. "Try to eat slowly."

"Aye!" the hulking blonde took a big mouthful and munched happily.

"Careful, Thomas," Victoria's voice purred behind them and they both looked over. "Too much pie and whiskey might give ye an upset stomach."

"Ach, I'll be fine." Thomas took another bite. "Oi, yer almost out of ale, pal! Le' me get ye another …"

"Is alright," Sam chuckled and kept the drunk man in his seat. "You eat, I'll go ge' a refill."

Satisfied that Thomas was occupied with his food, Sam walked over to Jackie's booth. Liz wasn't there, so he assumed she'd gone on a break as Jackie poured him another overpriced cup of ale with a grunt. Victoria stood next to him, but he hardly paid her any attention as she got her own drink. Finally accepting that she wasn't going to leave until he talked to her, he said quietly. "How are ye, Vicky?"

"I'm good, thanks. Yerself?"

"I'm alright."

"Still workin' on yer house, are ye?"

"Aye."

"Ye almost finished?"

"Aye, is' comin' along. Where's Ben?"

"Somewhere around here drinkin' with Liam and the others; he's no' missin' me."

Sam took a sip of his ale but didn't respond.

Victoria took a sip of her own ale and cleared her throat. "Wha' days are ye workin'?"

"Why?"

"Tha' light in me Jetta's come back on again."

"Come by anytime, if I'm no' there then Virgil will handle it."

"Yeah, well, I dinnea know Virgil."

"He'll be better able to fix it than I."

"I trust ye know wha' yer doin'."

Sam was starting to get annoyed by her forwardness and had a mind to tell her to bugger off when boisterous laughter interrupted them, and they looked over to the direction where the noise was coming from. Behind one of the food canopies, they barely caught a glimpse of Liz appearing to struggle with a figure neither of them could really see. Curious, Sam set down his ale and walked over with Victoria following him.

Liz was trying to walk back to her booth when Liam cornered her. Try as she might to get around him, he wouldn't let her escape and had even gone as far as to grab her wrist to stop her.

"Let go of me," Liz insisted, trying to wrench her arm free. But the giant, ratty redhead had a tight hold on her to the point where her wrist began to ache. "You're hurting my wrist!"

"Com'on, luv, jus' one li'le kiss?" Liam slurred his words together.

He was so close to her face, Liz could smell the strong alcohol on his breath and had to turn her head to keep from retching. Reaching with her other hand, she slapped him across his face as hard as she could but that seemed to only egg him on as he grabbed her other wrist and chuckled.

"Oi!"

The two of them looked over to see Sam approach.

"Le' go of'er."

Liam laughed. "Mind yer own, McKay. This doesnea concern ye."

"Liam," Sam growled. "Le' her go, now."

A small crowd heard the commotion and looked over before beginning to gather around the unfolding scene.

Smirking, Liam finally released Liz and watched her scramble over to Sam, who tried to usher her away. Before they got too far, Liam muttered something extremely derogatory under his breath just loud enough for all to hear, and Sam immediately turned around and punched the man to the ground with one swing.

Unbeknownst to anyone, Ben Abernathy had joined the growing crowd and had seen the confrontation. But when he noticed his wife standing behind Sam, that's when he joined the fray. While Sam wasn't looking, Ben came up from behind, turned him to face him, and gave him a good punch to the face, which made Sam stagger backwards. Sam barely had time to recuperate before Ben charged him and tackled him by the waist, sending them both backwards and into one of the booths behind them. The racket had gotten a lot of the surrounding Scotsmen's attention, including Thomas. As soon as he saw Sam stand up and punch Ben, the giant blonde immediately sobered and jumped up and away from his pork pie to rush over to help his friend when he was blocked by more of Abernathy's crew: Wyatt and the Lawder twins. Thomas gave a mighty roar and charged all three of them.

Though some people tried to move to a spectator position, many men had taken the opportunity to find something to punch the man standing next to them over and within moments, the festival had turned into a brawl. Vendors tried to move the crates of whiskey they'd brought out of the way before anyone could fall on them and break them, as dozens of grown men pushed, shoved, punched, and even bit one another. A few bystanders tried to simply duck out of the way but were not successful and ended up getting hit in the crossfire before ultimately deciding to join in the fray. It wasn't until the sounds of whistles rang through the air that everything started to calm down.

"OI! BREAK IT UP, THE LO' O' YA!" The head constable shouted as he and his men waded through the crowd, trying to stop the fighting.

Sam had Ben pinned down when he was pulled off by two men and dragged away. Ben jumped to his feet and tried to charge but was held back before he could.

Blowing his whistle again, the constable addressed the crowd. "Now tha's enough! Every one a' ya nyaff's back away now!"

Finally, the crowd had settled. Ben and Sam glared at one another as the constable reprimanded the crowd about keeping the peace and not causing another incident. After the threat of taking every single one of them to jail if another fight broke out, everyone was released and all began to walk away from the scene.

Liz ran over to Sam with a damp towel she had retrieved from the now ruined Jackie's booth; his nose was bloody and his left eye was already starting to bruise. Taking the towel from her, he held it up to his nose and watched Ben grab Victoria by the elbow and lead her away but not before yelling at Liam and the others to follow them. Glaring once more at the gang (but particularly Liam), Sam kept his eyes on them until they were well out of sight before he and Liz walked over to the booth.

Jackie was gathering up what little bottles of his brew had survived and cursing everyone under his breath. Despite being told to 'bugger off,' Sam worked alongside Liz to help clean up everything they could. It was well past dark by the time they were done, and even though the crowd hadn't thinned any, Jackie was preparing to leave as he had nothing else to sell.

"Away with the both of ye!" the short, bald man growled at Sam and Liz after they had loaded everything into his pickup.

"Do you want me to come help you unload?" Liz asked.

"Ach!" Jackie waved her off, got into the driver's side, and drove away.

Liz put her hands into the pockets of her jeans and looked at the ground.

"Dinnea worry," Sam nudged her. "He'll cool off by tomorrow. And he's no' mad at ye, he's jus' always been a grumpy bassard."

She smirked and looked up at Sam's face. "We should get you some ice for that eye."

"Ach, I'm alright."

"What about your nose? Did he break it?"

"If he did, then I'd have to shake his hand," Sam replied as he carefully pinched the bridge of his nose. Satisfied that it wasn't broken, he nodded. "Ben's strength is in his tackle, no' his punches."

Chuckling, Liz turned to see a banged-up Thomas stagger over to them. "The bawbags stole the rest of me pie."

Liz and Sam laughed heartily and quickly caught the large man as he began to fall.

"Come on, pal," Sam chuckled. "We best ge' ye home."

"Aye," Thomas nodded, his drunk state returning now that the fight was over. "Helen'll be plenty pished to see me pished."

"Mind if I tag along?" Liz looked up to Sam, her eyes giving away how shaken she still felt.

Understanding her meaning, he nodded. "Aye, come on."

The three of them walked through the crowds out of Highland Gathering and towards Thomas' flat. About halfway there, Thomas began to sway from side to side, and Sam had to practically drag him up the stairs of the two-story building. Holding his friend upright, Liz opened the door just in time for Sam to bring Thomas inside of the tiny flat and lay him down on the couch where the man had already begun to snore.

"Where's yer car?" Sam asked Liz as they walked back down the stairs.

"I parked right over there. Can I give you a ride home?"

"Aye, thanks."

Walking a little way back to the park, Liz gently rubbed her right wrist where Liam had squeezed it tightly.

Sam noticed. "Ye alright?"

"Yeah, I'm fine. Just hurts a little."

Gently, he took her wrist in his hands and lifted it closer to examine it. "Is' no' bad, ye might need some ice."

"I'm sure, after a couple pain killers, it'll be fine."

Still inspecting her wrist, he thumbed a particularly nasty bruise that was forming and couldn't help himself as he brought it closer to his lips and gently kissed it.

Liz could feel herself blush furiously at the tender gesture and watched him intently.

"There," Sam said as he released her. "All bettar."

Liz smiled and turned her head away, hoping he wouldn't notice her blush. She looked up when they got closer to her car and froze.

Sam turned to where she was looking and furrowed his eyebrows at the sight: her car had a broken windshield and a slashed tire. Walking over to inspect the damage, he could feel his blood boil. *I dinnea think Liam was* this *much of a rocket.* Turning his attention back to Liz, he walked over and placed his hands on her shoulders. "Hey, is' alright. I'll sort this out in the mornin' with the constables, and we'll get it towed to the garage where I'll fix it for ye."

"Yeah …okay …" Liz nodded but hardly seemed to hear him.

Growing concerned, he quickly led her away. "Come on, we'll take Thomas' car."

"How are we gonna get the keys? Didn't you lock his door?"

"After the first ten shots he wanted to drive to Aberdeen, so I confiscated them."

Liz chuckled. "Why? What's in Aberdeen?"

"His girlfriend: Helen."

Chapter Seven

Sam drove Liz back to her house. The ride was fairly quiet; despite talking a little, Liz's face was pale. He could hardly blame her, though, as she'd been assaulted only an hour before they'd discovered her car. But the way she held herself had him more than curious about what was going through her head at that moment. When he pulled into the drive, he noticed another car there. Liz was about to take off her seatbelt when he stopped her.

"Ye expectin' somebody?"

"What?" she asked and looked to where he was looking. Seeing another car that she didn't recognize, she began to shake.

"Stay here," he said gruffly, got out of the car, and walked towards the vehicle. Seeing that it was empty, he walked towards the house. The door had been kicked in, but had attempted to be shut again. Walking back to Liz, he told her to call the police and immediately steeled himself for a fight with whoever the intruder was before approaching the door again.

Pushing it open, it was eerily quiet inside. He tiptoed down the hallway and looked into the sitting room first but was relieved to find it empty. Next, he checked the kitchen which was also empty, but he grabbed a large frying pan before making his way up the stairs. The bedroom door was open and he saw a foot sticking out of it. Hearing a loud snore, he relaxed a great deal and flipped on the light. Liam was lying in the middle of the floor completely passed out. Sam set down the pan, picked up the drunk man, and carried him down the stairs before throwing him outside and onto the ground.

"Ach! Wha—" Liam woke up, but Sam happily punched him, knocking him down and out for the second time that night.

Liz raced out of the car and over to Sam, still visibly frightened. "How the hell did he get into my house?!"

"He knows his way around locks," Sam said matter-of-factly. "Dinnea worry, the police will lock 'im up, and he'll never bother ye again."

Like magic, they both heard the sounds of sirens wailing, and two police cars pulled into the drive. Sam did his best to keep Liz away from everything as he answered all of the constable's questions for the report, including mentioning her vandalized car. He scoffed every time the drunk Liam would insist he didn't touch the car and that he was only trying to get home but must've turned the wrong direction. Once the police were gone, Sam walked Liz into her house and leaned down to inspect the damage on the door.

"Sam?"

Liz's voice was near hysterics, and he turned all of his attention to her.

"I can't stay here tonight." She tried to hold back the tears, but her voice was cracking. "Between my car and then my house—"

"Is' okay, is' okay," Sam quickly pulled her into his arms and soothed her. "Shhh …he cannea do anythin' else, I promise."

She buried her face into his chest and shook from the sobs she was trying to hold back. Taking a few deep breaths, she pulled back and tried to speak. "I-I-I need to-to go to a ho-hotel."

"Ye shouldnea be alone righ' now …would ye like to stay at my house tonight?"

Heaving a sigh of relief, she nodded. "Yes."

Sam waited by the door while Liz went upstairs to pack something. He didn't have to wait too long until he heard a loud clunking noise and looked up to see her carrying a large suitcase in one hand and the finger-painted flower pot with a strawberry plant in the other. Taking the bag from her, he loaded it into the car while she sat helplessly in the front seat clutching the plant. They drove back to his house. The silence was even worse than before. Once they walked inside, he set to work making her a cup of tea. When she asked where some blankets were for the couch, he insisted she would take his bed, and he would sleep downstairs. He didn't know if it was because she was scared or tired that she didn't argue, but she took her plant upstairs, and he followed with the suitcase.

Checking for the third time that the bedroom window was locked, Sam turned to see Liz sitting on the edge of the bed and taking off her shoes. He could tell that she was still shaken, but at least she was breathing much more evenly. When she looked up at him and smiled softly, he relaxed and sat next to her.

"I know this is daft to ask, but are ye okay?"

"Yeah, I'm better now."

"Do ye need anythin'? I've go' a bottle of scotch downstairs, if ye feel like settlin' yer nerves."

She chuckled and shook her head. "No, thanks."

Sam watched her for a moment just to be sure there wasn't anything else he could do before he answered. "Well, goodnight lass."

He leaned over and kissed her cheek before he rose and walked to the door.

"Sam?"

He turned to look at her; she had stood up and walked over. Her face was flushed again and he clenched his fists together, trying to resist the strong desire to find out how far that pink color spread on her body.

Liz stopped directly in front of him and looked up into his eyes. She hooked her bottom lip in between her teeth and Sam held his breath. Then she stood on her toes to reach his lips; they were so soft and soothing, exactly the way he imagined the way her lips would be. He couldn't help but kiss her tentatively, and he felt as if he was melting; when he pulled back from her, Liz unknowingly sighed.

That sigh nearly made Sam lose all resolve to leave the room. Holding on to his last strand of decency, he forced himself to place his hands on her arms and take a small step back.

"Liz?" he whispered huskily. "I donnea think this is a good idea."

Her eyes shot open and she pushed her hair back again. "I'm sorry, I shouldn't have done that."

She began to back away, and he quickly recovered. "What? No, I thought tha' was nice. I just mean …ye've had a hard day, yer tired, and I donnea want' take advantage."

Blushing a furious pink color now, she nodded. "Yeah, you're probably right …Thank you, Sam."

Knowing if he stayed there any longer, he would lose all control. Sam quickly cleared his throat and bid her one final goodnight before shutting the door and retreating down the stairs to the kitchen where he could splash himself in the face with cold water. The temptation to walk back up the stairs and give in to the urges he'd been missing for more than a year was overwhelming, so he didn't stop until the cold water had quelled the raging heat he felt. Finally, he calmed down and walked into the sitting room. Getting as comfortable as he could on the couch, it took a long time for sleep to finally claim him but when it did, he couldn't be moved.

Later than he was used to the next morning, he woke up to see some toast and a cold cup of coffee with a note on his table that read: "Thank you for everything." Knowing he wouldn't need to check upstairs, he decided he would catch her later on and smiled at the thought that perhaps they could explore the previous evening's kiss a little further. His phone buzzed, and he picked it up to see an email from Rivera. Without a computer at the house, he was forced to read it on the small screen and had to hold it far away from his eyes to be able to make out each word:

Simon found everything you asked for.
Rivera.

Underneath, in the forwarded section, he saw the message and three attached files from Simon but couldn't bring himself to laugh at the twenty-three-year-old's goofiness. *Liz Harper? On the run from wha'?* He decided to shower and fix himself a decent breakfast first before looking into everything. Once he was settled at the table, he pulled up the first file, a missing persons report:

Elizabeth Brianne Harper
Date of Birth: August 14, 1989
Place of Birth: Stamford, Connecticut
Hair: Dark Brown
Eyes: Blue
Height: 5'9"
Weight: 168 pounds (at the time of her disappearance)
Sex: Female
Race: White

REWARD:
The FBI is offering a reward of up to $50,000 for information leading to the location of Elizabeth Brianne Harper and her daughter Natalie Iris Harper, and $25,000 for information leading to the identity of the person(s) involved in their disappearance.

DETAILS:
Elizabeth Brianne Harper, age 29 (at the time of her disappearance), and her daughter Natalie Iris Harper, age 5 (at the time of her disappearance), were last seen on June 10, 2018, at the Cleveland Museum of Art located at 11150 East Blvd, Cleveland, OH 44106. Elizabeth was last seen wearing a blue floral dress and white sweater. Natalie was last seen wearing blue jeans, a pink t-shirt, and white jean jacket. Elizabeth's stepfather reported her and her daughter missing on June 11, 2018. There have been no reported sightings of Elizabeth and Natalie since their disappearance.

Attached at the top left was a picture of Liz smiling. To the right was a picture of a little girl that was almost a mirror image of her mother, with the exception of having long blonde hair instead of dark hair.

Sam closed down the missing persons report and pulled up the next file, which was a news report video based out of Connecticut on July 28, 2018. A middle-aged woman serving as the news anchor said:

"As the search for Elizabeth Harper and her daughter Natalie continues, Elizabeth's stepfather Alexander Michaels held a press conference begging for the return of the two girls."

A man with a thin, clean shaven face and silver hair stood in front of several microphones and said tearfully:

"Please, if anyone watching this has Liz and Nattie, I'm begging you as a father to make contact. All I want is for them to be home and safe. I am offering a reward of $100,000 on top of the FBI reward for their safe return."

The video then turned to their pictures, and the news reporter's voice continued:

"The CEO of Ashworth Internet Security company also went on to promise a year of free service to anyone who had information regarding the missing girls on top of a cash reward."

Sam stopped the video and leaned back in his chair. *Wha' the hell is going on?* Staring at the final file attachment, he opened it and felt the blood drain from his face; it contained hospital and detox records for Elizabeth detailing the use of methamphetamines from the time she was twenty until the age of twenty-four. She had been clean for years until two days before her disappearance. He stared at the report and thought intently on her behavior since they'd met. There had been no indication she was using in all that time. But then the thought of the little girl came to mind, and he couldn't help but wonder where she was and whether or not she was safe.

Abandoning his barely touched breakfast, Sam ran out to Thomas' car which was still parked in the driveway. His gut told him he wouldn't find Liz at her house, considering how frightened she was the night before, but he decided to check anyway. Sam wasn't the least bit surprised to find it abandoned. He decided to try the police station next. Walking inside, he saw Ben Abernathy talking with the lead constable he knew as Harry, but he walked up to the counter anyway.

"Harry, has Liz Jordan been in to see ye?"

"Take a seat Sam, I'll be righ' with ye," Harry answered and turned his attention back to Ben. "Look Ben, the man was found inside a woman's house with the door kicked open. And i's been speculated tha' he damaged the same lassie's car."

"I dinnea touch anybody's bloody car!" Liam shouted from the cell behind the counter.

"Shu-up, Liam," Ben said. Turning his attention back to the constable, he continued. "Look, pal, he was drunk off his arse las' night and no' thinkin' righ'."

"That may be so, bu' he still has to appear before the judge before I can just le' him go."

"Isnea there anythin' we can do to le' him out?"

Harry looked over his shoulder at Liam and sighed. "I can see abou' movin' up his meetin' to this afternoon, and tha'll get his bail set, ye can come and check on 'im tomorrow mornin'."

"Cheers." Ben nodded and began to walk away.

Outraged, Sam stood up and walked over to the counter. "Ye cannea just le' him go! The man assaulted the lassy jus' las' evenin'!"

"According to ye, Sam. And so far, we cannea find any physical evidence tha' connects him to destroyin' her car."

"Tha's 'cause I *didn't* touch the bloody car!" Liam called again. "And comin' into her home was an accident! I though' it was mine!"

"Right," Sam growled. "And I suppose ye though' it was yer drink ye were spikin' tha' night at Jackie's."

Sam's statement caught Ben's attention, and he turned back around to look at Liam. "Wha'?"

Everyone turned their eyes towards Liam, who began to shift uncomfortably. "I dinnea know wha' yer talkin' about. Yer offa yer heid, McKay."

"Can ye prove this, Sam?" Harry asked.

Clenching his jaw, Sam shook his head no.

"Well, then there's nothin' more we can hold him for. The judge'll decide wha' to do with him this afternoon, and tha's tha'. Now as far as the lassy ye were inquirin' abou', no I havenea seen her today."

"Ach." Sam banged his fist down on the counter. "Alrigh', thanks."

Walking past a bewildered Ben (who was still watching a very shifty Liam in his cell), Sam then made his way over to Jackie's to enquire about Liz. There was a substantial crowd inside of the pub, and Sam had to fight his way over to the short, grumpy man behind the bar.

"Oi! Liz here?"

"No!" Jackie barked. "She never showed up for her shift, so I'm here by myself dealin' with these bampots!"

"Have ye called her?"

"Of course, I have, ye nyaff! But the bloody tone's dead!"

Shocked, Sam walked back out of the busy bar and decided one last ditch attempt at the garage might give him answers. *Maybe she'd get her car?* But Virgil hadn't seen her either, and Sam knew the answer to what he was wondering: she was in fact running.

After dropping off Thomas' car, Sam walked home feeling very confused and a little angry: angry at Liz, and angry at himself for sticking his nose into someone else's business. And for allowing himself to feel anything for the woman when he knew from the beginning he shouldn't get involved, his rage spiked. More than once, he pulled his phone out of his pocket and debated on calling Rivera to tell him to report her. Stopping in front of his house, he made up his mind that he would and pulled up the number when he stopped himself. Something was wrong, that was for certain, but he couldn't figure out what. His gut told him there was more to her story than the hospital reports and he sighed ... *Damn it, I cannea do it* ... Shoving his phone in his pocket, he walked inside of the house and decided to distract himself by replacing the upstairs bath tub and shower instead.

~~~

A few days later, on another rare and sunny day, Sam decided to take a break from fixing the cottage and instead go for a walk through the wooded hills. Even with the herds of sheep and a few cows he passed, the air smelled clean and fresh the further he walked, and he inhaled every breath. The further away from town he got, the denser the trees became, and he was glad he wore his jacket. Without much sunlight, it was colder in the woods. But the temperature did nothing to stop the surrounding fauna. The forest was filled with the sounds of life; a little mouse scampered away as soon as it saw him, but Sam didn't pay it any mind as he continued to walk. He stopped to rest when he came to a small stream and took a few handfuls of water to drink, when the sounds of a quiet sob caught his attention. Looking all around, he couldn't see anyone, but the sound came again. Curious, he followed it up the stream until he saw Victoria sitting on a rock in a small clearing, her head in her hands. A little voice in the back of his mind said he should turn around and walk back, but he couldn't. He cleared his throat.

Victoria snapped her head up when she heard the noise and looked at Sam. Just as quickly as she looked at him, she pulled her knees to her chest and turned away. But Sam had already noticed the red spot on her cheek and walked over, concern etched in his eyes. Kneeling in front of her, he gently took her face in his hands and forced her to let him inspect it. It was bright and angry looking, but it wouldn't leave a bruise. Still, it was enough that Sam felt his blood begin to boil.

"Tha' Ben's handiwork?" He asked her directly.

She sniffled. "He's nevar hurt me before, no' once."

"So wha' changed?"

Victoria looked him in the eye. Sam shook his head.

"Tha' was a long time ago, Vicky. I tol' Ben tha'."

"Aye, I know it was a long time ago. Doesnea mean I dinnea think about ye from time to time. Why do ye think I came out here?"

Sam looked around, and it suddenly dawned on him where they
~~~

were; memories of being sixteen, a stolen bottle of whiskey, and a hot night under the trees flooded him. He sat down on the ground next to her and sighed before reaching for a hanky in his pocket and handing it to her, which she gladly accepted and dabbed her eyes.

Folding his hands together, Sam asked. "Why'd ye marry him?"

"Why'd ye stop bein' pals?"

"Tha's no' yer business."

"Why I married him isnea yours," Victoria challenged.

Sam couldn't help but chuckle at her fierce attitude. "Aye, fair enough."

Victoria smiled and looked down to the hanky she was still holding, fiddling with the edges of it. "…I want to have a baby, but he dinnea want one."

He kept quit and waited for her to continue.

Taking a deep breath, she said, "He actually stopped bein' such an arse no' long after ye left. He was sweet and kind … guess he reminded me of ye. Bu' he dinnea want kids, says he's too afraid they'll end up like him, and he dinnea want to deal with tha'."

Sam scoffed. "Aye, I suppose he wouldnea like havin' t' face the consequences of his past."

"Alrigh' I answered yer question," Victoria challenged. "Now ye have to answer mine. Why'd ye stop bein' pals?"

Feeling the wet ground starting to soak the seat of his pants, Sam adjusted himself before he answered. "I'd had enough o' the bullyin."

She turned to look at him. "…He told me once that ye swam out Gare Loch to save Thomas when ye were kids. Tha' true?"

He nodded. "Aye."

"Was it his idea?"

"Aye."

He could feel her eyes on him as she waited for an explanation. "… Well, ye remember when we were kids how short and skinny Thomas was?"

"No one would know it now," She chuckled. "But aye, I remember."

"Well, is' like ye said, Ben and I were pals. And Liam, Wyatt, and the Lawders were part of our group, too. The six of us go' into loads of trouble togethar': stealin' from Mr. Stewart's store, destroyin' ol' Jackie's flowers, once we even stole a boat from the docks and went sailin' up and down the loch for hours before we got caught."

Victoria smiled as he revisited the memories with apparent fondness until his tone turned somber.

"…Then one day, a very cold and icy day, Thomas wanted to join up. Ben tol' him if he could wild swim across the loch and back, he'd be the newest member of the group. Thomas didnea hesitate and jumped right in Gare Loch, even though it was completely iced over …but he dinnea come back up. Ben and the others were laughin' and insisted I was worryin' for nothin', but I jumped in and pulled Thomas out. He nearly froze to death cause' …It was then and there I realized tha' I'd become a bully, and I dinnea wanna' be one."

She stared at him in shock. "…I never knew tha'."

"Aye. T'was a long time ago."

Looking down at her hands, Victoria cleared her throat. "…He fired Liam yesterday."

Surprised, Sam looked over. "Did he now?"

"Aye. He wouldnea tell me why, jus' said he'd crossed a line."

Sam couldn't help but feel impressed, despite how angry he was at Ben for hitting his wife. He pointed to her cheek. "Tell me abou' tha."

She sniffled. "Well, like I've done before, I tol' him we'd make sure our kids wouldnea be like him, bu' this mornin' he tol' me his answer was final. I was angry, so I said I wished I'd've waited for ye."

"Tha' when he hit ye?"

"Aye," she nodded. "I left after tha', didnea want his apology."

"No one can blame ye for wantin' to cool off."

"I've had plenty of time to cool off …just still confused." Tears began to flow again, and she buried her face in her hands.

The air around them grew thick; Sam's wet pants made him more uncomfortable by the second, but still he sat by Victoria as she cried until he decided to put his arm around her and rubbed her shoulder, doing his best to comfort her. He looked down at her when she finally raised her head and was met with her lips on his in a soft kiss.

After a moment, Victoria leaned away and blinked up at him. Sam saw the understanding in her eyes and smiled gently at her. "We're no' the same people anymore, Vicky."

"… I guess we're not." She nodded and pulled away. Looking at her feet, she mumbled a quiet, "Sorry."

Sam shook his head and removed his arm from her. He turned to look at the stream again. "Do ye love him?"

She nodded.

"Then go home and fix it."

Victoria took a moment to consider his words before she smiled to herself and nudged him. "Thank ye, Sam."

He watched her stand up and follow the stream back towards town. Rising and brushing off his pants, for all the good it would do, he turned in the opposite direction and continued on deeper into the woods. It wasn't until his stomach began to grumble that he turned around and started for home again, when he heard an email notification on his phone. Looking at the screen, he felt his heart flutter. *Is' Oliver!* He opened the message excitedly only to feel a horrible emptiness as he read the words:

Stop emailing me and leave me alone!

He would never cry, but he was completely in despair. He wrote back:

I love you, son

Sam couldn't hear anything around him as he walked home, but he certainly didn't feel hungry anymore. Instead of going into the kitchen, he sat down in his chair with a pen and paper and wrote another letter to his little boy.

Chapter Eight

Julie walked into her apartment intending to sink into a nice hot bath. It had been a particularly horrible day at work: SWAT was called out to rescue a kidnapped girl, and once again, she was told to stay behind and go over tactical approaches with the new trainees. *At least, on Sam's team, I could have been a part of the action ...* It was humiliating. She even tried to fight her case with her superior, only to be told that she was where she was needed. He 'politely' reminded her that it was either this or serving as a desk jockey for the local PD, which was the only reason she stayed. *This is better than sitting on my ass and answering phones all day, I guess ...*

Dropping her keys into the bowl sitting next to the door, she turned on the radio as she passed through the small kitchen and down to the bedroom. With practiced confidence, she removed her gun from the holster on her hip, as well as the spare she kept hidden behind her back, and threw them both on the bed before she began to fill her tub with boiling hot water. The bath was steaming, and she was about to step in when the doorbell rang. Frustrated, she put her robe back on and walked over to look through the peephole. Rivera was on the other side holding a bottle of wine and a plastic sack that she recognized from King Chen's Palace, and Julie couldn't resist. She opened the door, and he quickly stepped inside.

"Looks like I'm here just in time," he teased as his eyes raked over her body.

"First, let's see what you've got in the bag."

Chuckling, Rivera walked over to counter and pulled out each item. "Spring rolls, house Lo Mein, and Kung Pao Beef. I also got their famous coconut ice cream."

"And nothing goes better with coconut ice cream than a cheap chardonnay." Julie took the bottle from him and smirked. "I'll get some glasses."

Rivera set to work getting plates. "Rough day?"

"What makes you think that?"

"You're wearing your bathrobe, which you only do when you intend to take a bath, which you only do after a bad day of work."

She laughed. "You've been here too much."

When he wrapped his arms around her waist and moved her rich red hair out of the way, she could feel herself melting against him.

Rivera kissed her neck slowly. "Damn, babe, you've got a lot of tension right here … You know, there's another way to relieve it, and I could always help you."

"Mmmm … that depends on how good the ice cream is today."

He suddenly spun her around to face him and lifted her onto the counter. Julie gasped at the lustful hunger that blared in his eyes. *I love it when he's like this.* She barely had time to breathe before he was devouring her mouth with his. She wrapped her legs around him when his phone started ringing.

He looked at the screen and growled. "Hang on, this is important."

She nodded and hopped off of the counter. Grabbing a pair of chopsticks, she ate the lo mein while eavesdropping on his half of the conversation.

"Rivera … Yes, ma'am … Yes, ma'am, we can … Well, ma'am, I happen to know a guy who would be a perfect fit for the job … Yes, Director. I'll send you everything in the morning … Thank you. Goodnight." Rivera hung up the phone and clasped his hands together. "Yes!"

"Good news?"

"We just got the green light."

"For the smuggling thing, right?"

"Yup," he nodded and stole the bite of food she was getting ready to eat.

"Hey, that was mine!"

Chuckling, he leaned forward and kissed her. "Before we get back to where we were, I need to call Sam."

Julie furrowed her eyebrows. "What for?"

~~~

It was past midnight when Sam decided to go to bed; with Thomas gone all week visiting Helen in Aberdeen, he didn't have the urge to go to Jackie's much. So, he had kept to himself and stayed in his
~~~

house reading every book he owned. Having finished all the renovations almost a month before, there wasn't much else he could do to occupy himself other than walking through the woods and reading when he wasn't at Virgil's garage. The lax pattern was slowly driving him crazy.

Just as he was about to turn out the light and go to sleep, his phone started ringing. It was Rivera, so he decided to ignore it. *I'll call him in the mornin'.* He turned out the light, but Rivera called again. Groaning from how exhausted he felt, he turned the light back on and sat up.

"Wha's so important that ye have to call me in the middle of the bloody night?"

"A job."

Sam was awake instantly. "Wha' kind o' job?"

"Undercover. I can't give you too many details over the phone but the gist of it is you'll be working in West Virginia as a deputy of sorts."

"Come off it, man, I donnea do undercover. Tha's yer job. And even so, nobody's gonna hire me."

"Maybe they won't hire Sam McKay, but that'll be taken care of. This is on behalf of the FBI; you'll get a whole new identity."

Sam sighed. "I appreciate it, Rivera, but I dinnea have the money to come back to the states, especially for only part-time work."

"Don't worry about that Sam; you'll be compensated. Plus, what about that thing with the Harper woman? There's still an open reward on her. Even if you don't know where she is now you can still—"

"No. No, I won't do tha'." He answered in a clipped tone.

"Why not? The last time you saw her was two months ago, that's still a credible amount of time. And she's obviously on the run—"

"Rivera, drop it now." Sam growled.

He heard the man sigh. "Okay, fine … What if I get my boss to pay for your ticket?"

"Does yer boss know my history?"

"She knows that I think you're perfect for the job, and she trusts my judgment."

Sam rubbed his face anxiously as he thought about the offer, but Rivera continued.

"Come on, Sam. West Virginia is so close to Ohio, you'd be a couple hours drive away from your kid, max. Plus, this will help to rebuild your reputation that not even that son-of-a-bitch Green can touch you.”

The mention of being closer to Oliver sold him. “Alrigh’, alrigh, I’ll take it. When can ye have my free ticket ready?”

“How fast can you get packed?”

~~~

Sitting in the lobby wearing a visitor’s badge, Sam looked around the building of the FBI headquarters as he waited for someone to fetch him; though his ticket had been purchased the morning after he and Rivera had spoken, he wouldn’t be leaving for another week. He didn’t mind the delay, though, as it gave him enough time to get things in storage as well as get everything arranged with Hannah about renting the home again. After informing her that he would be gone for at least a year (as Rivera had promised the visa he would be provided with was good for that long), he’d said goodbye to everyone yet again, and Thomas drove him back to the airport. Even though it was short notice, Hannah had managed to get the day he was leaving off, and they had a tearful goodbye at the airport. Sam promised up and down that whenever she and Zander decided on a wedding date, he would fly back for it in a heartbeat. She smacked him and said, “Ye bettar!”

Thomas was also upset that he was leaving again and made that very clear the whole time leading up to the airport. “Ye’ve been gone for twelve years! Am I no’ gonna see ye for another twelve now?!”

Sam assured him that he would try to be better about visiting, even though both men knew that was a lie. Still, they shook each other’s hands and said their goodbyes, but not before Sam told Thomas to finally marry Helen and stop all of the long-distance nonsense they had going on.

“If I marry her, will ye come back for my weddin’ too?” Thomas asked him pointedly.

“To see ye leave the bachelorhood nest? I wouldnea miss it.” He replied with a grin.

That was only two days before, and now Sam was ready to get to work. He began to wonder if he was being sweated out on purpose,
~~~

until he saw Rivera coming around the corner.

"Hey, Sam," he smiled and shook his hand. "It's good to see you!"

"You, too."

"Come on, this way." Rivera led him down the hallway to the elevators and up to the third floor where they turned left and walked to the end of the hall before entering a conference room.

Inside, on the other side of a long table, sat an older attractive woman dressed in a black pantsuit that Sam immediately guessed was his new boss. She had snowy white shoulder-length hair and wore very little makeup other than maroon lipstick that complimented her pale porcelain skin. She also had the demeanor of an irritated cat. Sam could tell she was a force to be reckoned with and immediately got the feeling they wouldn't get along that easily.

"Sam, let me introduce you to the director of our office, Belinda Copper."

She stood up and shook Sam's hand. "Afternoon, Mr. McKay."

"Afternoon," he nodded.

"And this is Evan Dower," Rivera pointed to another man that sat quietly in the corner, almost completely forgotten. "He's going to be your handler."

Evan was much younger with black hair and a round, clean shaven face. He smiled enthusiastically and stood up to offer his hand. "Nice to meet you, sir."

Sam chuckled inwardly as he accepted and shook it. "My 'handlar?'"

"Yes, sir. I'll be the guy that you call with any and all information you find out. I'll make sure that you have access to everything that you need, whether it's information on the people you meet, backup support—heck I can even get you weapons if you need them!"

"Thank you, Evan," Director Copper stopped him. "But first we'll have to go over the whole assignment with Mr. McKay before we get to that point."

"Yes, ma'am. Sorry, ma'am." Evan said softly and sat down.

"Now, Mr. McKay, here's the situation: last year, there were arrests made in West Virginia which brought an end to one of the biggest multi-state drug trafficking organizations in the country. Over $120 million dollars worth of cocaine and meth was recovered at the time of the bust, and we were able to round up more than thirty distributors and buyers."

"Well done." Sam nodded his admiration.

"Yes, but it would seem that the operation was not as successful as we originally thought," Director Copper continued. "After the close of the investigation, which took more than eight months to carry out, the trafficking ring should have been dismantled, and the drugs that were recovered should have, at the very least, made a dent in the distribution sales. But according to our intel, it hasn't."

Sam furrowed his eyebrows. "Well, over 30 convicted is certainly nothin' to sneeze at, but I cannea imagine it would make too much of a difference with the drug distribution rate in the whole country."

"Sam, it hasn't made any difference at all," Rivera joined in. "The drugs that were recovered were basically restocked almost the next day."

"Ring leaders can be replaced; new buyers can be found. But distribution and shipment should have at least taken a dip, and it hasn't." The Director opened a manila folder that was sitting in front of her and showed Sam the charts inside.

Though he looked at it, Sam could barely understand what he was being told. "Meanin' wha'?"

"We have reason to believe that the drugs are being admitted through state borders by corrupted officials."

Sam narrowed his eyes. "Cops?"

"That is what we believe. There's no way for us to tell who or when the drugs are passing through, so we'll need to put someone on the inside."

"So wha' do ye want me to do? Become a drug dealer?"

"No, no, Mr. McKay. We have a special team that is assigned to oversee those particular assignments. Your reputation as an IA Detective has Rivera convinced you're the man for this job. That being said, you'll be serving as a deputy for the Sheriff's Department out of Wood County, and one of your responsibilities will be to serve at a weigh station."

"That's a spot where big rigs carrying things across country come to get weighed," Evan added excitedly.

"Why West Virginia?" Sam asked. "I though' ye said they were bein' shipped all over the country."

"Shipment *flows* throughout the whole country, but none of our agents have had any success capturing vessels carrying the drugs.

West Virginia has one of the highest drug rates in the USA. And as it happens, one of Wood County's deputies from the Mineral Wells weigh station is about to retire, and an opening has been posted. You will take his place and observe, investigate, and report back anything that you might find." The Director produced two papers and laid them out in front of Sam. "This one states that you agree not to divulge any information that has been shared, and this one is our insurance that you agreed to take on this assignment, and we didn't force you. However, if you're uncomfortable with your assignment, you are only required to sign the first one, Mr. McKay."

"One moment," Sam stopped her. "First I wanna' know wha' I'll get at the end of all this?"

The intimidating woman chuckled. "You have already been given a visa that is good for a year. If this mission takes longer than that, we will renew it. And I think you will find our compensation, noted here on line 25, more than fair."

"Bu' at the end of the year, ye cut me loose, and my visa expires, unless I meet the requirements and renew it on my own. Aye?"

"That would be what happens, yes."

Sam looked to Rivera and scowled.

"Rivera has informed me of your situation with Congressman Green," Copper continued. "I will see to it that the damage he inflicted on your record is expunged. You should then have a much easier time finding work and being able to stay in the states. I'm sure you have your reasons for wanting to stay, but don't mistake me for someone interested in hearing them."

"Never crossed me mind, ma'am, bu' I want everythin' ye jus' tol' me in writin' before I sign anythin'."

Director Copper nodded, took out a pen, and wrote her further promises down in the blank section underneath the initial compensation and signed her name next to it. Once she was done, she handed the pen to Sam, who took it without hesitation and signed his name as well.

"Good," the Director stood up from the table. "Now that the official stuff is taken care of, we can get you set up with your new ID and equipment. Good luck to you, Mr. McKay."

Sam watched Copper leave without another word. As soon as the door was shut, the young man Evan began to speak much more freely.

"Alright! Well, Mr. McKay, I've just got to say, it's going to be an honor to work with you!"

Sam turned to Rivera with a questioning look, but Rivera simply shrugged and chuckled.

"Sorry, Sir, it's just that we've all heard your name. You're one of the few people in the whole country who has had such an amazing and successful career as a hostage negotiator. I mean, you're like in the top five of the agency's lists! Anyways, in here," he pushed another manila envelope across the table, "is all of the information you need, as far as case specifics go, including potential suspects and such. We've also drawn up a dummy profile for you, and there's a list of potential names you can take your pick from—"

"Orson McGregor?" Sam eyed the list skeptically. "Donovan McCleary? Rory McHaggin? Ye migh' as well cast me in a bloody soap opera if yer gonna' give me names like this."

"Oh," Evan looked down sheepishly. "Well, those were just what immediately came to mind since you're Scottish and all …"

"Keep my first name. There are thousands of Sams in the world; nobody'll notice. As far as the last name goes, surprise me."

"Okay, yes, sir. I'll get right on that."

"Okay," Rivera jumped in. "Thank you, Evan. Why don't you go get Sam's new identity set up, and I'll walk him out?"

"Right. Well again, it was nice to meet you."

Sam nodded and walked out the door with Rivera on his heels.

"I know," Rivera said to him quietly, "he's very enthusiastic."

"Donnea ye mean he's seen a few too many spy movies?"

Rivera chuckled. "He should have everything ready for you in a couple hours. I'll bring it by your hotel later."

Sam nodded.

They rode the elevator down, and Rivera escorted Sam to the security desk where the guest badge was returned, and he was cleared to leave. A taxi was already called and waiting for him, and Rivera watched them as Sam rode away. He didn't hear the sounds of footprints sprinting towards him and turned just in time for Simon to run into him head on, knocking the both of them to the ground.

"Dammit, Abler!" Rivera growled and stood up, brushing himself off. "What the hell are you doing up here?"

"You couldn't take the time to tell me that the boss was here? I had to find out through the system! Where is he?!"

"Relax, fanboy, he just left."

"Well, why the hell didn't you tell me he was coming?!" Simon pushed Rivera's arm. "I wanted to say hi!"

Rivera couldn't help but chuckle. "I've got to take him some stuff later tonight, anyway. You can come if you want, then you'll get to say hi."

Simon clapped his hands together. "Yay! I'll call Julie! She'll want to see him, too! It'll be a big reunion!"

"Yeah, yeah good idea," Rivera nodded sadly.

Simon turned and bounded away, leaving Rivera at the door again. He berated himself for showing emotion at the mention of Julie's name, as she still insisted their relationship (though he wasn't sure he could even call it that) be kept a secret. It had led to the latest fight. He hadn't spoken to her in a week, not since the night he told her that Sam was coming back to the states. She had immediately retreated into her usual shell of business and practicality and started saying they would have to be careful while he was back. As much as he had tried to argue the point with her, she wouldn't give in, and eventually he had left her apartment angry.

His phone buzzed, breaking him out of his melancholy state.

"Rivera."

~~~

Three weeks later, Sam had moved into the tiny, 'new' and fully-furnished apartment that was to be home for the next year in Mineral Wells, West Virginia. As promised, the FBI had set him up with everything that he needed, including the actual interview for the deputy position. Using the cover that had been assigned to him, he was successfully hired under the name Samuel McKennedy, an immigrant who had just moved to the area. Given his old IA persona, even the Sheriff had asked him why he would want a Deputy position. "You're overqualified for this," he'd said, but Sam was hired all the same and under instructions that he would be working at the weigh station every Thursday and Friday. On Tuesdays, he would be on patrol throughout the city. When he wasn't working, the FBI informed him that he was to explore and observe the town, make friends, and gather as much information as possible. But if there was anything he didn't enjoy doing, it was using people, and
~~~

this assignment felt as though that's *all* he would be doing. His only consolation was that once it was all over, he would never see any of the people he came into contact with again. In the end, he knew he was doing all of this for Oliver, and that was the only reason why he would do it. He had even written to his son that he was moving back to the states, and that he wanted to see him, though he never received a reply. He thought about calling Meredith to get her to help him speak with Oliver, but anger at her lack of help with the relationship stopped him. He simply continued to send letters and emails to the boy every Tuesday without fail.

Sam's new position didn't require much training, and he had quickly established a routine of walking and observing on his off days. He made any notes he could think of as he worked. Only one week in, and everything was in tip-top shape, as he expected it would be. Knowing it would take longer than a week to crack open any secrets from anyone, he simply played his part of the hard worker and kept mostly to himself on the job. This went on for a few weeks, and the days were becoming a blur to him, making him even more surly than usual. *I need a lead, a project, somethin'!* he'd often think to himself. Still he kept up with the charade of going out and about town, learning everything that he could, until one particularly grey and rainy night he decided to explore the local night life. Some of his new co-workers recommended a little hole-in-the-wall bar and country club to him that was further north, so he decided to visit it.

With at least a dozen bars within a few miles of each other all over the town, it didn't surprise him that this club wasn't very busy. A few old men sat at the bar, there were a few couples sitting in booths laughing and chatting away, and a small group of men gathered around the pool tables at the back. Maybe twenty people in total, not including the servers. Though he didn't particularly enjoy the country music playing in the background, it did feel homely.

"There's a spot at the bar here, buddy!" The barkeep called to him. "Unless you got some friends coming, then there's an open table over there."

Sam walked over to the bar and sat down.

"What can I get ya?"

"Guinness."

The barkeep turned around to fill up a pint, and Sam noticed another figure further down the bar that caught his eye. She had her back turned to him, so he took the opportunity to admire curves that couldn't be hidden by the jeans and a loose t-shirt. Her dark hair was shorter than he normally found attractive, coming just above her neck and loosely curly, but he couldn't seem to stop admiring her when she turned to hand a drink to one of the old men at the bar.

"There you go," he heard her say and Sam froze. He knew that voice, and he knew those curves. She turned his way and their eyes met. He saw her freeze where she stood as they stared at each other, neither of them daring to look away.

"Here you go, buddy," The barkeep said as he placed the ale in front of Sam.

Coolly, he lifted the pint to his lips and took a long sip. He saw Liz swallow before she turned back to the other customers. Looking down at his drink, he couldn't help but think: *Well, shit ...*

Chapter Nine

Sam waited until closing time. It wasn't in his nature to borderline stalk anyone, but between all of the information he had read about Liz being a missing person, knowing she was actually a runaway, her drug problem, and memories of the heated kiss they'd shared on his mind, he didn't move from his spot. He didn't know how he would approach her or what he'd say, but he was going to get some answers and had decided that nothing would stop him from doing so. He'd kept his eye on her throughout the night. When the barkeep called her 'Erin,' he'd furrowed his eyebrows until he realized that was the new alias she'd given herself. Her body language suggested that she knew he was watching her though she never turned to look at him again.

Finally, the barkeep stood in front of him. "Okay, pal, it's closing time. Let's settle the bill."

Sam paid the man and stood up to leave, deciding to give up on his quest for the night and just try again tomorrow, when he heard Liz say. "I'm done, Keith, so I'm out for the night."

"Goodnight, Erin. See you tomorrow."

Sam watched her suspiciously as she grabbed a jacket and walked towards the door almost in step with him. They walked outside, turned towards the parking lot behind the bar, until finally Liz stopped walking. Sam turned to her and waited for her to say something, but she didn't move. He decided to go first. "Erin?"

Even in the darkness, he could see her shift uncomfortably under his scrutinizing gaze. He heard her swallow and whisper quietly, "Please …is there someplace we can go talk?"

"Wha's wrong with here?" His tone was a little sharper than he'd intended, but he held his ground.

She finally looked at him, and he could see the start of tears brimming in her eyes. Sighing, he conceded. "Aye, alright. Where's yer place?"

"Right around the corner. Follow me." She turned and began

walking, and he followed.

She wasn't exaggerating when she'd said she lived right around the corner; they walked for maybe five minutes until they came to a couple of old brick apartment buildings, and she made for the first one. Walking up the stairs in silence, they stopped at the very last door on the left, and Sam watched her pull out some keys and shakily open the lock. She walked in first and moved aside, giving him permission to enter. He walked in and took in his surroundings; it was nicer than the place he was living in, albeit much smaller and very bare. In the living room, he saw a new painting she was working on sitting on an easel with a lot of open paint supplies and brushes sitting on the ground underneath it. Looking over to the kitchen, which was enclosed by a long countertop, he recognized the same finger-painted strawberry plant 'Ronald,' and his curiosity piqued.

Liz shut and locked the door behind them and cleared her throat. "Um …I have a couple of chairs at the kitchen table if you want a cup of tea or something."

"No, thanks," Sam turned to her. "I donnea wanna stay too long."

She flinched at his words and reached up to push back a few strands of hair.

Crossing his arms over his chest, he felt the same as he did during the hundreds of times he'd scolded Oliver for doing something he wasn't supposed to as he waited for her explanation.

Liz swallowed again and began. "Okay, I … I don't even know where to start."

"Start with yer real name."

"You know my real name."

He took a menacing step towards her. "Do I, Liz? Because I'm confused. Is it Jordan or Harper?"

She shot her eyes up to meet his as soon as he'd said it. "H-how did you—"

"Doesnea matter how, and I donnea care why ye changed it. Why did ye leave, and wha' are ye doin' here?"

She turned away and tried to walk into the kitchen, but Sam grabbed her arm and turned her back around, forcing her to look up at him. "Jus' tell me the truth, woman. Have I ever given ye reason no' to trust me?"

"No, you haven't. But … I can't …" she couldn't finish her

sentence without tears threatening to fall.

His frustration was beginning to get the better of him, and he marched around her towards the door. "Fine. If yer no' gonna talk to me then I'm no' gonna help ye."

"You can't help me. Nobody can."

"Have ye let anybody try, Liz?"

Her silence gave him all the answer he needed.

"Tha's wha' I thought."

"Sam … please try to understand. I don't want anybody else to get hurt … especially not you …"

Her pleading words softened him; his pride told him he should just open the door, walk out, and never see her again, but his gut told him to shove that feeling out of the way. There was so much he wanted and *needed* to know, including the whereabouts of the young girl he saw in the report. But seeing the way she held herself in this moment, frightened and alone, somehow he knew Liz would never hurt her daughter, and there had to be a good reason for her behavior. Taking a deep, calming breath, he walked back towards the kitchen and sat down at the tiny two-person table.

After a moment, Liz joined him. "…Please …how do you know?"

"I tol' ye I'm a cop, I have my ways."

She furrowed her eyebrows. "No, you said that you *were* a cop. Has that changed?"

As much as he wanted to close the gap between them and tell her the truth about his own situation, he thought better of it and simply nodded. "Aye, it has."

"What are *you* doing here?"

"I cannea tell ye why either."

She leaned back in her chair. "Then here we are, two people who can't trust each other."

"Aye, t'would appear tha' way."

"What is it that you want, Sam?"

"I already tol' ye, I want the truth."

"To what end? You're not my knight in shining armor, and I can't be rescued."

"I'm no' here to rescue ye, Liz. I'm here because … well, I've come to care for ye, lass."

His words caused her to give an unexpected reaction of pity. "Sam … what I'm mixed up in … it's more than complicated. Believe me when I say that … we should just pretend that we don't know each other."

Sam swallowed hard. "If tha's what ye really want of me, I'll no' argue yer wishes."

Standing up from the table, he walked over to the door, fully intending to leave this time. Just before he shut the door, he cleared his throat. "Bu' fer the record, I've often though' of tha' kiss."

She opened her mouth like she wanted to say something but quickly shut it and nodded her head. Taking that as his cue, Sam left without another word and shut the door softly. His heart began to ache, a feeling he hadn't felt in a long time. Ignoring it, he made his way back towards the bar where his car was waiting.

~~~

"Hello, my programs aren't working. Can somebody come fix it please? Gah!"

Simon Abler raked his fingers through his hair harshly and knocked the glasses off his face. Though he managed to catch them before they hit the ground and suffer any damage, he was still beyond annoyed and did his best to appear menacing as he walked towards whoever the idiot who didn't know how to work a computer was. He didn't care that the people he passed by stared at him in amusement as he whispered to himself, "A whole …stupid …freaking year of being in IT and there's still *nothing else* available?! I'm gonna' be telling people to turn their computers off and on again for the rest of my life!"

It wasn't until he turned the corner to his destination and saw the face that belonged to the voice over the phone that he instantly stopped griping. She was new, he could tell that much, and obviously was still familiarizing herself with the FBI's databases as she tried to fix her computer without him. She was dressed in standard business attire, as was expected in the office. But the way her bangs were falling over her eyes, he sighed and instantly forgave her for the phone call. While she was still preoccupied with her console, he quickly straightened his short-sleeved button-up and adjusted his glasses before he knocked on her door. She quickly looked up at him, and he cleared his throat, "Hi, I'm Simon from IT? I believe you called about a program crash?"
~~~

"Yes, hi," she smiled genuinely at him, and he thought he would melt to the ground like ice cream on a hot day. "I'm so sorry I called you, I'm sure you're sick of having dumb things to fix, but I didn't want to tell my boss how I'd messed up a case because of a simple computer crash."

"Oh, don't worry about it. Honestly with all the excitement we get down in IT, having something simple to fix every now and again is great." Simon lied through his teeth as he grinned at her and walked over to the desk. "What happened?"

"I'm not sure, I entered my credentials and the whole thing just started acting weird on me. I only just started."

"Well, sometimes getting each individual agent's computer set up can take a few days. May I?"

"Thank you," she nodded and moved out of his way.

After forcing a hard restart on the computer, he turned to her and smiled his most charming smile. "I'm Simon."

"Kelsey," she smiled back and offered her hand.

He accepted it quickly and gave her a little more than a gentle shake, making her chuckle when he finally released her. "So, Kelsey, you're new. Where were you before here?"

"Oh, I just came over from Quantico."

"Oh, so you're a *real* newby. then?"

"Yeah," She giggled. "What about you?"

"Oh, I've been here for a while now. I was actually part of a white-collar investigation team when I first started."

"Really? What made you go to IT?"

She sat on the desk and crossed her legs; Simon gulped and did his best to concentrate on the computer as it finally finished restarting. He began clacking away at the computer and answered. "Oh, life just happened. I went to a different division for a while, and when I came back, there wasn't a position for me in White Collar anymore."

"Huh, well that sucks. I bet you were really good."

He felt himself blush; after hitting enter, he managed to bring back the files she had up. "There you go."

"Oh, thank you! You just saved my butt!"

"No problem at all," he winked at her. "Let me just double check there isn't any unseen viruses in the computer so this doesn't happen to you again …"

He noticed the page she had pulled up described a group of individuals that committed a home invasion. Curious, he sped-read the document and a few details stood out to him that reminded him of something important. He checked the computer for viruses as promised and emailed a copy of the documents to himself while Kelsey had her back turned. "Okay, well it looks like everything's working just fine. If it happens again, don't hesitate to call us and just ask for me."

"I'll make sure that I will. Thank you, Simon." She smiled and batted her eyelashes, and suddenly he couldn't remember how to say goodbye properly.

"N-No problem, bye!" he dashed out and practically sprinted back to his tiny office in the basement level. Once he reached it, he sat down at his desk and berated himself for not asking the cute new hire out for a cup of coffee or at least for her number. *Seriously, you idiot? You've never had problems with words before!*

He leaned back in his chair and couldn't stop thinking about the girl two floors above him when the notification in the corner of his screen reminded him of what he'd 'stolen' from her desktop. Clicking on it, he took his time to read the home invasion report thoroughly.

No fingerprint identification ... bomb was set off after the group left... victim had a bullet wound to the forehead ... wait a minute! He pulled up his personally-crafted search engine and began clacking away on the keyboard furiously until he found what he was looking for: the last case he'd gotten to do with Sam and the others. Per Sam's usual curious nature, he'd had the Cleveland PD send him all of the details as they unraveled the case so he could build his own profile. Simon was in charge of entering all of the information. They had hundreds of files filled with details, and a few of them had been solved, though there were still plenty that were left open. The bank robbery was one of them. Sam was never convinced that it was just a standard bank robbery, despite all of the evidence that said there was nothing otherwise, and now Simon was more than proud of his former boss as he read over the details of the only man that was killed in the incident: Brian Cairne.

Pulling up the ballistics report on the old case and the new one he'd just gotten, he compared the details, and more and more his eyes widened in amazement and his mouth stretched into an enormous smile. The bullets that had been collected were the exact same caliber. Furiously, he entered the specific details into his program, and five other cases were brought up with similar details: one person of interest was executed with a bullet to the head; there was an explosion as they left; and there was never any physical evidence left behind other than the bullets. The only difference with their case was a partial print had been recovered, but not enough to identify anyone. Other than that, the details were exactly the same.

Simon was glued to his computer. "… HOLY SHIT!"

His outburst startled the four other people downstairs with him, and they all looked over with questioning eyes.

"Sorry, sorry, finally finished that stupid boss fight!"

They all nodded and returned to their computers; Simon grabbed his phone and dialed Rivera. "Come on, pick up pick up pick up pick up!"

It was answered after three rings. "Rivera."

"Dude, it's Simon! Get down to my desk, quick!"

"I'm in the middle of something, Abler."

"Is it work-related?"

"Yeah."

"Is it important?"

"…No."

"Then get down here! Trust me, you're gonna want to see this!"

He hung up the phone before Rivera could argue with him and sent copies of the reports to the printer. As much as he hated paper, he knew better than anyone that a hard copy of vital information was never a mistake, and he wouldn't risk it now. By the time he'd finished printing everything and returned to his desk, Rivera was stalking over looking more pissed off than usual.

"Shut the door!" He hissed to him.

Rivera obeyed. "Alright, I'm here, now what's so important?"

"This!" Simon pointed to his computer screen giddily. "Tell me what you see here."

He watched Rivera walk closer and lean over him to read through the documents and waited, practically bouncing in his seat, as the hot-headed man began to piece together the information. When his eyes began to open wider with understanding, Simon began smiling and nodding.

"… Brian Cairne wasn't just a robbery victim; he was a contract kill ..." Rivera said softly.

"Yes!" Simon exclaimed. "There's been at least five other situations like this in the country where the whole incident ends in blowing up to destroy most of the evidence. The bombs are never the same, which explains why nobody thought they were all the same group, but there's always at least one or two people that are shot at point blank!"

"This-this is impossible! Why didn't anyone put this together until now?"

"Cause I'm down in IT instead of up there working crimes where I *should* be," Simon laid the sarcasm on heavy. "But don't you get it? If Cairne was a contract kill, then that means they were hired, and what happened was *definitely* not Sam's fault!"

Rivera leaned back, "... This could help to clear his name ..."

"Especially if we manage to figure out who it was that hired them ..."

Rivera looked down at him with a smile. "Nice goin', kid! Okay, save all of this into one of those secret stashes you've got and after—why is your computer doing that?"

Simon looked back at his screen, which started to get fuzzy and began to glitch.

"What the-no, no no no no no!" He typed on his keyboard every programming trick he knew as fast as he could to try and stop what was going on, to no success, when the whole computer shut down.

"What just happened?!" Rivera demanded.

"I don't know! I do a virus sweep on my computer *daily* so crashes won't happen! Hang on, it's restarting right now ..."

"What do you mean a crash? Can you get all that stuff back?"

"Yeah, yeah, totally. Just give me a second." Simon typed all of his credentials into the computer again, and his screen was brought up. He pulled up his search engine and quickly typed everything in but when the screen flashed 'No Results Found' at him, he started to panic.

"Abler, talk to me," Rivera started to sound angry. "What the hell is going on?"

"Something just deleted all of my files that relate to the bullet! Hang on a second, let me try something ..." he typed in 'Brian Cairne' and the autopsy report file re-appeared again. "This doesn't make any sense; the bullet wound information is right here, but it won't register when I search for it! Unless …"

"… Unless what?"

"Unless somebody used a *very* sophisticated program like … oh my God, it's the *Leviathan Bug*! I've only ever heard of that virus! It sort of rewired the whole search engine so that I can't detect—"

"English, Abler. Plain English please."

Frustrated, Simon sighed. "Okay, you ever play connect the dots before?"

"Of course."

"Well, a search engine is basically like that. Whenever you type in a keyword or phrase, it'll connect the dots for you and bring up everything that's related to what you ask for. You just have to dig for what you specifically want. *My* program is a little more fine-tuned than that, so whenever I enter something, it'll automatically piece together all of the cases that are similar and find me everything I need without having to do much digging for it. Now it's not doing it anymore, which means *somebody* has completely destroyed my algorithm and dropped my program down to *Google* level, the bastards!"

He could tell Rivera was still confused, but the man simply nodded, "Okay … can you fix it?"

"It took me years to write that algorithm, and now it's been obliterated by that Leviathan Bug, it'll take time."

"What about the files? Can you search for them individually?"

Simon typed in all of the information he remembered from both cases, but miniscule information popped up. "Most of them are gone, like they've been deleted …"

"What? That's impossible! Nothing can just be 'deleted' anymore!"

"Yeah, tell me about it. I still can't get those pictures I found of you in pink swimming trunks out of my head."

"You wha—never mind. Just *please* tell me you remember the specifics of those cases; we've got to write all that down quick!"

"Don't worry, I'm way ahead of you!" Simon lifted the small stack of papers on his desk. "As soon as I saw all this, I printed out copies just to be safe."

"Okay, good."

"And don't panic, 'cause you're right that nothing can just be deleted anymore. What I meant is the details have sort of been deleted, and that's why they're not coming up when I search for them."

"Abler, this Leviathan bug … it's not a standard bug or virus, is it?"

"Not by a long shot. Whoever sent it attacked *just me*. That's definitely not just a standard computer virus, or else the whole building would've been hit with it. We all share the same database. No no, this was *way* too good for that, like somebody knew exactly who and what they were looking for."

"… Somebody on the inside, you think?"

"Either that, or somebody who knew how to get through the firewall, and honestly I'd guess the latter based on how good the attack was. I think we can assume this is why nobody was able to connect the cases before; a bug like this covers the tracks of everything it wants gone."

Rivera stared at the computer for a long, hard moment, and Simon started to wonder what he was thinking, until he finally turned back to him. "Get those papers put somewhere safe, don't even tell me where they are, okay?"

"Yeah, yeah sure. What are you gonna' do?"

"I don't know yet."

"Well … you at least got a hunch on who might be responsible for destroying my program, right?"

Rivera shook his head. "Not a clue, kid. But until we find something else, we're going to keep these files out of the light and away from everyone. Got it?"

"Yeah, I got it. I promise!"

"Good."

Simon watched Rivera open the door to his little office and stalk back towards the elevator, and he suddenly felt nervous. *Nobody can hack my code, nobody!* He began to wonder if any of the four IT employees that surrounded him was secretly moonlighting as a master hacker, and he tried to slip the hard-copied files into his backpack as inconspicuously as possible. Taking a deep breath to calm himself down, he focused on fixing his program until another call came in for tech support. Too afraid of someone stealing the only evidence he had, he took the backpack with him.

Chapter Ten

Liz could barely contain her excitement as she drove along the highway towards Pittsburgh. Even though it was nearly 2:00 a.m., it was a three-day weekend, and she intended to not waste a moment of it driving to her destination. She'd had to work that night, much to her disappointment, which delayed her travel plans a bit, but she didn't dwell on it too much. *At least Keith didn't make me close,* she thought to herself. A passing road marker informed Liz she only had fifty more miles to go before she would be at her hotel, where she would get a good night's sleep (or at least try to). First thing in the morning, she would head to Shady Side Academy. With the strawberry plant sitting in the front seat and a packed bag in the trunk, there wasn't anything in her way in that moment. Her eyes were starting to droop by the time she pulled into the hotel, and she was grateful the clerk was just as anxious as she was to get her checked in and out of the lobby. Not even bothering to get undressed, she kicked off her shoes, collapsed on the bed, and fell asleep instantly.

Liz didn't even need the alarm to wake her the next morning; she was up long before the clock even rang. Even after showering, dressing, and unpacking her clothes, it was still too early to get to the school. She decided to try and kill some time by having some of the complimentary breakfast the hotel offered. Her stomach was in butterflies, and she could barely touch her waffles and coffee, but she forced herself to eat until it was finally time to leave. After retrieving 'Ronald,' she raced out to her car and drove to the Academy as fast as she could without going too far over the speed limit. Finally, she was driving under enormous, looming trees that signaled she was close to the grounds. When she saw the plaque that stated Shady Side Academy Boarding School, she thought she might burst. Due to the three-day weekend, there were lots of parents already there ready to pick up their children, and she was forced to park near the very back. Grabbing the plant, she practically sprinted towards the enormous, colonial style red brick building.

Running in to the office, she was so happy to see the face of her cousin and most trusted friend, Sienna.

"You made it!" Sienna beamed and walked around her desk to come hug her.

Liz hugged her just as tightly before quickly looking around. "Where's Natalie?"

"Out on the playground with the other children, this way."

Liz was led down a long hallway to the wing where children aged 5-8 were housed and out the doors to a large, colorful, and gated playground. They saw dozens of young boys and girls climbing, swinging, sliding, and playing games with each other. Looking all around, Sienna pointed to a smaller group of six kids playing on their own and away from the larger crowd. Liz followed where she was pointing, and tears sprang to her eyes to see Natalie in the middle of them. She wasn't quite sure what she was doing other than telling the other kids a story of some sort, but she appeared to have them all enthralled with whatever she was saying. Quietly, she snuck over until she was poised almost right behind her. The other children had stopped listening and were staring at Liz, forcing the little girl to look around curiously.

"Mommy!" Natalie jumped to her feet and ran into Liz's open arms.

Liz clutched her as tight as she could while smothering every part of her daughter's face with as many kisses as she could give her before the little girl asked her to stop. Wiping her eyes so Natalie wouldn't see her tears and ask why she was crying, Liz was content to just hold her daughter for a while, until the little girl pointed to the forgotten plant at her side.

"You brought Ronald!"

"Of course, I did," Liz laughed, finally releasing her from her grip. "And look, he's got some pretty big berries here."

"Can everybody have one?"

"Yeah, baby, if you want to share, you can. But we have to be careful, some people are allergic to strawberries."

"Not me!" one of the kids piped up.

"Me neither!" said another.

Liz laughed as all six of the kids reached and carefully plucked a strawberry from the plant and ate them in almost one bite. Other parents started to shuffle through the doors to find their kids, and Liz stood up, clasping Natalie's hand. "You ready to go?"

The little blonde angel beamed up at her mother and nodded furiously. Together, they walked back through the doors towards the office to see that Sienna had already signed a Natalie 'Dember' out for the next few days. She had the girl's small strawberry pattern backpack packed with clothes and ready to go. Ronald in hand, Liz led her daughter to her car and buckled her in tight before they started driving.

"So, what do you want to go do first, baby?"

"Can we go get ice cream?"

Liz looked at the clock and chuckled; it was only barely after 9 a.m., but she wouldn't refuse her daughter anything at that moment. "Ice cream is a great idea! What flavor do you want?"

"Pistachio!" Natalie began to bounce up and down in her seat, tugging against the seatbelt.

Liz pretended to make a disgusted face. "Pistachio? Yuck! You've got the same weird tastes as your daddy did."

"No, I don't!" the little girl laughed. "*You're* the one that's weird, mommy!"

They drove out of the forested grounds and back towards the heart of Pittsburgh until they found an ice cream shop where they gorged themselves on the biggest sundaes they could buy. Afterwards, they went to a public library. Liz was only too happy to spend hours reading Natalie every book she could find while she was curled up in her lap. After a late lunch, Liz took her back to the hotel to go swimming, and Natalie practically made Liz's eardrums bleed from her excited squealing at the new swimsuit Liz brought her: it was white with strawberries all over it. Finally, when it began to get dark, they locked themselves inside the hotel room, ordered pizza, and watched cartoons long into the night until Natalie had fallen asleep. Even after Liz tucked her daughter safely into bed, she constantly kept looking over her shoulder at her as she got herself ready to retire. She could hardly believe they were actually together again, even if it was only for a short while. Once she was ready to sleep, she slipped under the covers and wrapped her arms around Natalie as tight as she could without waking her and drifted into the most peaceful sleep she'd had in ages.

The next morning, the two girls brought their waffles back to the hotel room and ate them in front of the TV again until they were stuffed. They got ready for the day. Driving further into town, they took a day tour of a museum where Natalie had been for a class field trip, and Liz listened earnestly to every bit of information the six-year-old had to tell her, not once even remotely uninterested in what she had to say. She couldn't help but laugh at how excited her daughter got when they had burgers and fries for dinner, saying things like: "We *never* have hamburgers at school!"

Sienna walked in just as Natalie ran off to play inside the fast food playground. Liz smiled at her cousin and kept watching Natalie as the woman sat down.

"Sienna, tell me the truth. How is she doing at the school?"

"She's great, Liz. Honestly. Her teachers adore her; she's got a good group of friends; and she's so polite to everyone she meets."

Beaming, Liz wiped away another tear that threatened to fall. "And you? Has there been any…"

"Nope, I'm always careful whenever I check her out to come back to my house. Everybody believes that she's my niece and nothing else."

Liz nodded. Her cousin was about fifteen years older than her, never married, and had a little house on the outskirts of town. It had been left to Sienna when her parents were forced to retire and move into a nursing home. Liz never thought of Sienna as a plain woman, but she had never been interested in the advances of men growing up and had been terminally single for as long as Liz could remember. Her eyes were always set on getting a PhD in Child Psychology, and she had graduated from NYU with honors, before accepting a job as a counselor and teacher at the boarding school. Liz couldn't think of anyone better to watch after Natalie when her life fell apart, and Sienna had agreed to help out instantly, for which Liz would be forever grateful. No matter how many times Liz said thank you to her, it never felt like enough.

"When does the school year end?" Liz asked.

"June 7th, then it's a week off before Summer School starts. Have you found something permanent?"

Liz shifted uncomfortably. "I'm not sure, I'm not totally settled yet. I honestly thought I was in Scotland, as you know. But …"

She was unable to finish her sentence as her thoughts drifted to Sam; he had promised they would act as if they don't know each other, and he'd been true to his word so far. Still, she couldn't help but wonder if it would be a bad idea to bring her daughter to a town she'd barely been settled in for a couple months, especially with someone who knew she was hiding something so nearby. Despite the mountain of secrets between the two of them, she still felt like she could trust Sam, which was a dangerous notion. She couldn't help but wonder if he really would keep her identity a secret, or if she was setting herself up for disappointment.

"I'll hang on to her as long as you need me to, Liz," Sienna took her hand, bringing her out of her thoughts. "Don't worry about it. I can take the summer off, and she has all of her things in the second bedroom at my house. She'll be fine."

Liz nodded. "Thanks Sienna. The minute I get something together, I'll be back to get her, and you can get on with your life, I promise."

Her cousin scoffed. "Please, I love that girl more than my life of grading papers and counseling other people's kids; more than you think."

Liz laughed along with her, and they talked about Natalie's best subjects and her next birthday in about three months while the little girl continued to play. Once Natalie started to get tired, the three of them went out to see a movie together before Sienna departed. Liz and Natalie went back to the hotel and fell asleep to cartoons again.

Their last day together, Liz took Natalie to the zoo; out of the dozens of different animals they got to see, they spent the most time at the polar bear exhibit. Liz was only too happy to pose with Natalie in front of the life-sized polar bear statue for a picture (which she quickly made her new wallpaper on her phone). Having just enough money left to do an encounter with the Red Pandas, she watched with fondness as Natalie got to hand the little creature some food. She giggled as the little girl squeaked every time the panda would snatch food from her hands and munch on it right in front of her.

Picking up another pizza for dinner, the drive back to the hotel was quieter than it had been the last few days. Liz kept looking in the rearview mirror at Natalie, who kept looking out the window. Despite her ability to hide it well, Liz could tell the little girl was sad.

Liz turned to quickly poke her in the leg. "Hey."

Natalie looked at her through the rearview mirror.

"What's wrong, baby?"

"Mommy …I don't want to go back to school tomorrow."

"You don't? Aunt Sienna says you love school, especially your art teacher, Mrs. Benkins."

Natalie looked down at her feet. "Can't I come with you?"

She knew it was coming, but Liz's heart still ached to hear her daughter say those words. "I really wish you could, honey. But it's not a good time right now."

"Why not?"

"Because …mommy still hasn't found a good place for us to live yet. Honestly, Ronald barely likes where we live right now."

"Do you live on somebody's couch?"

Liz laughed. "What? Where did you hear that?"

"My friend Angie said her mom told her that her dad lives on somebody's couch, and that's why he doesn't get to be with them."

"No, honey, I don't live on somebody's couch. I just want to make sure that when you come to live with me, you'll get to stay with me forever. I don't think that'll happen where I live right now. Do you understand?"

The six-year-old nodded sadly. "Yeah, I understand."

They pulled into the hotel, and Liz did everything she could to get their minds off of their parting the next morning. They enjoyed more pizza and cartoons and even a pillow fight. The night ended with laughter but that couldn't stop the looming sadness Liz felt knowing she would have to say goodbye again in the morning. With Natalie tucked safely in her arms and sleeping soundly, Liz finally allowed herself to cry a few tears into the pillow. She fought hard to stay awake, as she wanted to spend as much time as she could just looking at Natalie, trying to commit every line and curve of her face to memory so she would be satisfied for the next few months' parting. Somehow, sleep finally claimed her.

One last breakfast together of more waffles, and they were driving back to the school. They got there thirty minutes before it was time for classes, and Liz helped Natalie unpack all of her clothing and get dressed in her uniform before they walked to her teacher's classroom. Getting down on her knees, Liz hugged Natalie as tightly as she could and tried to stifle the sobs as Natalie whispered. "I love you, Mommy."

"Oh, I love you too, baby." Liz whispered back. Leaning away, she kissed her forehead. "Now, you be good for your teachers and Aunt Sienna until I come to see you again, okay?"

Natalie nodded.

The bell rang, and Liz kissed Natalie goodbye one last time before she watched the little girl run into the classroom and take her seat. She stood outside the door and watched Natalie until a teacher asked if she needed some help. Finally, she forced herself away, knowing she would never leave if she didn't. Saying goodbye one last time to Sienna and thanking her again, she walked out to her car and made for the highway back to her little apartment in West Virginia. She constantly looked in the rearview mirror at the school until it was completely blocked by the trees. With the last vestige of Natalie out of sight, Liz pulled over, parked the car, and sobbed as loudly as she could into the steering wheel.

~~~

Tuesday patrols gave Sam the best excuse to truly observe the town and gather information. Driving up and down the streets, he took note of the people who behaved suspiciously as well as the people who didn't. Thinking of a time when he was a younger man and fresh onto the constable force, he chuckled as he remembered his first partner and mentor, Sgt. Gregorson. He could still remember the man saying to him, "Rule number one, never believe anythin' or anyone a' first glance." Sure enough, one day they were called out to a domestic disturbance. Sam's first impression was that the massive husband had been beating his tiny wife. Only later did they discover it was the other way around. He never forgot that lesson, and he never believed his first impression of anyone after that. And looking from the shady drug addicts to the soccer moms he passed by, he remembered his sargeant's advice.

After a few hours on patrol, he stopped into a little Chinese place for lunch. He had barely been seated when another customer walked through the door who caught his eye. Liz seemed to notice him, too, but quickly looked away, and he turned his focus back to his meal. It didn't help that the waiter seated them at tables next to each other, but they both did their best to eat in silence and ignore one another. It wasn't the first time he'd seen her around and had to do this; they'd run into each other a few times before in the last month at the
~~~

grocery store and even the same bank. Still, it was starting to get ridiculous, and he often thought about reaching out to her to start over. But the way she constantly kept silent, without so much as a smile, whenever they saw each other, had stopped him from trying.

Two speeding tickets and a public intoxication disturbance had been the end result of Sam's whole patrol shift, and he finished filling out the paperwork for all three within ten minutes and was out the door to go home. It was time for his usual routine of writing a letter to Oliver, and he thought that maybe telling him his dumb old dad finally got that boring job he'd thought about before was actually a mistake. Truthfully, he hated how quiet his work was; he almost felt useless. He'd been at the weigh station for nearly two months, and still there was nothing out of the ordinary, at least nothing he could see. Whenever he was there, everything was done perfectly and up to par, and every single truck that came in to be weighed and measured met every requirement. Even on the random searches he and whoever he was working with would perform, they would find nothing. He didn't have the first clue what he should be looking for that might give him a hint to who was allowing drugs to cross the country, and it was driving him crazy. At this point, being closer to Oliver was the only reason he stayed with the FBI assignment.

Trying to ease the frustration he felt, he tuned the radio to an old rock and roll station and bobbed his head to the Bruce Springsteen song that was playing. He was just about to turn left when he noticed a pretty beat up blue car further in the distance with someone hunched under the open hood. With nobody else around, he drove on through and parked behind it, ready to help.

"Dammit … dammit … dammit!" the familiar feminine voice said.

He chuckled. "Maybe ye should stick to walkin' 'cause it seems you have shite luck with cars."

Liz peered around the hood, saw him, shook her head in amusement and scoffed. "Dammit …"

"Wha's the problem, now? Did yer engine fall off this time?"

"It wouldn't surprise me if it did. Pretty sure my battery is really dead though."

"Le's have a look." Sam walked up. "Wha' are ye doin' out here anyway? I thought ye live on the other side of town."

"I was painting. There's a beautiful river nearby."

He stole a glance in the backseat and saw all of her painting supplies and nodded. Taking her place, he checked everything, including the serpentine belt (though that was mostly just to tease her), and asked her to try and start the car. It didn't make a sound. Chuckling, he leaned back up. "Aye, is' yer battery. I'll bring me car aroun' and give ye a jump."

In no time at all, Sam had the jumper cables in his trunk hooked up to both of their batteries, his engine running, and they leaned against their respective vehicles while they waited. Crossing his arms, he looked out to the green and forested hills on the other side of the road. Occasionally he would glance over at Liz, and she looked to be just as uncomfortable as he was. Finally, unable to stand it any longer, he cleared his throat and said, "Have dinna' with me."

The shocked expression she had on her face made him want to laugh, but he bit his tongue. When she didn't answer him, he continued. "Liz, this is ridiculous. We cannea keep pretendin' we donnea know each other when it's more than obvious tha' we do, anyone can see it."

"Shh," she looked around her nervously. "First of all, around here it's Erin. Secondly, what would be the point?"

"Does there need to be one?"

She sighed and shook her head. "Sam, you know I can't."

"Can't? Or just won't?"

She narrowed her eyes at him.

"Look, is' no' like I'm askin' ye to tell me all yer secrets. Is' just dinna'. Think of it this way, ye'd get a free steak out of it. No' to mention yer date looks a bit of alrigh', and he can be charmin'."

He had finally gotten her to giggle.

"Wine, steak, music … sounds like a pretty good evenin'. But no flowers though 'cause tha' might give ye the wrong impression—"

"Alright, alright, you've convinced me," Liz laughed. "I don't work on Thursday."

He didn't bother hiding his victorious smile. "7 o'clock alrigh'?"

"Sure," she nodded. "You remember where I live?"

"Aye, I think I can find it."

The tension in the air dissolved. Sam asked Liz to try and start her car, which successfully roared to life. With the cables disconnected, they said their goodbyes, and Sam watched her as she flipped her car around and drove off. Deciding that the day had gotten much better, he drove home smiling.

Chapter Eleven

Since the incident with Simon's computer, Rivera had been spending every spare moment he had going over the remaining report in the system of the robbery in Cleveland. With the new information of Brian Cairne being a contract and not collateral damage, all of the evidence that he revisited was being seen in a new light, and he would overlook nothing. Any and all physical evidence that could be collected from the wreckage had been carefully examined and recorded properly, and nothing was out of place. So, Rivera began to look into the investigation of Cairne's private life and found all evidence pertaining to that falling considerably short. There were a few interviews with the standard questions of "Did he have any enemies?" "What was he doing at the bank?" "Any problems at home?", etc., but nothing that really helped him. Not one of the witness statements appeared to be angry or uncooperative in nature. Checking out a copy of the interviews in the log, he took it back to his apartment and studied it further.

Cairne's daughter was the primary interviewee, but there was also his son-in-law Congressman Green and a few of the higher ups for Cairne's steel company. Despite knowing it was initially thought of as a robbery gone wrong, Rivera was appalled at the lack of information collected by the officers and decided he would personally undertake each interview one by one.

Though he had Simon hold onto the printed copies of the deleted reports, they had been meeting at his apartment regularly. Every night was spent over the details of every case and making comparisons to each of the victims to see if there might be a pattern, before determining that the robbers were, in fact, mercenaries hired to kill Cairne.

"What exactly are we doing?" Simon asked him one very late night. "Are we hoping we'll catch these guys or what?"

"For now, we're going to treat Brian Cairne's death as a murder and investigate it as such. At least we'll be able to put together a list of potential suspects that would want to hire a group of mercenaries to kill him, and then we'll go from there."

"Yeah, well, not a lot to go on here. What's the first move?"

"Re-interviewing everybody and anybody. We'll start with his family and then go from there."

"You mean *you'll* start with his family and go from there."

Rivera looked up from the report he was reading and over to Simon. "Yeah, yeah I'll be conducting the interviews, no problem."

"No, I mean you, literally, will have to do this by yourself. I'm in IT, dude. I can't exactly just take off whenever I need to like you. Call Julie and take her with you; I bet she'll be happy to get to do some real police work again."

Rivera stifled his groan; he knew Simon was right, but the last thing he wanted to do was speak to the woman he couldn't even really call an ex-girlfriend. Still, an unsolved murder and their friend's reputation were on the line, and he couldn't let his personal feelings get in the way of the investigation. Though he had no doubt Julie would do anything to help Sam, the question was whether she would feel the same way or not as far as the tension between the two of them went.

"Alright, I'll give her a call in the morning."

"Why wait? I'll just text her."

Before Rivera could argue, Simon had already sent Julie a message and received a reply almost instantly.

"She's on her way!" Simon smiled. "I'm gonna order another pizza."

"Don't you ever stop eating?"

"Hey, don't be jealous that my metabolism is better than yours, Mr. Spends-Three-Hours-A-Day-In-The-Gym."

Rivera rolled his eyes. *He's supposed to be a genius, but he sure can be an idiot.*

Just as the pizza arrived, Julie also walked through the door. "Hey guys, what's going on?"

"You remember the robbery case in Cleveland?" he asked.

"Yeah, what about it?"

"Brian Cairne wasn't a victim, he was a target!" Simon said excitedly. He shuffled around a few papers and showed them to Julie.

It only took a moment to read through them before she shot her head back up and demanded, "Why didn't anybody see this before?!"

"That's a whole 'nother can of worms," Simon grumbled. "Don't even get me started."

"The point is, we're now gonna' investigate Brian Cairne as a murder victim, and maybe we can figure out who wanted him killed. If we do that, we might just be able to unsmear Sam's reputation and get him back here for good."

At the mention of Sam, Julie smiled and nodded. "Alright, I'm in. I've got about two months of vacation time to use anyway."

"Perfect!" Simon clapped his hands together. "You and Rivera are gonna be interviewing people."

"And what are you gonna do, smart guy?"

"Go after the cockroach that destroyed my program."

She furrowed her eyes. "You're gonna … nevermind, if it's important, I'll figure it out."

Julie helped herself to a piece of pizza as she sat down at the end of the table next to Simon and began to make notes on where they should start. Whether she was ignoring his pointed looks or not, Rivera couldn't be sure, but he knew he wasn't too excited about how much time they were going to spend with each other.

A day later they were at Cairne Steel speaking to different staff members who either knew their victim personally or knew of his reputation. Everyone they spoke to all agreed that Mr. Cairne was a smart businessman and very shrewd in his dealings with others. None of his employees, of both high and low status, had anything bad to say about him. Rivera was starting to get a headache from the repeated statements as they talked to the last person on their list, a woman named Vera.

"Oh yeah, Mr. Cairne was a great employer. Honestly, everyone around here was sad when he died."

Julie nodded. "Can you think of anything out of the ordinary that happened that might have made a few people upset? Anything at all."

The woman took a moment to think before answering. "There was this one thing about an employee a few years ago, but it blew over pretty quick."

"What happened?"

"Well … looking back, it's pretty silly to think about now. There was an employee that worked here that kind of got special treatment. Not that Brian was ever unfair to any of us, it was just the little things, you know?"

Curious, Rivera jumped in. "Little things like what?"

"Like the guy would sometimes be late to work. Normally, after that happens five times, there's a written warning; two more times then you're on probation; ten times, and you're suspended. This guy was late all the time, but Mr. Cairne always excused it. It wasn't just that, though. He also frequently got advances on his paycheck, but he would make up for it by doing weekend work."

"What's the name of this employee?"

"I don't remember, I'll have to check my logs from a few years ago. Honestly, I'm not even sure it matters, because the guy died in a factory accident well before Brian died. Like I said, it all seems pretty silly now."

Rivera retrieved a business card from his wallet and handed it to her. "When you find everything, give me a call please."

"Yes, absolutely."

Their next stop was Cairne's family, which was his daughter, Georgia Green. Not a moment after knocking and the door was answered by a young Hispanic man.

"Can I help you?"

"Is Mrs. Green available?" Julie asked.

"It's alright, Beni," the woman herself said as she came from the kitchen in the back. Rivera couldn't help but note how much she looked like her father with her almond eyes and soft, friendly face. In comparison to Mrs. Green's home looking rich and modern in décor, the woman herself was dressed casually, but conservatively, in jeans and a nice sweater. She turned to the young man and added, "Would you mind taking care of the cookies? I think the timer is about to go off."

"*Si, Señora*," the young man nodded before retreating to the kitchen.

"I'm Mrs. Green. What can I do for you?"

"Mrs. Green, I'm Agent Rivera and this is my partner Agent Russell. We're investigating the circumstances surrounding your father's death. Would it be alright if we come in?"

Although the woman appeared confused, she nodded and stepped to the side. "I'm not sure how much help I'll be; I mean, this was a year ago."

She led them into the living room, and they sat on one couch while she sat on the other.

"Just do your best," Julie smiled. "Do you know why your father was at the bank that day?"

"No. He actually never went to the bank for anything. His accountants always handled the money."

"How often did you get to see your father?"

"Every Sunday," Georgia answered sadly. "He made it a point to always have family dinners and leave work at work whenever we were together, ever since I was ten."

Rivera was curious about the age detail she'd added, but Julie beat him to the question.

"Any special reason why?"

"My mother died when I was eight, and my dad didn't take it too well. He became a bit of a recluse. But, when I was ten, he turned that all around. Family dinners became very important. He never missed one since then until… well, until he died."

"Was there ever a dinner where he seemed agitated or nervous?"

"Not that I recall … could you please tell me what all of this is about?"

"Mrs. Green," Rivera leaned forward. "We have reason to believe that your father might have been murdered."

Georgia sucked in a breath. "Murdered? I thought he was a victim of the bank robbery."

"We believe that the robbery might have been a coverup."

"But … why would anybody want my dad murdered?"

The three of them heard the front door open, and the Congressman walked into the house. "Hey, honey, I've got an hour, and I thought we could go grab some lunch together. Beni can watch the kids for a few minutes—"

At the sight of Rivera and Julie sitting on the couch in front of Georgia, Green glanced to his wife before focusing on them. "I didn't know you had company."

Rivera bristled at the sight of the man; he could still recall the way he had screamed and threatened Sam a year before. Quickly collecting himself, he stood up from the couch and walked over with his hand outstretched. "Congressman, I'm Special Agent Rivera and this is my partner, Agent Russell."

Green accepted the hand and shook it. "Hello, agents. What is this about?"

"Jack, they think that Dad was murdered."

"What? He was killed in the bank."

"Some new evidence has come to light that suggests that was a cover, sir," Julie said. "We appreciate your help."

"Yes, of course," Green nodded and sat down on the couch next to his wife. "What would you like to know?"

"Well, right now we're trying to establish whether or not he knew someone would try to attack him. If either of you can think of anything out of the ordinary, leading up to the day he was at the bank …"

Georgia shook her head. "No, I really can't. Can you, honey?"

Green also shook his head.

"Wait …actually, now that I think about it, there was one Sunday dinner, about a few weeks before the bank."

Julie and River leaned forward as Georgia continued.

"We were here at the house, and dad was pretty short with everybody. He's not usually like that. He just said that something was going on with work and not to worry about it, though."

"Mrs. Green, were you involved with your father's business, much?"

"Not really. I mean he had me work there when I was in high school as an assistant to one of his secretaries so I could learn 'the value of hard work' and stuff, but all I did was Xerox some papers and do some typing, maybe a sandwich run or something."

"And what about you, Congressman?"

Green shook his head again. "No, not until he died. But the business was left to Georgia."

"Yes, but we just let the CEOs handle everything and report to us. I'm sorry," Georgia added. "I really wish we could be more helpful, but I can't think of anything else."

"Neither can I," said Green.

Leaving behind another business card where he could be reached, Rivera and Julie left feeling a little more than suspicious.

"What do you think?" He asked.

"I think that asshole Congressman knows more than he's telling us."

"Yeah, I think you're right. What do you wanna do?"

"I *want* to follow him around and see if I can find some dirt on him, but there's no probable cause to do that."

"Well, let's keep digging into whatever Cairne was doing a year ago and see if we can find something that will give us probable cause."

"Where to next?"

"Bank manager. You heard Mrs. Green. He never went to the bank, so there has to be a reason he was there that day."

~~~

Sam had just gotten out of the shower when his phone started ringing. Although the number wasn't in his contacts, he recognized it instantly and quickly sent it to voicemail. His date with Liz was in an hour, and he would not start the night off with a conversation with his ex-wife. He'd barely finished drying himself when the same number called again, and he sent it to voicemail again. Finally, a text came through that read:

Please pick up, it's an emergency!

He didn't have to wait very long when the phone rang once more, and this time he didn't ignore it. Putting it to his ear, he growled. "How did ye get this number?"

"Derrick gave it to me. Sam, you know I wouldn't normally call you, but this really is an emergency."

Meredith's hysterical voice had him at complete attention. "Wha's wrong? Is it Oliver?"

"...He's in trouble."

"Where is he?"

"He's been arrested."

Sam opened his eyes wide. "Wha?"

"He—he was caught with a gun at a gas station."

"Oh, Christ," he ran his hand over his face. "Where?"

"In Elyria. He's at the Cleveland Police station now, and I'm here too."

Sam looked at the clock, which read 6:03 p.m.; Cleveland was at least four hours away, and visiting hours would be over by the time he'd gotten to the city.

"Alrigh', go home, Meredith. There's nothin' we can do for him tonight. I'm on my way, and we'll figure out wha' to do when I get
~~~

there."

"Thank you, Sam," she sobbed into the phone.

Once he hung up, Sam set to work packing a bag before getting in his car and racing towards the freeway, when he suddenly remembered Liz. His mouth went sour at the thought of canceling their date on such short notice, but Oliver came first, no matter the cost. After quickly looking up the number to the bar she worked at, he called. The owner answered it and said that 'Erin' was busy. Sam's chest clenched with guilt as he asked the man to tell her that he would have to cancel their date because of an emergency. The man grunted that he would tell her and hung up before Sam could say thank you. Not dwelling on it, he continued on towards Cleveland.

The four-hour drive passed quickly enough, and before he knew it, Sam was driving into his old neighborhood and pulling into the drive of his former home. He barely had time to park the car when he saw Meredith running out of the bright red front door of the grey house with tears streaming down her face. Her black hair had gotten longer since the last time he'd seen her, but otherwise she was the same: dressed to impress for every occasion even down to her makeup.

Despite their history, Sam could never stand to see Meredith cry. He quickly pulled her into his arms, which she accepted gladly. He could feel his shirt start to soak with her tears, but still he held her and soothed. "Is alrigh', he'll be fine. Cleveland station's go' a good Juvenile ward there, and we'll be able to see him and start straightenin' things out in the mornin'."

Meredith nodded and they walked towards the house. He was surprised to see that, other than the furniture in the living room being re-arranged and a few pictures taken down or replaced, everything was just as he remembered. They sat down on the couch, and Sam leaned back. "Alrigh', tell me wha' happened."

"Oliver and these three other boys he's been hanging around lately were arrested after trying to rob a gas station. The cashier hit the panic button as soon as they started yelling, and the police were there almost instantly. They tried to make a run for it, but they didn't get very far."

"Have ye met these kids before?"

"Yeah, once or twice."

"Did they seem like troublemakers?"

Meredith looked at her hands and began pulling at her fingers. "I honestly didn't notice. Oliver hasn't wanted me around him much lately, so I've been giving him some space."

"How has he been at school?"

"His grades have dropped a bit since the divorce, which I honestly expected to happen but…his counselor called me and said he's been skipping a lot of classes lately."

Sam pinched the bridge of his nose and sighed. "Jesus, Meredith, why dinnea ye tell me sooner?"

"I don't know, I didn't think it would lead to something like this."

"Did ye try to talk to him about it?"

"Yes, of course I did, Sam!" She snapped at him.

He raised his hands in defeat. "Alrigh', alrigh', jus' askin'. Did ye see him?"

"Yeah, I was his phone call. I only got to talk to him for a few minutes before they took him back to his …cell…"

"Wha' did he say?"

"Just that he didn't do anything wrong, and this is a big mistake but …I think he's on something, Sam. He's been smelling a little funny lately, and he seemed pretty …out of it …when I talked to him."

Taking a deep breath, Sam nodded and stood up. "Alrigh' …try to get some sleep, I'll be back first thing in the mornin', and we'll get to the station."

"Where are you going?"

"To find a hotel for a few days."

"Don't be ridiculous. I'll get some blankets and pillows from the linen closet, and you can sleep on the couch."

"I donnea think tha's a good idea. Won't Ryan be upset?"

Meredith looked down at her feet. "He's not here, Sam. Look, I know you're not supposed to be here, and you're technically undercover, so let me at least give you a place to sleep for the night."

Exhausted from the long drive and the stress, he nodded again. "Alrigh', I'm too tired to argue with ye. No' tha' I'd ever win."

Meredith smirked at his comment and walked out of the living room, returning a few minutes later with a heavy blanket and a big fluffy pillow. They wished each other a tense goodnight, and Sam watched her retreat up the stairs before making himself comfortable.

He couldn't help but chuckle to himself at how often he found himself sleeping on couches because of a woman. Remembering that he had a shift the following day at the weigh station, he called dispatch, who promised to get a replacement for him without a problem, before he closed his eyes and was snoring in a matter of moments.

The next morning, after a quick cup of coffee and some toast, Sam and Meredith were sitting in an interrogation room waiting for their son to be brought in. It was the first time he would get to see Oliver in over a year and he was nervous; he wondered how much the boy had changed since the divorce. Would he look more like a man, or would he still see a little boy? He didn't have to wonder too long as within minutes after they sat down Oliver was brought into the room, his hands in cuffs and dressed in a jumpsuit, and placed on the other side of the table.

Sam took one look and sighed. *Meredith was right, he has been on somethin'.* The boy looked haggard and had dark circles under his eyes, his hair was longer and messier, and he looked skinnier. The officer who brought him in seemed to sense what Sam was thinking and nodded a confirmation. *This isnea good ...*

Oliver leaned against his chair and stared at the table. "What the hell are you doing here?"

"Watch yer tongue, young man."

"Your dad's here to help, honey," Meredith said softly.

"Aye, and I want ye to tell me everything tha' happened."

"Mom knows, I already told her."

"I'm askin' you."

Oliver finally looked up at him. "Why do you care?"

Sam took a deep breath. "Son, now is no' the time for this conversation. I cannea help ye unless ye talk to me."

Oliver remained silent and Sam was starting to lose his patience.

"Do ye realize where ye're at right now? You're in a police station, ye were found robbing a gas station, and ye're obviously usin'. Ye can be tried as an adult and go to prison for this, if the Judge decides to throw it out of juvenile court. Unless ye stop behaving like a spoiled little arsehole, tha's exactly wha's gointa' happen!"

His outburst finally had Oliver's attention, and the boy looked at his father. Though he was trying to hide it, Sam could see the tears threatening to fall in his eyes.

"I didn't want to do it, okay? Just the guys got hold of a gun and thought it would be funny …"

Meredith gasped in shock. "And you went along with this?!"

He looked down in shame.

"Did ye ever hold the gun yourself?" Sam asked him gravely.

Oliver nodded.

"Yer mum said ye tried to run away when the police showed up. Did ye threaten the officers when they caught ye?"

He nodded again much more slowly.

Sam raked his hands through his hair. "Alrigh' … here's wha's goin' to happen: ye're gonna' go back to yer cell, and they're gonna hold ye until ye see the judge."

"How long will that take?" Meredith asked.

"We should hear somethin' in 24-48 hours, bu' we might be able to find out when we leave."

"And then what?" Oliver asked, the panic in his voice satisfying Sam that he was finally beginning to understand the severity of his behavior.

"And then the judge will decide wha' ye're punishment is, or if ye'll be tried as an adult. So, if I were ye, I'd think about what ye've done and behave much more repentant and contrite when ye go to speak to him. Is tha' understood?"

Oliver nodded.

"Should we get a lawyer?" Meredith asked.

Sam shook his head. "No, no' until we know whether or not this will go to trial. Officer, we're done here."

The officer walked over and unhooked Oliver before leading him away from his parents. Sam and Meredith followed and walked to the front desk. An old acquaintance of Sam's was waiting and informed them Oliver would be seeing Judge Phillip Buckley at 3:30 p.m. that afternoon, to which Sam groaned inwardly and whispered to Meredith as they left, "Oliver better be beyond damn repentant if we're seein' Buckley."

They were at the courthouse by 3 o'clock with a suit for Oliver, which he grumbled about wearing. Sam warned him one final time. Phillip Buckley had a reputation for throwing the book at everyone brought before him, particularly the children of government employees, and Sam had no doubt the man would do just that to his own child if they were ever in trouble. Sure enough, Oliver didn't behave as well as Sam would have hoped, and Buckley didn't hold back in expressing how stupidly the boy had behaved. But miraculously, the judge sentenced Oliver to a detention center with counseling for six months to a year, depending on his behavior at a new trial in five months. Sam was more than relieved that he would not be charged as an adult and insisted to Meredith that the sentence could have been much worse as they left.

Later that night, Sam found himself sitting in a bar with Meredith. With the horrible day and new situation he had to deal with, he justified ordering a scotch instead of ale and nursed it heavily while Meredith sipped at her martini.

"What do you know about the detention center?" She asked.

"Is' no' the best in the state, and I donnea like the counselors much."

"Can we get him anywhere else?"

"We can get him transferred to a privately owned detention and addiction center if we appeal it, bu' it'll cost more than either of us can come up with."

"So, we just leave him?"

"No," Sam leaned back and shook his head. "They have family counseling sessions every Wednesday, and we're no' gonna miss one. Maybe we can get through to him if we finally talk to him abou' everythin'."

Meredith looked down, knowing exactly what he was implying. "I … don't know if I can, Sam. I honestly think it'll make things worse."

"It cannea make things worse than they are. He deserves the truth, Meredith."

"I know, I know. But right now is not the time to tell him the truth."

He sighed and took another sip of his drink. "Well, we're still going to the sessions. Maybe we'll ge' lucky if he sees that we both love him no matter wha'."

He noticed a tear run down Meredith's face, and he, reluctantly, rubbed her back. "It'll be alright, Meredith. I promise."

She nodded and took a heavy sip of her drink.

Chapter Twelve

Sam slept for a few hours on Meredith's couch but left very early the following morning. Ever considerate, he made sure to fold the blankets and fluff the pillows just the way Meredith liked them but didn't stick around to say goodbye to her. Being in the same house as her was starting to feel too familiar. Making it back to his shabby apartment, he managed to shower, shave, get dressed in his uniform, and clock in for his shift at the weigh station just as the sun was rising. The lack of sleep and the situation with his son weighed heavy on his mind; he knew the next six months were going to make things difficult, to say the very least, especially once the FBI discovered that he was going to be attending counseling meetings with Oliver regularly. He was certain that would not go over well.

And then there was Liz. He could feel himself getting a headache just from the thought of having to talk to her after so rudely standing her up at the last minute. Realizing that despite their history, he really did not know the woman that well, and he wasn't sure how she was feeling. Still, he knew he couldn't just never talk to her again. Knowing he would have to come up with a damn good apology, he resolved to stop and buy some flowers for her once his shift was over.

Not wanting to put her on the spot at her place of work, instead he waited until closing time before driving to her apartment. He saw her walking back just as he'd parked, looking very tired and ready to fall asleep at any moment, so he hurried up the stairs after her. But when he reached the right floor, he never expected to see her standing frozen outside of her apartment and looking in.

"Liz?" He called to her tentatively.

She jumped in surprise when he'd said her name. Turning to look at him, the horror in her eyes had him concerned, and he quickly joined her at her side. Looking to where she'd turned her attention, he dropped the flowers and retrieved his service gun from its holster before walking slowly inside.

The apartment was in ruins; her sparse paintings were cut to a state of ribbons, while the few pieces of furniture Liz owned were also toppled over. Every dish that she had was tossed about the kitchen and shattered to pieces, while every cupboard door was left open. Walking further down the hallway, Sam took note of the similar state of the bathroom. The bedroom had her clothes thrown about, and the mattress was flipped completely off of the bed frame. After looking in every nook and cranny and satisfied that there was no intruder hiding, he turned to Liz, who was directly behind him.

She shoved past him and ran to the closet where she produced a suitcase. Throwing it open on the ground, she began to grab every piece of clothing she could find and shoved them into the suitcase.

"Wha' are ye doin'?"

"I've got to get out of here!" She shrieked.

"Where will ye go?"

"I don't know, but I can't stay here!"

Setting the gun back in the holster, Sam walked towards her and tried to place his hand on her arm, but she pulled away as if his touch had burned her. Furrowing his eyes, he tried another approach. "Alrigh', jus' slow down for a moment and talk ta' me."

"No, you wouldn't understand!"

"Aye, yer right, I donnea understand. Nor will I, unless ye tell me wha' there is to understand." Finally, he caught her hands and forced her to stand still. "Liz, I'm yer friend, and I know people. I can help ye."

Liz heaved a sob. "Sam—"

"Just tell me the truth. Please."

She stood quietly, seeming to consider his request for a moment before replying, "First, take me somewhere safe, and then I'll tell you what's going on."

"Aye, ye got it."

Springing into action, Sam grabbed everything of hers he could carry including her ruined painting supplies and a toppled, broken 'Ronald,' before leading her to his car. They drove in silence back to his apartment. The distance from the center of town seemed to relax Liz a great deal, and she wasn't crying anymore when they arrived.

After making them some tea, Liz sat on one end of the couch while Sam sat on the other. He waited for an explanation. He watched her closely as she stared at her hands and took a few deep breaths before turning to look at him.

"... I'm in trouble."

"Aye, I gathered tha' much."

"There's someone that I've been trying to get away from for some time now."

"Who?"

She looked down at her hands again. "That's not important."

"Ex-husband?"

She shook her head. "No, I wasn't lying when I said my husband died. ... But what I didn't tell you is that I also have a daughter."

Sam tensed but remained impassive as he leaned back against the couch.

Liz cleared her throat and pulled at her fingers as she continued. "Her name is Natalie, and she's almost seven. Shortly after her father died, everything just fell apart, and the guy I'm running from threatened to take her away from me unless ... anyway. Things just got to be unbearable, so I staged our disappearance."

Her tone suggesting that the little girl was still alive made Sam relax. Out of the corner of his eye, he took note of the broken strawberry plant and smirked. "Ronald's hers, aye?"

Liz chuckled. "Yeah, she's always loved strawberries. When she was three, she plucked a strawberry fresh from a farmer's market, and the next thing we knew, we had to buy the plant 'cause she had eaten every berry. From then on, she wanted strawberries on her birthday cake, strawberries on her clothes, the works. So, for her fourth birthday, her dad bought her a strawberry plant to take care of, and she decided to name it Ronald. We finger-painted the pot and put his name on it, and she's taken care of it ever since until ..."

He could see the tears brimming in her eyes but pressed her further. "Why is she no' with ye?"

"You saw the state of my apartment; he can always find me. If he can find me while I still have Natalie ... I don't want to think about what he might do."

"Is she safe?"

"Yes, she's with my cousin. I get to see her whenever I can get away ... it's just that right now, I'm trying to find a place where he can't find us before I go back to get her. Leaving her was the hardest thing I've ever had to do, but I won't lose her, Sam. Not to him."

Sam breathed a sigh of relief. "Aye, I understand. So, yer plan is to keep runnin' until ye find a safe spot? Where do ye think tha'll be?"

Liz leaned onto her knees and dropped her face in her hands. "I don't know … I honest to God thought that being thousands of miles away in Scotland would be as safe as it could possibly get. I was just starting to feel like I could send for her when … well, you know what happened."

"Aye, but I'm no' convinced tha' bastard Liam didnea vandalize yer car."

"It wasn't him; I know it wasn't. He may have been a handsy drunk, but I honestly believe he was only drunk enough to break into my home but not touch my car."

Sam furrowed his eyebrows. "So tha's happened before?"

"Yeah. The first time was in Florida, about a month after I got settled. Next, I tried New York, and two months later, it happened again. And then I thought overseas might be a better chance, but when I realized I was wrong …I thought I might as well stay in the States where I can at least be a little closer to Natalie and see her more often. So, I did everything I possibly could to cover my tracks this time but—"

"Wait, so he's never broken into yer home before?"

Liz shook her head. "No, it's always just the car. And don't ask me why because I have no idea."

"But yer car hasnea been touched; I saw it as we drove away."

"So?"

"So, in my experience, criminals donnea defer from their patterns unless they have a reason to, or they're gettin' desperate. And from everythin' ye've told me, it sounds like they're jus' enjoyin' frightenin' ye and are content destroyin' yer car. So why would they go after yer apartment, unless this was just a random burglary and no' the man chasin' you."

Liz laughed incredulously. "I honestly wish I could believe that, but I can't take any chances, Sam. I can't let him find Natalie."

He leaned forward and took her hands in his. "Who is he, Liz?"

"I told you, that's not important."

"And I told you tha' I know people tha' can help. Remember tha' I was a cop here for a long time. I have a team here tha' I trust with my life."

"I believe you, but this guy has his ways. I've seen him buy people off before. I have no doubt he would try to buy the police if he even gets a hint about where Natalie is."

Sam moved closer to her and brushed a stray hair away from her face. Gently, he tilted her chin up to look him in the eye. "Liz, le' me absolutely clear about one thing: he cannea buy me."

Her eyes were red and puffy from how much crying she had already done, but that didn't seem to stop the fresh tears that gathered at the corners. "I can't run from him forever, Sam. I want my daughter back!"

Her vulnerability and brokenness made Sam feel a new sense of protectiveness over her. Wrapping his arm around her, he pulled her to his chest and held her tightly. "It'll be alrigh', Liz; it'll be alrigh'."

He felt Liz's arms slip around his waist as she heaved her sobs onto him. For a long time, he refused to move until he was certain that she was calm. There were moments when he thought she had gotten everything out, but then suddenly she would start crying again, so he remained quiet. Finally, about ten minutes after she'd settled down, he wondered if she'd fallen asleep and looked down to see her eyes drooping and even redder and puffier. Smiling, he kissed the top of her head. "Come on, lass, le's get ye to bed."

He stood and scooped her up into his arms and carried her to his bedroom before gently setting her down on the mattress.

As he was tucking her in, she looked up at him, "Sam—"

"Now, now, yer in no condition to go anywhere. Yer goin' to get some sleep, and we'll figure out wha' to do in the mornin'. And I want ye to promise me tha' you'll still be here in the mornin'."

He was satisfied to see a little smile pull at the corners of her mouth. "What I was going to say was: will you stay with me, please?"

Hesitating, he cleared his throat.

Liz leaned up and continued. "Before you tell me this is a bad idea because I'm just feeling vulnerable and scared, I can assure you that I already know that, and I still want you to stay here with me. I just … I'm tired of feeling alone."

He searched her face for any hint that she might be a little uncertain but couldn't seem to find one. *This is a bad idea,* he thought to himself, but that didn't stop him from taking off his shoes and climbing in next to her. The furnished bed was already too small for just him, and Liz had to snuggle up tightly to prevent falling off of it. Her hand across his chest and her face buried in his neck made Sam acutely aware of how long it had been since he'd held a woman this way. He did his best to hold perfectly still, resolving to get up and leave after she'd fallen asleep and not risk compromising anything between them. But then suddenly Liz's lips were on the base of his throat. They were so soft and featherlike, but the tender affection already began to light a heated fire throughout him. He held still, waiting to see if she would stop, but she continued kissing him over and over again.

Sam swallowed hard and clenched his eyes together. *She doesnea need ye to take advantage of her, ye horny bastard. Don't—*

His thoughts were interrupted as she leaned up and over him, her face too close to his for a comfortable level of tender civility. He opened his mouth, intending to tell her she'll regret her actions later, but was silenced by her lips on his. He groaned as they danced together in a kiss, the intoxicating ache he felt nearly drowning him. Finally, he grabbed her arms and pushed her away.

Breathing heavily, he growled her name, "Liz—"

"Don't," she whispered firmly, placing her fingers over his lips and silencing him. "I'm not a child; I know what I want. And right now, I want you."

Still he hesitated, his honor fighting with his body. He'd often wondered what being with her would be like, and now he had the chance to find out, and still he resisted. But when she leaned her head back down and kissed him again much more gently, her assurance was all it took for Sam to break his restraint. Letting go of her arms, he took her face in his hands and pulled her down to him. He tried to be slow, but need and hunger overtook him, and he rolled them both over.

Later, with Liz wrapped securely in his arms, a slight sheen of sweat covering the two of them, Sam was drifting off to sleep when she whispered, "I didn't peg you as a flowers kind of guy."

"Hmmm? Oh, they were supposed to be an apology."

He could tell she was smiling by the way she kissed his chest. "You're forgiven."

Julie looked over the bank statements for the hundredth time; it had taken them a week to see the man Brian Cairne had spoken with, as he was out of town when they'd first gone to the bank. When they finally got in touch with him, he was hardly willing to answer her and Rivera's questions about why Cairne was there that day in his office. They'd learned that he was setting up a rather large trust account for his daughter and grandchildren. The conversation played over in her head again as she looked for anything that might help them:

"Wouldn't a guy that rich already have a trust set up for his family?" She'd asked.

The bank manager (a man by the name of Richard Hughes) didn't bother looking up as he typed away on his keyboard. "I'm not in the habit of asking my clients for their reasons on why they do things, agent."

Julie scowled at him.

"Does Mrs. Green know about these trusts?" Rivera asked.

"No, he had finished getting them set up just before … the incident. But I was under strict instructions not to inform her of the trusts for the time being."

"Why is that?"

Hughes shifted uncomfortably before replying, "I'm afraid I'm not privy to give that information. Mr. Cairne expressed how important it was to keep these accounts secret for the time being, and it is my job to honor all of our clients' privacy."

"Even when it's the police asking?"

"Yes, agent, even when it's the police asking."

Julie eyed him coolly, getting the feeling that he just enjoyed pretending he was of a 'higher class' than they were. "And what if we had a warrant?"

"Then, of course, I'll be willing to finish answering your questions, madam."

"Fine. We'd like copies of all of Mr. Cairne's statements in every account, including the trust funds, for the last twelve months prior to his death."

"Yes, of course, after you produce the warrant we'd discussed."

They'd left the office feeling perturbed at the manager's attitude.

Thankfully, Julie knew a judge who owed her a favor, and they had a warrant within the hour. She smirked as she remembered the look on the man's face when they gave him the document: he looked like a child being scolded by the principle. Begrudgingly, he gave them everything they'd asked for, including the answer to their question: Georgia and her sons were not to know of the trusts until she was either divorced from Congressman Green, or the man had died. Adamantly insisting he never asked why, Julie and Rivera had more questions than answers, and they asked for a copy of the Congressman's bank statements as well, to which Hughes didn't argue.

They'd hoped they would learn more through the paperwork, but nothing stood out to them so far, and Julie was starting to feel impatient. It was late at night in Rivera's apartment, and her body was screaming at her to get some sleep. While Rivera was hunched over the table with her, she smirked to see Simon passed out on the couch. Deciding to start fresh in the morning, she stood up and started making her way for the door.

"Don't tell me you're quitting, too," Rivera said softly.

"I can't see anything out of the ordinary here, Derrick. And I'm tired. We'll try again in the morning."

When he yawned in reply, she chuckled.

"Alright," he nodded, "in the morning then."

She felt the air between them grow colder as he abruptly turned away from her. Rolling her eyes, she said under her breath, "Goodnight, you big baby."

"Excuse me?"

"You heard me; you're being childish."

"What are you talking about? I just stood up. How is that being childish?"

"You're kidding right? You literally just turned around to stomp away like I told you that you couldn't have your favorite toy."

"Ha!" he mocked her. "That's rich, coming from you."

"And what's that supposed to mean?"

"It means I'm tired of playing these games with you, Jules. We're two fully grown adults, and it's nobody's business but ours whether or not we're sleeping together."

"Shh!" She hissed as she looked over at Simon. Seeing that he appeared to still be asleep, she breathed out a sigh of relief. "Keep your voice down."

"Unbelievable," Rivera raked his hands through his hair. "You know what? I'm sick of fighting with you. Good—"

They were interrupted by his cell phone buzzing on the table. Julie stood there scowling right back at him before gesturing to the phone. "Well? Aren't you going to get that?"

He snatched the phone up from the table and growled into it. "Rivera."

His countenance grew less angry as he listened to whoever was on the line, and Julie couldn't help but feel curious as to what was going on.

"… Alright, where do you wanna meet? … Got it; we'll be there in ten minutes."

Julie waited for an explanation as he hung up and shoved the phone in his pocket. "That was the Congressman, he wants to meet."

"What for?"

"He says he has some information that concerns Cairne's death, and he doesn't want his wife to know. Are you coming or not?"

She hesitated for a moment before following him. "Just so you know, I'm still pissed off at you."

"The feeling's mutual. Come on."

After the tense ten-minute drive, they pulled into a parking garage off of 12th Avenue and went to the fourth level before parking and slowly walking through the rows of cars. Julie could feel the hairs on the back of her neck standing on edge as they searched for their contact. She peered out of the corner of her eye at Rivera, who appeared to be completely at ease. She placed her hands on both of her guns as they walked, beginning to wonder if they had been duped. She suddenly heard footsteps coming from behind them. Julie drew the guns from their holsters before turning around to see three shadowy figures coming closer.

"Whoa, it's us!" the Congressman said. "Hank, Bruno, lower your weapons."

Rivera put his hand on Julie's arm, and she lowered her own weapons before they walked towards the man who had set up the meeting and the two other shadows.

"Who are these guys?" She asked him sharply.

"My private security team, agent. I'm making a run for President, you know, and some people don't like that."

"You said you have something for us?" Rivera asked him directly.

"Yeah, here."

Green produced an envelope, which Julie opened. She pulled out photos of Brian Cairne in a hotel suite with what looked to be a dark-haired woman who had her back turned to the camera. There were many of the photographs, but the most notable was one where Cairne was hugging her, in another he had his hands on her arms, and in another they appeared to be talking.

"Okay, so what's this supposed to mean?" Julie asked Green sharply.

"Isn't it obvious?"

"Did you have your father-in-law followed, Congressman?" Rivera asked.

"No, you don't understand, *Brian* gave me these pictures. He told me that he'd made a mistake and had gotten … romantically involved with a member of his staff, and the whole thing had started to go south."

"South how?"

"She started demanding a lot of money—expensive hotels like the one you see in the pictures here—just typical gold-digging behaviors. I'd suspected that he'd been involved with someone for a while, and then one day he gave me these photos and asked me to hold onto them for safe keeping."

"Why you?" Julie asked.

The Congressman didn't blink. "Let's just say that I know people who are good at hiding and revealing things when they need to be revealed. I think Brian had a plan to use these pictures to get the woman to leave him alone."

"If she was so bad, why didn't he just fire her?"

"That's what I wanted to know, but all he told me was she had something on him that prevented him from being able to do that. I don't know what, maybe she planned to accuse him of sexual harassment or something. But if you look closely at the woman's finger, you can see a ring on it. Maybe he planned to show the photos to her husband or something. Again, I'm not sure."

"Why didn't you tell us this when we were at your house last week?" Rivera asked.

"You have to understand; my wife adored her father. She was his only child, and he gave her everything she ever wanted. I didn't want to tarnish her memory of him. And he gave me these photos months before he died. I didn't think anything about it, until you told us he was murdered. It took some time to recover them."

"Do you have any idea who this woman is?"

Green shook his head. "No. And he wouldn't tell me, said the less I knew the better."

"Is there anything else you want to tell us, Congressman?" Julie asked.

The man furrowed his eyebrows. "Like what?"

"Like why Brian Cairne would want his daughter to divorce you?"

Julie could see Rivera turn to her with scolding eyes, but she didn't care. Keeping her eyes trained on Green, she didn't move a muscle.

"What are you talking about?"

"He was at the bank that day setting up trusts for your wife and sons, but not for you. And the manager was put under strict instructions to not let her or the children anywhere near the money unless you were no longer around. So, it sounds to me like Brian didn't confide in you as much as you're trying to make us think he did."

Green shifted uncomfortably, and she felt a surge of satisfaction.

"Look," he cleared his throat, "… a few months before he died, Georgia and I were having some … problems. I was in the middle of a very tense race with my opponent and … well, let's just say that I didn't spend my nights alone. But I ended the whole thing immediately after the campaign was over."

"Did Brian approach you?" Rivera asked much more civilly.

"No, I didn't even know that he knew until you just said something because he never said a word to me. Obviously, he found out, though, as I can't think of any other reason why he would want Georgia and I to get a divorce."

The Congressman's body language and tone made Julie think that he really had no idea that his father-in-law was preparing for his daughter to leave him. She decided to table her suspicions for later, but she would be sure to read through the Congressman's bank statements again in case she was wrong.

"Look, I'm not proud of what I did. It was the lowest moment of my life, and not a day goes by that I don't wish that it had never happened. But please … don't tell Georgia about any of this."

Julie opened her mouth to speak, but Rivera beat her to it.

"We'll do our best to keep anything that doesn't need to be out in the open hidden. But now, according to these photos, we have a suspect. If whoever this woman is turns out to be the killer, your wife will find out sooner or later."

Green nodded. "I understand. Thank you, agents."

The man walked away, and Julie followed Rivera back to their car where they examined the photos a little closer.

"Should we take these to the company and see if she looks familiar to anybody?" she asked.

"Yeah, we'll go first thing in the morning. Maybe we'll get lucky. Did you drive to my place?"

"Took a cab."

"I'll drive you home."

Julie looked up at him. "I thought we were still fighting."

"We are, but one of us has to be the bigger person here, and it might as well be me."

She wanted to argue but felt too tired to do so. Rolling her eyes, she turned to look out the window at the street lights for the short drive.

Chapter Thirteen

The sun shone brightly through the window onto Sam's eyes, forcing him to roll away from it, when it occurred to him that he was alone in the bed. He sat up and looked around, feeling concerned that his companion had already disappeared again. Then the bedroom door opened, and Liz gingerly walked in with two mugs of coffee. His button-down shirt completely drowned her tiny-in-comparison frame, but the sight of her in his clothing was enough to make him ache for her all over again.

She smiled shyly at him and sat on the foot of the bed before handing one mug to him.

"Good mornin'," He said softly as he took the mug. He leaned in closer and kissed her tenderly.

"Morning," she sighed.

He took a sip of the steaming coffee (which was very bitter) and tried not to cough after he swallowed it.

Liz caught his reaction and chuckled. "I know, sorry. Can't cook and can't even make coffee."

"Tha's alright," he coughed again and set the mug down on the floor. "We can get coffee at the restaurant."

Getting out of bed and walking towards the tiny dresser, Sam set to work getting himself dressed when he felt Liz's hands wrap around him.

"You know I can't stay," she mumbled into his back.

Turning around to hold her in his arms, he whispered into her hair. "Where will ye go?"

"I don't know yet."

"Liz, ye cannea keep doin' this. It seems t' me tha' runnin' hasnea stopped him, so maybe ye should try a different approach."

Liz leaned away and looked up at him. "And do what? Fight? I don't know if I could do that."

"Why?"

"Because I can't."

"Can't or won't?"

Liz stopped herself from answering.

"Darlin', if there's anythin' I know is' tha' no matter how hard it gets, ye have to try."

She turned away from him. "I wish it was that easy."

He sighed and rubbed her shoulders. "Look, Liz, if ye wanna run again, I won't stop ye. Bu' I'm no' gonna chase ye, neither."

He saw her stiffen at his words but gently caressed her hair.

"… Do you really want to hear the whole story?"

"Aye."

She took a deep breath. "Alright. My mom raised me on her own; I never knew my father. One day when I was six, she got a job as a secretary and shortly after, started dating the guy that hired her. The next thing I knew, they got married. I remember feeling so excited knowing that I was finally going to have a dad. Alex was always so nice to me. He would take me to go get ice cream, to Coney Island, anything I wanted, all I had to do was ask and give him a hug. Then as I got older, the hugs got longer. One time when I was twelve, my mom was out getting groceries or something, and he asked me to sit on his lap. I didn't think it was a big deal because we'd been a family for a few years. But … well, after that, if I asked him for anything, I had to sit on his lap first."

Sam was no stranger to sexual abuse to children, as he'd been around plenty of cases in his career, but that didn't stop the bubbling rage he felt. "Did yer mum know?"

Liz shook her head. "I don't think she even suspected, and I never told her. I mean, my dad abandoned her as soon as she found out she was pregnant with me, and she was a single mom. I didn't want to make things hard on her over nothing."

"Liz, wha' he did to ye wasnea nothin'." He led her back to the bed, and they sat down on the edge.

"Well, I didn't figure that out until much later. One night, when I was seventeen, mom and Alex were out at a party, and I was at home doing homework or something. They'd had a little too much to drink, especially my mom, and when they got home, he asked me to help get her to bed. Then he followed me to my room and … well, anyway … He apologized, said it would never, ever happen again. And it didn't. Actually, he left me alone after that. Then I moved to college and met Daniel, my husband. He was this kind, romantic artist. He was actually the teacher's assistant, and we just hit it off. Shortly after we got married, my mom died from alcohol poisoning. A few years later, I was pregnant with Natalie and life had all of a sudden happened to us. Daniel went to work for his uncle; I was at home raising our baby. Things were really good."

Tears had gathered in her eyes and Sam retrieved some tissue paper for her. "Wha' happened next?"

She sniffled, "I got a call … Daniel had died in a work accident. Natalie and I got evicted, we were homeless. Alex came and said we could live with him until I could get a situation set up. Obviously, I was wary, but … I didn't have anywhere else to go. And I thought, since I knew what he was capable of doing, I could watch him and make sure he never touched Natalie the way he did me. Whenever I went for a job interview, I made sure she was at a friend's house or daycare. But I had absolutely no skills, no one would even give me a chance. And then one day, I came home and … he had picked Natalie up. She was sitting on his lap playing with a new toy he'd gotten her. It suddenly hit me that I really had no idea what he was capable of doing. For all I knew, he'd been doing the same things he did to me right under my nose, no matter what precautions I took, he was …"

"Grooming her," Sam provided.

"Yes! Exactly!" Liz sucked in a ragged breath. "I had Natalie go out to play, and I confronted him. I told him if he ever touched my daughter, I would kill him. He told me he would fight for custody of her and take her away from me, if I said that again. He said the court would see me as a neglectful mother with no job, and he could make a case that I was abandoning her all the time, that I'm unfit to care for her … That's when I realized that I had to get out, no matter what. I went to Daniel's uncle begging him for help, and he gave me a job as a secretary, go figure. But then he died and I was fired … we were homeless again, and Alex threatened to take Natalie away unless we moved back in …"

"Tha's when ye ran, isn't it?"

Tears streaming down her face, Liz nodded.

"How do ye know it's him tha's chasin' ye?"

"The first time my car was vandalized, there was a note attached that said, 'I know.' Who else would leave a message like that?"

"Why donnea ye come forth? Laws have changed, Liz, ye'll be

believed, and he'll never bother ye again."

She scoffed. "For what crime? I can testify all that I want against him, and his lawyers will throw it right back in my face that I was deluded, spoiled, on drugs, whatever they can concoct."

The moment she said 'on drugs,' Sam tensed; he remembered the detailed report that Simon had found for him, and he couldn't help but ask, "Were ye?"

"Was I what?"

"On drugs?"

Liz looked down at her hands in shame, "… Yes, for a time. I started when I met Daniel. But the minute we found out we were pregnant, we sobered up and said we'd never do it again, and we never did."

He wanted to ask about the night before her disappearance, but the way she held herself in shame at the admission stopped him. Instead, he wrapped his arm around her. "I believe ye. Wha' about Natalie?"

"What about her?"

"She can talk to a judge—"

"No," she shook her head sternly. "I will not force my daughter to sit in front of a bunch of strangers and be picked apart by lawyers. Besides, even if I wanted to, he never did more to her than have her sit on his lap. His lawyers would make me out to be a delusional lunatic, while he was just being a loving grandfather. I can't beat him, Sam. My only option is to get away."

"Alrigh', alrigh'. Have ye ever tol' anyone wha' ye just told me?"

"No, never."

"Well, then there's some good news."

"What?"

"Ye've got a friend on yer side now. And now tha' I know wha's goin' on, I can help ye."

"How?"

"I can have someone keep watch on yer stepfather, and if he tries to do this again, it'll be taken care of."

Liz chuckled. "Sam, I appreciate it … but he's a powerful man."

"We can at least try." Sam nudged her, and she smiled. "At least think about it."

"Where am I gonna' go? My apartment was broken into."

"Right, we'll have to get to the station, so ye can file a report."

"No!"

Her outburst caused Sam to furrow his eyebrows questioningly.

"I don't want to file a report. If you're right, and it was just a random burglar and not him, then that'll be the end of it because obviously, they didn't find anything. But if you put my name in the system, then he'll be able to find me for certain."

"Ye're usin' an alias, Liz."

"It hasn't stopped him before. I don't know how he does it, but he does. Please, Sam … just let this go."

The way she pleaded with him softened his resolve. "Alrigh', fine. But I'm changin' the doorknobs and locks, is tha' understood?"

"Yes," she nodded.

"And I'll be drivin' by once a week."

"Okay."

"And I want ye to finally give me yer number."

He couldn't help but feel amused by her surprised expression; he clarified, "so ye can let me know if somethin' happens again."

She nodded again and her stomach grumbled, making the both of them chuckle.

"I guess I'm hungrier than I thought," she said.

"Aye, le's get goin'. After breakfast, we'll stop by the hardware store and get ye some really good locks and new keys."

Smiling, Liz stood up and kissed his lips softly. "Thank you, Sam."

Sam watched her pick up their coffee mugs and retreat to the kitchen. As he finished getting dressed, he couldn't help but feel something was still off about the situation. *Why would he ransack her apartment? Hell, why would he only go after her car?* It didn't add up, but he promised to leave her out of the system, and he would uphold that promise. Deciding to quietly dig deeper after she was settled again, he pushed all of his doubts to the back of his mind and took Liz out for steak and eggs.

After replacing the locks and helping Liz put her apartment back together as well as could be done, Sam created a whole new routine. Taking it upon himself to drive by her apartment at least once a week, he made sure to circle the whole block as well to check for anyone suspicious, but couldn't seem to find anyone or anything out of place. Liz went back to work as if nothing was wrong, and every night (per his insistence), she would send him a text saying she was back in her apartment safely. For the next two weeks, everything was a queer normal.

Then came the first Wednesday of family counseling at the juvenile center back in Cleveland. Sam arrived a few minutes before the meeting was supposed to start and saw Meredith outside waiting for him. Together they walked in and took their seats just as Oliver was escorted into the room. The session went about as well as Sam expected it would: Oliver refused to talk about anything that related to what he'd done and turned all of his aggression towards believing his father had abandoned him and his mother. It took every ounce of willpower Sam had not to shout the truth at him, especially because Meredith refused to say a word about Oliver's feelings. Not knowing what else he could do, he sat there and let his son yell and scream at him for the entire hour. The therapist didn't help matters as she only encouraged Oliver to say everything he was feeling, without so much as acknowledging Sam or Meredith. When the session was finally over, he drove back to Mineral Wells in aggravated silence.

Just as he was pulling into his apartment parking lot, Dispatch phoned him and asked him to take over a shift for the night. Rather than sit at home where he could stew on the horrible meeting with his son, he readily agreed and made ready for work.

There was only one other guard there with him: a portly woman named Trisha who reminded him of a chatty aunt he had by the way she would continue to talk and talk to him throughout the shift. He would always grunt or give short one- or two-word answers in reply and nothing more but that didn't stop her overly friendly attitude. When 10:00 p.m. rolled around, he was secretly wishing the job would allow him to be alone again until midnight, when he could go home and sleep before having to return for his shift the next morning.

Other than Trisha, it was insanely quiet; a few cars passed along the highway now and then but no trucks until about 11:30 p.m. Per the flashing lights, the rig pulled in and onto the scale. Each axle measured under the express weight limits except for the front of the container, which was nearly 1,500 pounds over the weight limit. Grateful for the chance to be away from his chatty workmate, Sam grabbed his flashlight and the clipboard with paperwork and walked out to the driver.

"Good evenin', Sir. I'm afraid ye'll have to re-arrange the weight in yer shipping container, ye're too heavy back there."

The greasy overweight man appeared shocked by his accent (which he was accustomed to) but mumbled, "Okay, sure."

Sam waited on the side as he heard the driver move around a few crates. Curious, he looked inside to see crates of flowers. *Those cannea be tha' heavy, can they?* When the man had finished, he instructed him to pull off of the scale and back on again while he checked the computer. The rear axle had increased by about 400 lbs, but still the front of the container was too heavy. Securing his equipment, he walked back to the driver.

"Ye're still too heavy, sir, so I will be performin' a check on the container."

"Alright, go ahead." The man was getting somewhat perturbed but underneath the frustrated exterior, Sam got the feeling he was a little nervous.

"Step away from the container, please."

The man did as instructed, and Sam jumped up into the trailer; he shined his flashlight through the rows and crates of different flowers, but in his mind he counted the length of the trailer. Reaching the end of it, he smiled to himself. *Six feet too short to be a true container.* He looked back to the driver, who had beads of sweat starting to appear on his forehead, and smirked. Turning back to the wall, he tapped it and the sound that greeted him wasn't metal, but actually wood. An opportunity had been presented, and though part of him was saying to report this and confiscate the truck, his deal with the FBI reminded him that wasn't his true assignment. Turning back to the driver, he called him up into the trailer.

"Look, man, I just drive it. I don't ask what's in it," the man shifted around nervously.

Sam smirked. "Uh-huh. $1,500, and I let ye go without reportin'."

The man gawked. "What?! I don't—"

"Or we'll confiscate the truck and conduct a more thorough search. Wha' do ye think we'll find behind tha' wall?"

Sam stared the man down until finally, he nodded and pulled out his wallet. "I've only got a grand on me."

"I'll take all of it."

Sam shoved the cash in his pocket, and they walked back out of the trailer. Taking only a moment to memorize the details of the trailer in his head, he patted the rig and watched the man drive off before walking back into the station where Trish was waiting.

"Hey, that truck was still too heavy on the axle."

"Aye, we moved around wha' we could, and he was tired. I tol' him to take it slow on the drive and le' him go this time."

Trish watched him sit down before quickly turning to the many buttons and levers on the board. "Okay, if you're sure. Perfect timing anyway, we're done!"

They shut down and locked the station before walking to their cars that were parked in the back.

"'Night, Sam!"

"Aye, g'night, Trish."

Sam went to bed feeling a little better about the day. His gut told him he'd made the right decision letting the truck go, but he would only be certain if he reaped any reward from it, other than the $1,000 he'd confiscated.

Sure enough, the following day after finishing his shift, he drove to the bar where Liz worked, and an antsy feeling plagued him. He sat over his pint of ale, talking to Liz (but using her alias Erin) whenever she had a minute, and still the feeling wouldn't go away. Leaving an hour before closing time, he was walking back to his car when he heard someone walking behind him. He balled his fists together and spun around, ready for a fight.

"Gerald?" He asked, surprised to see a man he barely knew from the Sheriff's office standing there.

"Hey. Sam, right?"

"Aye. Wha' can I do for ye?"

"Actually, I wanted to talk about what I could do for *you*. How about you and I go get a bite to eat? There's a little place down the road that makes a damn good Rueben sandwich."

Gerald was much shorter than the average man with greasy blonde hair that he kept slicked back at all times. Though Sam never talked to him much, he knew immediately after their first meeting he wasn't the sort of fellow he would want to be around socially. But the sudden friendly midnight offer had him more than curious, and he accepted the invitation.

Sitting in a little booth and digging in to what Sam agreed was a good Rueben, Gerald took out a pen and wrote down something on a napkin before sliding it over. Sam looked down and saw "1%" written on it.

"Tha' supposed to mean somethin' to me?" he asked.

"You let a truck slip through last night; why?" Gerald asked him directly.

I knew it, Sam thought to himself triumphantly, but he kept his poker face trained on the little man. "T'was late at night; the driver was tired, and I decided to le' him go with a warnin'."

"Uh-huh, and was this before or after he paid you a grand?"

Sam shifted in his seat. "I donnea know wha' ye're talkin' abou'."

"Well, this number should give you a pretty good idea of what I'm talkin' about. Sometimes we get trucks that don't measure up the way that they should. If you were to cut these drivers a little bit of slack, then you're looking at a 1% ... let's call it a bonus."

Yes, I'm in! Don't be too eager. Sam straightened his shoulders and took another bite of his sandwich.

Gerald watched him intently, that smug smile still on his face. "Think about what I'm offering you here, Sammy. You work three days a week, live in a shitty apartment, and from what I gathered from Gloria at dispatch, you've got a kid in a bit of trouble."

Sam bristled at the mention of Oliver.

"Think about what this money could do for your kid, hell, even for yourself. You tellin' me you're not even the least bit interested in making a little bit of extra dough? Come on, Sammy."

"Is' no' Sammy, Sam will do."

"I apologize, Sam, but as I was—"

"Two."

Gerald stared at him blankly before laughing. "You're a negotiator, huh? Well, two is pretty steep. But ... I think 1.5 is doable."

"And jus' how would I be collectin' my payment?"

"Now now, no need to trouble yourself with all the details just yet. But here's your first installment for last night," Gerald reached into his pocket and produced a small but thick envelope and slid it across the table to him. "I think you'll find it's more than adequate for one night of work."

Smirking, Sam stuffed the envelope in his back pocket and offered his hand. "I believe we have a deal. One las' question, how do I know these trucks?"

"Oh, don't worry; you'll get information as you need it. Good to have you on board, Sam."

He drove back to his apartment quickly. Finally, after almost two months, he had something to report, and he knew that would make the FBI happy. Once he was back in his apartment, he locked the door and looked around before calling the number to his handler Evan.

"Hello?"

"Is' Sam."

"Hey! Pretty late, but what's up?"

"Ye can tell Director Copper tha' I'm in."

Sam heard the sounds of Evan scrambling before he answered. "Seriously? Okay, what happened?"

"Had a suspicious truck pull up at the weigh station, sure enough the trailer was too short on the inside."

"Too short? What do you mean?"

"Shipping containers are normally forty feet long; this one was only 34 feet when I walked it. The back wall was wood, no' metal."

"A fake wall? Seriously? Well, what did you find?"

"Nothin', I dinnea look. But the driver was nervous, he knew wha' he was carryin'. He paid me no' to report him. And tonight, I have been made a member of the dishonest cops club."

"Ha! Excellent work, Sam! This will definitely make the Director happy! Who was it that invited you in?"

"Fella' by the name of Gerald Mebbin, a Deputy."

"Anybody else?"

"No' yet. I've only jus' been let into the circle; it'll be some time before I know more."

"Yeah … yeah, you're right. Well, excellent work, Sam! I'll tell the director first thing in the morning!"

"Bye, Evan."

"Goodnight, sir!"

After depositing the evidence money Gerald and the driver had given him into a safe box hidden in the closet, Sam went to bed feeling triumphant. After two long and tedious months, he was finally making headway on his assignment, and he no longer felt useless. But as he laid there listening to the crickets outside his apartment window, the words that Gerald said about having enough money to help out Oliver rang out in his mind. He thought of the cost of rehabilitation centers and how that problem could be easily fixed, if he just kept a little of what he confiscated. His stomach turned at those thoughts, and he quickly shoved them deep down and away before he drifted off to sleep.

Chapter Fourteen

"When I find you, you stupid … stupid … stupid …" Simon glared at his computer screen as his fingers flew across the keyboard furiously. Every minute of his spare time was spent trying to rebuild the search engine that had been destroyed by the Leviathan, but every time he thought he was close to completion, a new error would pop up, and he'd be forced to chase down that particular problem before he could move forward. "I'm gonna … gah!"

Another error in his coding appeared, and he decided to give up for the time being and slammed his laptop shut. It was almost quitting time, and it had been a particularly slow day in the IT department at the office, which was the only reason he'd been able to spend so much time focusing on his code. But he was looking forward to tabling that particular problem for later, as it was time to meet up with Rivera and Julie again, after he picked up the photos the Congressman had given them from the evidence lab. Every night for over a month, they'd been conducting their own investigation into Brian Cairne's murder, and the best lead they had were those photos. Rivera and Julie had taken them back to Cairne's company the day after they'd gotten them, but the woman in the photos was completely unrecognizable. Most of the people they talked to pointed out that many women would look that way from behind. Therefore, Simon took it upon himself to have a friend working in digital forensics look them over and enhance any images she could. He had to win her over with coffee and a bear claw before she agreed, but they were ready, and he hoped it would give them more to go on.

Walking out of the office, Simon couldn't resist taking a peek at the pictures when a slap on the shoulder startled him. Looking over, he groaned to see Cole Terry standing there. "Hey, Abler!"

He quickly shoved the photos back into the file. "What do you want?"

"Oh nothing, just haven't heard anything from my favorite crew in a while. But it looks like you've got something juicy on your hands."

"I don't have anything for you."

Terry mocked a pained expression and covered his heart with his hand. "That hurts. Especially because I heard through the grapevine that you guys are trying to solve your last case with Sam."

Simon gulped; the only people who knew what they were up to were Rivera, Julie, and himself. None of them were fans of the annoying blog reporter. Chancing that Terry was only venturing a guess, he bluffed. "Looks like you better find a new grapevine, because I have no idea what you're talking about."

"Oh really? Then how come I saw him around town last week when he was deported over a year ago? Not to mention those photos you have in your little folder."

"You must've seen somebody that looked like Sam. And this is official FBI business. Now, go away and bother somebody else."

Cole smirked and tried to hand him a business card, but Simon raced away to his car. Finally away, he took a deep breath and tried to drive as inconspicuously as he could over to Rivera's apartment.

Rivera opened the door for him, and Simon noted that Julie was already there, still tearing through paperwork. Simon took his seat at the table next to her with his laptop. "Anybody else hungry? I can order—"

"No more pizza," Rivera groaned. "Shake it up a little bit for all our sakes, will ya?"

Julie nodded. "Yes, please. I vote Thai."

"Okay, okay, geeze. Oh, got the photos back today. And guess who's back to dogging us for a lead?"

Rivera and Julie both raised their eyes in concern.

"Yeah, he tried to look at the pictures, but I wouldn't let him. Not to mention he saw Sam in town … guys, he knows what we're doing."

"That's impossible," Julie argued. "None of us have said anything outside of this room, right?"

"I know I haven't," Simon agreed.

"Guys, relax," Rivera answered. "He's probably just seen us all getting together frequently and took a wild guess, and there's nothing more he has to go on. Okay?"

"Yeah, yeah … you're right," Julie said.

Simon took a deep breath and nodded. "Yeah, that's all. Okay, getting back to the photos, out of curiosity, I looked into Cairne Steel's standing in the stock market for the last year. It dropped by about thirty points shortly after the man died."

"Okay, so what does that mean?" Julie asked.

"Well, they had to adjust for the lack of funding, and there was a 10% cutback on the staffing. Even after the company was left to the Greens, it still hasn't really recovered. It's actually losing points a little at a time. I wouldn't be surprised if they claim bankruptcy in the future."

"Huh … we should take a look at the company's financial statements and see if there's anything else going on that would cause that," Rivera said. "Did that woman ever get back to us about the name of the guy that she mentioned? What was her name …"

"Vera," Julie provided. "And no, not yet. I'll give her a call first thing in the morning."

"Hey, guys, I know this is a long shot, but I'm gonna' see if I can get a list of names of the people that were let go after Brian's death," Simon said as he pulled up his faulty program.

"What for?" Rivera asked.

"I dunno, maybe something will stand out."

"Did you get that thing fixed?" Julie asked, and he waved her off.

"Don't even get me started. I've got enough here that I can do a few things but it's gonna be a while longer before I get it back to normal … Eureka! I'm in the Cairne Company database!"

He didn't notice that Rivera had grabbed the envelope with the photos sitting next to him until he looked up. The man was staring at one photo intently.

"What is it?" said Julie.

"Got a clear picture of the woman in the photos. The lab was able to enhance the mirror in the background so we could see her face. Simon, look familiar?"

Taking the picture from him, Simon looked closely at the reflection, and his eyes opened wide. "No way … is that who I think it is?"

Rivera came over next to him. "Yup. Look through Cairne's database and see if you can find her anywhere."

Simon moved his fingers across the keyboard like a man possessed before hitting enter. "… Huh."

"What is it?"

"Well, yeah, she worked for him alright, but it was only for six months. And I think she was related to the guy who died in that accident Vera told you about. Look: Daniel Harper."

Julie leaned forward. "Brother and sister?"

"Hang on," Simon clacked away again. "… Husband and wife. Looks like she went to work at the same company a few months after he died."

"This doesn't make sense," Rivera said quietly. "Why would she be at a hotel with the man who owned the company where her husband died? … Simon, can you see if Daniel had life insurance, or if there was a payout to his widow?"

"… No, no life insurance, and the company didn't give her anything."

Julie piped in. "Green told us that Cairne had these photos taken because of an office romance gone wrong. And he couldn't fire the girl because of complications … what if she was trying to get close to him so she could get a payout for losing her husband? And then after Cairne caught onto it, he decided to fire her but couldn't because there would be a lawsuit over the death?"

"Well, if that's true, why would he have these pictures taken? How was he hoping to blackmail her with them, if her husband was already dead?"

"Unless he didn't have them taken," Rivera said softly.

Simon and Julie looked up at him but he was staring at the computer screen intensely. "Maybe he got them from somebody else who had them taken and gave them to Green for safe keeping … Can you access all the financial statements of Elizabeth Harper?"

"I can try," Simon nodded. "What am I looking for?"

"Large amounts, going in or out, anything that suggests she's guilty of something."

"Okay … are you going to tell Sam?"

"… Not yet, not until we piece together what's going on."

Rivera walked away from the two of them and towards the kitchen; Julie followed him shortly after. Sighing, Simon began to tear even deeper through the life of the woman his boss had him look into months before.

Another boring Tuesday patrol left Sam feeling frustrated; as excited as he was for the break into the corruption circle, that didn't make his other duties less monotonous. It had been almost two weeks since Gerald paid him for letting the truck through, and there hadn't been any other suspicious trucks during his weigh station shifts. He supposed it would be some time before there was another one, and he would have to just be patient. Still, he was already bored and wished something else would happen. Just as he stopped for some lunch, he noticed a suspicious-looking character walking on the other side of the street: their face was well-concealed with large black sunglasses, their head was covered with a hoodie, and they were looking around as they walked. Certain he'd been in Mineral Wells long enough to at least know quite a few of its occupants, he was certain he'd never seen this one before and decided to keep an eye on the figure. He watched them walk up the street a bit before turning into an alleyway. Sam jogged over and peeked around the corner. He couldn't quite see who the person was talking to, but it was clear that some sort of money exchange was happening. Just as he was about to walk in and expose the situation, the second figure moved into his eyesight. He felt his blood freeze before quickly hiding, as the two suspects parted ways.

Sam watched Liz continue down the street, acting as if she'd just stopped to pick up the mail and nothing more. While he wanted to go after her and demand an explanation, his gut told him to follow the mystery figure instead. Turning down the alleyway, he quickly but stealthily followed whoever was behind the sunglasses as they kept walking. He managed to follow them for another block undetected before they quickly bolted around the corner. Sam chased whoever it was as fast as he could but lost track of them almost immediately. Frustrated and confused, he walked back to his car. The more he thought on the situation, the more he was convinced Liz was lying to him. He decided he would confront Liz that night when she was off of work.

Getting back in his car, he continued his patrol throughout town. No matter how much he tried to people watch, his mind kept wandering back to the extremely suspicious encounter he'd witnessed in the alleyway. He started to wonder what more Liz was not telling him, and before he knew it, he was driving near her apartment complex. He turned the corner and slammed on his breaks: another mysterious figure was next to Liz's car, and he'd bet his salary it was the same man from the alleyway he was chasing. Backing up before he was spotted, Sam parked the car, withdrew his gun, and inched towards the scene. When he heard the sound of something hitting metal, he rushed forward.

"OI! Hands in the air, now! Donnea make me shoot ye 'cause I will!"

The figure turned to bolt, but Sam was quicker. He fired his gun and was pleased to hear a man's voice shriek in pain before the figure dropped to the ground.

"You shot my leg!" The figure wailed.

"I tol' ye to put yer hands up," Sam said simply as he withdrew a set of cuffs, recited the Miranda rights, and yanked off the sunglasses and hood. The man was bald with a dark five o'clock shadow framing around a chiseled jaw, but he didn't spark any familiarity. Looking back to where he'd heard the noises, Sam noted that it was Liz's car that the man had hit with the crowbar that was on the ground near it, and he furrowed his eyebrows in confusion. *What the hell? Weren't they just talkin?* Knowing that the middle of the street was no place for a confession, he hauled the man back to his patrol car and drove for the station.

Later that day, after processing the suspect, Sam watched as he was hauled away to the cells in the back. He had a mind to ask the Sheriff to let him interrogate him himself, but first he needed to know why, and he intended to interrogate Liz for every detail of information that evening. Shift over, he changed out of his uniform and turned his cell phone back on and saw three missed calls from Rivera. *This cannea be good ...*

Once he was back to his own car, he called him back and was answered after the first ring.

"Sam?"

"Aye, wha's up?"

"Are you sitting down?"

"I'm in my car, do I need to be home?"

"No, that's as good a place as any. Okay, remember the guy that was shot and killed at the bank? Our last negotiation assignment together?"

"Aye, Brian Cairne," Sam nodded; he could never forget the names of the people he couldn't save.

"Yeah, him. Well, there's a lot I need to bring you up to speed on, but the short version is Julie, Simon, and I discovered that his death wasn't just because of a botched robbery. He was murdered."

Sam leaned back in his seat. "Wha'? Are ye sure?"

"Oh yeah, we've combed through everything, we're positive. Simon found something that connected him to similar cases. He was a hit by a professional team with the same MO: they stage a robbery of sorts and kill their victim by a point-blank shot."

"Who are they?"

"We don't know. These guys are good, and we can't track them. But Julie and I have put everything and everybody under a microscope. We did find enough evidence to support the theory that he was murdered, and we're sure we know who did it. Do you understand, Sam? This means we can clear your name; we can prove there was nothing you could do, and you can get your reputation back!"

It was the best news he'd heard in months; Sam sighed and allowed a little smile to cross his face. "Who was it?"

"Our prime suspect is a woman it appears he was having an affair with, or at least he thought he was having an affair with her. Her husband had died a few months before, and she was using him for money. When he'd tried to cut it off, she had him killed. Boss … it's that woman you had me look into: Liz Harper."

For a moment, Sam didn't think he could breathe. "Wha'? That cannea be right."

"It is, Sam; we checked everything. She was depositing a hell of a lot of money into her account every month until about a month before Cairne's death. Then a week after he died, she withdrew it all: $100,000 in total. Sam … it's her. And I have to ask, do you have any idea where she is?"

Sam stared out of the windshield. *She killed him? She used me?* "… Aye, I know where she is."

Someone knocked on Sam's window, and he jumped, recognizing Gerald. "I have to call ye back."

He hung up and quickly rolled down the window.

"Hey, Sam," Gerald smiled, "Who was on the phone?"

Shit, of all the times to be caught off guard, he was sweating as everything was running through his mind all at once. "Gerald, hallo. What can I do for ye?"

"Who was that on the phone?" the man repeated.

"Ach, no one important," he tried to sound innocent, but the way Gerald looked at him made him wonder if he'd completely blown his chance at getting deeper into the ring. Trying to recover, he said, "Actually, it was my ex-wife, she's on me arse abou' money again."

"Awe, sorry to hear that. Well, I just wanted to let you know that we've got a couple people who are curious about meeting you. Here," he handed Sam a small slip of paper with an address on it. "Sunday at 11 p.m., you got that?"

"Aye, got it," Sam nodded. "Thanks, Gerald."

"See you around," the man nodded and quickly walked away from the car.

Sam stuffed the paper into his pocket and headed for home, stewing about the entire situation. *Wha' the hell is goin' on here? Wha' is she really up to?* He thought about everything she ever told him over and over again, and he knew there was a lot missing from her story. And yet the more he thought on it, the more he believed he couldn't truly trust her to give him the entire truth. Once he was in his apartment, he called Rivera back.

Late that night, standing outside of Liz's apartment, Sam shifted back and forth on the balls of his feet. Straightening his shirt, he could feel the wire that was taped to his chest underneath his shirt and quickly turned it on before knocking on Liz's door. He knew she was home. He was sitting in the car with his old team as they watched her walk back. He watched her with an icy glare; he could barely feel Julie's hand on his arm as they waited. Once they were sure she was back inside, he was set up with listening equipment.

"Are you sure about this, boss?" Simon asked him sincerely.

"Aye," he said quickly. "Before we arrest her, I want to give her the chance to tell me her side of things. If ye need to move in, I'll le' ye know."

He looked in the backseat at Julie and Simon, who simply nodded. Turning to Rivera, who was handing him a gun and a set of cuffs, they nodded to each other before he set out towards the apartment.

Now, standing in front of her door, he felt a mixture of sickness and rage bubbling up inside of him. He didn't want it to be true, but all of the evidence suggested that it was. This was her last chance, and he hoped she would take it. He knocked on the door again, and Liz opened it a few moments later.

"Oh," she smiled at him. "Hi. I wasn't expecting you tonight."

"Aye," he nodded. "I though' I'd drop by. May I come in?"

"Yeah, absolutely." Liz stood to the side and shut the door behind him. "Would you like some tea?"

"No thanks, I'm alrigh'." Sam glanced around the apartment, not sure exactly why, but it seemed better than just staring at her. His eyes fell onto a large suitcase sitting near the hallway. "Are ye goin' somewhere?"

Liz looked over at the bags and shifted nervously. "Um, yeah. I was thinking about going to see Natalie again soon, maybe this weekend."

He nodded and looked into her living room where he saw a new painting she had sitting in an easel. Walking closer, he realized it was turning into a portrait, even though it was still in unrecognizable stages. He nodded towards it. "Anyone I know?"

Liz chuckled behind him. "I should hope so, it's supposed to be you. Sam, is something wrong?"

Taking a deep breath to steady himself, Sam turned and looked at Liz directly. "Liz, I saw ye talkin' with someone in the alleyway earlier."

Her countenance changed instantly, and Sam probed her further.

"Who is he?"

"Just … an old friend," she said softly.

"And wha' did he want?"

"Nothing," she said a little too quickly and took a step backwards from him.

"Then tell me abou' the money."

"What money?"

"Liz, stop it!" Sam snapped. "I saw ye givin' him money before he handed ye somethin', jus' please tell me wha' it is!"

"I told you, it's nothing! Why are you asking me this?"

"You tol' me tha' yer stepfather's been chasin' ye, but tha's not true, is it?" Sam walked towards her.

"What? Of course, it's true! Why would I lie about that?"

"How well did ye know Brian Cairne?"

He saw the confusion flash across her eyes.

"He … he was my husband's uncle."

"The uncle ye went to work for after yer husband died?"

"Yes, like I told you."

"How well did ye know him?"

"Not very well. I only really talked to him after Daniel died just to get a job."

Sam withdrew one of the photos that his team had brought with them from his pocket. Unfolding it, he pointed to Liz's reflection in the mirror. "Tha's you, isn't it?"

Liz turned pale right in front of him. "Where did you get that?"

"If ye dinnea know him tha' well, why were ye with him in a hotel room?"

"Why are you asking me these things?! I told you, Brian was helping me!"

Sam threw the photo to the side and clenched his fists, desperately trying to keep his anger under control. "Liz, I'm givin' ye one las' chance to tell me the truth. Why were ye with him in tha' hotel? And wha' was the reason ye talked to tha' man today?"

She looked up at him defiantly. "Are you arresting me?"

He knew somewhere inside of him that he didn't want to, but her lack of faith in him drove him to make the hard decision. Dissapointed, he shook his head. "… Aye, I guess I am." He put his hand to his ear where an earpiece was and said, "Come on in."

The front door opened and Rivera, Julie, Simon, and a few other officers poured into the apartment and seized Liz. Sam watched her being taken away in handcuffs while his team surrounded him; none of them would touch him, but he knew they wanted to be close to show him their support.

The four of them drove together back to Cleveland's FBI headquarters, but the trip was anything but friendly; Sam stared out of the windshield with hardened eyes, unable to hear any of the ambient noise around him. When he felt someone put their hand on his shoulder, he turned to look at Julie.

"Hey, you couldn't have known. Don't do that thing that you always do, where you beat yourself up over not knowing."

He turned to look back out of the window. He poured over every detail since the day he'd met Liz, trying to think of every time something didn't add up with her. Thinking about the man he'd arrested again caused him to voice his thoughts out loud: "Why would she pay someone to destroy her car?"

"What was that?"

"She tol' me tha' she ran from place to place because someone had destroyed her car where she was stayin'. Bu' I saw her payin' the man tha' was about to before I stopped him. She didnea' wanna' report when her apartment was broken into, so I doubt she'd report her cars bein' vandalized either. Which means we cannea corroborate her claims of someone followin' her. Bu' still, why would she pay tha' man to destroy her car?"

"Because it makes her look innocent," Rivera said. "She gets your trust and makes sure she doesn't look like she's guilty of anything. Didn't you say that her car was trashed back in Scotland, too?"

Even though his blood was beginning to boil, he couldn't shake the feeling that something was still off about the case. "Ye said she withdrew $100,000? Where did it go?"

"We don't know yet," Simon said, "I can't find anything that suggests where it is, but I'll keep looking. If you ask me though, she probably paid those hit guys in cash so that it couldn't be traced."

"And unless she gives us any good reason why she had all that money, there's no reason to suspect otherwise," Julie said.

"Still, why would she use all tha' money jus' t' have Cairne killed?"

"Revenge for her husband dying," Rivera said, "I've seen people kill for less."

Sam rubbed his face with his hands. "I wanna' lead the interrogation."

"No way, boss."

He turned to Rivera.

"Look, you knew the whereabouts of a fugitive for months, and it's obvious you're a little confused right now. If you go in there, we could lose the whole case, and then you'll be right back in Scotland. Let us handle it, okay? We've come this far."

Sam hated to admit it, but he knew Rivera was right and nodded his head in defeat. It was nearly 4:00 a.m., by the time they pulled in front of the FBI building, and he watched intently as Liz was led from the other car in handcuffs.

Chapter Fifteen

Sam stared through the two-way glass of the interrogation room at Liz; apart from being exhausted, her eyes were red from the tears she'd been crying, and she kept shifting her wrists in the handcuffs.

"Did she ask to call anyone?" he turned to Simon, the only other person in the room with him.

"No," he shook his head. "She was offered a phone call, but she refused."

"Has anyone contacted her stepfather?"

"Yeah, as soon as we parked. One of the guys said he was on his way, so we should see him soon."

The door to the interrogation room opened, and Sam watched Julie and Rivera walk inside and sit on the other side of the table. As entertaining as it was to see the two of them play off of each other during an interrogation, Sam was in no mood to smile.

Rivera was carrying a manila folder that he placed on the table and pulled out the hotel photos. Liz looked down at them. "We'd like you to explain these."

She remained quiet.

"Okay, let me tell you what we see: we see a young woman in a hotel room with our murder victim."

Julie then pulled out some printed papers and pointed to something specific on them. "We also see multiple deposits of about $5,000 in your bank account for about six months, then there's a sudden withdrawal of $100,000 shortly after our victim was killed."

Rivera kept his eyes trained on Liz as he added, "Now, none of this makes a whole ton of sense at first glance, mind you. But the witness who gave us these photographs says that Brian Cairne gave these to him and intended to use them against you."

Julie leaned forward onto the table. "But you know, we think that *you* are the one who had them taken to try and blackmail him for more money. But when he wouldn't go along with it and stopped giving it to you, you had him killed, took the money he had already given you, and ran off."

Liz didn't move.

"Do you know what the penalty for murder in the state of Ohio is, Mrs. Harper?" Rivera asked her. "It's a life sentence, with the potential for the death penalty."

"On top of being our prime murder suspect, you're being charged with kidnapping." Julie pulled out a photo of Liz's daughter Natalie and placed it in front of her.

Finally, Liz reacted; she glared at the both of them and said quietly, "I didn't kidnap my daughter."

"Then tell us where she is."

"No."

"Why not? We can make sure that she's safe."

Liz shook her head and looked at her hands again. "That's what you think, but she's safe where she is."

"Do you not understand the severity of what's going on here?" Rivera snapped. "Kidnapping and murder are serious crimes, and there's enough evidence against you to get you capital punishment!"

"You have got everything wrong!" Liz screamed, the tears pouring out of her eyes. "I had nothing to do with Brian's murder! Yes, he was giving me money, but he stopped when I asked him to!"

"Okay, then explain what all of this is to us. Why were you in that hotel room with Brian?"

"Because he was trying to help me!"

"Why would he help a complete stranger?" Rivera asked in a much softer tone.

"He wasn't a complete stranger; he was my husband's uncle. After Daniel died, I needed work, and he gave me a job and was trying to set me up with a place to live."

"Let's assume that you're telling us the truth," Julie said. "Then explain why he was just casually handing over $5,000 every two weeks to you."

Liz sighed. "Secretaries don't make a lot of money; it wasn't enough to support us and … it just wasn't enough, okay? So, he sent me extra out of his own pocket. I tried to do more work for it, I even offered to take a job on the factory floor since that position made more, but he insisted that this arrangement would work just fine."

Julie and Rivera looked at each other before Rivera asked, "What did you do with all that money when you withdrew it?"

"I used it to disappear."

"$100,000 couldn't buy you a whole new life?" Julie spat at her.

"I thought it could at least get me started," Liz said angrily. "But it didn't matter where I ran, I was always found! I'm not lying!"

Sam watched the interview intently; while his gut told him that Liz was indeed not lying, her story seemed too shaky. He'd already had a chance to look over the records at Cairne Steel, and Daniel was not the first person to die on the factory floor. But he was the first family member, and Sam supposed that would certainly make one feel responsible for any family left behind. He wanted to stop the interview when what Rivera said next threw him off.

"You say that Brian Cairne was your husband's uncle, from who? A brother? Sister?"

"I don't know," Liz shook her head. "I never really asked."

"Well, maybe you should have because Brian Cairne was an only child; in fact, he was the son of two only children."

Liz looked up. "… What? Why would Daniel lie to me about that?"

The door to the observation room opened, and Sam and Simon looked over to see an agent stick his head in. "Hey, there's a guy here named Alexander Michaels, says he's here for our suspect."

Curious, Sam followed the agent to the lobby where he saw the same clean-shaven, silver-haired man from the news clip months before.

"You found Elizabeth? Is she alright?" he asked earnestly. "Where's Natalie?"

Sam walked forward and offered his hand. "Mr. Michaels, I'm Sam McKay. I'm afraid yer stepdaughter has been placed under arrest."

"What? For what charges?"

"Please, if ye'll jus' follow me somewhere we can talk a little more privately …"

Sam led the man to a small, comfortable room with some plush-looking furniture and took a seat in a chair whilst Alex sat on the couch opposite from him.

"Okay," Alex asked in a panicked tone. "Why has my daughter been arrested?"

"Mr. Michaels, do ye know anyone named Brian Cairne?"

Alex furrowed his eyebrows. "No, should I have? Oh, wait! Wasn't he the man who died in that robbery a while back? Owned a pretty big business, right?"

"Aye, tha's him. Well, it would appear tha' his death was actually murder. And Liz is the prime suspect."

"What?! That's preposterous! I demand to see my daughter, now!"

"And I'll be happy to take ye to her, Mr. Michaels, but first I have a few questions for ye. Liz is sayin' tha' she ran away and hid her daughter. Can ye think of any reason why she would do tha'?"

The silver haired man stared at Sam for a moment before leaning back against the couch, "She told you I molested her, didn't she?"

Sam kept his face emotionless.

"God … I should have known this would happen." Alex shook his head sadly. "Liz was a troubled child. I met her mom when she came to work for me and instantly fell in love, with Liz too. After we got married, it was only then that I saw how bad things really were. My wife, Bianca, was an alcoholic. I don't know how I didn't see it for so long, but one night I got home from work, and she was yelling at Liz while the poor girl was cowering in a corner. I quickly got my wife out of there and went to comfort Liz, and I ended up staying the night. She was just so upset; it took a long time to get her to stop crying. The next day, I had Bianca committed to a rehab program, which really upset Liz. I told her it was the best thing we could do for her mom and that after she got better, her mom wouldn't be so mean anymore. But … I think all that did was make things worse, because Liz just wasn't the same after that. I thought therapy might help, so I called a friend of mine who's a psychologist, and he started seeing Liz regularly. Once Bianca had completed her program and came home, Liz was doing much better. Bianca still had her moments, but then she would go back to her therapist and deal with them while I tried to assure Liz that her mother would be alright.

"Liz moved to college and met Daniel … he was bad news from the beginning. Some of the same behaviors I saw my wife do, Liz fell right into them. When we found out she was on drugs, and she was going to marry this boy … it just destroyed my wife. She drank herself to death shortly after the wedding. What could I do? Liz was a grown woman, and I couldn't force her to go to rehab. When she told me she was pregnant, I told her it would be better to kill the baby than let it be born an addict."

Sam watched the man rub his face and sigh.

"I instantly regretted saying that. But before I could apologize, she walked out the door and told me she'd never talk to me again. But I think something good came from it because the next thing I knew, she and Daniel had gotten clean, and Natalie was born. Then the accident happened … please understand, I was afraid that Liz would go back to doing drugs, and Natalie would have the same type of upbringing that Liz had. So, I went to her and we reconciled, and I offered for her and Natalie to move back home until Liz could get something sorted out. When she told me she had gotten a job, I was thrilled for her. I encouraged her to keep working hard but insisted she was always welcome, and there was no rush to move out. Then she started coming home later and later, I thought she might have been returning to some bad habits. One night she came home and she was very … out of it. Thinking she was on drugs again, I told her she had to stop, or I would take full custody of Natalie, and she would have to get completely clean before she could even see her again. Then one day she came home and took Natalie without a word; I couldn't even get her to talk to me. She just packed Natalie into a car and drove away, I assumed to a hotel or something. And then I found out they had gone missing. At first, I wanted to think that they had been kidnapped, but as time went on …"

Leaning forward, Sam cleared his throat. "Why didnea ye tell the police any of this?"

"I honestly don't know … I think I wanted to protect her? Maybe I was afraid if she was arrested, Natalie would never forgive me. Please, do you have my granddaughter?"

"No, I'm afraid we donnea know where your granddaughter is. Liz was alone when she was arrested."

Alex looked at Sam sternly. "Please take me to Liz. She's done answering questions until my lawyer gets here."

Leading him back to the interrogation, Sam knocked on the door, and Julie answered it. He heard Alex say the interview was over, and he barely caught a glance at Liz as Rivera and Julie exited the room. She looked nervous and angry at her stepfather, but the door closed before he could see anymore.

"Did ye find out anythin'?" Sam asked.

Julie answered. "No, she's insisting that she's innocent and had no idea Brian's death was a murder. She won't tell us where the kid is, either. What did he have to say?"

"Tha' Liz grew up with an alcoholic mother, and she's an addict herself."

"Well, he wasn't lying about that," said Simon. "She has a couple charges for drug use, but she was acquitted, probably thanks to her stepdad's lawyers. But from what I can tell, she's been clean for the last five years, other than an overnight stint in the emergency room right before they dissappeared."

The memory of Liz running out of Jackie's suddenly came to Sam, and he couldn't help but wonder if Liam had drugged her after all, or if it was a relapse on Liz's part.

"Well, it doesn't matter now, she's lawyered up. And unless we can prove that she paid those mercenaries to kill Brian, or she gives us a confession, we can't charge her for much more than kidnapping." Rivera looked to Sam for any more information, but he just shook his head.

The interrogation room door opened, and Alexander Michaels walked over to Sam and his team. "She won't tell me where Natalie is. Please, agents, you have to find her. She's only six."

Sam was at war with himself: one part of him said that Liz was innocent, but the other couldn't deny all of the evidence she had stacked against her or her elusive behavior since he'd met her. Knowing she would go to prison for some time, he concluded it would be better for her young daughter to be with family for a while rather than think her mother had abandoned her. He turned to Simon. "Can ye track the movements of Liz's alias?"

"As long as nothing was paid in cash, absolutely."

"She's been goin' by Erin, but I donnea know wha' last name. I do know the bar she was workin' at, ye can get any information from her boss in the mornin'."

"I'll get right on it." Simon nodded and walked away.

"Mr. Michaels," Julie turned to the older gentleman. "Why don't you go home? The minute we find your granddaughter, someone will contact you."

Alex looked back at them anxiously before nodding his head. "What about Elizabeth?"

"We'll be holding her here for a few days until we get the rest of her paperwork processed, then things will move to a trial."

"Agents, tell me the truth, what is she looking at?"

Rivera stepped in. "Kidnapping and possibly murder … it won't be good, Mr. Michaels."

Alex squared his shoulders. "Then I guess it's time for my lawyer to earn all that money I've been paying him."

Julie led the man away, leaving Rivera and Sam alone. Sam rubbed his tired eyes and pretended to ignore the pointed look his old partner was giving him.

"How long were you sleeping together?" Rivera asked.

Knowing there wasn't any point in lying, he answered. "Jus' one time."

"Jesus, Sam. You do know that you can't be involved with this anymore, right? If this gets out then it could get thrown out in court. Not to mention make things worse for *you*."

"I know tha', which is why I'm leavin' now. In case ye've forgotten, I've go' my own assignment to worry about."

"Alright, good. But you're in no condition to drive home. Here," Rivera reached into his pocket and pulled out his keys. "Why don't you head back to my place and sleep for a couple of hours?"

"No thanks, I'll ge' a taxi."

"That's way too expensive. At least let me get somebody to drive you."

"Fine, jus' hurry up."

Rivera nodded and gave the order to a passing agent, who nodded and hurried off to get a car. Turning back to Sam, he offered his hand. "I'll let you know what happens as the case progresses. Hopefully, if we can prove the murder, then you won't be stuck in Mineral Wells forever."

Sam smirked and shook his hand. "Ach, is no' tha' bad. Jus' do me one favor and have Simon send me all the files. I'm no' gonna' ge' involved, I'm jus' curious."

Rivera chuckled. "Will do. Goodbye, Sam."

"Aye," he nodded and walked towards the door where the agent and the car were waiting along with somebody else.

"Sam!"

He turned and groaned. "Oh fer the love a'—wha' do ye want, Terry?"

"I knew it! I knew you were back!" Cole Terry smiled

enthusiastically and thrust a recorder towards him. "What brings you and the FBI together? Who was the woman seen taken into the building? Does it have anything to do with the last case you worked here before being deported?"

Sam snatched the recorder out of his hand and threw it to the ground before stomping on it.

"Hey! Those aren't cheap!"

"If ye know wha's good for ye, ye'll back the hell off now," Sam growled. "I'm tired, I'm goin' t' get some sleep."

Opening the door to the car and settling into the back seat, Sam gave the address for Liz's apartment and found little satisfaction in leaving the annoying blogger in the dust. Knowing there was nothing else to do for the time being, he closed his eyes for the four-hour drive and tried to get a little sleep, but the tiny car made it impossible to be comfortable. It was nearly 8:00 a.m., the sun shone through the car brightly, and Sam stretched as much as he could in the backseat of the black company car as the agent turned and said, "Sir? We're here."

"Aye, thanks, agent …?"

"It's Gill, sir."

"Safe drive, Agent Gill."

The car drove away as Sam walked towards the building and Liz's apartment. Stepping past the caution tape that barred the door off from the public, he breathed the scent of vanilla and pears deeply. His gut clenched in guilt from turning her in, but his head kept insisting that he had done the right thing. Spying what he was looking for on the kitchen counter, he walked over and picked Ronald up before vacating the apartment. As angry and confused with Liz as he was, the story she'd told him of Natalie plagued his mind, and he couldn't seem to let it go. Strawberry plant in hand, he walked to his own car and drove the rest of the way back to his shabby home.

Grateful it was his day off from being a deputy, he had every intention of collapsing in bed and sleeping the day away. But the moment he walked through the door, he felt something hit him on the back just below his neck. Dropping Ronald, he collapsed to the ground in pain. He tried to get up when he was kicked in the ribs by his attacker, and he cried out. Another blow to the back of the head, and everything began to swim and become distorted. He turned to try and see his attacker when he was hit again, then he heard the gunshot. Everything went black.

~~~

Sam tried to open his eyes, but one of them was swollen shut, and the pounding headache he felt made it harder. Despite the tube in his nose, he could smell disinfectant and clean sheets, which made it easy for him to guess that he was in a hospital. He tried to sit up but immediately regretted the action as he felt a terrible pain in his chest and torso.

"Two cracked ribs, a hole in your side, and a pretty nasty concussion. You're a tough customer, Mr. Mckay, but you won't be going anywhere for a while."

Gently, Sam turned his head to the familiar voice. Belinda Copper sat in a chair, her legs crossed, and by the look on her face Sam could tell he was in trouble. "Director, I dinnea think ye cared."

The older woman didn't react beyond an irritated stare. "Did you get a look at who your attacker was?"

"No, dinnea ge' the chance. He attacked me from behind. How long have I been in here?"

"Five days."

Sam opened his good eye wide. "Is' Monday?"

"Mhmm," she answered coolly.

"Shit! I was supposed to meet more of the corrupted police las' night!"

"I'm aware. The hospital called Evan after you were brought in, and he found the note in your pocket with the address. It turned out to be an abandoned mill outside of town. We put a watch on it, but no one has turned up. I'd put my money that the man who gave you that information, Gerald Mebbin, was the one that attacked you."

"Tha' would explain why I was hit on the back first; Gerald is a short fellow." Sam gingerly pulled himself up into a sitting position in the bed. "Di' ye catch him?"

"Yes, we have him in custody."

"Aye, good. How long will I be in here?"

"The doctors say they'll let you go in three to four days. Then you'll have two days to pack and get your affairs in order before your flight."
~~~

Sam furrowed his eyebrows. "I beg yer pardon?"

Director Copper stood up and smoothed out her skirt. "I came here to tell you that your cover's been blown, Mr. McKay. You're no longer of any use, and therefore our deal is null and void. We will cover your hospital stay and your ticket back to Scotland, but your visa has been frozen, and you are unwelcome in the United States for an indefinite period of time."

"… All tha' for my cover bein' blown? Tha's bullshit, and ye know it, Copper!"

"It's not just your assignment, Mr. McKay. I've had time to look over the report regarding the murder of Brian Cairne. You've known the whereabouts of a fugitive for months—"

"I dinnea know Liz was a fugitive until the other night!"

"But you did know that she was a runaway, and the FBI has been looking for her and her daughter for well over a year, didn't you? Don't play coy with me; I know you're a smart man, McKay. I don't have any doubt that you would investigate her yourself. Withholding that kind of information doesn't exactly put you in my good graces. Under normal circumstances, I'd have you arrested for obstruction of justice, but given the fact that you were able to discover one of the corrupted policemen and give us a lead, I am choosing to be lenient. You are being deported, Mr. McKay, and that's the end of it."

Ignoring the pain he felt in his body, Sam started climbing out of bed with the intent to physically fight the woman if he had to. Holding onto his IV drip, he towered over her and growled. "Over me dead body, it is."

"I assure you that can be arranged," Director Copper said as she looked up and stared at Sam directly in the eye, completely unaffected by the height advantage he had over her. "You've been given two days to get your affairs in order, I suggest you save your strength for them. Try not to do any heavy lifting."

Sam glared at the Director as she left without another word. Sitting back on the bed, he breathed deeply and tried to think of what he could do. He thought of Oliver and how he would be unable to see him again far into the foreseeable future. He then thought of asking Rivera to have a word with the insufferable woman but immediately decided against it. *He's put his neck out on the line for me enough.*

A knock at the door broke him out of his melancholy, and he

looked up to see a nurse walk in carrying a tray of food. "Good to see you awake! Now let's see if you can manage a few bites, and then we'll see if we can get that feeding tube taken out."

Chapter Sixteen

Against the doctor's recommendations, Sam checked himself out of the hospital a day early. The pain medication prescribed to him suggested that he not drive, but of course he wouldn't let that stop him. He only took half of the recommended dose; just enough to take the edge off, but not enough to impair him from behaving normally. After getting back to the apartment (and thoroughly checking around everywhere with a bat in hand), he set to work packing what little he had and loading his car, including the broken strawberry plant Ronald, which he scooped into a small box with the intent to fix the pot as best as he could. He was about to leave when he remembered the little safe deposit box of money from his assignment and quickly ran to check that it was still there before loading all of it into his suitcase. *A' least now I've go' somethin' to help me ge' settled again,* he thought to himself spitefully. Getting into his car, his first destination was Cleveland. Rivera informed him that he'd called Meredith to explain the situation, and Sam would be stopping by before he left. Meredith arranged for a meeting between him and Oliver at the center the next day, and Sam was determined to be there.

Sitting side by side, he and Meredith were in a comfortable waiting room as Oliver was brought in. Relieved that his son looked much healthier than the last time he'd seen him, Sam couldn't help but hope their spur-of-the-moment meeting would be a good one.

"Okay, I'm here," Oliver said bitterly. "Now what did you want to talk to me about?"

Sam rested his forearms onto his knees as he leaned forward. "Jus' came to tell ye tha' I love ye very much, and to listen to the counselors here."

Oliver cocked his head curiously. "Yeah, I'm already doing that. It's not like I have a choice, do I?"

"Oliver … I cannea be at every meetin' anymore. I'm bein' sent back to Scotland."

Sam would have sworn he saw a flicker of disappointment in Oliver's eyes, but it was immediately replaced with the cold, uncaring exterior he'd been portraying for weeks. Oliver folded his arms across his chest and said quietly, "What a surprise."

Meredith spoke up. "Oliver, you know your father wouldn't do this if he didn't have to."

"Whatever."

Sam took a deep breath. "I know ye donnea believe me, son, but I don't have a choice in the matter. If I did—"

"I said whatever! Thanks for at least giving me a heads-up this time. Have fun in Scotland." Oliver stood up from his seat and walked out the door before Sam and Meredith could stop him.

"'This time?' Wha's he talkin' about?"

"I have no idea," Meredith shook her head in bewilderment.

Looking down at his hands, Sam sighed and shook his head in misery.

As they had ridden in the same car, he and Meredith grabbed a bite to eat before heading back to her house. Sam didn't argue when she insisted that he could spend the night again as his flight was the next morning, and he wanted to be well rested before being stuck on a plane for half a day.

He'd just finished arranging the pillows on the couch when he turned to see Meredith standing behind him holding a glass of scotch. Smirking, he accepted her offering and swallowed it in one gulp. "Sláinte."

She chuckled and took the empty glass away before handing him another full one. "Can they really do this to you?"

"Aye, is' already been done. My visa will be frozen the day after tomorrow, and I'll be an illegal if I'm still here."

"Well, what can you do to unfreeze it?"

"Nothin'," he shook his head sadly. "Tha' takes time and a whole new application. And now tha' the FBI knows me personally, they're no' likely to accept tha' application any time soon."

Meredith chuckled as she sat down on the couch opposite of the one he intended to sleep on. "That's funny considering usually everyone who meets you likes you."

Sam took a small sip of the strong, earthy liquid before he sat down next to her. "Ye'll be sure to no' miss a single meetin', aye?"

"Not one. And I promise that I'll email you all of the details after every one of them."

He stopped himself from making a quip about how that would be a change and instead nodded his head and uttered, "Thank ye."

The two of them sat quietly for a moment and listened to the crackling fire in the fireplace. As Sam wondered what he could possibly do to stay in the states, he turned to look at Meredith when she cleared her throat.

"You know … I think there might be another way to stop you from leaving."

He leaned back against the couch and eyed her curiously.

"There's two ways to get a visa, right? Working and marriage. Since you're here on a working visa, they can't exactly stop you from getting a marriage one."

Unsure if he heard her right, Sam opened his eyes wide. "I beg yer pardon?"

"I know … I know this is ridiculous of me to say to you, and I know that I have absolutely no right to. But … Sam, the truth is that I've missed you. I made a huge mistake, I know that, and not a day goes by that I don't regret what I did. And before you ask, the reason why I never told you or talked to you before was because I didn't think I had the right to. I know you're angry with me for everything, including taking full custody of Oliver … obviously I've been doing a shitty job as a single mom. But … there was a time when you wanted to work things out, and I was an idiot to not do it back then … But maybe we could do it now?"

Sam was in shock. Not at her proposal, but the fact that she was the one to propose it. It was true, he'd wanted to try and work things out from the beginning, after they'd both had time to cool down. He thought about the past eighteen months since the divorce, about how often he'd thought of them reconciling and being closer to his son again. One part of him was jumping for joy at the thought that it could be a reality; they could truly be a family again, or at least work their way back to being one. But then his thoughts turned to what had driven them apart in the first place: his work had demanded a lot from him, including their time.

It was as though Meredith could read his thoughts because she continued. "I know that means you wouldn't be a cop anymore, but maybe that's not such a bad thing. I make more than enough money at my real estate agency. Things are stable, so you could retire and spend more time with all of us. Oliver would love that. Don't you see, Sam? It's perfect."

He set the glass down on the coffee table and rubbed his face. "This is … unexpected. And i's a lot to consider."

"What's there to consider?"

"The las' eighteen months of no' even talkin' to each other for a start."

Meredith looked down at her hands in shame. "… I shouldn't have just sprung this on you. You're right, I should have reached out more during our time apart. I don't know why I didn't …"

"And where do ye get off jus' askin' me to marry ye again?"

"I'm just trying to be helpful, Sam." She quickly softened her offended tone and continued. "Look, I know it's a lot to take in, and obviously you don't have to make a decision tonight."

He sighed, "Lass, I cannea make a decision like this in the next few days, le' alone one night."

"Then how about this: why don't you go back to Scotland and think about it for a while. If you want to do this, I'll buy a ticket and come out to you and then we'll work out the rest of the details that way, okay?"

He closed his eyes and shook his head; he hated how she could use words to make everything sound so good and manipulate her way into getting what she wanted sometimes. But at that moment he was too tired and a little too drunk to think, so he nodded his head and said, "Aye, I'll do tha'. I've go' an early flight in the mornin'."

"Okay, I'll let you get some sleep." Meredith took the glasses and deposited them in the kitchen. Before ascending the stairs for the evening, she leaned down and kissed his cheek and whispered, "Goodnight, Sam."

"Goodnight, Meredith."

He heard her walk up the stairs, but his focus was on the fire. Confused didn't begin to cover how he felt. He thought he should be happy; this was a way to be closer to Oliver after all. Meredith's proposal was sound in reasoning and, from what he could sense, she really was willing to work on the problems between the two of them. But anger overshadowed the joy as he considered all that had happened between them, from the day she sent the divorce papers until the night she'd called him to ask for help. There was so much to process, and the scotch's dizzying effects were already in motion.

He couldn't make a decision in that moment, and certainly not drunk. *Think on it ... jus' think on it ...* he repeated the mantra in his head a few times before laying his head down on the fluffy decorative pillow and quickly passing out.

~~~

"Ladies and gentleman, welcome to Glasgow International Airport. It's a bright and sunny 25 degrees Celsius, or 77 degrees Fahrenheit for our American friends on board with us today. Thanks so much for traveling with us, and we hope you enjoy your time in Scotland. "

Sam walked out of the terminal and saw his sister Hannah waiting next to her car for him. Smiling, he walked over and hugged her tightly.

"Thanks fer comin' to ge' me."

"Well, I happened to be in the neighborhood," she smiled and wagged her ring finger at him to show a wedding band behind the engagement ring.

Sam chuckled. "Ye and Zander eloped after all, eh?"

"Aye, an' his mum was pished when she found out."

"Where'd ye go?"

"Dublin, jus' go' back a few days ago, and we've been stayin' in Glasgow for a few more," she giggled. "I would have tol' ye sooner, bu' t'all happened s'fast!"

"Ach, nevermind tha'," he smiled and placed his hands on her shoulders. "Wha's important is tha' yer happy. Are ye?"

"Aye, I am," she nodded and the bright, beaming smile on her face assured him. "Come on, le's go home."

"Are ye sure I'm no' puttin' the two of you out? I can find an inn to stay at for a few days."

"Donnea be a bampot. Ge' in the bloody car, Sam. Ye can stay at our place until the cottage is vacant again, then I'll give ye a ride back to Rosneath."

The hour drive back to Stirling was spent discussing Hannah and Zander's plans for the future: saving for a house and trying for a baby all at the same time. Sam was happy for her and frequently told her how proud of her he was. When they'd arrived at her tiny flat, he wasted no time in giving Zander the 'big brother' treatment of threatening his life if his sister's heart was ever broken. When
~~~

Hannah elbowed him in the ribs, he finally stopped and shook his new brother-in-law's hand tightly and sincerely congratulated him.

A few days later, he'd gotten word that the family cottage had been vacated, and he was free to move back in again. Hannah drove him back to Rosneath on the weekend when school was out and helped him to get settled into the white with blue trim house before wishing him goodbye once again, but only after he promised that he would come for dinner once a month. After she left, Sam wandered into town and towards Virgil's garage, hoping his old job would still be available, but was disappointed to discover that it wasn't, so he headed to Jackie's for the evening instead and found Thomas already at the bar waiting for him.

"Oi, over here, big man!" the bristly, blonde giant called.

Sam smiled and joined him. "Hallo."

"Jackie, two pints!"

The short, bald man grunted before filling the two glasses and setting them in front of them. Sam chuckled and barely got a sip in before more patrons started coming over and saying hello, asking why he was back so quickly, all of their usual questions, before Thomas shooed them away so they could drink in peace.

"Di' ye do wha' ye hoped ye would in America?" Thomas asked him after downing half of his pint.

Rather than directly answer the question, Sam just nodded and stuck to his drink.

"Di' ye get to see Oliver?"

"Aye."

"… And how is he?" Thomas probed.

"He's go' himself in more than a wee bit o' trouble. He's in a juvenile center for at least six months."

"Awe, Christ," Thomas shook his head sadly. "I'm sorry, big man."

Before Sam could answer, the bell over Jackie's door sounded, and he turned to see none other than Victoria and Ben Abernathy walk inside. If he didn't know any better, he would think that they were newlyweds by how happy they looked. Before he could ask Thomas what was going on, Ben's voice rang over the crowd:

"This rounds on me, chums. I'm gonna be a da!"

The pub erupted in cheers and laughter before every patron rushed the bar for their free drink.

Sam sat there in shock before turning back to Thomas for an explanation.

"I dinnea hear the whole thing, bu' after Liam go' his arse in jail, Ben fired 'im and Wyatt, too. No one's seen 'em around here since. Bu' Ben's proved he's no' such an arsehole after all."

Sam felt a delicate hand on his shoulder and turned to see Victoria standing over him with a huge smile on her face. "Hallo, Sam."

He smiled in return. "Hallo, Vicky. I guess congratulations are in order."

"Aye," she nodded excitedly. "We jus' go' back from the doctor, the wee lambie will be here in six months time."

Suddenly Ben was standing next to her and looking directly at Sam. For a moment, the whole pub hushed as they watched the encounter, curious as to what would happen next. But Sam only smiled and offered his hand out to him. "Congratulations, Ben. Ye'll make a fine da'."

A slow smile crept across Ben's face, and he placed his hand in Sam's. "Thank ye."

The whole pub let out a breath of relief before turning back to their drinks.

Sam and Thomas were on their second pint for the evening when Ben walked over and tapped Sam on the shoulder. "Can I have a word?"

Curious, Sam followed him outside. "Wha's up?"

"I wanted to thank ye … fer talkin' to Victoria, I mean."

Sam nodded. "Aye, yer welcome."

"Are ye back for good, then?"

"T'would seem so."

"Ye workin' back at the garage, then?"

"No," Sam shook his head. "Bu' I'll find somethin'."

He wondered if that was all Ben wanted to say to him when the man cleared his throat, "… Di' ye hear how I le' go of Liam and Wyatt?"

"Aye."

"Well … I've been a wee bit short-handed since I did. No' many in this town can handle the physical demands I pu' on them when it comes to buildin' a house. But ye know yer way around a hammer, don't ye?"

"Are ye offerin' me a job, Ben?"

"Aye, if ye can handle me bein' yer boss."

Sam couldn't help but chuckle. "I suppose I'll jus' have to learn to listen to ye."

Ben smiled and turned to walk back into the pub. "Ye start Monday mornin' at seven, and I donnea tolerate lateness."

Sam followed him and took his seat back at the bar next to Thomas, who asked him urgently, "Wha' was tha' about?"

"He offered me a job."

Thomas's eyes looked like they were about to pop out of his head, causing Sam to laugh.

"Well, then … does this' mean the great rival between Sampson McKay and Benjamin Abernathy is no more?"

"Aye, I suppose Rosneath will have to find a new scandal to cling to now."

When 'last call' sounded, Sam and Thomas left Jackie's and said their goodbyes, but not before Thomas gave him back his bike. Pushing it home, Sam pondered on his situation: even if he did accept Meredith's offer, it would be some time before he could see Oliver again. But he could also make a life in his hometown as well. He had the cottage, a job, and there were no strange women to upset his lifestyle anymore.

Once his mind turned to Liz, he felt melancholy. So much evidence was stacked against her; any jury would see that she was involved with Brian Cairne's murder, or at the minimum, kidnapping her own daughter, possibly under the influence. His gut told him everything was as it should be, and Alexander Michael's lawyers would do their best to get her the lightest sentence possible; she would be taken care of. And yet he couldn't help but feel there were too many unanswered questions, making him curious. That was his curse: he would always feel curious when something didn't add up perfectly.

He told himself he had no reason to think about the case, it was closed. Rivera, Julie, and Simon had set out to try and help his reputation so he could stay in the states. Despite their success, Sam only made the situation worse because of his involvement with Liz and blowing his cover on the assignment the FBI had given him. He would never be permitted back in the states again, at least not unless he and Meredith remarried. Thinking about her plan, the idea of an early retirement left a sour taste in his mouth. He didn't feel old enough to retire, but he didn't feel young enough to start over either. Knowing Meredith, she would want him to be at her beck and call much like early in their marriage, and that thought wasn't very appealing. Yet the glimmer of hope she'd given him of them working out their problems still had him considering the offer.

Setting his bike down next to the small, thriving garden, Sam walked inside the cottage and started getting ready for bed when his phone buzzed. It was an email from Rivera. Curious what he would want to tell him, he opened it and read:

Sam-

Liz had her trial and she's been found guilty of kidnapping. There wasn't enough evidence to support aggravated murder, so those charges were thrown out. Michael's lawyers were able to keep her out of prison, and she's been admitted to a recovery center for drug addiction for the next five years. Good thinking on tracking her alias, btw. We found Natalie hiding out in Pittsburgh, Pennsylvania with a woman claiming to be Liz's cousin. She's been arrested for accessory to kidnapping, but Michaels didn't press charges.
I'm sorry we failed. I'll keep my eye on Oliver for you.
Rivera

Sam set down his phone and sighed. *Is' over ... there really is nothin' left to do.*

⁕⁕⁕

Chapter Seventeen

For the next two weeks, things were a quiet normal for Sam: he worked at Ben's construction company five days of the week and joined him and Thomas at Jackie's in the evenings. Another family counseling session with Oliver had taken place, and Sam was grateful that Meredith had kept her word of sending him the details of it. At least he felt involved. With no other way of communication with his son, he went back to his routine of writing at least one letter a week to Oliver and sending it to Meredith so she could take it to him.

One night after working in the rain all day with Ben, Sam decided to go home instead of joining Ben at Jackie's. He discovered a large package sitting on his front step. Once he was inside and drying off in front of the fireplace, he saw the name Simon Abler on the return sender and opened it, only to smile at a note sitting on top of a thick file which read:

Sorry it took me so long to get this to you, the director has been on my butt since we solved the case. We miss you!

-Simon

Setting the note down, Sam stared at the file with hesitance. He thought about just throwing it in the fire and not concerning himself with something he had no control over. He had all but made up his mind to get rid of it when he saw the repaired but heavily cracked strawberry plant he had sitting in the corner. Taking a moment to stare at Ronald, he shook his head and sighed, *Goddamn me* ... He tore open the file and pulled out every piece of paperwork his team had managed to collect, along with all of the pages of notes they'd made throughout the investigation.

Three hours later, Sam was starting to get very tired and nearly fell asleep on top of the mountains of financial statements. Though he had no doubts about his team's capabilities, he had to be sure there wasn't anything they were missing, and he wouldn't rest until he was certain of it. Brian Cairne's personal financial statements were pretty straightforward, other than the incident of setting up trusts for his daughter and grandsons, but his team had made doubly sure of those records, so he set them to the side and focused on the others that lay before him. Every charge dating nearly six months back looked to be standard and nothing out of the ordinary until Sam noticed a $600 charge at a doctor's office a month before he died. Upon further checking, it was not the same doctor that Brian Cairne had listed on his personal records as his go-to physician. *Why would he pay tha' much at a visit?* Furrowing his eyes, he checked the time and decided it wasn't too early to call Rivera.

~~~

Rivera finished his coffee and piled his dishes in the sink; just as he was walking out of the door to work, his phone rang.

"Sam?"

"Did ye look into this $600 charge at Williamson Clinic's office?"

"What? What are you talking about?"

"Brian Cairne saw someone at the Williamson Clinic a month before he died. According to his file, his main physician was a Doctor Gregory Johansen at the Johansen Clinic. So why was he at a different clinic, and why did he pay $600 out of his own pocket?"

"Maybe he was switching doctors."

"Then why didnea he run the charge through his insurance? And wha' possible reason could there be to pay a doctor $600 on the first visit?"

Rivera was stumped. "… I'll send Julie over to check it out immediately."

"Good, call me as soon as ye know somethin'."

"Sam, get some sleep. It'll be a few hours before I can call you anyway."

"Ach, jus' call me when ye know wha's up."

Sam hung up before Rivera could argue, so he dialed Julie. It was sent to voicemail after three rings. "Hey, Sam just called me. There was a $600 charge in Brian Cairne's financial statements made by Williamson Clinic, and Sam said Cairn's doctor never worked there. Can you go check it out, please? Call me when you find out, thanks."

His duty fulfilled, he walked out the door to work.
~~~

Julie sat in a room at the Williamson Clinic impatiently; the nurse at the front had been less than helpful until Julie flashed her badge and demanded to see the doctor who treated Brian Cairne. Finally, she was taken back and told the doctor would be with her in a few minutes, but that was twenty minutes ago, and she was starting to lose her patience. Finally, the door opened and a middle aged, attractive looking woman walked inside.

"Hi, I'm doctor Regina Williamson. I understand you're here to discuss a patient of mine?"

"Well, I don't think he's your patient anymore, considering he died over a year ago," Julie muttered and pulled up the picture of Brian Cairne she had on her phone. "My name is Julie Russell, and I'm working with the FBI. Brian Cairne came to see you a month before he was killed and paid $600 for the visit. I need to know why."

The doctor stared at Julie for a moment, seemingly weighing the information she was given, before nodding. "Alright, come with me to my office, and I'll pull up my records."

Julie walked around the woman's small office, looking at the doctor's pictures of her standing with various people including some high-end millionaires she recognized from the news, while the doctor sat at her computer entering information.

"… Okay, I've got it here. Brian Cairne was here for a grandparent DNA test."

Julie rounded the desk. "What? For himself?"

"Yes, he wanted this to be confidential and requested that I not have his records transferred over from his physician."

"Who was he being tested against?"

"I don't know, he brought in a blood sample, and we took his blood here, but he wouldn't give the name."

Julie furrowed her eyebrows, "Okay … what were the results?"

"A probable match. Whoever's blood he brought in is most likely his grandchild."

"Why only probable?"

"Well, Agent Russell, a positive paternity test would show that at least half of the DNA fragments belong to the biological parent. You would think that means there would be a 25% match against grandparents, but in reality, it is more of a luck of the draw. There's no way to determine how much of your DNA would be passed down to your grandchildren. Children can lean more on one side of the biological DNA from one parent than the other. But in this instance, 37% of this child's DNA matched Mr. Cairne's, which makes it highly probable that it is in fact his grandchild. However, a paternity test would be much more conclusive."

"Did you tell him that?"

"Yes. I even offered to do a paternity test, but he insisted that he couldn't get samples."

Julie stared at the computer screen for a moment. "Do you still have the blood samples?"

"No, they were promptly thrown away at Mr. Cairne's insistence. Not that we needed them anymore, we have the DNA on file and as long as we have the results, we can match it to anyone else's blood or saliva."

"… Can you tell whether the child is a boy or girl?"

"Two X chromosomes in the sample, which means the blood belonged to a girl."

… *He has grandsons,* Julie thought to herself. "Okay, last question: did Mr. Cairne ask about anything else while he was here?"

Doctor Williamson shook her head, "No, he just asked for a copy of the results before he left, but that was it."

"Okay, thank you for your time, doctor."

"My pleasure."

Julie ran out of the office and called Rivera as soon as she was in the car. He answered in two rings. "Hey, you're not going to believe this."

~~~

Sam refused to sleep, even though he knew he would regret that choice in the morning. The oddity of the doctor visit only refueled his curiosity, and he began to notice a few other details in the files that didn't make sense. In the other mercenary hits, there was never any physical evidence left behind, and yet the police managed to find a partial print that didn't belong to any of the victims the day Brian Cairne was killed at this robbery. In one of the other reports, the
~~~

hostage negotiation officer had noted that the perpetrator sounded Swedish, but he distinctly remembered that the man he'd spoken to had a Latino accent. Too much didn't make sense, and he needed answers. And when Rivera called him back and told him about the DNA test with an unknown sample, he was glad he followed his instincts as his mind was going a million miles an hour.

"Got any theories on who this mysterious kid might be?" Rivera asked.

"Aye, one. I need ye t' patch me to Simon."

"Hang on, I'll go find him in the basement. Let me call you back."

Sam paced his floor for what seemed like an hour until his phone finally rang again.

"Hey, boss! What's up?" Simon's cheery voice sounded over the phone.

"I need a passport, visa, and an FBI ID."

"… Okay, but why am I doing that?"

"Because we arrested the wrong person for Brian Cairne's murder. Liz is innocent."

He could hear Simon gulp on the other line. "Sam … you do know I could lose my job over this? Go to prison?"

"Do ye wanna spend the rest of yer life fixin' computers?" Sam asked him a little too harshly. Taking a deep breath, he said in a much calmer tone, "Please, Simon."

After a beat, he heard the sound of keyboard letters being typed furiously. "Okay … done. Your passport's unflagged, and you're all set."

"Good, I'm catchin' the next flight outta' Glasgow. Tell everyone I'll see them in 24 hours."

He hung up and raced up the stairs to pack a bag; it was the middle of the night and freezing, but that didn't stop him from riding his bike into town and to Thomas' flat. It was nearly 4:00 a.m. when he pounded on the door until he heard movement on the other side.

"Go away, ye dafty bampot! Is' too bloody early to be bangin' on—" Thomas ripped the door open ready for a fight when he stopped himself. "Sam? Wha' the hell, big man?"

"I need yer car, or a ride."

"Wha' for?"

"I need to get to the airport. Please, Thomas."

Thomas rubbed the sleep from his eyes before he nodded. "Aye, alrigh'."

Sam started up the rusty Hillman Imp and prayed it was still as faithful as ever as he sped along the road towards Glasgow while Thomas slept in the passenger seat. Once they were at the airport, he said a quick goodbye and raced towards the desk where he was able to purchase the last ticket to America. Grateful he'd kept the money from his botched assignment, he paid in cash and rushed towards the gate just as they were loading the passengers. Once the plane took off, Sam forced himself to quiet his mind and rest for the long journey, knowing he would need it as there would be a lot of work to do once he got there. Sixteen grueling hours and two flight changes later, he was walking out of Cleveland Hopkins International with new purpose. Rivera, Julie, and Simon were ready and waiting at the door, and the four of them headed to the nearest hotel.

"Okay, boss, who's the kid?" Simon asked as he took a bite of pizza.

"Natalie, Liz's child."

The three of them stared at him as he grabbed a slice of his own pizza.

"Wait, then who—"

"Liz's husband, I'd bet me life on it." Sam pulled a typed confession out of the file he'd packed. "She said Brian was her husband's uncle, bu' he had no brothers and sisters."

"Well, if that's true, why didn't Cairne ever come forward about it?" Julie asked. "Do you think he knew?"

"If he did, t'wouldn't make sense for him to wait a year after his son's death to investigate. Somethin' must've happened tha' pushed him to prove it."

"Assuming Daniel Harper really is his child," Rivera said, "we'd have to prove that first. Besides, how would he even get a blood sample from her?"

"Blood is no' as hard to get to as everyone thinks it is, Rivera, ye know tha'. He could have paid a doctor to get a sample for him, hired a private investigator, maybe she scraped her knee once when he was visitin' Liz and took a swab."

"Well, again, this is all really fun to think about, but we can't prove it."

"Luckily, we know exactly where we can find our proof," Sam smiled. "We know where Alexander Michaels lives, go and get a

DNA sample from Natalie."

"Sam, we can't do that without a warrant."

"Ye donnea need one if Michaels isnea in the room with ye. The both of ye go, say ye jus' have some follow-up questions for Michaels about Liz, and take a swab of her mouth when he's no' lookin'. If I'm wrong, then tha' will be the end of tha' theory. Bu' if I'm right, then we'll know exactly wha' to look for next."

Julie and Rivera looked back at one another before nodding their agreement.

"What about me, boss? What can I do?" Simon asked eagerly.

"First, I need ye to find out who Daniel Harper's parents are, and if there's any connection to Brian Cairne. Then we'll go pay them a visit. You two will go get the DNA in the mornin' and take it straight back to the doctor for comparison."

Once the pizza was gone, the team left Sam in the hotel for a much-needed night of rest.

~~~

"You've got the test?" Rivera asked Julie as he pressed the doorbell of the Michael's home.

She reached into her pocket and wrapped her fingers around the sterile swab and test tube kit and nodded just as the door opened.

Alex's eyes opened wide when he saw the two of them. "Oh, I wasn't expecting either of you."

"Sorry to intrude, we just had a few follow up questions to the Brian Cairne murder case."

"Didn't you hear? Liz isn't responsible for the murder, and she was convicted for kidnapping only. And she's serving her time in a rehabilitation center."

"We're looking at a new suspect," Rivera lied. "We just want to make absolutely sure that everything is all accounted for while we build our case. It'll only take a moment of your time."

Julie eyed Michaels carefully; he looked over his shoulder before turning back to them. "Alright, but not in front of Natalie."

He moved to the side and led them to a large sitting room adorned with Victorian style furniture. Julie smiled when she saw the little girl playing with a dollhouse as big as her in the middle of it, but her expression was sad.
~~~

"Nattie, sweetheart, I need you to stay here for a few moments while I speak with these nice people, alright?"

"Yes, grandpa," the little girl muttered.

Julie took that as her cue and walked over to the little blonde child. "I'll tell you what, they don't need me. Is it okay if I play with you for a few minutes?"

Natalie looked at her grandfather with pleading eyes until he nodded. "Alright, I'll be back in a minute."

Rivera and Michaels left the room and Julie picked up one of the dolls. "So, what are we playing?"

"House," Natalie smiled. "I'm the mommy, you be the baby."

"Okay," Julie smiled back. "So what does the baby do?"

Natalie opened the top of the house and moved Julie's hand to the top room. "The baby needs to take a nap; it's good for her."

"Oh, is it? What if the baby wants to play?"

"There's a time to play and a time to nap," Natalie insisted.

Julie chuckled and rose to her knees to put the doll in the room Natalie had suggested. Another doll was sitting in there and she gestured. "Is this the daddy?"

"No, that's the grandpa."

"Really? And what's the grandpa doing?"

"He's watching over her, making sure she's safe while she sleeps."

Julie furrowed her eyebrows and looked directly at the little girl. "… Does the grandpa do that a lot?"

Natalie nodded her head, "Yes, he's always watching over her. Especially when mommy has to leave."

"… Where does the mommy go when she leaves?"

The little girl shrugged her shoulders and kept playing with her doll. Julie wanted to probe her further, but the sounds of Rivera and Michaels coming back through the hall stopped her. Reaching into her pocket, she pulled out the test kit and a lollipop. "Hey, do you like suckers?"

"Mhmm," Natalie smiled and nodded.

"Well, here, I can give you this one. But first, can you show me how many teeth you have?"

Natalie opened her mouth without another thought, and Julie quickly rubbed the inside of her cheeks with the sterile swab before locking it in the plastic tube. "Wow, you have so many teeth! I bet you have more than I do."

"I've got a loose tooth here!" The little girl smiled and pointed to a top one.

Julie chuckled and unwrapped the lollipop. "Well, here, this should hopefully make it looser. If it's loose enough to come out, I've heard that the tooth fairy will stop by to get it."

Natalie giggled and sucked on the candy happily.

"I'm sorry, Agent Rivera, I don't know how much more information I can give you."

Julie quickly pocketed the test before Michaels could see it and smiled at Rivera as the two men walked back into the sitting room.

"No, I apologize for wasting your time, Mr. Michaels. Like I said, we just wanted to be thorough and make sure we didn't miss anything. Agent Russell, I believe our work here is done."

Julie nodded and turned her attention back to Natalie. "Well, thank you for letting me play with you. I'll see you later, okay?"

"Okay. Bye-bye."

"Bye, sweetie," Julie smiled down at her.

"Natalie," Alex said sternly. "Did you thank the nice agent for the candy?"

"Thank you, Agent Russell."

"You're welcome," Julie giggled and waved. "Bye."

They walked out the door and all the way back to the car before Rivera turned to her. "I'm sorry I couldn't give you much time. Did you get it?"

"Course I did." Julie pulled out the test to show him.

"How?"

"I asked her to show me her teeth." She chuckled at Rivera's amazed expression.

"Wow ... I didn't know you were so good with kids."

She shrugged, "I love kids, Derrick. I just don't want to have them."

He looked like he wanted to say more but quickly turned his focus to the steering wheel. "Come on, let's go see if Sam's right."

Chapter Eighteen

"Have ye go' anythin' yet?"

Sam was pacing up and down the hotel room while Simon sat at the small desk typing on his laptop furiously.

"Here we go: on-file records state that Daniel Harper was born September 8, 1987, at a hospital in Grand Rapids, Michigan, to Charles and Elaine Harper."

"No adoption records?"

"None, and I triple checked that."

"What can ye tell me abou' his parents?"

Simon clacked away for a minute. "Charles Douglas Harper, born February 15th, 1951, in Kalamazoo, recently retired from a 45-year career as a teacher. Elaine Ruth Harper, maiden name Jones, born October 24th, 1953, also in Kalamazoo. There's no employment record on file for her until ten years ago when she started working for a little fabric store in Grand Rapids; she was probably a stay-at home-mom."

Sam pondered the information for a moment. "… When did they ge' married?"

"June 26th, 1971. But what does that have to do with anything?"

"Tha' would have made them 20 and 19 years old."

"So?"

Sam chuckled. "Simon, do ye know what the average marryin' age during the 60's and 70's was?"

"No."

"Between 20-23 years of age for both men and women. And shortly after tha', usually within' the first year or two, is when they would star' havin' families."

Simon furrowed his eyebrows in understanding and nodded. "So why did they wait 17 years to have Daniel?"

"Exactly. Di' they have any other children?"

"No … it looks like Daniel was an only child. And I can't find any prenatal visits on record that aren't related to him."

"I donnea think Daniel was a miracle baby."

Simon's eyebrows shot to his hairline. "You think Mrs. Harper has some explaining to do?"

Sam picked up his coat and keys. "I do. Where are the Harpers now?"

"They haven't moved since they got married. Their house is in Eastown Grand Rapids on Carlton Avenue."

"Okay, tha's a … four-hour drive from here, so we best ge' goin'."

"Yay, a road trip!" Simon smiled and jumped up to follow him.

With Sam driving, they reached Eastown just shy of 1:00, and ten minutes later found themselves in front of a cute yellow two-story house with a large tree in the front yard. Sam wasted no time in knocking on the door, but the silence on the other end made Simon shift back and forth on his feet.

"Do you think we should have called first?"

"No, I find we ge' the truth with genuine reaction."

"Well, maybe they're not home."

"Car's in the drive; they're home." Sam tried the doorbell that time and heard a little movement on the inside. The door was answered a moment later by an old man wearing shorts and a golf shirt and leaning on a cane. "Hallo, is this the Harper residence?"

"Yes," the old man nodded. "Can I help you?"

"Are ye Charles?"

"Yes, and you are?"

"My name is Sam McKay, and this is Simon Abler, we're with the FBI."

"Oh, are you here about the cannabis? Because I was told that's legal now."

Simon snorted.

"No, Sir," Sam shook his head. "We'd jus' like to ask ye a few questions."

The man raised his eyebrows. "Alright, would you like to come in?"

"Aye, thank ye." Sam followed Mr. Harper inside with Simon right behind him.

The little house was adorned with pictures on nearly every wall of a younger version of Charles, a very attractive woman with curly hair that Sam presumed was his wife, and a handsome blonde boy that Sam could only assume was Daniel. They ranged from when the boy was a child all the way until he was an adult. A few pictures had a little blonde girl which Sam immediately guessed was Natalie, their granddaughter, and only a few of the pictures also contained Liz.

Mr. Harper led them to the living room and gestured to the floral couch with a wooden coffee table in front of it. "Would either of you like some lemonade? Hungry? I just fixed my wife and myself some lunch. In fact, she should be home soon."

Right at that moment, they heard the front door open and a light, airy voice call, "Charlie? There's a strange car in front of the house. Do you know who's it is?"

"In here, Elaine, we have company."

Sam and Simon looked over to see the woman from the pictures walk in; her hair was white and a few wrinkles had gathered around her eyes, but there was no mistaking she was the same woman in the photos. "Oh, hello."

"Mrs. Harper, we're sorry to impose on ye."

"Darling, they're from the FBI." Mr. Harper said.

"Oh no, we were told that it was legal to take cannabis for pain. Charlie's leg has been acting up for some time, and it's the only thing that works."

Simon snorted again, and Sam had to nudge him before shooting him a look that said, 'Be quiet.'

"No, no, they're here about something else."

"Oh … would either of you like some lemonade or perhaps some lunch?"

"No thank ye," Sam shook his head.

"And what about you, young man?"

Simon (who had been quiet the whole time) stuttered. "O-oh, um …"

"Please, Agents, it's really no trouble. And we wouldn't want to be rude and eat in front of you," Mrs. Harper smiled. "See, Charlie has to eat regularly, or else his blood sugar gets too low."

"Well, when you put it that way," Simon smiled. "I wouldn't say no to a sandwich."

Mrs. Harper smiled and turned back to Sam. "And for you?"

Chuckling, he conceded. "Ach, alrigh'. Thank ye, Mrs. Harper."

"Can I come help you?" Simon offered but quickly sat down when the elderly woman waved her hand and walked away towards the kitchen.

"Your accent is interesting," Mr. Harper said as he took a seat in one of the floral chairs across from them. "Are you from Scotland?"

"Aye, Helensburgh."

"Ah, I thought so. I taught geography for years. Elaine and I have discussed going to Scotland for a few weeks, do some sight-seeing and maybe some golfing."

As if like magic, Mrs. Harper re-appeared with a serving tray carrying four plates of egg salad sandwiches, chips, and apple slices as well as four tall glasses of lemonade. After she had given each of them a plate and sat down in the other floral chair next to her husband, she asked, "Does this have anything to do with Liz's arrest?"

"Why would ye think tha', Mrs. Harper?" Sam asked, suspicious of how quick the woman was.

"You don't really think she's capable of murder, do you? That girl loves Nattie more than life, she would never do anything to risk losing her."

Sam took a bite of the sandwich (and hummed his appreciation at the delicious simplicity) and asked, "Wha' makes ye say tha'?"

The older couple looked at one another before Mr. Harper spoke. "When Liz and Daniel first met, they weren't … in a very good place. Daniel was addicted to heroine, and he dragged Liz into it. It continued on even after they got married. But once they found out they were pregnant with Natalie, both of them cleaned right up and never went back to the drugs again."

"There's no way Liz would have gotten addicted again, not even after Daniel died." Mrs. Harper insisted. "And we stand by that. That's what the whole trial was based on, wasn't it? She was back on drugs and that's what forced her to kidnap Natalie?"

"Ridiculous," Mr. Harper agreed. "How can a court try a mother for kidnapping her own child that she already had custody of?"

"Actually, Mr. and Mrs. Harper, we're here to ask a few questions about your son," Simon said after swallowing a bite of his own sandwich. "This is delicious, by the way."

Mrs. Harper smiled and nodded, "Thank you, young man. You're here about Daniel? He died a few years ago in a work accident."

"Our investigation actually has t'do with a man named Brian

Cairne," Sam said and watched the two of them carefully.

Neither of them reacted beyond looking at each other before looking back to Sam.

"What about Brian?" Mr. Harper asked. "He died in a robbery, didn't he?"

"Ye knew him?"

"Yes, we knew him very well. He was a dear friend of ours. In fact, without him, we would have never had Daniel."

Simon and Sam looked at each other with puzzled expressions.

"Brian and I knew each other from our Army days. He was as close to a brother as I'll ever have."

"Shortly after we got married, Charlie was drafted for the war in Vietnam," Mrs. Harper filled in. "And Brian helped to keep him safe so he could come back to me. And once he did, we decided to start having our family."

"We tried for years to have children," Mr. Harper continued, "But … unfortunately it just wasn't meant to be without a little help. About a year after he was discharged, we got an invitation from Brian inviting us to his wedding. While we were there, he asked how things were going, and I told him how we were trying for a baby, but things weren't moving along. He patted me on the back and said he was sorry, and I thought that was the end of it. But then, about five years later I think, I get a letter from him containing a newspaper clipping about a man in England who had invented in vitro fertilization. He said he'd been talking to some people and knew of a doctor that would be willing to help us."

"Of course, the treatment was experimental at the time and extremely expensive. There was no way we could afford that on Charlie's salary as a teacher. But Brian had gotten his business in the steel industry off of the ground by then and insisted he could help cover the cost."

Sam was amazed by the story. "… No offense, bu' why would he jus' hand over tha' much money without loanin' it?"

Mr. Harper laughed. "No offense taken, Agent McKay. You see this?" he tapped his cane. "Brian not only kept me safe, I saved his life, too. Pushed him out of the way when I saw a grenade coming at us. A little piece of it got lodged in my hip, and I was sent home, but I've had to use this damn thing ever since."

Mrs. Harper smacked him on the arm and uttered. "Watch your

language, Mister."

"Sorry, darling," Mr. Harper kissed her cheek before continuing. "I've had to use this *darn* thing ever since. Believe me, we pointed out to him how ludicrous it was to just give us that much money. We even insisted that we pay him back for it over time, but he wouldn't hear anything about it. He played the 'you saved my life; I want to repay you' card, and we couldn't argue with him no matter how much we tried."

"So, he found a doctor and arranged for us to meet with him for the procedure. He wouldn't even let us *look* at the bill," Mrs. Harper smiled sadly.

"When we found out he was killed in the middle of the robbery … I can't even express how heartbroken we were. There just aren't connections like that anymore. I mean lifelong friendship connections."

Sam and Simon glanced at one another again before Sam cleared his throat. "If ye donnea mind me askin … di' the doctor ever tell ye wha' the problem was? On why ye cannea have children alone?"

Mr. Harper shook his head. "Not at all. My sperm count was a bit too low."

Sam furrowed his eyebrows. "So … was Daniel …"

"Oh no, agent, he's still my son. It was a little too low to have children the old-fashioned way, but there was just enough for the procedure to be successful."

"We had decided that if the in vitro didn't work, we weren't going to try again. Brian had even offered to help in a very … unusual manner that the doctor had suggested was possible," Mrs. Harper's cheeks turned slightly pink as she spoke. "But you have to understand that this was the 80s, and this was very brand new. Having another person's child, even if it wasn't out of infidelity, was very taboo at the time. We just couldn't keep a secret like that."

"But, thankfully, it worked on the first try, and we had Daniel," Mr. Harper smiled and took his wife's hand in his. "And he was all we needed."

Sam peered out of the corner of his eye at Simon, who was watching the two of them with fondness.

"That's … a beautiful story," he smiled.

Sam nodded before continuing. "Mr. and Mrs. Harper … yer daughter-in-law Liz tol' us tha' Daniel called Brian his uncle. Could ye clarify tha' claim?"

"Nothing to clarify, Agent. We owed Brian a great deal so we made him Daniel's Godfather, but he insisted he could just go as Uncle Brian." Mrs. Harper stood up and put all of the dishes back on the serving tray.

"Oh, no, Mrs. Harper, allow me to get that," Simon stood up immediately and took the tray from her before walking away to the kitchen.

"I'm sorry, but what does all of this have to do with Brian's death?" Mr. Harper asked.

Sam answered. "Some new evidence has come to light, we're jus' tryin' to chase all the loose ends."

The couple nodded their agreement.

"Jus' one more question before we leave. Have ye kept in contact with Liz?"

The two of them looked down at the floor, obviously ashamed of their answer, before Mrs. Harper replied, "… When Daniel first brought Liz home, we weren't as supportive as we could have been. Things between the four of us were … rocky, to say the least. Even after he died, we didn't really want to see her. That's our shame, though. Not hers. But she tried to send us pictures of Natalie now and then, as you can see from how many we have on the walls."

"Agents, can you think of anything that *we personally* can do to help her now? We didn't give her a chance like we should have back then, but the girl doesn't deserve to lose her daughter. No one should lose their only child."

Sam sighed. "The bes' thing ye can do is support her, publicly and personally. A visit wouldnea hurt either."

"We tried to, but the doctors at the facility she's at say she's not allowed to have visitors for the time being. We're not even allowed to write to her."

"Wha' about yer granddaughter?"

"Michaels keeps insisting Natalie is too shocked by everything that's going on and says he wants her to get used to being home again before he'll let us visit," Mrs. Harper answered, her tone very spiteful. "We never did like him much either."

Sam nodded, his suspicions of Liz's stepfather growing more by the second. "Well, thank ye fer lunch. We donnea want t' take more of yer time, Mr. and Mrs. Harper."

The elderly couple smiled and thanked the two of them before escorting them to the door.

Back in the car and driving back to Cleveland, Simon cleared his throat. "So … do you think they're telling the truth?"

"Aye," Sam nodded. "Neither of them acted even remotely guilty except for their treatment of Liz. I think I was wrong abou' who Brian Cairne's mysterious grandchild is."

Simon's phone pinged with a text alert. "… Maybe not."

"Wha' do ye mean?"

"Rivera just texted me that the DNA of Natalie they got is a match to the one Cairne brought to the doctor."

Sam looked over. "Are they positive?"

"Yeah, Rivera said the doctor checked twice. But if it's a match, and Daniel's not Cairne's kid—"

"Then *Liz* is," Sam said quietly. "Liz's father was Brian Cairne."

━·⊰ ❧⊱·━

Chapter Nineteen

Back at the hotel room, Sam and his team were eating Chinese food while looking through the same information with new eyes. While Sam kept his focus on the photos of Liz and Brian in the hotel room, his team kept spinning ideas about Liz.

"Do you think she has any idea?" Julie asked.

"No way," Rivera answered. "You were there in the interview, she kept insisting that Brian was trying to help her, but she couldn't give us a good reason why."

"You mean she *wouldn't* give us a good reason why."

"Whatever. Either way, I think he never got the chance to tell her."

"But he must have at least been preparing to," Simon said, his mouth full as he reached over the mountains of paperwork to put some pot stickers on his plate. "He was giving her money and trying to get her set up into a place of her own."

Julie took a bite of noodles. "But why wouldn't he just come out and say it? Especially after having the DNA results from Natalie?"

"Come on. You spend your whole life without a father and then suddenly one just walks into your life? Not to mention the shock *he* must have felt after discovering a child he never knew he had before. If I were in his shoes, I'd want to be delicate, too."

"Plus, there's the matter of *why* Liz wanted to disappear in the first place." Rivera looked over to Sam (who hadn't even touched his food). "You know her the best, Sam. Got any answers for us?"

He nodded sadly. "She tol' me Alexander Michaels had molested and raped her when she was younger."

Julie nearly choked. "Her stepfather?"

"Aye."

The three of them looked at him with horror in their eyes before Julie asked in a hushed voice, "… How old was she?"

Sam sighed. "She said he had started to groom her ever since she was her daughter's age … she was 17 when she was raped."

"That sick bastard—"

"Why wouldn't she tell us that?" Simon interrupted. "I mean, if I got arrested for something I didn't do, I would reveal everything I could to the police to make them look deeper."

"She was scared, and I cannea blame her." Sam set his plate down and picked up a paper that was sitting in front of Julie. "She's been tryin to ge' away from him ever since she was fired, bu' he always seemed to find her. She tol' me once tha' she'd seen him buy the police before. I imagine she felt tha' none of us would listen to her anyway. No' to mention she would do anythin' t' keep Natalie safe from Michaels; fer Christ's sake, she stayed separated from her in hopes tha' Micheal's wouldnea find the little girl."

"Well, it sounds like we need to look into Alexander Michaels a little bit more."

"After talkin' with Mr. and Mrs. Harper, I agree. Have we go' anythin' on him?"

Simon had already pulled out his laptop and was clacking on his keyboard with zeal. "Just that he owns an internet security company, graduated with his Masters in computer science from NYU in '81, married only once to a Bianca Gulliver, who died of alcohol poisoning. Nothing else is coming up."

"Come on, he's got to at least have a speeding ticket or something," Rivera asked with an annoyed tone.

"Nope, the guy is clean as a whistle."

"God, I hate guys like that," Julie muttered. "So slick that you can't find anything on them."

"Aye, and even if we could ge' Liz to agree to say somethin' on her behalf, the incident is already past the statute of limitations and wouldnea do anythin'."

"It might hurt his reputation," Rivera jumped in. "But that still wouldn't be enough to exonerate her."

Julie raised her hand. "Hold up. Why would Alexander Michaels want to kill Brian Cairne? The guy owns a prestigious software company, so it's not like he's in a position to lose anything. And if he's smart enough to keep his dirty laundry out of the spotlight, why would he risk someone finding out? What would his motive be?"

"Maybe he just wanted to keep Liz quiet," Simon suggested. "Maybe she threatened to tell people. Maybe she already did. Maybe Brian was not only helping his daughter, maybe he intended to make

Michaels pay for what he'd done."

"If I found out my daughter was being molested by some sicko, then I'd sure as hell want a piece of him," Rivera agreed.

"Aye," Sam nodded. "And according to Liz, he was startin' to groom Natalie as well. She tol' me she saw him doin' some of the same things he used t' do to her."

"What things?"

"Makin' Natalie sit on his lap, buyin' her gifts in return."

Julie gasped and everyone looked at her questioningly. Setting her food down on the table, Julie gulped, "… When we went to get the sample, I was playing dolls with her. She had me put the baby doll down for a nap in a room where there was another doll. She said it was the grandpa who was watching her sleep. She said the grandpa does that a lot whenever the mommy wasn't home. I thought it was odd, but I didn't get the chance to ask her more about it. What if …"

The whole team fell silent; Sam clenched his fists together.

"Boss … we have got to get that little girl out of there," Julie insisted. "Who knows how long it will be until he does something worse to her?"

"We will, Julie, we will. Our first priority is solvin' Brian Cairne's murder. Once we do tha', we can help Liz ge' her daughter back."

"Then the first thing we need to do is prove that she actually *is* Brian Cairne's child. The doctor said a paternity test would be more conclusive than the DNA test against Natalie. Liz is being held at a private mental health and drug institution near Bedford; Julie and I can go get a sample right now." Rivera started to rise but stopped when Sam stood.

"I'm goin'."

"… Sam, you're involved, and you're not even supposed to be here—"

"Anno, bu' I owe'r an explanation. She may hate me, bu' out of the four of us, I'm the one she might trust the most. I think I can ge' her to cooperate when she sees I'm on her side."

Rivera opened his mouth to argue but stopped himself. "Alright, just be careful. What should we do?"

"Dig deeper into Alexander Michaels. Either he is our murderer or he isn't, bu' I want somethin' tha' we can pin 'im for. Understood?"

"You don't have to sell me on that," Julie nodded.

"I'm scouring the dataverse as we speak, boss," Simon smiled.

"And abou' these—" Sam picked up the photos of Liz and Brian together and handed them to Rivera, "—find out who the hell took 'em."

<center>~~~</center>

It was just past nine o'clock, and the moon was shining brightly when Sam walked up to the rehabilitation center. He knocked loudly on the glass door after discovering it locked. A beep came from his left and he looked over at an intercom.

"Visiting hours are from 10:00 a.m. to 4:00 p.m. Monday through Friday, come back in a couple days," a grumpy voice answered.

"Agent Sam McKay of the FBI, I'm here because I need to ask one of yer patients a few questions."

"Hold on, please."

The intercom went silent for a few moments, and Sam debated on pounding on the doors again when finally, the voice returned.

"Show your ID to the camera, please."

Holding up the fake ID Simon created for him, he did as instructed.

"… Just a moment, please."

Eventually a heavyset, bearded and bald man wearing scrubs came into view and unlocked the door, allowing Sam to enter into an open foyer with a large table sitting in the middle of it.

"The manager on call said that you're allowed no more than ten minutes then you'll have to leave and come back during visiting hours."

"Fine," he nodded.

"Which patient are you looking to talk to?"

"Elizabeth Harper, she's new."

"Yeah, I know her," the man smiled. "Nice girl, drug addict. Follow me."

Something about the nurse's comment made Sam's gut twist, but he kept his face emotionless. They walked through the foyer and down a large, beige hallway until they came to a metal door where the nurse had to scan his hand before they could enter. This part of the facility was bright white and smelled heavily of lavender and disinfectant, not to mention the long hallway made Sam feel very uneasy.

"Are ye the only staff member here at night?"

"Yup, but just on the weekends. Curfew is 9:00 p.m., which is when all of the room doors automatically lock, and then it's lights out at 10:00 p.m. This wing is where our newest patients come for at least the first two months of their stay, or until our on-site psychologist says they're stable enough to be moved to the general public quarters. There they share a room with one of the other patients."

"And wha' about Mrs. Harper?"

"I'd have to check out the doctor's notes on her. Here we are."

They stopped in front of a door with the number 18 painted on it. The nurse knocked on the door before sliding open a slot and saying, "You have a visitor, are you decent?"

"… Yes," came a timid reply; she was so quiet Sam could barely hear her voice.

The nurse then pressed a button on the right which made a loud buzz sound before the door clicked.

"Wait here for a second, I have to sweep the room and make sure there's nothing she could use to hurt you. Not that you'd need any protecting, big guy like you."

Sam ignored the quip and nodded as the large man opened the door. As the nurse looked all around the very bare space, he kept his eyes on Liz and felt his heart wrench with guilt. She looked positively haggard. Dressed in a white jumpsuit, dark bags under her eyes, her beautiful dark hair was shaved almost completely off, and she was holding her knees to her chest on a cot that hardly looked comfortable.

"Okay, you're good, man. Remember, ten minutes. No more." The nurse walked out and allowed Sam to enter before shutting the door. Sam heard the loud buzzer and the door click again before he heard heavy footsteps walking away.

He turned his attention back to Liz, but she hadn't even looked up at him. Not knowing where else to start, he said, "I know yer innocent."

That made her look up from under her eyelashes at him, but he didn't get any further response than that.

"I'm sorry, Liz. I know tha' doesnea mean much, bu' I promise ye tha' my team and I will no' rest until we get ye out of here." He pulled the sterile swab and plastic tube kit from his coat pocket. "I need to swab the inside of yer mouth."

"Why?" she asked him quietly, but that didn't disguise the malice in her voice.

"To prove tha' yer Brian Cairne's daughter."

The absurd answer should have made her start, but she didn't move.

"Did ye no' hear me? Brian Cairne was yer father, Liz."

"That's ridiculous."

"Is it? Ye said tha' he was helpin' ye, very generously if ye ask me. Liz, Brian go' a blood sample from Natalie somehow and had a DNA test done against him, is' a 37% match. And we already checked ou' yer late husband's parents, they confirmed tha' Daniel was their son. Brian was his Godfather of sorts. Tha' means the only other explanation is ye're his daughter."

Finally, he had gotten a reaction out of her; she sat up and stared at him intently. "That's not possible. My father abandoned my mother after she was pregnant."

"Did she tell you tha'?"

Liz's face paled. "… Alex told me that one night after he and mom had been drinking a bit … I think I was eight. But … if it's true, and Brian was my father, why didn't he just tell me?"

"I dunno, bu' it may help to prove yer innocence. Now, please?" He held out the swab.

Liz sighed and opened her mouth. Sam rubbed the cotton tip all along the inside of her mouth for a good minute, making sure he had more than enough DNA on it, before placing it inside of the plastic tube and sealing it shut.

"We'll know for certain in the mornin'." He tucked the test back into his pocket again before turning his attention back to her. "Tell me the truth, are ye bein' treated well here?"

Tears brimmed in her exhausted eyes as she gingerly rubbed her nearly bald head.

Sam felt his blood begin to boil with rage. "Wha' else have they done to ye?"

"Nothing, Sam. It's just … they've taken everything away from me, even my picture of Natalie. Oh, God, is she alright?"

The guilt he felt intensified. "She's alrigh', Liz, hush now. My team saw her personally, they said tha' she's fine, bu … they know abou' yer stepfather."

"Sam, don't leave her there with him, please," Liz pleaded as the tears started to stream out of her eyes.

Not knowing what else to do, he placed his hand over hers. "Liz, my team and I will fix this. I promise."

His words seemed to sate her hysteria a little, and she nodded.

"I need to ask ye a few questions before I go. Did ye tell Brian about yer stepfather?"

"Yes," she sniffled.

"When?"

"A few months after he gave me a job. It was right after I'd confronted Alex about what he was doing to Natalie, and he first threatened to take her away from me. I wasn't making enough to get us out of there fast enough, so I went to Brian to ask for more work, overtime, anything. He said he was more than happy to help me, but he asked why I needed the money so badly … so I told him."

"And wha' did he say?"

She thought for a moment before shaking her head. "Nothing really except that I'd never have to worry about Alex again. Then he drove me home to pick up Natalie before driving us to a hotel. Actually, now that I think about it, I think it was the same hotel that was in those pictures your people showed me."

Sam nodded. "Okay, this is good. Liz, when ye went to ge' Natalie, where was Brian?"

"I don't know, in the car waiting, I think?"

"Think harder. Di' he come inside? Walk me through exactly wha' happened when ye went to get Natalie."

Liz took a shuddering breath and rubbed her temples with her forefingers. "I don't know Sam. I was just in a hurry to get us out of there as fast as possible. I walked inside and straight past Alex, who was sitting in the den, and ran upstairs to pack a bag for us. Natalie was playing in the playroom. I got her and then we walked down the stairs and got in the car. I heard Alex yelling and carrying on, but I didn't even look at him. I was so focused on Natalie, making sure she was alright. The way he was carrying on … she was so scared."

"Can ye remember anythin' he was yellin'?"

"Just things like 'What do you think you're doing? You're not leaving. I'll take her away.' Et cetera. Things like that … but then I heard something break. Something glass. I didn't look up to see, I assumed that he'd just thrown a vase, which was unusual because I've never seen him throw anything before, but I didn't want to question it."

"Can ye think of anythin' else?"

She shook her head, "No. A few minutes later, we were being driven to the hotel. Brian paid for a suite and left us for the night."

"Alright. Now abou' the pictures. Why did Brian come to see ye?"

"Just to assure me that he'd taken care of things, and I wouldn't have to worry about Alex again."

"When?"

"I don't know, a couple nights later, maybe? I'm not sure. … You said that he'd gotten some blood from Natalie?"

"Aye."

"… She came out of her bedroom just as he was getting ready to leave. She'd had a nightmare. He had brought her a little present, a brand-new book. He offered to read it to her to help her calm down. I was a little hesitant about it, but he didn't give me the same feeling Alex did, so I said it was okay. When she opened the page, she got a nasty paper cut. He must have gotten some of her blood that way when I went to go get her a band aid."

"Aye, is possible," Sam nodded. "We donnea know *how* he got it, we jus' know tha' it was a blood sample he'd brought."

Liz wrung her hands together and breathed heavily. "God … this is so much to think about … I wish he'd've told me."

They heard the sound of heavy footsteps coming back.

"Liz," Sam whispered, "I promise, I am goin' to ge' ye out of here and back to Natalie."

She nodded just as the buzzer sounded again.

After the click, the door opened and the nurse said, "Time's up, man. You'll have to come back during visiting hours if you want to ask her more questions."

"Aye," he nodded. "Thank ye, Mrs. Harper."

Liz nodded timidly, and Sam vacated the room.

After the nurse locked the door, they began walking back towards the entrance when he said, "So, according to the notes in her file, she's going to be in this wing for a few more months before she'll even get a chance at the General Public area."

"Wha'?" Sam furrowed his eyebrows. "For wha' reason?"

"The psychologist notes say she's still extremely dangerous to herself and others. Heck, she even tried to choke herself with her hair, and believe me that was a sight to see. In this wing, we can keep a closer eye on her until she's stable."

Sam had to stop himself from punching the nurse. *Doctors notes indeed ... this is tha' arsehole Michaels' doin' ...* Just before leaving, he took a business card from the front desk and pocketed it, deciding to have Simon look deeper into this facility later.

Driving back to his hotel, Sam pulled over when he saw a quiet spot and got out of the car to pace around it. Angry energy coursed through him as he thought about what Liz and her daughter were being forced to go through, and he wished he'd never told Rivera where she was in the first place. Unable to think clearly, he punched the engine hood of his car and left a dent in the metal. The pain he felt told him he had possibly fractured a knuckle, but he rubbed it gently with his hand and sat down on top of the dent. ... *I have to fix this ...*

Chapter Twenty

Rivera and Julie walked into the headquarters of Jackson Green's busy campaign and were immediately stopped by an extremely thin young woman with jet black hair pulled back in a tight bun, wearing a black skirt suit.

"Excuse me, just where do you think you're going?" she demanded.

Badge already in hand, Rivera flashed it to her. "FBI, we need to speak to Congressman Green."

"Do you have an appointment?"

"Does it look like we need one?" Julie answered her.

The woman glared. "The Congressman is in an interview right now and cannot be disturbed. I'm Rosie Newt, his chief of staff, and I'm handling all social calls."

"Good, when somebody comes to socialize, we'll let you know." Rivera pushed past her with Julie on his heels, and they made their way to the back of the building.

"Agents! This is unacceptable! If you don't leave at once, I'll be forced to call the Congressman's private security!"

"There he is," Julie pointed at some glass doors.

Rivera looked and saw the Congressman sitting next to a desk across from a woman with cameras facing them. He marched over and opened the door without knocking.

"As President, I promise to get illegal drugs off of our streets and away from our children—" Green stopped talking and looked to Rivera and Julie curiously.

"I'm sorry, Jackson," Rosie said much more sweetly. "I'll call Nick and Zane over at once."

"That won't be necessary, Rosie, thank you. Agents, please come have a seat. Sophie, guys, could you give us ten minutes?"

The interviewer and the camera crew nodded and left without a word.

"Rosie, could you have Dana bring us some coffee and some of those cinnamon buns somebody brought?"

"Okay," she nodded and left after casting one final glare at Rivera and Julie.

Rivera and Julie kept their eyes trained on Green as the doors closed. "That's quite the promise you're making, Congressman."

"I can assure you that it's one I intend to keep, agents. Now, how can I help you?"

Rivera retrieved the packet of photos and tossed them down in front of Green. "You said that Cairne gave these to you?"

"That's correct."

"And told you to keep them safe."

"Yes."

"Tell me about that conversation and spare no details."

The politician furrowed his eyebrows. "There's honestly not much to tell you that I haven't already, Agent Rivera. I was working late one night and then Brian texted me saying he was going to send me some photos, and I needed to keep them safe because he was in trouble."

"Wait a minute," Julie said. "He *texted* you?"

"Yes. Did I not mention that when we spoke last?"

Rivera eyed him coolly. "Conveniently not. I don't suppose you have the conversation saved in your notes or an email or anything?"

"No," Green shook his head. "Brian told me to delete the message as soon as we were finished and not to mention it again … As I think about it, it was very odd. He's never texted me before. I don't think he's ever texted anyone, actually. He preferred calling and talking on the phone with people or speaking to them face to face. Heck, whenever he came to visit Georgia and the kids, he would always leave his phone with his keys at the door. He was one of the few men I knew who didn't use his phone like it was oxygen. Anyways, we haven't changed our phone company in ten years. I'm sure they'd have the conversation somewhere on file, so you can check there."

"We will," Rivera nodded. "You said that you were working late that night, so I imagine there are plenty of staff around that would be able to corroborate your alibi?"

Green sighed and looked down at his desk in shame. "… Rosie … I was here with Rosie that night. Yes, I know, it's a cliché to sleep with someone on my staff, but it's been over for a year now."

Rivera glanced over at Julie, who never took her eyes off of

Green, and nodded. "We'll be back."

"I'm sure you will be."

They left before the promised coffee and cinnamon buns arrived and walked until they found the thin, bitter woman again.

She looked them over with disapproving eyes. "Are you finished now, agents?"

"We have one question for you before we go," Rivera said.

"Are you and the Congressman having an affair?" Julie said just loud enough for the passing staff members to hear.

Rosie's eyes widened; she looked nervously around at the other people walking by them. Rivera smirked when he heard Julie snicker at the reaction.

"Come with me, please," she whispered and led them to another small room and shut the door. "How dare you ask me such an impertinent question!"

"That you haven't answered," Rivera replied. "Are the two of you having an affair?"

Rosie stood there with the shocked expression on her face for a moment too long before she swallowed and nodded. "We were … until it ended about 11 months, 3 weeks, and two days ago."

"And were you with him the night he received a text from his father-in-law about some photographs?"

"… I don't know anything about photographs, but there was a night when he got this text that he said was pretty strange. He told me to go get a bottle of champagne while he took care of it, and when I got back … well anyways." She folded her arms around herself and looked to the ground.

"How often were the two of you sleeping together?" Julie asked.

"… Probably three or four times a week, always at night after the rest of the staff had gone home."

"Did he ever get any other strange or important calls during that time?"

She shook her head.

"Thank you, Miss Newt," Rivera said.

"Is Jackson in trouble?" She asked quietly.

"We're looking into every avenue during this investigation; that's all you need to know. Have a nice day."

Julie walked to the door first, and Rivera followed. Once they were back inside of their car again, Julie sighed. "That poor, deluded woman."

"Excuse me?" He asked, surprised. "I thought you didn't like her."

"I don't, but didn't you hear her answer on how long since the affair? Anyone who keeps track of the days since a breakup for *this* long is obviously hoping there's still a future. It's just pathetic and sad."

Rivera swallowed and turned his attention to driving away. *So, what does that say about us, Jules?* He thought to himself as he drove, suddenly feeling foolish for knowing it had been exactly 21 days since their breakup.

"What do you think about the whole texting answer?" Julie said.

Grateful for the change in topic, Rivera cleared his throat. "Ehem, I think it's either a really good lie because he couldn't make up a story about the conversation, or he's telling the truth, which makes this tougher."

"Yeah, anybody could have taken Brian Cairne's cell phone and quickly texted that conversation. So how do we find out who?"

Rivera thought about it for a moment, "… Maybe we should just go straight to the source of the photos, track down the person who took them."

"Sounds great, except we're not even supposed to be working this case. How are we going to find the source if we can't use the FBI's resources?"

"Don't worry, I know someone." Rivera dug through the contacts on his phone to a number he hadn't dialed in a long time, but couldn't ever bring himself to get rid of. After pressing the call button, he raised it to his ear and waited.

... Ring … Ring … Ring ... "Hello, Derrick."

He breathed deep and smiled. "Hey. Can I meet you for coffee in an hour?"

"You never did like to waste time," the sultry voice giggled. "Always straight to the point. Lucky for you, I've had a slow day today."

"So that's a yes?"

"Always is. Our place?"

"Yup."

"I'll be there."

The call ended before he could get another word in. Rivera

couldn't help the silly smile when he put his phone away, even though he could see Julie making a curious face at him from the corner of his eye.

"Who was that?"

"Someone who knows their way around photos."

"So, we're going to meet them in an hour?"

"No, *I'm* going to meet them in an hour. I'll drop you off at Sam's hotel so you guys can look into the cell phone records while I find out where we can find the guy who took the pictures."

Exactly an hour later, he was sitting at a small booth in a quiet and quaint coffee shop called Bea's outside of Central on 55th. It had been nearly four years since he'd last been there, but the place hadn't lost any of its peculiarity. With bright orange walls and dark forest green accents, it still smelled like burnt coffee and butterscotch cookies (which was the house pastry and really the only reason anyone came to Bea's). A plate of six sat in front of him. As he took another bite out of a cookie, the bell over the door rang, forcing him to look up and see the woman he was waiting for: Hadley Palomino, the girl he'd met way back in Quantico. They'd graduated from the same class in the top 20%, but while he went off to work for the FBI, she had decided to become a pivate investigator. Their torrid relationship had lasted for all of six months, but he had never forgotten her. She was still wearing her favorite bright red lipstick, which went perfectly with her mocha skin, and suddenly his head started to swim. She looked all around before she spotted him and smiled. Finally, she wandered over and took a seat across from him.

"Black, one sugar, no cream, right?" Rivera smiled.

"How sweet, you remembered." Hadley took a sip of the coffee and tried not to cough. "God … still very bad. Remind me why we chose this as our place again?"

"Because of these," he chuckled and shoved the rest of the half-eaten cookie in his mouth.

"Right, nothing beats Bea's butterscotch cookies." Hadley picked up one and took a bite. "How many of these have you had already?"

"I was nice and only had one while I waited."

"Ha! You really *do* need a favor. What's up, Derrick?"

He pulled out the envelope and handed it to her. "I need to know who took these."

Hadley pulled out the photos and looked through all of them

carefully. "Don't you have big shot forensics experts for this?"

"This case is off the grid, Hadley. Do they look familiar?"

"... Doesn't look like anybody's work that I know."

"Don't PIs share some of their surveillance techniques with each other?" Rivera teased.

"Not as often as you might think, but if you give me a couple of days with them then I can find their photographic fingerprint and let you know."

"Thanks, I owe you one."

"Yes, you do," she winked at him. "I'm still expensive."

"I remember."

"Which is why I'll be taking these as a down payment." She scooped up the remaining four cookies and stood up.

"Hey! Two of those were for me!"

"Like we agreed, I'm still expensive."

Rivera chuckled and shook his head. "You're leaving already?"

"This is urgent, right? Might as well get started." She turned and sauntered away from him. Rivera kept his eyes on the way she swung her hips as she walked. "I'll let you know when I've got something!"

Just as quickly as she was there, she was gone again, and Rivera felt the need for a cold glass of water. Chuckling to himself, he walked to the barista at the counter and purchased two more cookies before he left.

~~~

Sam stood behind Rivera as he rang the doorbell to the Michaels residence. Julie was certain that she would behave in a manner that would compromise their case now that she knew Michaels was a predator and insisted she not go to the questioning. Instead, she would take the saliva sample Sam had collected to Dr. Williams. Sam was more than happy to go in her place and look Michaels in the eye when they questioned him, especially with the new information Simon had managed to find that supported Liz's claim about something glass breaking.

The door was opened by none other than Natalie, and Sam smiled when he finally got to see her in person. The little blonde angel looked so much like Liz; his heart ached.
~~~

"Hi, Natalie," Rivera said to her cheerfully. "Do you remember me?"

"Mhmm," she nodded. "You're one of the people that came to talk to Grandpa. Where's the lady that gave me the lollipop?"

"She wanted to come, but she had something important to do. Is your grandpa here?"

Michaels appeared behind Natalie as soon as Rivera asked. "Agent Rivera, what can I do for you?"

"We need a few more minutes of your time, if that's alright."

"Of course." He turned his focus to Natalie. "Sweetheart, why don't you go upstairs and play? Grandpa'll be up in a minute."

The little girl nodded and bounded up the steps without another glance.

"Please, come in." Michaels led them past the stairs and through the hallway until they reached a very posh office, to Sam's standards. In the middle of the room sat a large, cherry wood desk with a computer on the corner, a red leather chair sat behind it, and two other red leather chairs sat facing it. The room smelled like cigars and cognac. Michaels gestured to the chairs. "Please, have a seat."

"No thank you, we won't take up too much of your time," Rivera said calmly. "We needed to ask you a few questions about Brian Cairne."

"I thought we had already gone over this, Agent Rivera. I don't know anything about him other than what I've read in the news."

"You've never met him in person before? Maybe had coffee together?"

"No, Agent. I have never talked to the man in my life."

Sam was already impatient. He stepped forward. "Now I think we all know tha's no' true."

Michaels kept his face emotionless.

"Tell us abou' the day Liz and Natalie left."

"I believe I told you that Liz was falling back into her drug problem, and I said I would pursue custody of Natalie if she didn't get clean. One day after work she came home and took Natalie without a word. Then I found out they had run away."

"Tha' must've upset ye."

"Of course, it did, agent. My daughter was putting herself and my granddaughter in danger."

"Why didnea ye try to stop her?"

"I tried to talk her out of it."

"If ye were so worried about Natalie's safety, why didnea ye call the police?"

"I didn't want Natalie to hate me."

On cue, Rivera pulled out a piece of paper and laid it in front of Michaels. "This is an Emergency Room record on you, Mr. Michaels. According to these notes, you went to get some stitches in your side the same day the girls left. Is that true?"

"It must be if it's on the hospital record," Michaels answered, perturbed. "But what does this have to do with anything?"

"Why did you go to the hospital that day?"

Michaels looked down at the paper but didn't answer.

Sam answered. "Liz tol' Brian wha' ye were doin', and he came to help her leave, and she heard ye break somethin' glass. And here we have an ER visit for stitches. I think Brian came to confront ye on molestin' her and Natalie, ye go' angry and tried to throw somethin' at him, or maybe he threw somethin' at you, and ye got cut."

Michaels rolled his eyes. "Very interesting conjecture, agent. But for the record, I was being careless in the kitchen and accidently cut myself with a knife that was sitting on the counter in an odd position. And I've *never* touched my daughter nor my granddaughter."

"Must be a very sharp knife to be able to cut through clothin' and skin just sittin' on the counter."

"You don't have to believe me, but you can't prove otherwise."

"I'm sure tha' yer neighbors wouldnea forget a row like tha'."

Michaels leaned forward onto his elbows. "The nice thing about my neighborhood, agent, is that everyone keeps their business to themselves. And even *if* your theory was right, what would that prove, hmmm? Absolutely nothing."

"It would prove that you lied to us about knowing Brian Cairne," Rivera said. "And it would also give you a motive to kill him."

Michaels scoffed. "For supposedly hurting me with broken glass?"

"I've seen men kill for less. But no, for taking Liz and Natalie away where you couldn't hurt them."

"And perhaps he threatened ye," Sam continued. "Brian Cairne was rich, powerful; he even had a son-in-law runnin' fer president, which would give him some pull if he really wanted to use it. He could've taken everythin' away from ye, if he wanted to. Tha' kind of pressure would drive anyone to kill, wouldn't ye agree?"

"I'm afraid I'll have to take your word for that," Michaels said simply. "You can look at my record, agents, I've never done a violent thing in my life. I don't run in *any* of the circles Brian Cairne did. If I have ever been in the same proximity as him, it was probably while we were both stuck at the same traffic light."

"Oh, aye," Sam growled, "I's obvious ye're a smart man. Ye'd make sure there's no possible way any of this is connected to ye, wouldn't ye?"

Sam stared into Michaels blank, cold eyes before the thin, graying man said, "From now on, any questions you have can go through my lawyer. And if the two of you *ever* come back here to harass me again, I'll make sure it'll be your last time. I'll escort you to the door."

"No need, we know the way out," Sam growled before turning and walking away with Rivera on his heels.

<center>~~~</center>

Back at the hotel, they found Julie standing over the computer with Simon.

"Good news," she said as she showed them some new papers. "It's confirmed! Liz is Brian Cairne's daughter! Now please tell me you got something out of that sick son-of-a-bitch."

"Not enough to prove anything," Rivera answered her in an angry tone. "But he's definitely guilty of something. You should've seen him, that smug little prick was just *waiting* to rub our noses in how untouchable he is."

Sam walked over to the table. "Simon, have ye found the Green cell phone records yet?"

"Yeah … looks like Green was telling the truth about the texting." Simon sighed. "Listen to this:

"Jackson, I need a favor."

" 'Sure, what's up?"

"I'm sending you a package that you need to keep safe for a while."

"Can I call and discuss this with you?"

"No can't talk right now. Delete this message when we're done ok?"

"Okay. What's the package?"

"It's photographs, I'm having some trouble at the factory with a woman. These photos will get her to leave me alone."

"Why not just fire her?"

"Wish I could. Just keep them safe, don't tell Georgia."

"Okay, you got it."

"Delete this message".

"And that's it." Simon ran his hands through his hair.

Julie came to his side and looked over the text conversation. "Geeze, whoever took Cairne's phone and typed this is either really bad or really good. This conversation is so … technical, it feels like a computer wrote it and not a person."

Sam joined them behind the laptop and looked over the details. "And yer sure tha' Brian never texted anyone before?"

"Yeah," Simon nodded. "I had to sift through a ton of emails and documents just to find this. The guy had never sent a text message in his life."

"Wha' about yer contact, Rivera. Has she go' anythin' with the photos yet?"

Rivera shook his head. "Not yet, but she's thorough. She won't quit until she finds something and then she'll let me know the second that she does."

"She sounds perfect, why don't you ask her out?" Julie murmured under her breath just loud enough for Simon to hear.

He looked at her curiously before turning his attention back to Sam. "So, what now?"

"Gah, there's go' to be somethin' we're missin' here!" Sam rubbed his face and began to pace the floor.

Julie joined him for a few moments before she finally voiced her thoughts out loud. "Okay … let's just assume for a second that Michaels *didn't* do it."

"What?" Rivera practically barked at her.

"As much as I would love to throw the book at that guy, just hear me out," she continued. "What if Brian Cairne's murder does have to do with Liz, but not in the way we *think* it does. What if it has nothing to do with what happened to her, but rather what was *going* to happen to her?"

Sam stared at Julie. "Wha' do ye mean?"

"Well, Brian was investigating whether or not Liz was his daughter, right? And along the way he was trying to set her up with a better life. Well, what if he intended to do more than that? What if he was planning on publicly announcing she was his daughter?"

"Guy that high profile would make his plans for the future pretty public," Rivera agreed.

"Doesnea tell us who might have a problem with tha' though. Brian's daughter would be the obvious choice, bu' per the note in his will, Georgia inherited the company after his death. Her husband is runnin' fer President and is still the CEO of the international bank En Passant. Hell, he even had two new trusts set up fer her and the boys. Even if Cairne intended to split his daughter's inheritance between her and Liz, she's still a millionaire."

"Some people don't like sharing anything, Sam."

"Aye, perhaps. But me gut is tellin' me Georgia wouldnea have her own father murdered … Maybe his murder has nothin' to do with Liz, and she's jus' a poor bystander."

"Who just happens to be his long-lost daughter?" Julie argued.

"Tha' could jus' be a coincidence. Whoever did this did an excellent job of coverin' their tracks, so we best start thinkin' outside the box." Sam picked up the Cairne Steel Industries paperwork and looked over the company's financial paperwork again, when something peculiar caught his eye. "I may not know much abou' how to run a bloody business, bu' doesn't it seem odd to anyone tha' fer the last six months of his life, Cairne's company was sendin' smaller than usual payments to somethin' called A.R. Sway?"

"Someone, not something, boss," Simon answered.

"Who is it?"

"A professional corporate spy of sorts," Simon answered. "He's basically the computer PI for big time businesses, goes undercover to get information and has some unsavory means of getting answers for people. He's almost a ghost."

"So how do ye know 'im, Simon?"

"Please, any computer hacker worth his salt knows this guy. I've even had a few run-ins with him in the vast dataverse."

"Not that corporation work is my forte, but Brian was most likely doing some digging on his competition, Sam," Rivera added. "It's probably nothing."

Sam furrowed his eyebrows. "Every witness ye've interviewed has described him as shrewd in business but fair and honest. Hirin' a corporate spy doesnea seem tha' honest to me."

"I guess that would depend on what your definition of 'shrewd' is, wouldn't it?"

"No," Sam shook his head. "Somethin' abou' this doesnea add up. We should talk to this A.R. Sway and find out wha' exactly Brian hired him for."

Simon cleared his throat. "That's easier said than done, boss. This guy is good, I mean *really* good. I've heard that just to get a meeting with him requires a deposit."

"How much?"

"Last I heard, it's somewhere close to five grand."

Julie sighed. "I doubt we'd get funding approval from the Director, and I don't have that much money on me."

"Me neither," Rivera agreed.

"Ditto," added Simon.

Sam paid no attention to them as he rummaged through his suitcase for the last of the cash Gerald had 'paid' him. Doing a quick count, he was pleased to discover $4,600 left. "Can the rest of ye pool $400?"

Chapter Twenty-One

Sitting on a bench at the Public Square, Simon tried to sip his coffee inconspicuously and kept his eyes trained on the Fountain of Eternal Life. Glancing at the time on his phone, he started to feel nervous as the mysterious A.R. Sway was ten minutes late. He adjusted the earpiece for the tenth time when he heard Rivera's voice growl at him.

"Will you chill out, kid? You're making me nervous."

"How come *I* have to be the one to meet this guy?" he tried to answer quietly, only to earn a confused look from a passerby.

"Because yer the computer savvy one; ye'll be able to speak his language," Sam's voice answered.

"You guys know that I don't do undercover work, and this is why. I'm too easily discovered."

"Simon," Julie said. "Just take a deep breath and drink your coffee. The minute Sway appears, we'll walk you through what to do. We're right here with you."

Julie's soothing and assuring tone helped to calm Simon a touch, but not enough to stop his insides from shaking. He looked down at his phone again when someone sat down on the other end of the bench. Curious, he looked over and recognized the cute girl with the bangs from the FBI sitting there with a large bag at her feet. *Oh, great,* he thought to himself, *exactly what I need right now.*

Almost as if Rivera could read his mind, he heard him say, "Take it easy, Romeo. Remember what we're here for."

But the way those bangs fell in front of her eyes had him mesmerized, and he had a hard time looking away. She was no longer dressed in business attire, but rather flowery leggings and a Black Sabbath t-shirt with her hair in a bun. He couldn't help but think how beautiful she looked and suddenly had a hard time breathing. But then she looked over, and he tried to recover by drinking his coffee only to have it spill on his shirt.

"Smooth," Rivera chuckled.

"Hey," Kelsey smiled at him. "Don't I know you from somewhere?"

"Um, yeah, I fixed your computer at the office once." Simon gulped.

"Right ... it's Silas, isn't it?"

"Simon, actually."

"Stop socializing, say you're there to meet someone," Rivera said in a very annoyed tone.

"Shut up, Derrick," Simon mumbled under his breath. "So ... what brings you to the Fountain of Eternal Life?"

"Oh, I'm just meeting someone."

"Yeah? Hot date?"

Kelsey chuckled. "You could say that."

"She's lying," Julie said urgently. "She's not dressed for a first date."

"Are you kidding?" Rivera argued. "People are always dressing crazy these days, that's no way to tell she's lying."

"She's not even wearing earrings. Every girl wears earrings on a date. I'm telling you; she's lying. ... She's gotta be Sway!"

Simon sat still and stared at Kelsey as the two of them argued until finally, Sam told them to be quiet. Realizing how awkwardly he was behaving, he furrowed his eyebrows and tried to maintain his cool. "So ... you going to get lunch together?"

Kelsey eyed him for a moment longer before grabbing her bag and standing to leave. "You know what? I think I got stood up. It was nice to see you again."

"What? You just got here."

"Yeah, well, she's late. See ya'."

"Simon, donnea le' her get away!" Sam growled into his earpiece.

"Hey, um ... I think who I'm meeting isn't coming either. Wanna go get some coffee?"

"You already have coffee," Kelsey chuckled.

"Yeah, but ... you don't."

"Sorry, Simon, but I'm not really into guys. Bye."

Suddenly Sam, Julie, and Rivera were standing in front of Kelsey. She looked around her furiously until Julie stepped in front of her and said, "That's alright *Miss Sway*, you can get coffee with me."

Back inside Sam's hotel room, he kept his eyes trained on Kelsey; her arms folded behind her head, she was lying down on the bed calmly and staring at the ceiling.

"Kudos to you guys for figuring it out so quick," she said. "I think this is my first … what do you call it? Sting operation? Not that I've done anything illegal, of course. But I think I should let you know that I don't betray my clients, and legally you can't hold me longer than 24 hours. And the last I'd checked, *you"* —she nodded at Sam— "are not supposed to be in the country, am I right?"

Sam didn't say a word.

"But then again," she turned to Simon. "Your skills are almost as good as mine, so who's gonna' question it?"

Rivera pulled out a photo of Brian Cairne and held it up for her. "You know him?"

"Not familiar."

"His name's Brian Cairne, you worked for him last year."

She shook her head. "Doesn't ring a bell."

"Okay, chicky, let me lay it out for you," Julie said in a clipped tone. "You illegally broke into the FBI and stole some files, which is a federal offense. How does fifteen years in a prison cell and never touching a computer again sound to you?"

"Yeah," Simon added. "I'll testify that I saw you in there."

"Save the whole 'good cop bad cop' thing for somebody that you can actually intimidate." Kelsey got up from the bed and stretched.

Sam stood up and towered over her, causing her to subtly flinch. Taking the photo from Rivera, he showed it to her again. "We're no' interested in sendin' ye to prison, Kelsey. Ye help us, we let ye go, and we never met. Is tha' simple."

Kelsey kept her eyes trained on him, weighing his promise carefully. Finally, she took the photo. "… You said his name is Brian Cairne?"

"Was, he was murdered last year."

She looked up at Sam, shocked. "… If you guys think—"

"We know ye didnea kill him; we're tryin' to find who did, and we think ye might have the answer. Wha' company did he hire ye to spy on?"

"See, that's what people normally hire me to do, but this guy was different. He wanted me to do some digging on someone in particular. I told him to hire a regular PI for that, but he insisted he needed someone that could go deeper and stay hidden. He even paid me double for it."

Julie suddenly produced a picture of Liz. "Was this who he wanted you to look into?"

"No, I remember it was a guy that I was investigating. If you let me get my laptop, I can look back through my files and tell you who."

Simon produced her large bag. As soon as she was sitting at the table comfortably, Kelsey began to move her fingers across the keyboard like lightening. Sam smirked as he watched Simon stare at her work in complete awe.

"You always keep the information you collect for your clients?" Rivera asked.

"Only the interesting things," Kelsey answered. "Here it is, the only personal case I've ever had: your guy wanted me to do some digging on Jackson Green."

"What?!" Rivera, Julie, and Simon shouted at the same time.

Kelsey jumped at their outburst. "Jeez, you guys really are hard up for a lead, aren't you?"

"Why did he want ye lookin' into Green?" Sam asked with a level tone.

"I didn't ask. But here," she produced a zip drive from her bag and copied the files over. "Here's everything I found on him. I encoded it so anybody sneaking around would have a hard time getting to my stuff, but I'm sure your guy can handle it. I gave the laymen's terms version to Brian, and he seemed to appreciate my work, but I never heard from him again after that."

"How did you get all of this, if you don't mind me asking?" Simon said.

"That's okay, I don't mind at all," Kelsey winked at him, making him blush and look down. "Okay, I helped you. Will you let me go, now?"

Sam nodded. "Aye, thank ye Miss Sway. If we have more questions—"

"I'm sure you'll be able to find me," she smiled as she packed away her computer. Looking back up at Simon again, she said, "Oh and by the way, sorry about the whole Leviathan Bug thing."

"That was *you?!*" Simon demanded. "What the hell did I ever do to you?"

"Hey, man, you stole my files!"

"That you were *illegally* collecting," Julie reminded her. "If you're so smart, why did you need Simon to fix your computer?"

Kelsey chuckled, "My line of work, I've found that flying under the radar is the best way to do my job, and sometimes you have to use somebody else's credentials to do that. Look, I'm sorry all the same. I just couldn't risk you looking into my client's business, so I sent you the bug to delete everything before you could ask too many questions."

"Yeah, well, you should be sorry, because that program took me years to perfect and I still haven't worked out all the kinks!" Simon answered her disdainfully.

"Well, here," Kelsey produced another zip drive and handed it to him. "This should get rid of the rest of those kinks. It's the antidote to my Leviathan Bug. We cool?"

Begrudgingly, Simon accepted the drive and nodded.

"Great, see you guys around!" Kelsey said as she shut the door behind her and left.

Rivera gave a hearty laugh as he nudged Simon. "I think she likes you."

"Shut up, meat-sicle," Simon muttered.

"Simon, pull up the files," Sam instructed. "I wanna know why Brian Cairne was lookin' into his son-in-law."

Within moments, the files Kelsey had left them were pulled up, and Simon was working through the coding to get everything together. Everyone could tell that Simon's pride had been hurt by the way he furiously clacked away on the keyboard, so they stayed out of his way. Finally, they saw readable English on the screen: suspicious names were opening loan accounts through Green's bank En Passant, and Kelsey had discovered that they were connected to the Rios Cartel in Mexico. Green was collecting a 7% profit in an 'offshore account' for looking the other way while the money laundering was taking place. In another file was a list of names of the people who worked for Green in his private security company. No more than two dozen, Sam scanned over the list until his eyes landed on the one he knew instantly: Gerald Mebbin.

"Oh … my … God!" Julie exclaimed.

"I don't believe it," Rivera added. "Green's on the bankroll of the Rios Mexican Drug cartel! You know what, actually I *can* believe it."

"I don't understand," Julie said. "The OFAC Sanctions List has all of these names on there, and it's illegal and prosecutable for any bank in the world to do business with them. In fact, all of their computers are programmed to send an alert to the FBI if any of those names are found in the banks' systems, aren't they?"

"Yeah, but it's not programmed to look for subtle variations, Jules," Rivera answered her. "Look at the names, they're not intact. They're separated by periods and dashes, only the naked eye could catch that and not the algorithms."

"Big word for you to use, Rivera," Simon chuckled. "I'm proud of you."

Rivera shoved him.

Ignoring their banter, Sam pointed to the private security names. "Rivera, tha' name look familiar?"

"If Mebbin is on his bank role … Green must be the guy controlling the smuggling operation I had you looking into; he's who's paying the cops to look the other way on the shipments."

"Aye, and ye can bet tha' every one of these men are in on the ring. He must have them transfer around as his private security to get updates on the shipments and arrange payment in untraceable cash."

"You have to admire the genius of it," Simon added. "Not to mention the irony. The guy is running for president, and his campaign slogan is he's promising to decrease the drugs on the streets. He's in cahoots with one of the biggest drug cartels in Mexico and has access to the shipping, so he follows through on his word while still allowing drugs to flow into the states in smaller numbers."

"That definitely makes him look like the perfect president; he'd get another term easily after that," Julie nodded.

"Aye, and somehow Brian caught on tha' he was up to no good and jus' needed proof," Sam agreed.

"What do you think happened?" Simon asked. "Brian went to confront him, so Green had him killed before he could turn him in?"

"Aye, tha' would explain why he was taking precautions to prepare his daughter for a separation … wait!" He practically pushed the others out of the way as he ran to the mountains of paperwork and searched each page until he found what he was looking for. "Of course! Accordin' to the notes in one of the mercenary encounters, they spoke to someone with a Swedish accent. The man I spoke to was Latino!"

Rivera was shocked. "Sam, are you positive?"

"Aye."

"So, Green just called on his cartel buddies to kill his father-in-law, and they made sure it looked like a copycat hit," Julie said. "But how would they know how to do it just like those mercs did? That information isn't made public."

"I have no doubt the cartel has methods of gettin' information," Sam answered.

"Okay, but how does the texting play into all of this?" Simon asked. "Green has an alibi with the woman he was sleeping with."

"Please," Julie waved her hand nonchalantly. "With how blindly in love that woman is, I have no doubt she'd lie to the ends of the earth for him. Green easily could have sent himself those messages one night when he and Brian were in the same place."

"Then we'll jus' have to confirm tha' alibi with his wife, won't we?" Sam said.

~~~

It was Wednesday at 11:00 a.m., perfectly within visiting hours at the Rehabilitation Center, and no one would have a reason to stop Sam from talking to Liz. He sat on the faux leather couch and tapped his feet on the ground until finally, a nurse approached him, and he stood up.

"We have Mrs. Harper waiting for you in the visitation room of the East Wing," the older woman said sweetly. "Just follow me, please."

She led Sam down the hallway and to the heavy door he remembered. After she scanned her hand, and the door opened, he was led through the hallway that smelled like heavy lavender disinfectant, past the patient cells, to a common room of sorts. There was a couch, a table, a circle of chairs, but only one patient. Liz looked just as haggard as she had a few days prior, but the way she sat on the couch and stared off into space told Sam things were worse than before.
~~~

"You should know, agent, that she had an episode a few days ago," the nurse said as they walked closer. "The poor thing went into a fit of hysterics and got a nasty cut on her head. She had to be restrained and heavily sedated, so she may not be able to answer your questions."

Swallowing the bubbling rage he felt, Sam nodded. "Understood, thank ye."

"Elizabeth, honey? You have a visitor. Agent Sam McKay has come to talk to you."

Liz acted as though she didn't hear a word the nurse said; Sam clenched his fist together and took a deep breath.

"As I said, she's not in a very good state right now. Perhaps you'd like to come back another time?"

"I'm already here, so if ye donnea mind, I'd still like to try and speak with Mrs. Harper."

"Of course. Would you like me to sit in with you?"

"Ach, n'thanks," he replied as calmly as possible. "I'm sure I can handle the wee thing meself."

The nurse chuckled at his quip. "If you need anything, I'll be just down the hall. And if there's any trouble, we'll be able to see it."

The woman pointed to a camera in the corner of the room and left without another word. Sam's eyes flicked back and forth between the position of the camera and the angle that Liz sat in: she was sitting away from the camera so that it couldn't see her face. When her eyes darted to his, he did his best to not let his smile show. "Clever lass."

Liz gave a much more broken smile in return before ever so subtly nodding her head at the seat next to her. He followed her instructions and finally got a look at her worn and tired face. The ugly red mark above her right eye made him want to throw the table across the room, but he kept his wits about him and peered over her head at the camera.

"Your mouth should be blocked at this angle," she said softly.

"Aye, we've go' a minute then."

"Sam ... Alex was here."

"When?"

"Monday morning." Liz took a shuddering breath but kept her posture perfectly still.

"He give ye tha'?" He nodded subtly to the mark.

"Yes."

"Why?"

"Because I attacked him. He told me that you went to his house and threatened him, so he's going to push to have me declared legally insane, so I never get out of here. I lunged at him, and he pushed me into the corner of the cot. Then he called the nurse and …" Liz closed her eyes, and a few tears squeezed out and down her cheeks. "He'll never let me get Natalie back."

Sam leaned forward a little. "I won't le' tha' happen."

Liz took a deep breath before opening her eyes again. "Please, tell me that you found something."

"Aye, a lead on why Brian was murdered."

She sucked in a breath of relief. "Oh, thank God! What happened?"

"I cannea tell ye everythin' Liz, bu' he was investigatin' someone close to him and discovered tha' man was involved in a lo' of illegal activity."

"Okay, so what does this mean for me?"

"It means yer story has much more weight now, and once we prove it, ye can appeal yer sentence."

The smile Liz had on her face quickly faded. "With what lawyer that Alex doesn't own? I don't have any money, Sam. And by all outward appearances, Alex has done everything he can for me by getting me in here and keeping me out of prison."

Though he knew that she was right, he was not about to let her give up hope. He couldn't tell if it was the toxic smell of disinfectant or the maddening blank white walls that were making his mind race, but still he tried to think of everything he could do that would help Liz. Finally, the memory of the bald man he'd arrested came to mind.

"Christ, of course!" he hissed under his breath.

Liz flinched at his words but looked at him curiously.

"Liz, tell me who it was ye were talkin' to tha' day in the alley."

She furrowed her eyes at him. "Gabriel. His name's Gabriel. But what does he have to do with this?"

"Gabriel who?"

"I don't know his last name."

"How do ye know him?"

She looked down at her hands. "He's the one who helped me and

Natalie disappear.”

“Wha’ were ye talkin’ to him about?”

“He was collecting his payment for a new ID.”

“Wha’ for?”

Liz looked up at him, and Sam could see the shame in her eyes as she answered, “… I was getting ready to run again. Sam … what happened between us … I thought I was letting my guard down and … it’s just that bad things have happened whenever I let my guard down. I’m sorry.”

Sam didn’t react beyond a blink. “I caugh’ him tryin’ ta smash yer car an’ arrested him.”

“What? Why would he do that?”

“At first I though’ ye hired him to do it to make sure ye looked innocent, bu’ now I think he was hired by whoever killed Cairne to do it. How did ye find him?”

“Actually, he found me. After Brian died and I was fired, I started to panic. I still had contact with some people that used to … supply me when Daniel and I were using, and I asked if any of them knew someone who was good at faking IDs. Nobody did, but then one day when Natalie and I were coming back to the last night at the hotel, I found a note slid under the door with a phone number on it. I called, and he said his name was Gabriel, and he could help me get a new identity. I was running out of time, and I didn’t know what else to do, so I hired him.”

“And he helped ye to disappear the next day?”

“Yeah,” Liz nodded gently. “I went to the bank and closed my account. We met at the Stamford Museum; he gave me the new ID, and I gave him cash. Then we hopped on a bus, I got Natalie settled, and I headed off to Florida. A few months later my car was vandalized, and I had to call him again. But … you’re saying Alex had him following me from the beginning?”

“Is’ possible,” He nodded. “And now tha’ I have a reason to look into him, we can find out. Donnea worry, I promised ye I’d fix this, an’ I will.”

Liz’s sad smile made his heart ache, and he took both of her hands in his enormous one.

She didn’t look at him. “… Are you mad at me? For trying to run again.”

“Mad, no,” he answered too quickly and she looked in his eyes.

"... Alrigh', perhaps a wee bit. Bu' I understand why, and I cannea fault ye for tryin' to be cautious. I jus' wish ye trusted me."

"I do."

Liz curled her hands up and laced her fingers through his. When she began to stroke the top of his hand with her thumb, he closed his eyes and sighed. "... I wish I could kiss ye right now."

She smiled sadly, "Me too."

Sam glanced back up at the camera again and playfully weighed just how much of a risk he would be taking if he caved in and kissed her, if only for a moment, when he heard the sounds of footsteps coming closer, and he quickly pulled away. The old nurse reappeared, "I'm afraid that is all the time I can permit today, agent. Mrs. Harper needs to return to her room and rest now."

"Aye," he nodded before turning his attention back to Liz. "Thank ye for yer time, Mrs. Harper. Get well soon."

Liz didn't react beyond a blink, and Sam took that as her goodbye. After the old woman escorted him back out of the facility and to the door; he made quick work to call the old Sherriff's department in Mineral Wells and was pleased to discover that Gabriel hadn't been processed yet. Then he quickly called Rivera and said, "Oi, the man tha' I arrested for destroyin' Liz's cars hasnea made bail, and his court date is no' for another two weeks. Go get him."

Chapter Twenty-Two

Rivera and Julie escorted Gabriel into a holding cell at Cleveland's Third District Police Department, Sam's friend and colleague Chief Humbar's department. Sam was already there and waiting in the observation room. When the bald man with unkept facial hair was cuffed to the table, Rivera and Julie walked out the door and into the observation room where Sam and the stocky Chief Humbar stood watching the suspect through the glass.

"His name's Gabriel Hayes." Rivera handed a file to Sam (who looked it over while he continued to speak). "No record, guy's pretty much a law-abiding citizen. Recently divorced, father of three, got a house in Shaker Heights, worked at a little accounting firm until he was recently let go. The secretary at the Sheriff's department was more than accommodating when I asked her for the file, but I did have to listen to a bit of crap to get it."

Sam smirked. "Aye, Trish's a talker. How long do we have?"

"I can let you have the room for a few hours for now," Humbar said.

"Can you keep him in lockup for tonight, if we don't get him to crack?" Rivera asked.

"He's technically in FBI custody, but I can give you two nights before somebody has to take him."

"Alright, if we have to, I'll get him into my facility," Rivera nodded.

Sam kept his eyes trained on the man in the room; he took note of how his eyes shifted all around him, his tense posture, even the way he held his hands suggested that he was more than nervous.

"I don't think it'll take that long to crack him," Julie said. "I mean look at him, his body language suggests that he's guilty of something, and he's just itching for it to be over. Hell, he doesn't even look like the criminal type."

"No, he doesn't," Sam agreed. "Julie's gonna' join me in the interrogation."

"Really?" Rivera asked somewhat annoyed. "After I just spent eight hours in a car dragging his ass here?"

Julie smacked his arm. "You mean *we* spent eight hours in a car dragging his ass here."

Sam interrupted their banter. "He frequently made contact with Liz, which suggests he's go' a soft spot for the ladies. If two men go in there, he's gonna' feel trapped." Sam turned to Julie. "He'll look at you like a savior. Jus' be sure to act sweet and understandin', aye?"

"Got it, boss," Julie smiled. "You leading?"

"No, technically I'm jus' a citizen, and yer the official. Ye'll lead, bu' … le's give 'im a minute to sweat, then we'll take a shot at 'im."

"Well, since we're gonna' be here for a while, might as well get some coffee."

"Sorry to tell you guys that it's still as horrible as ever," Humbar chuckled as he opened the door for them.

As Julie followed Humbar to the mess, Sam turned to Rivera and said, "Tell Simon I wanna know everythin' abou' this man. Who he is, wha' he loves, and how the hell he's connected to Alexander Michaels."

"What? I thought we were going after Green?"

"We are, bu' is' all fer naught if Liz is locked up. Jus' ge' started, alrigh'?"

"Yeah, you got it," Rivera nodded.

Sam was nearly finished with his coffee by the time Gabriel Hayes looked ready to explode. Still handcuffed to the table, he kept rubbing at his wrists as well as he could, and beads of sweat were peppering the top of his bald head. What interested Sam was that he refused to look at the two-way mirror during the entire time he sat in the room waiting for something to happen. Hayes would look all around him, mostly at his hands, but never at the mirror.

"Why doesnea he look at the mirror?" Sam wondered aloud.

"Because he's guilty of something, and he knows that we know it," Rivera said absently.

"No no, look at 'im: he's shiftin' about like he's more than uncomfortable …"

Julie joined him at his side. "… Maybe he has anxiety, like officially diagnosed. He's in a high-pressure situation, so his senses are on overdrive. Pay attention to whether or not he looks us in the eye, and try not to be loud when we talk to him.”

“Aye,” Sam nodded. “Ye ready?”

“After you,” Julie gestured to the door.

Folder of evidence in hand, Sam opened the door to the interrogation room and took a seat at the table across from the very nervous Gabriel Hayes. Julie joined him and had a kind, albeit tiny smile pasted on her face. Gabriel took a look at her and relaxed his shoulders somewhat.

“Gabriel Hayes,” she said sweetly. “I’m Agent Julie Russell, and this is my partner and observer, Mr. Sam McKay. I believe you two know each other.”

“Do ye remember the first time we met?” Sam asked him gruffly.

Gabriel gulped, “… Yes …”

“I caught ye preparin’ to vandalize this woman’s car.” Sam took out a picture of Liz and placed it on the table. “But I also saw ye talkin’ to her in the alleyway no’ an hour before tha’. Now, accordin’ to her, ye supplied her with false identities. And then ye turn around and destroy her car? Curious. Care to fill in the rest of the blanks for us?”

Gabriel gulped again and shook his head. “Nope.”

“Come on, Gabe,” Julie said sweetly. “You don’t have a record of any kind. From what I’ve seen, you’ve been a pretty upstanding guy since the day you were born. If you help us, we can help you. We can make sure none of this sees the light of day. You’ll go back to a normal life. All you have to do is tell us why you planned to wreck this woman’s car.”

Gabriel looked back down again and shook his head.

“Wha’ about Scotland?”

That seemed to get the bald man’s attention, as his eyes flitted up to Sam’s before looking back down again.

“And there’s Florida and New York as well,” Julie continued. “Gabe, we know all about it.”

Gabriel took a deep breath. “I don’t have anything to say to you.”

“Come on. We’re talkin’ abou’ vandalizin’ cars here, tha’ can be erased from yer record with our say-so. We know ye were put up to it by this man: Alexander Michaels.”

Sam laid out another photo. Gabriel glanced down before returning to look at his hands.

“We jus’ wanna know when he contacted ye and why. How does

an accountant ge' involved with a man like tha? Why would he pay ye to harass his stepdaughter?"

"We're your best chance here, Gabe," Julie added. "Please take our offer, and let us help you."

Gabriel sat quietly before shaking his head again and keeping his focus on his hands.

~~~

Rivera watched the scene in the interrogation room with annoyance; convinced that Sam's plan of attack was a mistake, he wanted to walk in there and raise a ruckus to make the suspect talk. Every question asked would only be answered with a 'no' or a 'nope' or just a shake of his head. It was starting to drive Rivera crazy, and he had all but made up his mind to barge in there, when his phone started buzzing. He pulled it out to see Simon's name on the screen.

"Hey, what did you find?"

"Absolutely nothing that connects Alexander Michaels to Gabriel Hayes. No phone records, no bank payments, they don't even live within ten miles of each other."

"So, we've got nothing, is what you're saying?"

"I didn't say that," Simon chuckled. "On a hunch, I decided to look for anything that might connect Hayes to our dirty Congressman, and guess what? It turns out Gabriel Hayes and Jackson Green went to the same high school and were even on the same basketball team. Outside of that, they don't run in the same circles. Heck, they don't even have the same bank. He's got a sealed juvi record, and I'm working on getting in it as we speak. But I did find something else interesting: over the last eighteen months, Hayes made four pretty hefty deposits of about $7,500 each, and then he purchasesd a plane ticket right after each deposit. He's been to New York, Florida, Scotland, and then this last one he was in Mineral Wells."

"So, we can prove that wherever Liz was, he went."

"Pretty much. Knowing that they knew each other, I did a search on Green's personal financials of any withdrawals for the same amount and found four as well. The withdrawals and the deposits were all done within two days of each other, but it was all cash, so there's no way to technically prove that Green paid Hayes anything
~~~

at all. It could be just a coincidence.”

“Well, it’s a start anyways. Thanks, Simon.” Rivera hung up the phone and knocked on the window to the interrogation room before walking out to meet Sam and Julie in the hallway. “It’s not Michaels, Sam. Green’s the guy that’s been paying him.”

Sam leaned back in complete surprise. “Wha’? Are ye sure?”

“Positive. Simon found a money trail that proves Hayes harassed Liz everywhere she went, and there are withdrawals of the same amount from Green’s personal accounts that line up. The only problem is it was all cash, so there’s no way to prove that Green was paying Hayes without a confession.”

“Anythin’ else?” Sam asked.

“Hayes has got a juvenile record that Simon’s trying to crack as we speak, and he and Green were on the same high school basketball team. Doesn’t look like they’ve had had any contact since then, though.”

“Except when Green called him up to harass Liz after he murdered his father-in-law,” Julie said disdainfully. “But Hayes won’t admit that, unless we can pick everything apart until we’re all he’s got left to run to. What do you wanna do here, boss?”

Sam sighed. “Have Humbar put him in lockup fer the night, maybe spendin’ some time with more seasoned criminals will scare him into talkin’ to us tomorrow. Then everyone go home and ge’ some sleep, and we’ll start again in the mornin’.”

They all nodded when Rivera spotted the familiar snowy white hair that belonged to Director Copper; she was behind Sam and walking into the precinct.

“Shit,” he hissed under his breath and Sam furrowed his eyes. “Sam, don’t turn around. Walk past me and wait in the men’s room.”

“Wha’ the hell for?”

“Copper’s here,” Rivera answered evenly. “Go.”

Sam took a deep breath and strode away as inconspicuously as he could, cursing his height for making it harder to be incognito than normal.

The moment Rivera saw the FBI Director walk through the door with her company tailing her, he knew that she was there to arrest Sam. The Director looked around before making eye contact with Rivera, and she strode over.

“Follow my lead,” Rivera whispered to Julie and she nodded.

"Director Copper, what can I do for you, ma'am?"

"Where is he, Rivera?" The Director asked evenly.

"Who, ma'am?"

"Don't play games with me; you know damn well who."

"I'm afraid that I really don't, ma'am."

The Director narrowed her eyes at him. "Sam McKay, the man you brought in to go undercover, the man we deported, who apparently is illegally back in the states."

Rivera mocked a surprise expression. "Ma'am? Sam's never done an illegal thing in his life. As far as I know, he's back in Scotland where you shipped him off to."

Director Copper looked over at Julie who quickly added. "Haven't seen him since the day we arrested that woman. What was her name again?"

"You certain that's how you want to answer, Miss Russel?"

"Yes ma'am," Julie said quickly, defiantly.

Director Copper kept her eyes trained on Julie for a long moment before she turned her attention back to Rivera. "Then perhaps you can explain a phone call to me made by Alexander Michaels? Something about two of our agents, Rivera and McKay, came to his house to harass him?"

"That is odd, ma'am."

Rivera held his ground as the Director tried to stare him down, until the finally the woman straightened her posture and leaned forward to tell him softly, "Sampson Angus McKay is now here illegally and will face severe consequences when we find him. I suggest you remember what consequences will be in store for you when that happens."

The older woman turned and marched back out the door.

Rivera turned to Julie (who released the breath she had been holding) and sighed. "We're runnin' out of time here, and now Sam's got the FBI after him."

"He won't leave until he solves this, Derrick; you know that as well as I do."

"Yeah," he ran his hand over the back of his neck. "Damn stubborn Scotsman."

Julie nodded. "We'd better get him out of here before the Director decides to search the place. I'll go get the car and meet you out back."

"Right," he nodded and turned to the men's room.

~~~

The following morning didn't prove to be anymore fruitful with Gabriel, and Sam was starting to lose his patience; no matter how much evidence they presented, insisting that they knew Green had hired Hayes and that the Congressman would do nothing to help him, their witness refused to say a word. Sam was about ready to explode upon the unrelentingly quiet man, when Julie suggested they take another break. Watching his only link being escorted back to a holding cell again, Sam rubbed his face and pinched the bridge of his nose as he tried to think about what else they could try to get Gabriel Hayes to talk to them.

"I'm telling you, the calm approach isn't working," Rivera said, his frustration getting the better of him. "Let me go in there, and I'll get him to sing like a canary."

"And risk him filing police brutality charges while your boss is watching our every move? Yeah, that's a great plan, Derrick," Julie said.

"Well, you batting your eyelashes at him every two minutes certainly isn't getting us anywhere."

"Unless ye've got somethin' constructive to say, will the two of ye shu-up?" Sam barked.

Rivera and Julie glared at one another but kept their mouths closed as Sam kept rubbing his eyes.

Rivera's phone buzzed. "… My contact says that's she's found out who took the photos, and she's trying to figure out who hired him for us."

"How?" Julie asked.

Rivera smirked. "She has her ways."

His remark made Julie bristle, but she quickly composed herself before anyone could notice. "So, what do we do now? We've only got one more day with Hayes before he has to be transferred somewhere, and we haven't made any headway with him."

Sam sighed. "Wha' doesnea make sense is why Green would keep harassin' Liz after gettin' away with the murder … maybe we need to put a little more pressure on the man himself."

"What are you thinking?"
~~~

"His political career is havin' a good run, bu' a scandal would ruin it, and he'll never be able to recover."

"With how much money that guy has, all of the stuff Sway gave us will be picked apart by his lawyers: illegally obtained evidence. And our only link to Liz is refusing to talk," Julie said.

"I'm talkin' abou' Green's wife."

Rivera eyed him curiously. "What do you suggest? She already confirmed that her husband was out just about every night during his campaign."

"Yeah," Julie nodded her agreement. "And I doubt she'd do anything to incriminate her husband."

"Maybe tha's because she donnea know he's been sleepin' around on her. Never underestimate the power of a woman scorned."

While Julie rolled her eyes at his quip, Rivera looked at Sam uncertainly. "Who's to say that she'll believe us?"

"Why would we lie?" Sam countered.

"Look, boss, going after a presidential candidate with what we've got is a one-way trip. And if we're wrong, and Mrs. Green doesn't cooperate, our careers are over."

"Not to mention what will happen if the FBI catches you," Julie added. "I highly doubt the Director will cut you some slack this time."

"You le' me worry abou' meself," Sam answered defensively. "And yer FBI, Rivera, ye've go' some pull and can convince the Director to look deeper into Green's dealin's. Bu' this is abou' solvin' a murder and provin' Liz's innocence. Now go ge' Mrs. Green."

Sam walked away from Julie and Rivera who, reluctantly, headed towards the car without another word.

~~~

Georgia Green had just finished cooking some pasta for dinner when the doorbell rang. Setting aside the marinara sauce, she opened the door and was surprised to see the two agents who told her that her father had been murdered on the other side of it. They asked her to come to the Third Precinct. Thankfully, Beni hadn't gone home yet and had agreed to stay with the boys until she got back. Now sitting on a less than comfortable and ugly couch, she was sipping a cup of
~~~

terrible coffee as the man named Rivera sat in the chair opposite of her.

"Agent, could you please tell me what this is all about? I thought I had answered all of your questions in regards to my husband's whereabouts."

Rivera presented a picture of Rosie Newt and laid it on the coffee table. Georgia eyed it and felt her stomach begin to clench. Though she already knew what they were going to ask, it still hurt to hear it. "Mrs. Green, do you know who this woman is?"

"Yes," she answered without hesitation. "That's Rosie Newt, my husband's Campaign Manager … and yes, they were sleeping together."

The two agents looked at each other in surprise, until Julie cleared her throat. "Mrs. Green, may I ask why you didn't tell us about this before?"

"I didn't think it was relevant," she answered quietly. "And because, as far as I knew, Jackson had stopped sleeping around about a year ago. He started to spend more time with me and the kids; he was bringing me flowers; he just … was acting so differently. I thought it was all done, and we could move on with our lives."

"So, you never told him that you knew?"

"No … look, agents, I know what you're thinking, that it's ridiculous for me to stay with my husband even knowing that he was cheating on me."

"It's not our business to judge that, Mrs. Green," Julie said kindly. "But … we do have to tell you that your husband has now become the prime suspect in our murder investigation."

Georgia snapped her head up. "What? What are you talking about?"

"Before your father was murdered, did he talk to you about your husband at all? Say anything unusual?" Rivera asked.

She thought hard and shook her head. "No, not that I'm aware of. I mean, like I told you before, he was acting a little odd at a particular Sunday dinner, but he insisted that it was work stuff."

"How did you and your husband meet?"

"We went to the same high school; a mutual friend of ours was having a party."

"What do you know about his job at En Passant Bank?" Julie

asked.

"Not much … Agents, could you please explain to me what any of this has to do with my dad's murder?"

Rivera and Julie had a silent conversation with each other again, until Rivera finally answered. "Your father hired someone to do some digging on your husband and found a lot of illegal activity."

"What kind of illegal activity?"

"It's a bit tricky to explain," Julie answered her. "But the sum-up is that your husband is working with some very dangerous people in Mexico."

Georgia gaped at them. "… Drugs? You're saying that my husband is involved with drugs?"

"Not necessarily the buying and selling part, but he is doing money laundering and shipment with them."

Georgia sat there in shock as she tried to process everything that was being told to her.

"Mrs. Green, I know that this must be difficult for you," Rivera said. "But we believe that after your father found out about this, he intended to confront your husband and turn him in to the authorities. He had even set up those two new trusts for you and your sons just in case things didn't go the right way. Unfortunately, he was killed, so it didn't pan out."

Though she could barely hear the words being said to her, Georgia wiped away the tears that were threatening to fall and looked back up at the agents to ask "What trusts?"

"The trusts that the manager of your father's bank told you about after your father died."

"I don't know anything about any new trusts."

"Are you positive? You didn't receive a letter or notice in the mail about them?"

"Agents, my sons and I already have rather large trust funds from my father. Why would he give us more? And why would I only get access to them, in particular, after he was killed?"

Rivera and Julie looked at one another before back to Georgia, who continued: "Look, this is a lot to take in, and I need to process it … would you mind giving me a few minutes, please?"

"Of course," Julie nodded. "Please let us know if you need coffee or anything."

After they had closed the door behind them, Georgia dropped her head in her hands and began to sob uncontrollably.

Sam watched everything through the window; Georgia reacted as could be expected from a woman who received such devastating news, and there was no hint that she had any clue about her husband's doings. Sam couldn't help but feel optimistic that she might help them. Still, he was going crazy not having any answers and decided he would try and interrogate Hayes again for the tenth time. Turning to the nearest officer, he instructed him to retrieve his suspect again, which he did almost instantly. As the suspect was led to the interrogation room, Sam was busy getting himself a cup of coffee, when he noticed Georgia Green staring through the window. Sam looked over to Hayes as he was being escorted to the observation room; the man was normally shifty and kept his head down, but his eyes never left Georgia Green's as he walked. Sam's mouth dropped open in realization. *No, it cannea be tha' simple ...* but the way the two people looked at one another stated perfectly clear that it was: they knew each other.

Chapter Twenty-Three

Georgia Green was looking all around the interrogation room as Sam and his team discussed her.

"Boss, she could have just been curious about Hayes and that's why she was looking," Julie insisted.

"The entire time we've had Hayes in custody, he hasnea done more than admire me shoes," Sam argued. "No, they know each other, and this cannea be a coincidence."

Rivera's phone buzzed. "… Simon got into the juvi record on Hayes, and it turns out he got caught making and selling fake IDs way back in the day. Did a little community service for his sentence, and he's never stepped out of line since."

"Well, tha' explains how he could help Liz, bu' it doesnea tell us *why* he went out of his way to find her."

"And you think Georgia knows why?" Julie asked.

"I think we havenea been askin' her the right questions. The two of ye get in there and ask them, and we'll find out whether or not I'm right."

Knowing they wouldn't be able to argue with him, Julie and Rivera looked at one another before nodding and entering the room. The Congressman's wife appeared eager to know why she was suddenly moved to a much less friendly room and waited for the two of them to make an explanation. Rivera presented a small stack of papers in front of her.

"Mrs. Green, can you please confirm for the record that these are your personal financial statements dating back over the last year?"

The woman looked down at the papers placed in front of her and nodded. "Yes, I believe so."

Julie then presented a photo of Hayes. "And do you know this man?"

Georgia was visibly unnerved; Sam stared at her intently and held his breath, waiting for an explanation.

"Yes," she finally answered.

Sam sighed in relief. *I knew it.*

"How do you know him?"

"Gabriel and I used to date in high school; then we broke up and I met Jackson."

"Have you had any contact with him since then?"

Georgia looked down at her hands and sighed. "Yes … about two years ago I was out shopping … I had figured out that Jackson was having an affair, and I went to clear my head, trying to think of what to do. I stopped to buy a coffee, and Gabriel saw me and said hello. He was going through a divorce with his wife, and we just sort of … bonded over our misery." Georgia sucked in a shaky breath. "We met for coffee a few more times after that, and … suddenly it was like we were back in high school again. I felt happier than I had in years every time I was with Gabe."

"You were having an affair?"

"Yes," she nodded, a tear slipping from her eye.

"Are you still having an affair?"

"No, I ended it about six months ago. After Jackson finally started behaving differently, and his affair was over, I was still angry with him, but I didn't want to leave him. I saw what Gabe's divorce was doing to his kids; I didn't want to do that to my sons. But after six months … I just knew I couldn't keep doing it. Jackson was legitimately trying, and I felt I owed it to our sons to try with him."

"Mrs. Green, were you giving Gabriel Hayes money?"

"Yes, sometimes."

"Could you tell us what for?"

"Shortly after my father died, Gabe lost his job. He had alimony payments he had to make to his wife, and I offered to help."

"And your husband never noticed?"

Georgia scoffed and shook her head. "At the time, I would have had to walk around wearing a necklace worth a million dollars for Jackson to object to anything that I was doing. And after dad's company was left to me, I'd had more than enough money, so it really didn't matter. I wanted to help him."

"Always in cash?"

"Yeah," she nodded. "I could convince Jackson that I was making cash charity deposits; we didn't want to risk him finding out about us."

"So … you had an affair with him, but you didn't want your

husband to know that you were giving him money?" Julie asked incredulously.

Georgia sighed. "Agent Russell, all I know is that I had someone who made me feel happy again, and I didn't want to share that with anyone … not even my boys knew."

Rivera gave Julie a look before clearing his throat. "Mrs. Green, can you think of any reason why Gabriel was harassing Elizabeth Harper?"

"What are you talking about?"

Julie pulled out the financial statements of Hayes and showed her the highlighted amounts. "These deposits match the amount of money you were giving to Hayes, then he would turn around and use it to fly out to where Elizabeth was."

"What for?"

"To scare her, then he'd turn around and make a new ID for her."

Georgia stared at the paperwork for a moment before shaking her head. "I had no idea he would do that."

"What do you mean 'do that'?"

Rivera leaned onto his elbows. "Tell us what you know, Mrs. Green."

"Dad had just come over for a visit, and I saw a package sitting by the door addressed to Jackson with no return address. That's not unusual, most of the time it's just business-related. So I opened it, expecting to find paperwork or something, and I found these pictures of my dad and this woman in a hotel room. Not naked pictures or anything like that, it just looked like they were talking. I couldn't understand why they were addressed to Jackson, but I asked my dad about them after the boys had gone to bed, and he insisted it wasn't anything to worry about."

Rivera quickly pulled out a copy of the photo of Liz and Brian Cairne and placed it in front of her. "Is this the picture, Mrs. Green?"

Her eyes opened wide. "Yes, but … h-how did you get this?"

"What did you do with the photos?"

"Gabe and I were meeting up a few days later, and I showed them to him; we were just wondering what they meant. Then I put them away, and that was the end of it."

"Did you give these photos to your husband?"

"Yes … I sealed them in a new package and sent them to us again, thought it might be better if he didn't think I was snooping through his mail. I tried to ask dad about them again, but he just told me everything was fine, and there was nothing scandalous about the photos. He insisted I drop it. I trusted him, so I did.”

“Mrs. Green, did you ever tell your husband about these photos in false pretense?”

Georgia furrowed her eyes. “How do you mean?”

“Just in passing, a phone call, maybe even a text from somebody else’s phone?” Julie asked.

Georgia shook her head. “No, nothing like that. I just left the pictures alone after sending them to Jackson again.”

“Alright. Getting back to Hayes, why do you think he went after Elizabeth Harper?”

“I honestly don’t know. After dad was killed, I ran to Gabe, and he told me everything would be alright. Shortly after that, he told me he’d been laid off and needed some help. I had no idea he planned to use it to harass this woman.”

Sam’s mind reeled as he thought about everything Georgia was saying. Knowing he finally had some leverage to use, he quickly exited and told the nearest officer to bring Hayes into another interrogation room. Once the bald man was handcuffed to the table, Sam walked in with confidence.

“I get it Gabe; you donnea want to do anythin’ to hurt her; ye love her.”

His statement caused Gabriel to look up.

“Georgia Green, yer in love with her.”

Gabriel kept staring.

“Ye only wanted to help her, right? Ye pieced together tha’ somehow Liz was important to wha’ happened to her father, and ye wanted to ease her burden somehow. Did ye think tha’ findin’ Liz, ye could get some answers?”

Gabriel breathed heavily, but Sam kept his eyes trained on him, daring him to answer. Finally, Gabriel nodded and mumbled. “Yes.”

“Ye made fake ID’s when ye were a kid, and somehow ye go’ wind tha’ Liz needed to disappear, and ye put yer skills to use once again. Ye created a whole new identity for her and helped her disappear, right?”

“Yes.”

“Yer no’ a killer, Gabriel, I can see tha’. Bu’ ye did want some justice for Georgia.”

"Yes."

"Ye thought tha' by scarin' Elizabeth, ye'd be punishin' her for wha'ever she did to Brian."

"Yes."

Sam smiled inwardly, feeling his triumph. "How did ye find Liz, Gabe? Did Alexander Michaels help ye?"

Gabriel looked at him confused and shook his head. "I swear I don't know who that is."

The hopeful feeling Sam had in his chest was gone instantly.

"A few days after Georgia told me about her dad's death, I was on my way to work when I noticed a hotel that looked familiar and then I saw this woman who resembled the one in the pictures from behind. … I did a little investigating on her, and when I saw that she worked at Cairne Steel, I figured she had to be the woman that was in the photos with Brian. After she was fired and needed a new ID, I worked out which hotel room she was in and left my number for her."

Sam stared at him intently. "And yer sure ye never had any contact with a man named Alexander Michaels? Never ran into him fer coffee? Never had a complete stranger say somethin' to ye tha' inspired ye to take action?"

"No," Gabriel shook his head. "No, I swear, nothing like that."

Sam gave a frustrated sigh and rubbed his face with his hand. "Did ye ever tell Georgia ye were doin' this?"

"No, I knew she'd tell me to stop and that it wouldn't help anything. Georgia isn't a vengeful person, Mr. McKay. Even when … Please," Gabriel asked quietly. "Do you know why this woman was meeting with Brian?"

Deciding it couldn't harm anything to tell the man the truth, Sam answered. "She's his daughter; he'd jus' found out and was tryin' to tell her."

Gabriel opened his eyes in shock. "Does Georgia know?"

"No' yet."

"You better tell her, she wanted to know who that woman was more than I did. What's going to happen to me now?"

Sam eyed the bald man for a moment, trying to decide how much harm he had actually caused, before answering. "Yer court date's in a couple weeks. Ye'll probably pay a fine for damaging the car and runnin' from an officer, then ye ge' to go home."

Without another word, he got up and left the dead-end witness in the room. Julie and Rivera were standing outside of their own interrogation room as Mrs. Green was leaving the precinct.

"She say anythin' else?"

"Nothing useful," Julie shook her head. "Just kept saying she had no idea that Hayes was using her money to harass Liz."

"You get anywhere with him now?" Rivera asked.

"He finally broke down and talked ta' me, bu' he jus' corroborated her story," Sam shook his head. "Poor numpty was only tryin' to give the woman he loves a little justice the bes' way he knew how."

"Well, I don't think Mrs. Green will be a Mrs. much longer after learning that her husband is responsible for her father's death."

Sam nodded his agreement. Julie was staring out in front of her, deep in thought, and he nudged her. "Wha's up?"

"I was just thinking about what Georgia said: she didn't know anything about the new trust funds and Brian's been dead for almost two years. She should have heard *something* about them by now, shouldn't she?"

"Aye," Sam nodded.

"A bank manager at En Passant could very easily be on the Congressman's payroll," Rivera turned to Julie. "How much do you want to bet the bank manager lied to us about the accounts?"

"I'd love to go charge Hughes with obstruction of Justice," she smiled.

"Go," Sam nodded. "And call me as soon as ye ge' answers."

~~~

Julie and Rivera arrived at En Passant Bank just before the lunch hour, only to be informed that the manager had called in sick a few days before and hadn't been to work since then. Fearing he had fled the country, they raced to his apartment on the Eastern Banks and hoped they were wrong.

Rivera pounded on the door. "Richard Hughes, it's the FBI, open up!"

No one answered.

Rivera withdrew his gun and Julie followed suit. Taking a step backwards, Rivera kicked the door open, and they entered to find a
~~~

ransacked apartment: furniture was overturned, broken glass littered the floor, cabinets were flung open, and various items had been thrown about.

"This doesn't look like the work of someone who was trying to make a quick getaway," Julie noted as they assessed the damage.

"No kidding," Rivera nodded. "Not unless he was particularly attached to his coffee maker and packed it with the rest of his stuff."

"Do you think he was trying to stage a robbery?"

Rivera opened the bedroom door and stopped to cover his nose when the smell of decay hit him. Looking in, he saw the body of the bank manager lying on the floor with a bullet wound in his forehead. "No, I'm pretty sure he was a hit."

Julie walked over to him and had to stop herself from retching from the smell. Finally composed, she saw the body and shook her head. "Green's taking care of every loose end."

"Call 911," Rivera nodded as he brought his phone up to his ear. "… We were too late, Sam. Green got to him first, Hughes is dead."

~~~

Back in Sam's hotel room, the team sat in silence as they watched Sam pace back and forth, deep in thought; his arms folded and his eyes glaring into the space before him, he looked like a bull ready to charge if anyone crossed him. Back and forth he paced until finally, Simon was brave enough to clear his throat.

"Look, boss, we've got enough here, we could at least convince the FBI to look into Green. And once this gets on the news, he'll be looked at under a microscope. Somebody will definitely find something to charge him with."

"Bu' no' murder," Sam growled. "And Liz will still be in jail."

"Boss," Julie said. "Think about this for a second: even if we *do* prove he ordered the hit on Cairne, how exactly will that help Liz anyway? The murder charges were thrown out of court, she's being held for kidnapping."

"And given her history of drug abuse, along with how well Michaels has covered his tracks, it's unlikely to be appealed," Rivera added. "Look Sam, we started this so we could un-deport you. This has to be enough to at least do that."

Sam finally stopped pacing and glared at all three of them. "So yer
~~~

sayin' we shoul' quit while we're ahead."

"Nobody's quitting—"

"I'm disappointed in all of ye," Sam continued. "Ye know damn well tha' Liz is innocent, and Brian's been murdered; hell, the whole family has been wronged! And yer tellin' me tha' we've done enough? I donnea accept tha'!"

While Julie and Simon stared at their feet in shame, Rivera walked over and stood in Sam's path. Despite the fact that Sam still cleared him in height by nearly a foot, Rivera held his ground and snarled. "Let me remind you that Simon was the one who discovered it was murder in the first place. And Julie has used all of her free time to try and find a way to help clear your name."

"This isnea abou' me, Rivera."

"Yes, it is! And every single one of us has been here every minute of the day because you asked us to. All of us have put our careers— our *lives*—in jeopardy because you said there was more to this. We found more, Sam. And we'll continue to find more once we take a step back to think. We're not quitting, but maybe you should take a minute to recognize what all of us have been willing to do for you. Until you can do that, we're done."

Rivera turned towards Simon and Julie and ushered them to the door, to which they obeyed quietly. Completely alone in his room, Sam stood dumbfounded and lost in his tracks. He sat down on the bed and dropped his head in his hands. Though he didn't want to admit it, he knew that Rivera had a good point. Since they had worked and schemed to get him back to the USA and solve this case, not once had he even said thank you to any of them. Blinded by anger, stress, and the desire to help the woman he'd come to care for, he couldn't see the path in front of him anymore. He couldn't help but wonder if he'd strayed away from the path some time ago. Sampson Angus McKay was supposed to be a fair, compassionate but stern, smart man. And in that moment, he certainly didn't feel like any of those things.

Chapter Twenty-Four

Rivera stood on the balcony of his apartment and took a deep inhale of his cigarette, his mind split between his loyalty and his anger. He was due for another surveillance assignment in two days, and he knew he couldn't ask anyone in his department to cover for him any longer, or else the Director would have his head. The fight with Sam was giving him all the more reason to go and leave his friend (though he wasn't sure he would have called him that at that moment) hanging with the remainder of this case. Taking another puff, he closed his eyes and savored the nicotine, when his doorbell rang. It was almost midnight, and he couldn't think of anyone who would want to talk to him this late. Setting his cigarette down on the balcony, he walked over and opened the door, only to be surprised to see Julie on the other side of it.

"Hey," she said softly.

"Hi."

"Can I come in?"

He stepped to the side and allowed her to enter before returning to the balcony and his abandoned cigarette.

"I thought you stopped smoking a few years ago?"

"Yeah, well, I think the events of the last few weeks give me a good reason to indulge," he answered by taking another puff.

Julie leaned against the door with her arms crossed and stared out at the city lights.

After a beat, Rivera asked. "Something on your mind, Jules?"

"Nothing important."

"Tell me anyway; I think we could use 'not important' right now."

She smirked. "I was thinking how your angry side is one of the things I like about you."

He laughed and took another puff.

"And I wanted to say thank you … for being so patient with all of us … me especially."

"I think you're the first person to ever use the word 'patient' as part of my description."

He finally got a real laugh out of her and smiled heartily. But the moment was over quickly, and they both looked back out to the lights again. The one thing Rivera truly liked about Julie was that there were no awkward moments between them, not even in their fights, and he was particularly thankful for that as they stood there in comfortable silence on the balcony. Just as he took another puff, he felt Julie come up behind him and slip her arms around his waist. He froze as she leaned her head down against his back and sighed deeply, making it impossible to ignore the way her body was curving against his. Knowing this was as close to an apology as he would ever get from her, he had half a mind to turn around and lead her to his bedroom, when his phone started to ring.

"Perfect timing," he grumbled to himself and growled into the phone. "Rivera."

"Did you miss me?" Hadley's voice purred, and he was instantly alert. Julie leaned away from him and he cleared his throat.

"I was beginning to wonder if you were keeping my photos for ransom."

"Ha! I'd never do that to you," she giggled. "But enough foreplay, I tracked down your photographer. The pictures were taken by a PI named Adam Trevors. His office is in Asiatown on Payne and 36th."

"And what do you think of him?"

"Bit of an idiot, way over his head. But then again, he's only in his twenties. I did a little digging and found out that he couldn't pass the psych eval to be a cop, so he became a PI instead."

"Think he'll crack if we put a little pressure on him?"

"Oh, honey, there's no need for that. I took the liberty of finding out who hired him for this job for you. You're looking for a woman named Maria Juarez. Ring any bells?"

"Not to me, we haven't had anyone by that name pop up in this investigation. You didn't by any chance get a description of her from him?"

"Like I said, he's an idiot. He apparently has this new thing he's trying out: online ordering to help his clients feel a little bit more private. That was the name on the order, and he was instructed to mail the pictures to a P.O. box, which he did only after receiving the full payment plus extra for not doing the meet and greet. In my seasoned opinion, it's never a good idea to do a job without meeting the client first."

Rivera sighed. "Alright, thanks Hadley. I owe you one."

"I'll send you the bill." He could almost hear her winking at him as she said her goodbye and hung up.

He turned back to Julie. "We didn't run across anyone named Maria Juarez, did we?"

"Not that I recall," she shook her head. "And without a description, we could just be dealing with another alias."

He had a feeling she had overheard the whole conversation. Judging by her change in body language, he could tell she wasn't happy about Hadley's banter.

"Maybe Simon will dig something up." Julie walked back into the apartment and towards the door before turning back to him and ushering him to follow her.

Though he wanted to clear up the misunderstanding, he could tell she wasn't in a listening mood and decided to drop it for the moment and follow her out.

~~~

Sam walked through the doors of the Rehab Center when he was stopped by the same nurse that he'd met the first night of coming to see Liz.

"I'm sorry, sir, but I'm gonna' have to ask you to leave," the large man said gruffly.

"I'm here to speak with Mrs. Harper," Sam answered firmly.

"Her stepfather has informed us that she will not be answering anymore questions without a lawyer present. Her lawyer isn't here, so you're not going in."

"And di' her stepfather also tell ye not to worry abou' strange cuts and bruises she suddenly acquires after his visits?" Sam growled. "No' tha' she could defend herself with how much drugs you people have her on."

"Agent, people who are a danger to themselves find ways to hurt themselves all the time. You are not allowed to be here, and if I have to, I will call on a few of my boys to escort you out myself."

Sam clenched his fist together and stared the man down, inwardly begging for a reason to punch him, when his phone started ringing. Finally, admitting to himself there was no way he'd be able to speak
~~~

to Liz, he turned and walked out of the facility and back to his car. He practically yanked his phone out of his pocket and looked down to see Rivera calling him. "Wha' is it?"

"Sam, you're on speaker," Rivera answered.

Simon's voice popped up and shouted. "We know who took the pictures! A PI was hired by a woman named Maria Juarez to follow Brian around."

"Who the hell's Maria Juarez?"

Julie's voice answered. "Once upon a time in Mexico about forty years ago, she was a dancer at a strip club until she went missing in 1993."

"Missin'?"

"The area of Mexico she lived in is in the territory of the Rios Cartel," Rivera answered. "I called a buddy of mine in the Mexico Headquarters and asked if he knew anything about this woman. He said that during that time there was a huge war going on between the drug lords until Fernando Rios, the head of the Rios Cartel, decided to start combining their clans through the marriage of his only son, Joaquin, to the daughter of his main competitor, Luis Delgado. There was a rumor that Joaquin had fallen in love with a different woman, and the whole operation was threatened, so Fernando had her taken care of before his plan could be thwarted."

"He had her killed?"

"No one wants to go snooping around in the cartels dealings, so by all appearances it looked that way."

"But then I found something in U.S. records, boss," Simon picked up. "Around the same time of Maria Juarez's disappearance, there was an application for U.S. citizenship by a Maria Vargos that was rushed through and accepted instantly. I know that doesn't prove anything, but Joaquin making two visits to Texas, where she lived, can't be a coincidence. Odds are it's the same woman."

"An' where is she now?"

"That's the funny part, boss," Simon said, "She's dead. I haven't found any record of a Maria Vargos since 2002, when she was killed in her home in Amarillo. She lived in a rough area, so the cause of death was chalked up as gang violence."

"I'd bet good money that Joaquin tried to sneak her out of the country before his father could kill her," Julie said. "Son of a drug lord would have his own pocket cash to use; he could have paid somebody to rush her through the system, so she would be safe."

"Until Fernando Rios found out and ordered a hit on the only woman stoppin' his son from combinin' the cartels," Sam whispered his agreement.

"Exactly!" Simon exclaimed. "Thank God for the cartel's sloppy approach in trying to copycat the hit on Brian, otherwise we'd've missed all this."

"Bu' who could use the cartel's resources, to go to all this effort, tha' would have this kind of information?" Sam tried hard to think as he drove back to the hotel when an idea suddenly popped in his head. "Di' Maria have any children?"

"Twins: a boy and a girl, born a few months after their mom came to America."

"$100 says they're Joaquin's kids," Rivera said.

"I'd take that bet," Julie answered. "They were found by the police and placed in the foster system after Maria died."

"And where are they now?"

He heard Simon typing on his computer before answering. "The girl ran away from her foster parents three years after placement, when she was thirteen. There's still a missing person's poster for her. It looks like the boy stayed in the system but disappeared as soon as he turned eighteen. Nobody's heard from either of them since."

"Wha's the name of the foster parents?"

"Greg and Alice Newt, why?"

Before Sam could answer, Julie began to yell excitedly. "Newt! Rosie Newt! Green's campaign manager is who had Brian followed!"

Sam chuckled inwardly at her enthusiasm.

"What do you think she's up to, Sam?" Rivera asked. "Trying to get some of grandpa's respect and earn a spot in the family business?"

"She's worked hard to ge' there: sleepin' with the manager of an international corporation in order to ge' him to agree to look the other way while money is bein' laundered through his bank on behalf of the Rios cartel. And now he's runnin' fer office, and she'd be able to use his power to allow shipments of only her family's drugs into the U.S. and crack down harder on the other cartel's shipments."

"If I were Papa Rios, I'd want her on my team, too."

"Aye, bu' she made the mistake of usin' her mother's name to send a message. Simon, dig up everythin' ye can abou' Rosie Newt. Rivera, Julie, meet me at Green's campaign buildin' in an hour."

"You got it," Simon answered.

"And send a copy of everythin' to Cole Terry," He smirked. "This'll ge' him to shu'-up. And drop Director Copper an anonymous tip with everythin'."

He could hear Simon gulp as he asked, "E-everything to Copper?"

"Everythin'." Sam hung up the phone and raced back to Cleveland. He didn't stop until he was pulling in front of Congressman Green's house. He saw Georgia Green and her two sons walking out of the house, followed by a young man carrying some suitcases. Sam got out of the car.

"Where are we going, mom?" the youngest boy asked.

"To Grandpa's old house for a few days," she answered sadly.

"What about dad?"

"Dad's not coming," the older boy said bitterly.

Sam walked up and cleared his throat. Georgia looked at him before turning back to her sons. "Boys, I need you to stay here with Beni for a second while I talk to this man."

"What are we supposed to do?" The oldest asked in an annoyed tone.

"Pull out your iPads and play some games. I won't be long," Georgia sighed. "Do you mind, Beni?"

"Not at all, *Senora*," the young man answered.

When her sons were occupied, she turned and walked towards Sam. "Can I help you?"

"Mrs. Green, I'm Sam McKay, I work with agents Rivera and Russell."

"What is this about, Mr. McKay?"

"Please call me Sam, and this is abou' Liz Harper."

Georgia sighed and folded her arms across her chest. "Look, Sam, this really isn't a good time to be discussing a woman I don't even know. I've already told the other two agents everything I know about her, and as you can see, I'm in the middle of leaving my husband."

"Aye, anno, and I'm sorry to intrude, bu' ye said ye dinnea know why yer father was meetin' with her, and I can tell ye."

His quick answer piqued her curiosity and she moved her hands to her hips. "Alright, why was he meeting this woman?"

"He found out she's his daughter, lass."

Georgia's eyebrows shot to her hairline. "Wh-what?"

"Mrs. Green, if ye donnea mind me askin', when di' yer mother die?"

"When I was ten."

"How di' yer father take it?"

"… Not great. He withdrew into his work and hired a nanny to take care of me for a few years … I hardly ever saw him during all that time. Then one day Bianca just left. I guess she must have said something to him because he said he was sorry for pushing me away, and he promised never to do it again, and he never did."

"Wha' did ye say the name of yer nanny was?"

"Bianca, why?"

Sam couldn't believe the coincidence and started to chuckle.

Georgia eyed him curiously and said, "I must have missed the joke in there."

"Forgive me, Mrs. Green. Bianca wasnea jus' yer nanny, darlin', she was Liz's mother."

Again, she stared at him in shock. "… Why are you telling me this?"

"Because ye aren't the only one tha's been hurt by yer father's death. Yer father intended t' help Liz after her husband, the boy he'd known fer years, was killed. I suspect once he saw Liz, he instantly recognized yer ol' nanny and began his own investigation. He even took DNA samples to a doctor downtown to confirm it. Bu' before he could explain everythin' to her and to ye, he was killed."

Georgia stood silently, doing her best to process everything that had been told to her, when Sam continued, "Mrs. Green, there is nothin' tha' I can say tha' will bring yer father back or make wha' yer husband did right. Bu' ye have a chance to help someone—yer sister—like Brian wanted to do."

"What do you mean?"

"Liz has been wrongfully accused of this and framed fer kidnapping her daughter when all she was tryin' to do was protect her. Her daughter, Natalie is her name, is bein' watched over by a verra, verra bad man. Ye're the owner of yer father's business; ye have access to the bes' lawyers in the world now." Sam withdrew the business card of the Rehabilitation Center he'd been keeping in his wallet and gave it to her. "Help her ge' her daughter back. Help yer sister. Please."

Georgia gingerly accepted the card from him; Sam thanked her and went back to his car, leaving her to stand and ponder over the information he'd given her. He hoped and prayed with all his heart that she would listen to him. She was Liz's only chance now.

Turning his attention back to putting Brian Cairne's murderer to justice, Sam got the address from Simon and raced deep into the heart of Cleveland. He stopped in front of the posh office building where Congressman Green's campaign was, and Rivera and Julie were out front waiting for him; the three of them walked inside and marched towards the back where Congressman Jackson Green was addressing the rabble of reporters.

"Thanks to the support of the people, I am pleased to announce that I will be entering the presidential race as a candidate for the Republican Party."

The crowd erupted in applause as the Congressman waved his hands and said thank you to every one of them. Sam looked around the room until his eyes fell on the person that, for once, he was happy to see and smirked. *This is gonna' be good.*

Cole Terry stood up and raised his hand as the next round of questions began. "Congressman! Should you win the presidential race, will your promise of cleaning up the streets from illegal drugs continue to be your main priority?"

"Of course," Green answered with a nod. "I will make the war on drugs my top priority in office."

"And you have a plan of attack?"

"Yes, we will be cracking down on border and shipping legislation. I intend to provide more jobs for Americans by increasing border patrol openings."

"Do you intend to use the money from the cartels to fund this plan?"

The room suddenly filled with the sounds of murmurs and whispers; the Congressman stopped short and turned pale. "I-I beg your pardon?"

"Your bank, En Passant, has several accounts that are connected with persons and organizations listed on the OFAC Sanctions List. In fact, there are rumors that you were receiving major payouts for looking the other way as they conducted their money laundering schemes. How do you respond to these accusations?”

Rivera, Julie, and Sam were pleased to see Green begin to shift nervously. The crowd of reporters began shouting questions until the Congressman replied. “Whatever rumors you may have heard, I can assure you they are baseless and otherwise false.”

“On the contrary, Congressman, I have proof of your dealings with the Rios Cartel, including bank account numbers that are directly connected to you.”

The trio’s intended target, Rosie Newt, stepped forward and took the microphone, “We have no comment on this matter. This interview is now concluded, thank you everyone.”

The room filled with shouts once again as Green and Newt quickly walked out of the scene and towards the office in the back, but not before making eye contact with the ones there intending to arrest them. Sam and the others heard the sounds of FBI agents walk inside and announce arrests, but they quickly slipped out to follow Green and Rosie, who had suddenly disappeared.

“What the—where the hell are they?” Julie demanded.

“Rivera, go recruit some of yer co-workers,” Sam barked. “Julie, with me.”

While Derrick did as he was instructed, Julie withdrew her gun and handed her spare to Sam. The two of them raced to the back of the building and saw their intended targets run out of the fire escape door and into the alleyway, setting off the alarm as they did.

Sam charged through the door with Julie on his heels and yelled, “FREEZE!”

Rosie Newt and Jackson Green kept running until Julie fired her gun and shot a piece of trash that stood not two feet in front of them. The shot did as intended, and the two of them stopped running just long enough for Julie to yell. “The next two are going into your knees! Turn around and put your hands on your heads!”

The two crooks raised their hands and slowly began to turn around when suddenly, Rosie ducked behind Jackson and produced a gun to his neck.

“Rosie, what the hell are you doing?!” Jackson asked in a panicked tone.

“Shut up or I pull the trigger,” she growled at him.

“Is’ over, Rosita!” Sam called to her; the use of her given name caused her to look up at him, and he continued. “The FBI are here and have the buildin' completely surrounded; there's nowhere to run to."

"I think I can manage! I've disappeared before!"

"Aye, bu' we know who ye are now! We know ye're the daughter of Joaquin Rios, and ye've been helpin' him launder money and drugs into the U.S. We know ye used the cartel to stage the murder of Brian Cairne when he started snoopin' around the operation, and we know ye framed Elizabeth Harper to take the fall if anybody pu' the pieces together!"

"Rosie, what are they talking about?" Green whimpered. "You had Brian killed?"

"Shut up, Jackson," she hissed to him.

"Yer a smart woman, Rosita," Sam continued. "Ye had it all planned out, even down to the patsy! Bu' ye couldnea resist usin' yer mother's name as a message, could ye? Ye had to honor her and tell yer grandfather tha' he'd made a mistake."

Rosie pulled her hostage backwards with her. "Either walk away, or I kill this man right here and now. I'll send someone to take care of you, too! I've done it before! The Rios cartel is not to be messed with!"

"I cannea do tha' even if I wanted to, Rosie. Jus' drop the gun."

Green whimpered as Rosie pressed the gun deeper into his throat. "Last chance! I'll kill him!"

Suddenly, Rivera and a few agents were at the other end of the alley and advancing on the situation. "Drop it, Juarez!"

Rosie jerked her wrist and a shot rang through the air. Green cried out in pain and dropped to the ground just fast enough for Rivera to fire his gun at Rosie. The bullet hit the woman in the back, causing her to fly forward and drop the gun. Rivera and his team advanced on her, past the crying Congressman, and kicked the gun away from the criminal.

Sam turned to see the smoke billowing out of Julie's gun and nodded. "Nice shot, darlin'."

"I was aiming for *her* leg," Julie countered. "But I guess I still saved his life … plus he deserves a bullet in the knee."

Sam chuckled as they walked forward to Rivera.

"She's dead," he confirmed for them.

"Thank you," Green whimpered behind them as he was picked up and loaded onto a gurney. "Thank you all so much. I promise that

I'll take care of—"

"Shu'up," Sam growled. "Ye're goin' to jail."

"Jackson Green, you are under arrest for laundering drug money and criminal intent, and I'm sure there's a few other things we can find along the way," Rivera said as he signaled for the agents to watch him.

"What? This is preposterous! I had no idea what Rosie was doing! I swear! You can't arrest me!"

Sam stood there smiling as the Congressman was wheeled away. Turning back to see the body of Rosie Newt on the ground, however, made that smile disappear just as quickly as it came. With her dead, there was no way to legally prove her operation, not to mention find out why she had picked Liz specifically to frame. Still, he had a pretty good idea of who it was who gave her the notion.

"We did it, Sam," Rivera said, patting Sam on the shoulder. "We solved Brian's murder."

"And we uncovered a huge scandal," Julie added. "I know we couldn't do any more for Liz, but—"

"I's alrigh'," Sam shook his head. "I have a feelin' Liz has more than jus' us watchin' out fer her."

"What makes you say that?"

"Jus' do," he said. Clearing his throat, he added. "Look, um … the three of ye did spectacular, more than anyone could even reasonably expect of ye … and I thank ye."

Julie showed her forgiveness with a smile, but Rivera took a moment to size Sam up before offering his hand to him. When Sam accepted it and shook it, Rivera said, "Just try not to forget that so easily from now on, right?"

"Aye, ye got it."

Rivera gave a small smile in return before nodding to the alleyway. "Why don't you get out of here before Copper sees you? We'll clean this up."

Chuckling, Sam nodded and walked towards the mouth of the alley and back to his car. As he drove back to his hotel, he thought about Liz and at that moment, he could only hope that Georgia Green had taken what he'd told her to heart. The more he thought about the Congressman's wife, the more he felt calm. If the woman was anything like her late father, he knew she would do the right thing.

Chapter Twenty-Five

The blank white brick walls of the tiny Rehab Center cell (as she had come to call it) seemed to be getting closer and closer to Liz as she stared at them. Her hours outside the cell had been reduced, and the only human interaction she would get during the day was when the nursing staff came at night to force her to take medication. More than once, the thought of taking the blanket that she was allowed to have in her room and turning it into a rope for her neck had crossed her mind. The only thing that prevented her from acting on those thoughts was Natalie. Knowing she could not leave her daughter to the hands of her stepfather, Liz repeatedly told herself that she would get out of this hellhole if it was the last thing she ever did, no matter the cost. It was the only motivation she had to still keep going, even though there was nothing that she could go to. Even now, she couldn't remember what day of the week it was, let alone what time it was. But still she woke up; she did everything she could to remain sane and alert. Between counting the painted bricks on the walls and how many bird chirps she could hear during the day, she just had to keep going.

Finally, the one day of the week had come when she was allowed to leave her cell and go sit in the common room under the leering gaze of the nursing staff. Still, she needed the change of scenery and did her best to enjoy it; she would get an hour or so to watch the TV and maybe go outside, then it would be back to her cell for the remainder of the day. As she blankly stared at the *Three Stooges* re-run, Liz almost missed the argument in the hallway.

"You're not allowed in here without proper authorization from the patient's guardian!" the head nurse insisted.

"I think you'll find everything in these documents stating we have the proper authorization," a strange male voice said. "And Mrs. Green is now Mrs. Harper's new guardian. We will be moving Mrs. Harper to a different facility today."

At the mention of her name, Liz looked over to the doorway to see a woman she didn't recognize standing there. She could tell the woman had money by the way she was dressed in a matching pale pink skirt suit, but her face was perplexed as she looked at Liz with a mixture of awe and pity. Finally, the woman walked forward and pointed to the other end of the couch.

"May I sit here?"

Liz, though still very unsure as to what was going on, nodded and whispered. "Go ahead."

The woman took her seat and folded her hands across her skirt. Liz could feel herself shrinking in shame under the woman's deep gaze and quickly turned her head so she wouldn't have to see it. Finally, the woman cleared her throat and said, "My name is Georgia Green."

Though Liz heard her, she refused to look at her.

Mrs. Green continued. "I believe you knew my ... our father, Brian, very well."

At the mention of Brian, Liz finally looked at Georgia with hope in her eyes.

"Yes," Liz mumbled. "He was my husband's unc—Godfather of sorts."

Georgia smiled softly. "Daniel, right? I remember the day dad went to your husband's funeral, he came home and told me he loved that boy like he was his own son."

Liz nodded.

"Did he ever tell you?" Georgia asked. "That you're ... I mean ..."

"That I'm his daughter, too?" Liz provided. "No, I didn't even know until about a month ago when a friend told me."

"Mr. McKay, right? He told me as well. Actually, it's because of him that I'm here."

The mention of Sam made Liz even more hopeful; he'd promised he would get her out of this hellhole after all.

"Per his insistence, I've had my lawyers look over your case. It would seem that your stepfather's lawyers conveniently forgot a few details for your defense, and considering all of the discrepancies, they've appealed a mistrial."

Liz could feel the tears brimming in her eyes; her voice shaky, she asked, "Wh-what does that mean?"

"It means you'll be getting out of here very soon," Georgia

smiled. "But for the time being, I'm having you moved to a different facility, that's closer to me, where I can make sure they're not mistreating you. If you would prefer that, I mean. I don't want to assume anything on your behalf as we ... well, we don't know each other that well ..."

Liz could hardly believe her ears as she listened to everything Georgia was telling her: she would get to leave? And be released? It was almost too good to be true.

"My daughter," she said quietly.

"Mr. McKay has informed me of your situation, and I've instructed my lawyers to formulate a solid battle for custody. I promise, you'll get your daughter back very soon."

Tears flooding her eyes, Liz stared at Georgia and prayed she could tell how thankful she was. Not knowing what words could even come close to portraying the emotion and gratitude she felt, Liz leaned forward and hugged her as tightly as she could. Though taken aback at the sudden contact, Georgia slowly wrapped her arms around her in return.

"Thank you," Liz sobbed. "Thank you so much!"

"... I've always wanted a sister," Georgia answered with a smile.

~~~

One Week Later ...

Sam packed the last of his things into his suitcase. He'd worn out his cover in the U.S. long enough and knew it wouldn't be much longer until Director Copper would find him and charge him with anything she could think of for ignoring his deportation. Liz was being released that day, and Georgia's lawyers had won the custody battle with Alexander Michaels. Sam intended to personally retrieve little Natalie from the slimy man himself. Just as he finished zipping up the suitcase, his phone began to ring.

"Sam McKay," he answered gruffly.

"I found it, boss!" Simon answered excitedly. "I found a connection between Rosie Newt and Michaels! It's not anything that a jury will buy, because it's too circumstantial, but seriously what
~~~

are the odds—”

“Simon, the point.”

“Right, right, sorry. Okay, so I was able to track the whereabouts of Rosie’s movements through her phone for the last few months before Brian died, and there was a coffee shop she frequented. Which isn’t unusual, everybody has a spot that they like and people don’t like to change—”

“Simon!”

“Hang on, I’m getting there. So, Michaels is on the other side of town, and he has his own coffee shop that he frequents and never likes to change. But on February 11th, a month before Brian died, he was at the same coffee shop that Rosie Newt goes to for the whole day! And I crosschecked the times; they were definitely in the same shop at the same time for about an hour!”

“So, he di’ pu’ her up to framin’ Liz,” Sam seethed.

“I found an ATM photo that shows them talking to each other, but without a testimony from Rosie there’s no way to prove it.”

“Tha’s enough for me. Good work, Simon.”

“Hang on, boss, there’s still one question we haven’t answered yet: how did Green get those texts from Brian? I haven’t been able to find any programming codes that suggest a hack into the phone.”

Sam thought long and hard. “… Can ye tell me the name of the boy? Maria Juarez’s twin boy tha’ disappeared?”

He heard Simon typing furiously in the background. “Benito.”

“… The Greens have a butler named Beni. I donnea think tha’s a coincidence.”

“Wait, are you actually telling me that you think the butler did it?” Simon laughed heartily.

“Send this t’ Copper, I have a feelin’ she’ll look into it. Good work.” Hanging up the phone, Sam grabbed his suitcase and the medium sized box with the label ‘fragile’ he had Hannah mail to him, and walked out the door to his car.

Pulling up in front of the large Michaels estate, Sam was pleased to see Rivera and Julie there, as well as a few other police officers from Humbar’s precinct. They rang the doorbell and waited for Michaels to answer. Once the door was open, Rivera held Michaels back with the legal documentation while Sam and a handful of the officers walked inside and spread out to look for Natalie, who was playing with the absurdly large dollhouse in the living room. The little girl looked up from her dolls at Sam and the other men standing there, and he could feel his heart melting at the sight of her angelic face. She truly was the spitting image of her mother, other than the blonde hair she inherited from her father.

Sam walked forward and squatted down in front of her. Smiling, he said, "Hallo, Natalie. My name is Sam."

She smiled back and answered. "Hi. Would you like to play with me?"

"I'd love to, bu' I've go' a better idea. How would ye like to see yer mum?"

The mention of Liz caused Natalie to become more animated. "You know my mommy? Where is she?"

"Aye, sweetheart, I'm a friend. She's no' here with me, bu' I can take ye to her if ye'd like."

Sam offered his hand to her, and Natalie accepted it with enthusiasm. Sam had to stay hunched over as he walked with the little girl, but he dared not let her go as they walked past Alexander Michaels.

"Bye, Natalie," Michaels said. "I'll see you soon."

Sam recognized the veiled threat and stopped dead in his tracks before turning to Julie. "Natalie, do ye remember Miss Russell?"

"You're the lady that gave me a lollipop!" the little girl answered excitedly.

"That's right, sweetie," Julie smiled and offered her hand. "Here, why don't we get you all set up in Sam's car?"

"Okay!" Natalie took Julie's hand and bounded away.

When they were far enough away, Sam turned back around and got directly in Michaels' face. "I know ye pu' Brian's murderer up to framin' Liz. And tha' was a mistake, because now I'll be watchin' ye every moment of the day from now on."

"I don't have any idea what you're—"

"Shu'up while I'm talkin' to ye, ye son-offa-bitch," he growled. Taking a deep breath to steady himself, Sam continued. "Ye may have gotten rid of Brian, bu' it takes a lo' more than a drug cartel to get rid o' me. Ye come anywhere near Liz or Natalie again; hell, if ye even *think* abou' harmin' those girls ever again, I will come back here and end ye. And I will make sure tha' no'one ever finds the pieces of ye."

Michaels appeared visibly shaken by Sam's words, but that didn't stop him from turning to Rivera and saying, "You heard him, he just threatened me!"

"I don't know what you're talking about, Mr. Michaels. Do you, guys?"

"No idea, sir," one officer answered, shaking his head.

"Not a clue," the other added.

Michaels fumed but couldn't bring himself to say anything else for the fear of Sam's wrath.

Sam stared him down for another moment, reassuring him that his threat would be honored, before he finally turned away and walked to his car, where he saw Natalie buckled up in the backseat with Julie. He quickly took a deep breath to calm himself before getting in the car and following the entourage of cop cars to the new facility Georgia had Liz moved to.

They arrived just as Liz was walking out of the doors and making her way through a rabble of reporters. Wearing a white wraparound dress and earrings that were obviously picked by her new sister, she looked so much healthier than the last time Sam had seen her. The rage he felt was instantly quelled; Georgia had done exactly what he'd hoped she'd do and more. He barely had the car parked before Natalie opened the door and was running to her mother across the parking lot.

"Mommy!" the little girl cried.

Upon hearing Natalie's voice, Liz turned to see her running and sprinted towards her until she could pick her up and swing her around. Tears running down her face, Liz hugged Natalie tightly and kissed every part of her face until the little girl was asking her to stop, but she couldn't bring herself to.

"Mommy, how long until you have to leave again?" Natalie asked timidly.

"Oh, honey, I'm not going anywhere ever again."

"You promise?"

"Yes, baby, I promise."

Holding each other in the parking lot, Liz didn't notice that Georgia had come up behind her until she felt her tap her shoulder.

"Oh," she was flustered, wiping the tears from her eyes. "Natalie, this nice lady is Georgia. She's the one that helped get you and mommy back together."

Georgia dropped to her knees in front of the little girl and smiled.

"Hi, Natalie. Wow, you are so pretty! I love your hair!"

"Thank you," the little girl beamed. "Mommy says I have daddy's hair."

Georgia giggled and looked up to see Sam approaching carrying a mailed box. Liz followed her gaze, and more tears fell when she saw him, so happy to see her friend and savior there.

"I'm sorry t' interrupt," Sam said. "Bu' I have somethin' for ye, Natalie."

"A present for me?" Natalie asked excitedly.

"Aye, sweetheart. I hope ye like it." Sam opened the box and pulled out the heavily damaged, but still repaired, strawberry plant.

"Ronald!" Natalie squeaked. The little girl jumped up and down excitedly until Sam handed her the plant, then she settled down and became very gentle. "Why does his house look broken?"

"He unfortunately had a bit of a bumpy ride, darlin'. Bu' I fixed 'im as best'I can. I'm sure yer mum would love to help ye paint a new house for 'im."

"Can we, mommy?"

"Of course, baby," Liz smiled, tears flowing freely.

"Thank you, Mr. Sam!" Natalie ran to him and wrapped her arms around his neck while still holding the plant awkwardly, but Sam didn't mind at all as he hugged her in return.

When she finally let go, Sam's eyes turned to Liz's, and Georgia noticed. She cleared her throat and turned back to Natalie. "Hey, if you want, and if it's okay with your mom, you can meet my sons AJ and Asher and show them Ronald."

"Can I?" Natalie pleaded.

"Yeah, honey. I'll only be a minute."

Georgia took Natalie's hand and walked with her towards the limo that sat not too far away. Georgia's two sons were sitting in the backseat.

Finally alone, Liz looked at Sam and folded her arms across her chest. "Sam, I … I'll never be able to thank you enough for all that you've done."

His genuine smile caused her to sigh inwardly. On habit, she brought her hand up to push back her hair again only to be reminded that her hair was barely starting to grow again. She giggled nervously, and he chuckled along with her, "I miss my hair."

"It'll grow back in no time, darlin'," he assured her.

Liz swallowed the lump in her throat; looking up at him, she asked, "So, what will you do, now?"

"Go' a flight to catch this afternoon. I'm technically no' supposed to be here, after all. Wha' about the two of ye?"

"Georgia has invited us to stay with her for now. I don't care where I am, as long as I have Natalie."

"Aye, she's a beautiful little lassy, jus' like her mother."

Liz blushed furiously. Taking a deep breath, she summoned up all of her courage and took a step closer to him. "I think, maybe in a few years, when things settle down, and when Natalie's not in school, we'll do some traveling. We might even start with Scotland, since I have some good memories there … Would it be alright if I looked you up when we do?"

In one mighty step, Sam closed the distance between the two of them and brought his fingers under Liz's chin. Gently, he raised her face until she was looking him in the eyes before leaning down to kiss her. Liz lost all sense of time as she stood there with his lips on hers, and when he stepped back, she could barely breathe. It wasn't until he spoke that she finally opened her eyes.

"I'd like tha'," he said to her. Running the back of his fingers against her cheek, he kissed her once more before he pulled away completely. "Goodbye, Liz."

"Goodbye, Sam," she smiled. Without looking back, she turned and strode towards the limo where her daughter and new family were waiting.

Sam kept his eyes on the woman he'd come to care for until she was safely tucked away inside of the limousine. As he watched them drive off, he sincerely hoped that she would look him up one day. But for the moment, it was enough to know that she wouldn't have to run away anymore, especially not without her daughter. Heading back to his own car, Julie and Rivera stood side by side waiting for him just as Simon pulled up in his own tiny environment-friendly vehicle.

"I don't care if Copper gets pissed at me for taking a longer than usual lunch break, you're not leaving without saying goodbye to me, boss," Simon said firmly with his hands planted on his hips.

"Are you sure about this?" Rivera asked. "I have a few more strings I can pull to get your visa back."

"Yeah, Sam," Julie nodded. "We don't want you to go."

"Ach, bugger off. The three of ye were fine without me before; ye'll be fine again."

"We probably will, but that doesn't change the fact that we like working for you."

"Apparently, I havenea been hard enough on you lot if ye're tha' sentimental."

Rivera, Julie, and Simon chuckled at his harsh reply. Though Sam maintained his outward façade of gruffness, truthfully, he was going to miss all three of them: Rivera and his short-fused yet gentle, brotherly ways. Julie with her no-nonsense drive was something he would always admire. And not hearing Simon's sarcastic remarks every day would certainly leave him wanting. Still, he knew there was nothing more that could be done. He'd come back to make sure Liz was free and with her daughter; his task was finished.

A small smile graced his lips as he offered his hand to Rivera, Simon, and then to Julie. Rivera shook it strongly, Julie leaned forward to kiss his cheek, and Simon insisted on a hug before the three of them said their goodbyes.

Driving to the airport, Liz's reunion with Natalie made Sam think of Oliver and the offer Meredith had laid out for him before he'd been deported. As tempting as it was to pretend, for their son's sake, that nothing had happened to break apart their relationship, he knew in his heart that things would never be the same. And even if he wanted to try again, the words Meredith told him of how he could retire from being a cop kept bugging him. He loved what he did, and seeing Liz permanently reunited with Natalie only fueled that further. Like magic, his phone pinged with a text from her that said:

Have you thought more about what we've talked about?

He looked at the clock; his flight didn't leave for another two hours, and he'd get through customs in forty-five minutes. He had enough time to lay it out for Meredith.

Ring … Ring … Ring …

"Hey," Meredith said cheerily. "I thought you might still be asleep. I didn't wake you, did I?"

"Ach, no, I was already awake."

"Oh, good. Well, listen, I'm not trying to rush you. I just haven't heard from you in a bit and wanted to know if you were still thinking about it or not."

"Aye, I've though' about it, Meredith." Sam took a deep breath.

"And I'm afraid we cannea go back to the way things were."

"I know that, Sam, and I don't expect things to go back to how they were. But they could be better."

"No, darlin', they can't. Meredith, we're divorced, and I think we should stay tha' way."

The silence on the other end of the phone told him she was shocked. Rubbing his eyes, he waited for her onslaught of questions. "What do you mean? I thought this was what you wanted."

"A year and a half ago, yes it was."

"So, what's changed? Is it me? I told you I'm sorry. I was stupid; I admit it. It was a mistake."

He sighed. "Perhaps if ye'd only shagged the bassard once, I would believe ye. But six months, and thinkin' I didnea know about it? Tha's a lot of mistakes."

His brutish reply caused a tremble to her voice that he couldn't miss. "… You were always gone. There was always another case to solve, another problem to fix, everyone else was the great Sampson Angus McKay's top priority … but I wasn't. Sam, I was lonely."

"Did ye think I wasn't?" He asked her sternly.

"I don't know! God knows you never told me how you felt!"

Taking a deep breath to calm himself, Sam said, "In all the time I was away, I never cheated on ye. No' once."

"… Weren't you tempted?"

"Tempted? Aye, absolutely. Bu' there's a difference between bein' tempted and givin' in to temptation. Meredith, you and Oliver were my whole world, and I love the two of ye … but ye made yer choice, ye chose Ryan."

"… And I asked him to leave, too. Right after the divorce."

"Tha's irrelevant. Wha's done is done. And even if I still wanted to try again, I cannea change who I am. I love wha' I do, Meredith. And if there was a time when I could have given up bein' a cop for you, is' long since passed."

He could almost see the tears falling down her face at his words, but Sam held his ground. Finally, she answered. "… Alright. Well … I hope that you'll still get back here someday, Sam."

"I appreciate tha' Meredith. Goodbye."

"Goodbye," she answered tearfully before disconnecting the call.

Sam stared at his phone. He knew the conversation was going to leave him in a sour mood, which would make the flight back to

Scotland even longer. But knowing that Meredith had actually set him free gave him some hope. He could go back to Rosneath and start fresh now. As much as he wished he could stay near his son at all times, he had to believe that this situation would be better for them in the long run. Shaking off the melancholy he was feeling, he grabbed his suitcase and walked into the airport.

Finally through customs, Sam still had an hour before it was time to board, so he walked into a bar and grill for a pint. It was busy, as airport restaurants usually were, so the waitress seated him at the bar before hurrying off to attend other customers.

"What can I get you?" the young and lean barkeep asked him.

"Guinness."

"I've only got Murphy's on tap."

"Fine. And I'll have a plate of those fried mushrooms."

"I'll have the same."

Sam looked over his shoulder at the familiar voice and was shocked and worried to see Director Copper standing there.

"Coming right up," the young man nodded. Like a flash of lightening, he had two pints of ale drawn and placed in front of Sam and the woman who joined him. "Mushrooms will be ready in a few moments."

"Thanks," Sam nodded and took a sip of the ale. The rich toffee flavor was a little too sweet for him, but not altogether unpleasant. He took another sip before turning to the director. "Ye here to arrest me?"

"Now what gave you that impression, Mr. McKay?" Copper answered him simply.

"Ye donnea seem like the type to buy a plane ticket jus' to have an overpriced pint."

"Good thing I can say it's a tax write off as I'm here on business."

"Oh? Mus' be important for ye to make an appearance."

Copper chuckled so softly that Sam almost missed the noise. "I thought you might like to know that the Green's butler, Beni Juarez, confessed to everything the minute he was picked up: texting from Brian's phone, murdering the bank manager, he confirmed his sister's activities, and the money laundering in Green's bank."

"Tha' was a fast arrest."

"I got a fast tip," she answered and took a sip of her own ale. "In the short week since your computer lackey fixed your visa, you have managed to solve a cold murder, unravel a political scandal, and free an innocent woman. All in one fell swoop. I'd be lying if I said I wasn't impressed, Mr. McKay."

The barkeep produced the two plates of fried mushrooms, and Sam popped a large one in his mouth before answering. "Ye're givin' me too much credit, ma'am. T'was my team tha' discovered Brian Cairne was murdered in the first place. An' he was the one tha' discovered the scandal and left us the clues to expose Green, as well as give Liz the life he wanted to give her. I dinnea do much."

"You saw the lines that connected all of that together, and you had the balls to come back here, despite the criminal charges you would be faced with, in order to make sure justice was served. You can spin it however you want it, McKay, but that's what I see. Frankly, law enforcement could use more men like you."

"Big, grumpy bassards tha' donnea know when to quit?"

"Good leaders that won't quit just because it's easier to. You say your team uncovered most of the details, but why do you think they did that? They're certainly not being paid enough to solve crimes in their spare time."

Sam couldn't help but chuckle. "Aye, I suppose ye have a point there."

"Glad we found something we can agree on," Copper nodded and took a small, lady like bite of one of her own mushrooms.

"So, di' ye come all this way to compliment me? Or is there another reason behind this praise?"

"You're really going to make me spell it out for you?"

"Aye."

Copper chuckled. "Fine, I'm here to offer you a job, Sampson McKay. I want you to work for me as part of a special investigative task force. As I'm sure you're aware, the system is flawed and sometimes even the best can miss things. But, as I've said, you're an asset to be reckoned with. There is so much good you can do. And I'd be an idiot not to have you on my team."

Sam stared at her blankly, trying to process everything that was being said to him. "And wha' do I get if I say yes?"

"The ban on your visa will *officially* be lifted; you'll be granted full U.S. citizenship; and you'll get standard pay, just to name a few things."

"Ye said 'special investigative task force,' meanin' a team?"

"Considering your activities, I assumed you would want Rivera, Miss Russell, and Abler on the task force. And I can tell you that they'll be getting their official assignment papers tomorrow, providing you say "yes," of course. But if you're not interested, I'll let you finish your snack in peace and wish you a safe flight." Copper looked at Sam directly as she waited for a response.

He held her gaze without fear. "… How long di' ye know wha' we were up to?"

"After I got the flag that your visa had been cleared."

"Then why dinnea ye search the precinct tha' day?"

"Because I wanted to see what would happen; that would determine whether or not I had to deport you again."

Sam laughed and popped another mushroom in his mouth. "This is shapin' up to be a hell of a day."

Belinda Copper magically withdrew some cash and laid down enough in front of the barkeep to pay for both of their meals. Sam looked at her questioningly. She shrugged and answered. "I already told you, tax write-off. I'll see you tomorrow morning for a full debriefing, Mr. McKay."

"Aye," Sam nodded as he turned to watch the Director leave, but very quickly lost sight of her amidst the bustle of people rushing to get to their flights. Taking one more sip of the sweet ale, Sam thanked the young man, grabbed his suitcase, and headed back to the entrance of the airport.

Hell of a day, indeed, he smiled to himself.

⁕ ❧ ⁕

Chapter Twenty-Six

Two Days Later ...

Sam looked in the mirror and adjusted his tie; Copper was nice enough to give him a day to find an apartment and a suitable suit for his new position, with the understanding that he would start work the next day promptly at 9:00 a.m. He tugged and pulled on the knot to loosen it up around his neck before deciding to forgo it. *She only said buy a suit, no' a tie,* he rationalized. The clock said 7:23 a.m., and he knew he wouldn't have enough time for breakfast if he wanted to see Oliver before work, so he quickly filled his thermos with coffee and smeared some marmalade on a piece of toast before grabbing his suitcase and running out the door.

Twenty minutes later, he walked into the office of the Juvenile Center and met Meredith. Though she acknowledged him, calling her about an hour after their painful discussion to tell her he'd been brought back to the U.S. and would be able to live nearby again made the situation more than awkward. Sam sat down next to her and cleared his throat.

"Nice suit," she said coolly.

"Thanks."

"So, the therapist said we can only do this once. After today, the sessions will be every Wednesday evening like usual. No more exceptions."

"Aye, I'll make tha' work."

"Good." Meredith straightened herself and kept her eyes on the door.

Deciding it wasn't worth a fight, Sam rolled his eyes and let her have the last word. The two of them sat together in awkward silence as they waited for someone, anyone, to come in with Oliver and let the session begin. Finally, the door opened, and the therapist, Patricia Neeves, and the thirteen-year-old boy walked inside and sat on the chairs across from them.

Upon seeing his father there, Oliver growled. "What the hell are you doing here?"

Only too happy to see the boy again, Sam ignored his rude tone and answered. "I'm here for our session."

"I thought you went back to Scotland."

"Aye, bu' I'm back now. This time fer good."

Oliver rolled his eyes and muttered. "Whatever."

"Oliver, your father is showing you that he cares," the older woman who was their assigned family therapist said. "He's here, and he's participating. Isn't that what you wanted?"

Oliver shifted uncomfortably before grunting his reply.

"Alright, we're going to try something different today. Oliver, up to this point we have let you and your mother do most of the talking in regards to how you feel. Mr. McKay, today I'd like for you to start off this session."

"Oh, um …" Sam cleared his throat. "Well … wha' should I talk abou'?"

"Why don't you talk about how you felt when you heard that Oliver had been arrested?"

Though he was doubtful of the therapist's tactics, Sam tried hard to think back to the frantic phone call he'd received from Meredith. "Well … I was worried, obviously."

"Why were you worried?"

"Because I thought he—"

"Speak to Oliver, Mr. McKay, you need to tell *him* what you're feeling."

Sam sighed and looked directly at his son, though the boy wouldn't meet his eyes. "I was worried because I though' ye were hurt, Oliver."

Oliver kept his arms crossed and his gaze hidden under the shaggy dark hair.

"Oliver, what do you think about what your father felt?"

The boy snorted. "I've gotten hurt tons of times before."

"Aye, bu' this is the first time ye were arrested."

"So that's what it takes for you to be worried? Me getting arrested?"

"Of course, no'," Sam answered angrily. "I'm yer father; I'm always worried about ye."

"YOU'RE NOT MY FATHER!"

Oliver's outburst more than surprised Sam, and he turned back to look at Meredith. Her eyes were widened with horror. Calmly, he turned back and asked, "… Why do ye say tha'?"

If looks could kill, Oliver would have already killed Sam ten times over by the way he glared at him. "A month after the divorce, I found your marriage license: January 15th, 2008. I was born in 2006, and you didn't come to the USA until 2007. I'm not an idiot!"

It was finally out in the open; while Sam was relieved that Oliver finally knew the truth, the boy wasn't any less hostile, and that made the situation more difficult. He took a deep breath. "Is tha' why ye're so angry with me?"

The boy didn't answer beyond folding his arms and looking down.

"… Alrigh', it's true. I'm no' the man tha' fathered ye, bu' ye mus' know tha' never mattered to me. Oliver, when yer mother and I met, I fell in love. And when I met ye, I knew I loved ye, too. Yer my son, no matter wha'."

Oliver finally lifted his head and looked at Sam with tears in his eyes. "Then why didn't you stay?"

"Son, believe me, I wanted to. Bu' sometimes things donnea work out the way we hope they might, and yer mum and I couldnea work things out."

"You could have tried! Isn't that what you were always saying to me when I was a kid? 'No matter how hard things get, Oliver, you have to try.' You can't even follow your own advice! Yeah, you're a *great* dad. You abandon my mom and you expect me to—"

"Le' me explain one thing to you, boy," Sam barked, earning a jump from his thirteen-year old. "I dinnea abandon her, nor you. If I really wanted to run off and no' be around, I wouldnea be here now! I wouldnea have sent ye all those letters! Yer mother and I will no' be gettin' back together, tha's the fact of it, whether ye like it or no'! Bu' don't ye *dare* sit there and think tha' I donnea love the two of ye; I'll no' stand for tha'!"

Oliver's eyes widened at Sam's outburst, and the therapist finally interrupted.

"Okay, this is good, Mr. McKay, but let's try bringing it back a few steps. Why don't you tell Oliver how you felt when you and Mrs. McKay divorced?"

Blown away by how she completely ignored the earlier revelation of how complicated their family was, Sam rubbed his forhead and sighed, "I dunno' … angry."

"Why angry?"

"Because I dinnea want tha'."

Though he barely caught it, he noticed how Oliver seemed to relax his shoulders at his confession. "What did you want?"

"At the time, to fix things."

The boy's eyes sunk to the ground. "But not now?"

Sam rubbed his face. "Oliver … yer mother and I are no' good people when we're together. To be honest, I'm realizin' now tha' gettin' divorced was probably the bes' thing we could do fer each other and fer you. I never wanted for ye to grow up in a broken home, bu' i' would be so much worse if ye grew up in a chaotic one."

Sam wanted to continue, but the alarm on his phone told him it was time to go to work. Sighing, he stood up and straightened his coat. "I love ye, Oliver, and ye are my son. Whether ye want to believe tha' or no' right now is up to ye. Bu' I promise ye this, I'll keep comin' here every Wednesday until ye do."

The way the boy looked at him suggested that he did, in fact, understand, even if only a little. But that had to be enough for Sam. Clearing his throat as a gesture of goodbye to Meredith and the therapist, he left the session without another word.

~~~

At FBI headquarters, Sam was greeted by Rivera and led to his own office on the third floor. Looking around him, he took note of the lone desk in the room with the arrangement of cubicles sitting in the main room outside.

"Not bad, right?" Rivera smiled. "Pretty close to old times if you ask me."

"I donnea like it," Sam answered. "Do I look like the big man tha' enjoys bein' above everyone else?"

Rivera laughed. "You may be over six feet, but you can relax. No one thinks that. If I were you, I would take this as a big vote of confidence from Copper."

"There are four cubicles out there, bu' only three of ye."

"So?"

Picking up his suitcase, Sam pushed past Rivera and made himself
~~~

comfortable in one of the cubicles. "This is my desk, out here with you lo'."

"Well then, can I have the office?"

"Shu' up and take a seat, Rivera."

Rivera chuckled, setting down his own briefcase just as Julie and Simon walked in through the hallway.

"Damn, nice digs!" Simon gushed as he looked all around. "Way better than the dungeon with no windows known as IT!"

"Not bad," Julie concurred, nodding her head in appreciation.

Rivera smirked and walked over. "By the way, Jules, the Director wanted me to inform you that she expects you to perform on every case to the best of your ability."

"What? Did she think I was going to slack off?"

"I assured her that you wouldn't, but her exact words were 'injury or not, I only accept the best in my headquarters.'"

Julie beamed at the praise before quickly composing herself. "Great, thanks Rivera. Now where's the coffee machine around here?"

"Yeah, I'm feeling a bit thirsty myself," Simon nodded.

As the two of them walked off, Rivera heaved a deep, disappointed sigh; Julie had been giving him the cold shoulder ever since his conversation with Hadley, and he had no idea how to broach the subject, let alone what to say to her. Even when Julie and Simon returned, she seemed to avoid looking him in the eye.

The four of them made quick work of choosing their permanent residency desks: Sam took the biggest one, Rivera was across from him, Simon next to Rivera, and Julie next to Sam.

"God, I've missed this!" Simon mused.

"What?" Rivera asked. "Getting the chance to snipe me with your smart-ass comments?"

"Hey, and now I get to do it full time, workmate!"

Simon winked, and Julie laughed. "I don't need to separate you two already, do I?"

Sam smirked but made sure his team didn't see it. Just as he'd finished arranging his desk to his liking, Director Copper walked around the corner with a file under her arm.

"I take it that all of you find your accommodations agreeable?"

"Yes, sir—ma'am … Director … ma'am!" Simon answered nervously.

"Relax, Abler, I only fire the employees that are silly and otherwise frivolous."

Rivera snorted and whispered under his breath, "Well, *you* won't last long."

Simon had to stop himself from retorting and quickly lowered his head as the Director made her way to Sam.

"McKay, follow me, please."

Following the commanding woman into the abandoned room, Sam stood with his hands in his pockets as Copper looked around before addressing him. "I'm afraid I don't see the problem with your office, Sam."

"No problem, Belinda, I jus' donnea want it."

"I thought the job description was very clear: you'll be leading this team. A leader requires an office."

"Well, unless I missed the line tha' says I'm required to *stay* in my own office, I'll be stayin' with my team."

Copper chuckled softly. "Should I assume that all of our interactions will be disagreements?"

"Mos' likely," Sam smirked. "Bes' we no' start our professional relationship off on the wrong foot over an office."

"Oh, I'm certain we're past the start of this relationship." Copper handed the file she'd been carrying over to Sam. "Your first assignment: an arsonist."

Opening the file, Sam flipped through the pages. "Anythin' else I need t' know?"

"As a matter of fact, there is, McKay; you will never address me by my first name again. Understood?"

Sam smirked. "Aye, understood."

"Very good, then it's time to work."

Copper walked out without another word while Sam read over the case file: there were five fires in the last two years, all started with the same chemical fluid, and at every fire at least one person was caught and burned alive. Pulling out the gruesome photographs, Sam examined them as closely as he could as he turned back to his team, who were still arguing with each other.

"What's the matter, Abler?" Rivera asked in a cheery tone. "No witty comeback?"

"You know, it's pretty pitiful that you had to call the principal just to get the upper hand, Rivera," Julie teased.

"Hey, the game had to turn in my favor at *some* point."

Simon skulked in his desk, refusing to answer, despite the constant goading. When Sam cleared his throat, the three of them quit talking and looked up.

"If you lo' are finished muckin' about, we bes' ge' started."

The End
Sam and his team will return.

About the Author

K.M. Hardy has held an interest in solving crimes since childhood. Graduating with a degree in Criminal Justice in the top ten percent of her class, she went on to work for the government for ten years. Her experience in Law Enforcement and Corrections has given her invaluable insight to the world of crime and politics, which had earned her a finalist spot in a ghost writing competition for the renowned James Patterson. She currently resides in the mountains of Utah with her husband, their three children, and their faithful German Shepherd.